HAVEN 6

A NEW DAWN, BOOK 3

A NEW DAWN SERIES

HAVEN 6

A NEW DAWN, BOOK 3

AUBRIE DIONNE

Entangled Publishing, LLC
2614 South Timberline Road
Suite 109
Fort Collins, CO 80525
Visit our website at www.entangledpublishing.com.

Edited by Kerry Vail and Stacy Cantor Abrams
Original cover design by Kim Killion
Cover art by Heather Howland

Print ISBN   978-1-937044-85-5
Ebook ISBN   978-1-937044-86-2

Manufactured in the United States of America

First Edition September 2012

To Brianne

CHAPTER ONE
UNEXPECTED CALLING

Matching request denied.

Eri stared at the response on her computer screen as reality prickled the hairs on her arms and then sunk like a bomb in her stomach.

Alea iacta est.

The die has been cast.

She thought of all the ways to express disappointment in the languages of Old Earth: *apogoitefsi* in Greek, *rozczarowanie* in Polish, *die Enttäuschung* in German, and *désappointement* in French. Such useless knowledge. Her linguist mind teemed with words, making her the most archaic and impractical colonist on the *Heritage*.

Not only was her job obsolete, but now she'd never have a computer-designated match.

An oscillating holopicture of her parents' faces drew her attention. She refused to blame them for her predicament. As an illegal DNA crossing resulting from an unrecognized pairing, she knew the computer would never consider her DNA acceptable for lifemate pairing, especially at her ripe age of twenty-five. Her profile had too many question marks, plus a few propensities for disease.

She should have known from the start. She shouldn't have persevered, pressing the Matchmaker for a decision she couldn't make because of the rules. How could the Matchmaker argue with a system that had worked successfully for hundreds of years? Eri's determination raised her own hopes only to crash them down in the end each time she sent a request.

Well, this was the last time, wasn't it? She clicked off the screen. All of the men her age were taken, and the age discrepancy between her and the graduating class was scandalous. She wiped her eyes. *If I can't work within the system, then there must be some way to beat it by hacking into the matching program or changing my genetic report.* Would the Matchmaker catch it? How embarrassing would that be? What would the punishment be?

Her computer alarm beeped.

Fifteen hundred.

Aquaria's pairing ceremony.

Damn!

She scrambled through her desk, overturning broken light sticks and soybean wafer wrappers to find something to tame her hair. Using the black computer screen as a mirror, she clipped her frizzy strawberry curls with tiny plastic clips. How could she let so many hours slip away?

Daydreaming about having her own pairing, that's how. She shot up from her desk and pulled her arms through the ceremonial blazer of her uniform. The *Heritage*'s coat of arms badge decorated her left breast pocket. Pressing the portal panel, she watched the particles dissolve like her dreams.

The corridors lay as empty and silent as a barren world. The Guide dictated that all colonists must attend each pairing ceremony.

Eri shook her head. She had lamented her own lack of pairing to the point of disobedience. Her boots clunked on the chrome as she rushed through the clear glass corridor connecting her small bubble of offices to the belly of the ship. Stars sparkled like pinpricks all around her. One point in particular glittered like a giant diamond, outshining all the others. The sparkle wasn't a star.

Haven 6.

Despite her tardiness, she stopped halfway down the walkway to trace Haven's circumference with her finger on the glass. Yesterday, it was the size of her fingernail, but now it glowed beyond her entire fingerprint.

Soon we'll all leave this ship behind.

A wave of melancholy tinged with hope washed over her. Maybe the computer would reassign her a more meaningful job. With plenty of resources, and couples allowed to have as many children as they wanted, maybe Commander Grier would deem the pairing system obsolete. Maybe.

Eri wanted to stay and fantasize, but she'd already wasted enough time. Would her sister notice if she rushed in ten minutes late with puffy skin around her eyes? Probably. Aquaria noted every new freckle on her arm, as if skin cancer were a problem when they had no sun. *It will be a problem soon enough on Haven, though.*

She tore herself away from her future and entered the main corridor connecting to the ceremonial viewing deck.

Rows of uniformed colonists sat on either side of the aisle. Aquaria stood at the podium, holding hands with Litus Muller, her perfectly chosen lifemate. She reminded Eri of the ancient beauties in her translation texts. A lacy ceremonial gown that Eri would never get to wear flowed to the last steps of the stage. Aquaria's long black hair shone dark as deep space and her skin glowed in the simulated candlelight. While Aquaria inherited their mom's loveliness, Eri had her dad's Irish heritage, and with that, his wayward radish-colored hair and blushing, freckled skin. If it wasn't for the infamy of the scandal, no one would know they were half sisters.

She spotted a vacant seat in the last row and tiptoed over as Aquaria and Litus recited their vows. Eri switched the sound off the locator embedded in her arm. The thought of pressing a button by accident, causing a shrieking alarm to go off, made her always check twice.

"I pledge my loyalty to you and the Guide…" Aquaria kept her gaze on the podium, as if straining to remember her lines.

"I'll uphold all customs…" Litus's voice rang out, strong and certain.

Yada, yada. Eri blocked their words and focused on the pair. Aquaria's mysterious blue eyes contrasted with Litus's perfect curls of blond hair. They were two opposites, like a moon and a sun, and yet they complemented each other.

Eri shifted as they recited their final vows. The congregation applauded, a roar of sound changing the solemn atmosphere of the room. People stood from their seats as if Commander Grier'd had them glued there all day. Ushers carried platters of food from a dwindling biodome harvest. The sweet scent of fresh fruit filled the room. Eri slipped through the spaces in between groups to grab an apple and congratulate Aquaria before the receiving line grew too long.

"Eri! There you are! I kept looking for you in the crowd."

Aquaria threw her arms around her and squeezed. "I'm sorry, Aquaria, I came in late and had to sit in the back."

"What's wrong?" Her sister's eyes shone so bright, Eri saw her disheveled appearance reflected in them.

"Nothing. I wanted to congratulate you."

"Nonsense." Aquaria waved away the ceremony like she was shaking off a chore. "Something happened. Are you sick?"

"No. You should be with Litus. I'll tell you about it later." Shining the apple with her finger, Eri suppressed a wave of guilt. Her sister shouldn't spend her reception worrying.

Aquaria took her hand in a viselike grip, her lacy sleeve tickling Eri's arm. "I'm not going anywhere." Aquaria tugged her away from the crowd, and they ducked behind the podium. "Not until you tell me what's got you so upset."

The scent of artificial lilac tickled Eri's nose as they stood over the vent. She struggled to keep her composure. She was the older sister by two years, after all. Swallowing a lump in her throat, she met her sister's penetrating gaze.

"The Matchmaker turned down my pairing request again."

Aquaria's mouth fell open. "That's not nothing. That's everything you've been working for. And to have to come to my ceremony afterward…Eri, I'm so sorry."

"I'm the one who's sorry. I'm worrying you on what should be the happiest day of your life."

"Litus is important, yes, but so are you. My relationship with him doesn't diminish what we have, and it never will." Her voice fell to a whisper. "And you deserve to have a lifemate just like everyone else, especially if you want one. I don't care what the computers say."

Eri stepped back, shooting a look across the room to make sure no one was eavesdropping. She'd never heard her sister talk blasphemy against the Guide.

The locator on her arm vibrated, and she checked the sender, relieved to have something else to look at other than her sister's overly compassionate face.

A single message scrolled across the miniscreen.

REPORT TO THE MAIN CONTROL DECK IMMEDIATELY.

Eri almost choked when she saw the sender.

Aquaria grabbed her arm. "What is it?"

Eri began to shake, and her knees weakened. "It's a message

from Commander Grier. She wants me to report to her. Now."

Because I showed up late? Impossible. How could the commander oversee every operation on the ship and keep track of each colonist at all times? Commander Grier had never acknowledged her in any way, not even a stray flick from her computerized eyes.

She's just a brain connected to the mainframe. Maybe she has nothing better to do.

Aquaria blinked in surprise. "Well, you'd better go now, you lucky star. It's not every generation someone of our status gets to meet the commander."

Wouldn't Aquaria rather enjoy her pairing ceremony than meet the commander?

Eri shook the thought off and gave her a quick hug. "You're right."

❧

The corridors to the main control deck stretched before Eri like a forbidden land. No one passed beyond the row of guards without sufficient clearance. People worshipped the commander like some demigod because she was the last of the Earth generation. She couldn't have all her devoted followers kneeling at the main control deck's portal.

Eri would much rather sneak back to her office and read ancient Greek plays. But in a ship surrounded by deep space, she had nowhere to hide. No one disobeyed the commander.

A guard three heads taller than her scanned her locator and allowed her through with a narrowing of his eyes. Eri returned his stare as she passed. After the denied matching request, having someone question her importance churned her stomach.

The portal to the main control deck fell away like a million swirling stars, and she stepped onto a viewing platform that spanned the entire length of the front hull. Galaxies stretched out in smears of cosmic dust, and nebulas swirled in bright reds and blues. Haven 6 glittered at the center, like a diamond stuck on a painter's easel.

A giant screen lowered in front of her. The pixels flashed to life, and the commander's sharp features and bright green gaze studied her.

Eri wasn't fooled. The image was only a recreation of who Ursula Grier used to be. In reality, the commander's brain floated in pink embryonic liquid in a locked glass tank behind the screen.

She bowed before the pixels. "Eridani Smith at your service, Commander."

"Excellent." The commander's eyes moved from Eri's scuffed space boots to the clips in her raging hair. Did her cheek twitch, or did the pixels just flash?

"I need to know the extent of your dedication to our mission on Haven 6."

Eri swallowed hard. Was the commander questioning her because of one tardiness in all her history? *Stick to the truth, and your voice will come out strong.* "I'm looking forward to landing more than anything."

The commander's eyes narrowed. Eri resisted the urge to squirm, feeling like an insignificant fly. *Can she see my intentions to hack into the matching system? My continual cursing of my archaic job?*

The image of the commander's face grew so large, her eyes took up the whole screen. "Would you do anything to ensure the survival of the mission?" Her voice boomed, echoing over the glass sight panel.

The commander's gaze simmered, searing Eri's mind, and Eri straightened up, standing as tall as a five foot two woman could. She thought of Aquaria, her parents, even Litus. "Of course."

The commander's face returned to its normal size. "Good. I have a mission for you."

Eri dropped her jaw, and then snapped it back up. Did Ursula Grier want to learn French?

"I know this comes as a shock. Sit down before you pass out. Let me explain."

The commander flicked her gaze to a row of stools against the sight panel. Not wanting to seem insubordinate, Eri nodded and climbed onto the nearest one, pushing off a film of dust.

Not many guests for the commander.

Eri's short legs dangled, and she tensed her muscles to hold them in place. Now was not the time to look childish.

The commander's image fizzled for a second, then blinked back on. "We reach Haven 6 in a week. As you know, scouts sent out hundreds of years before we left Earth reported it uninhabited by humanoids or any other intelligent species."

Eri nodded.

"Last night we reestablished contact with the scout droid sent to Haven 6 hundreds of years ago. Using its interface, we rebooted the satellite orbiting the planet. The satellite picked up images that would suggest the initial scout readings were wrong."

The commander's lips set in a grim line of disapproval before her face disappeared. Blurred images of a forest with brown thatched roofs poking out from the canopy filled the screen.

Eri leaned forward, eyes wide. Intelligent life? Not one scout ship had ever picked up even a sliver of proof they weren't alone in the universe. Since the space pirates severed all communication among the colony ships, there was no way to tell what any other colony ship had encountered. The commander's image reappeared before Eri could get a better look at the alien settlement. "Which leads me to alter my plans. I've appointed you part of an advance mission before colonization. A research ground crew."

Eri steeled her knees so she wouldn't collapse off the stool into a puddle of mush on the floor. "Why me?"

"You're our only linguist, Ms. Smith. You must decipher the alien language and root yourself into their society. Only then can you estimate their abilities and any imminent threat to us."

Did the commander choose her because she was expendable, or truly because of her linguist skills? She shot down the first thought and continued to listen. *Maybe for once I'll be important.*

"We're not going to land on a planet that may endanger the lives of the people on this mission. You, along with a small team, are to befriend whatever creatures reside on Haven 6."

Eri's heart almost burst with pride. "You want me to represent the *Heritage*?"

Grier's lips tightened like she was mildly annoyed. "This is precisely why all colony ships have at least one linguist—in case they encounter extraterrestrial life."

"Of course. I-I knew that." Eri stuttered over her words. "It's just—I'm so shocked. I'm honored and humbled you've chosen—"

Grier interrupted her. "Report all of your observations to me directly. I need to know their intelligence level, their advancements, and any weaponry these aliens possess."

Eri saluted. "Yes sir, Commander."

❦❧

The mention of weapons did raise a red flag, but Eri squashed the concern down. The commander was just protecting all of them, making sure no one from the ship would get hurt. Besides, this was the first time she'd been assigned a task that would make a difference, and she wanted to prove herself and make the commander proud at the same time. *By the time I'm done, they'll be begging to promote me. Then, I'll have my choice of a lifemate…gorgeous eyes, chestnut hair… someone to talk to, grow old with…*

The commander's rigid voice startled Eri out of her daydream. "Report to the briefing at seventeen hundred in Bay 6. Don't repeat this to anyone without code nine clearance. Project reference: Delta Slip."

Eri bowed, her curls falling on either side of her face. She snapped up and turned on her heel, thinking of all the language syntax refreshing she had to do.

CHAPTER TWO
MATCHING EYES

The breeze raised every hair on Striver's arms as he crouched behind a fern cluster, downwind of a bathing swamp boar. The smell of wet hair and mold assaulted his nostrils. The beast stank when it was alive, but roasted on a spit, the smoked meat tantalized his taste buds. He ran his tongue along the tips of the feathers on his arrow for a slight spin when launched.

The boar rose from the water, its hairy hide, over a meter long, prickling the surface. Striver lifted the arrow and cocked his bow.

Holy Refuge, this beast is huge.

Taking a deep breath, he calmed his nerves and sharpened his focus. The boar would feed the entire village for two days, but if it sensed him and charged, its sheer weight alone could crush him. Never mind the cloven hooves. Its snout wiggled, wrinkling up between its curved tusks as it sniffed the air.

No way it'll sniff me out.

Striver had wrapped swamp weed around his biceps, streaked mud across his forehead and cheeks, and wore a velvety mire leaf on his back. He reeked so much like a swamp rat, he wouldn't be surprised if one nested in his hair.

Just a little higher and he'd have a direct shot.

The beast sunk until only its black eyes crested the water and Striver cursed under his breath. What was it waiting for?

Leaves rustled across the bog. Striver spotted the boar's quarry. A weasel worm poked its head from the shoreline, whiskers twitching. The swamp boar stilled.

No, no, no. Not now.

Maybe the weasel worm would squiggle back into the log?

Luck was not on Striver's side. The small mammal slithered across the shoreline in his direction.

His father's teachings came back to him. *Wait for opportunity to show itself. Don't run from fear.*

The swamp boar took off, water rippling as it swam across the bog and reemerged on Striver's side, chasing after the weasel worm. Sludge dripped from its jaw and hefty flanks as it climbed ashore and gained momentum. Then its black eyes locked on his. He aimed and released the arrow faster than his heart could beat.

The beast charged as the arrow slipped through the air like a silent secret and plunged into its chest. Striver fell sideways as the boar roared in pain and slid across the ground, its massive body flattening all the vegetation in its path. Swillow wisps launched in flight, and the weasel worm darted into the undergrowth as if using Striver as a distraction had been its plan all along.

Upturned leaves drifted back to the forest floor. Striver waited until silence fell before emerging from the ferns. He approached the beast from behind, walking through the upturned brush without a sound. It stared into the trees, bleak and unresponsive. He watched the chest for movement, but the boar had released its last breath. Relieved and humbled, he tied the feet with a rope and dragged it away from the shore. He could not bear its weight on his own, so he'd have to ask the villagers to help. Using a few palm leaves, he hid the boar from other predators.

Noting his current coordinates, he slipped the disguise off his arms and circled the bog, using the sun poking through the canopy as a guide. He'd traveled far tracking the beast.

Almost to the border.

Striver paused, leaves rustling around him as a breeze cooled his tense muscles. It would only take a few more steps to reach the wall. The odds of any sign of Weaver were slim, but he'd promised his mother. He had to try. Turning back, he circled the bog and headed to the wall.

The stone fortification rose from the trees like an impenetrable wall surrounding his village's territory in a semicircle from the mountains in the north to the sea in the south. The stone cast an ominous shadow in the forest. As he approached, the undergrowth tapered off, the darkness too absolute for much growth. Only the tallest trees rivaled the concrete. He touched the cool surface, feeling a mix of wonder and disgust at the only sign of technology in an otherwise natural world. Built by his ancestors, it was meant to segregate the law-abiding from those who wished to follow the pirate legacy.

Metal rungs led to the top, where knife-sharp shards of wood and flint protruded like the hairs on the boar's back. Striver hung his bow around his chest and climbed, hoping the Guardians didn't notice his detour. He reached the top and peered through the sharpened pricks. A façade of slick concrete fell to a moat so deep, the water churned black. The tail of a leecher swept up, slapping the surface, and disappeared. But Striver wasn't interested in the moat waters. He looked beyond the dense trunks, tempted to call out his brother's name.

"He won't come." The voice came from the sky. Striver turned as a ten-foot wingspan blocked the sun.

Phoenix. Had he been watching the entire time?

The Guardian spiraled down, landing on the branches of a nearby tree. He folded his winged arms, iridescent feathers settling behind him, and regarded Striver with pale, opaque eyes. His beaked mouth chirped once, a melancholy sound. "You must let him go."

Ignoring him, Striver gritted his teeth and climbed down. "I'm never going to give up on him."

"His life path is his own choice." The words lilted like sweet birdsong, but to Striver they soured in his stomach.

"I know the rules." Striver jumped the remaining meter to the ground. The Guardian flew from the treetop and joined him on the forest floor.

Striver resisted meeting his gaze. Phoenix's controlled emotions frustrated him. Sometimes he wondered if the Guardians felt anything at all.

"I mourn Weaver's loss as well," Phoenix said.

Striver pulled his bow over his head and secured his arrow bag closer to his shoulder. "He's not your brother."

"We are all brothers here."

"Of course." As if he'd forgotten. He knew very well the colony's unity, taught by the Guardians, was their strength. He just didn't want to hear it now.

Striver gestured toward the bog. "I felled a boar. Will you help me carry it back?"

"That's why I came to get you." Phoenix's large eyes glistened in a patch of sunlight and, for a moment, he looked amused.

"Must you follow me everywhere I go?"

"The chosen leader of the people has to remain safe. You take risks, just like your father did. Besides, I was guarding the border. I only spotted you when the swillow wisps rose from the trees."

Striver quieted with the mention of his father. They walked the remainder of the way in silence, listening to the calls of den micers and the pattering feet of weasel worms. The putrid bog air turned to the crisp smell of fresh leaves.

A horn wailed over the forest, and they paused, searching the shadows around them. Striver whispered, "Which direction did it come from?"

Phoenix craned his head. "South. By the *S.P. Nautilus*."

"Of course."

Clutching his bow, Striver darted through the undergrowth as Phoenix rose to the sky. The Guardian flew swiftly, but he'd be damned if he let the birdman beat him to the call. Jumping over a brook, he landed on the other side and his boots slid along the embankment. He regained his footing and sped forward, following others as they rushed along the border.

When he reached the southern portion of the wall, men perched along the ridge, firing arrows across the moat on the other side.

Weaver. I hope he's all right.

Scrambling two at a time, Striver climbed the rungs. He reached the top just as Carven released an arrow. Lawless men and women braved the moat, carrying lengths of rope to storm the wall. They wore boots made from thick boar hide up to their waists to protect against the sharp teeth of the leechers.

"Damn pirates have come for the ship," Carven growled, reaching behind him to pull another arrow from his bag.

Striver let an arrow fly as a warning and turned to Carven, wondering how a father of four could look so fierce. "They'll never make it across. The water's too deep."

Carven shook his head, streaks of gray hair making him look older than his years. "They don't have to."

"But their arrows will never reach—"

One man waded into the waters and held up a black bow, made from bray wood and strung with swamp thickets. He raised it to the top of the ridge and let an arrow fly with a rope attached. The arrow hit Thrift, the potter from their village, and he fell backward off the wall until the rope pulled taut. Lawless hooted in triumph.

Striver's heart sank. *I know that bow.*

Weaver had equipped the army with Striver's latest invention, the Death Stalker. They'd made them together for the last hunting season. He'd been so proud of his brother for helping him design it. Never did he think Weaver would use the great reach of the bows to scale the other side of the wall.

Never did he think his brother would side with the enemy.

As he gawked, Lawless flooded the wall with arrows, securing ropes. Three men dangled from the first rope, climbing closer to the top of the wall, hand over hand. A team of men on the banks covered them. Guardians flew above the mass, dropping nets to confuse and contain the horde. At a time like this, Striver wished their culture allowed them to act more aggressively.

"There's too many; I can't keep them all back." Carven's voice wavered.

"Hold your position. Focus on the banks." Striver shouted the orders to the others on the fence and grabbed an arrow from his bag. The chaos around him muted as he focused on the rope. He saw every twine of fiber and the bulge of the three-part braid.

Now.

His arrow sailed across the moat and severed one of the braids. The men on the rope held on as their lifeline bounced but didn't break.

Damn!

An arrow whizzed by his cheek. A moment later he stood, aiming for the same spot. The men hung only a meter away from the unguarded part of the wall where Thrift had been stationed. Striver swore he could smell their unwashed clothes and fresh sweat.

Carven gritted his teeth as he ducked behind the wall. "They're coming."

"I got 'em." Striver pulled the bow taut, feeling the familiar stretch of his arms. He released the tension and the arrow flew a millimeter lower than the first one, slicing the rope in two. The men writhed in the air as they fell to the moat. The leechers swarmed, and the water boiled with their wrath.

Blocking their screams, he turned to the other ropes and raised his bow. This time his arrow sliced two at once, each rope sending more men and women into the murky waters. Carven hollered in triumph by his side, but Striver felt no accomplishment in sending men to their deaths.

Carven shouted over the wall. "Take that, you Lawless pirates!"

Disheartened by their comrades' plunge, and writhing in the nets the Guardians had dropped from the sky, the Lawless retreated to the water's edge and into the safety of the dense forest, pursued by the Guardians above.

"Well done, Striver." Carven saluted him. "You've driven them back."

Disgust overwhelmed him as he watched the leechers swim in and out of the pile of empty clothes floating along the surface. "If only they'd stay in their own lands and stop bothering us. No blood would be shed."

Carven put a hand on his shoulder. "As long as we have the *S.P. Nautilus*, they're going to keep coming."

"I'm tempted to destroy it. As much as it is a reminder of where we came from, it holds too many secrets. If the Lawless got their hands on that technology…"

"They won't. We'll protect it like we always have."

Striver sighed, the adrenaline rush wearing off. "I hope so."

As the last few men disappeared into the forest, Striver spotted a head of chestnut hair a shade lighter than his own.

Was it him?

"Weaver!" He picked his way through the razor-sharp protrusions on the ledge.

Carven called after him, "Striver, wait! It's too dangerous with

Lawless still out there."

The older man grasped his pants leg, but Striver pulled away, a razor edge slicing his pants cuff. "I have to see if it's him."

Just as he dangled over the fence, the man's head of chestnut hair turned back. Green eyes bright as his own glimmered over a tight-lipped scowl that sank Striver's heart in swamp sludge. Weaver ducked under a moss-laden branch and disappeared.

CHAPTER THREE
SECRET SPUNK

Eri paced outside Aquaria's new family cell, her redheaded halo reflecting in the dull chrome.

Should I disobey the commander and tell Aquaria about my mission?

She could trust her. Only her sister knew of her pairing requests, and she'd never spoken a word of it to anyone. But could Aquaria keep the information from Litus? Lifemates didn't have secrets. Eri didn't want to stand in the way of her sister and Litus. But she also didn't want to leave without saying good-bye.

Eri buzzed and her sister's heart-shaped face flashed on the hailing screen. Tears streaked her cheeks and she wiped red, blotted eyes. "Eri, I was hoping you'd stop by."

Thoughts of her new mission fell away.

Her voice quivered, and Eri leaned toward the screen. "Aquaria? Are you okay?"

The screen flashed off and the particles of the portal dematerialized. Aquaria ducked out and checked both ends of the corridor before pulling her in. "Come and sit with me on the couch."

The smell of brewing vegetable stew made Eri's stomach gurgle. Passing by a wallscreen of daises bowing and lifting in a silent wind, Eri settled into the cyber-green plastic couch, wondering if the furniture had come with the apartment. Aquaria favored blue. "Is everything okay?"

"No."

Her sister sat beside her and took a deep breath. "Commander Grier assigned Litus to the exploratory team."

"Oh." Of course. It made perfect sense she'd cry for Litus. Eri put an arm around her shoulders. *Maybe today isn't the best time to tell her of my assignment.* "I'm sorry."

"That's not all. He said you're on the team, too." Aquaria stared at her, as if daring her to deny it.

Eri frowned and watched the daisies. "I saw tree huts. The inhabitants are hardly anything to worry about. I'm just so excited Commander Grier asked me to be a part of the team."

"It makes perfect sense. You're an excellent linguist, the best that's ever lived on this ship."

"It's a galactically spectacular opportunity to advance my career."

Aquaria sniffed. "This is it—your chance to make a difference. Your destiny—everything you've been preparing for your entire life. You have to go out there and live it. I only wish it wasn't so dangerous."

"Dangerous?" Eri hadn't even thought of it that way. More like advantageous.

Aquaria took her hand. "She didn't tell you about Delta Slip?"

Eri leaned forward, denial blocking any open thoughts. "Yes, she did. I'm supposed to gather information and root myself in the aliens' culture. Befriend them."

Aquaria's features grew solemn. "I don't think that's all she means to do."

"What are you saying?"

"Litus hasn't told me everything—he can't." Aquaria's gaze darted to a holopicture of their wedding on the far wall. "He shouldn't have even mentioned the fact that Haven 6 was inhabited, but I pressed him. I mean, what's a marriage if you can't even tell your spouse what's going on?"

Aquaria clenched her hand into a fist and jutted out her chin.

Eri wanted to help, but she wasn't a marriage therapist. She needed to figure out what Aquaria was trying to tell her about the mission. "What *did* you learn?"

Aquaria took a deep breath like she was repressing feelings Eri shouldn't know of. "From the cryptic answers he gave me, I got the impression that you'll be collecting information to use against the inhabitants."

Acid burned Eri's stomach. "The commander said I was to befriend them…learn their language…"

"Think about it, Eri. What kind of information did she want from you?"

Here was the red flag Eri had blatantly ignored. "She did mention weapons, but I thought it was only to protect us." Even as Eri defended the commander, doubts crept in. "Her mission is to look out for us. Not any other species. If they did present a threat…"

Aquaria nodded conspiratorially. "Commander Grier would make sure they wouldn't get in the way. In the most thorough manner she could."

Eri ran her hands through her curls. "Which puts me in quite the predicament."

Aquaria shrugged, her intense gaze turning to the blowing daisies. "Maybe we're worrying over nothing. You said you saw thatched trees huts. Maybe they're not a threat at all. I don't mean to belittle your mission. In fact, it's probably the most important mission in all of this ship's history. I'm just asking you to keep your eyes open." Her voice fell to a whisper. "I snuck a look at the mission's supplies. They're bringing gallium crystal void rays."

Gallium crystal void rays hardly sounded diplomatic. Eri covered her face with her hands. "I don't want to be a spy."

Aquaria grabbed her hand, squeezing so hard, her fingernails dug into Eri's skin. "Listen to me. You're going to have to find out if these creatures are peaceful. If they are, you're going to need to decide."

"Decide what?"

"Whether or not to warn them."

Eri froze. Blasphemy leaked from her sister's mouth.

"I can't go against the commander or the Guide."

Aquaria nodded and looked away. "That's a decision only you can make." She spread her hand over the layout of her new family cell. "Look at me—I'm hardly one to speak. I follow the Guide to the letter, and what has it gotten me? A cyber-green couch and a wallscreen full of daisies."

"And handsome Litus."

Aquaria's gaze roamed to a distant place Eri couldn't see or understand. "How could I forget? I just wish I knew more about him. I want to know who he is inside, not the façade he puts on for everyone else."

Eri's mouth snapped shut. Maybe the façade *was* the real him. For Aquaria's sake, she hoped not.

The wallscreen beeped and a smooth-toned voice sung out, "Fourteen hundred."

Aquaria dabbed at her eyes, brushed off her pants legs like she had crumbs all over her, and stood up. "Litus will be home soon. Come, I'll make you a cup of tea." The change in her voice and her composure was a shock, like walking from the rainy biodome into the fluorescent halls.

Eri balked, unwilling to get up from the couch or leave their conversation. So many questions lingered.

As if on cue, the portal dematerialized and Litus stood in the doorway in his navy officer's uniform. Aquaria walked over and gave him a peck on his cheek. "Welcome home, hon."

He noticed Eri on the couch. "I didn't know we had company."

"Eri stopped by to see our new place." Aquaria disappeared into the kitchen.

Eri stood up, plastic crinkling, hoping the cyber-green didn't melt onto her white uniform. "I like the daises on the wallscreen." She didn't mention the couch.

Litus set his workbag down by the portal. "That was Aquaria's idea, right, dear?"

Aquaria shouted back a response between gurgles of the food congealizer. "I thought it would brighten up the room."

"Are you staying for dinner?" Litus turned to Eri, his face somber and unyielding. Eri wondered what thoughts swam behind his unwavering blue gaze. He seemed to size her up, calculating her inner feelings.

"No, I have a lot of work to do." Not wanting to burn in his gaze any longer, she ducked her head into the kitchen. "Bye, Aquaria."

"Good luck, Eri. Remember what we talked about." Aquaria whipped her head around from the countertop preparation to give her a steady stare.

"I'll remember."

As Eri passed by Litus, a faint smile brightened his handsome face. "See you tomorrow."

"Tomorrow?" Was Litus coming by to learn Spanish?

"The first training session for Delta Slip."

"Oh, yeah." Aquaria's new information had blindsided her so completely, she'd forgotten. "Of course."

"Looking forward to it, I hope. It's an honor to be chosen for the team."

Eri traced the doorframe with her pointer finger, collecting dust on her fingernail.

An honor. Yeah, right.

శ్రీ ✦

The laser-training arena sat in a bay near the library. Eri had walked down the corridor countless times to research old texts and run her hands over real books from Old Earth. She'd never had a reason to stop for target practice in the arena. She almost passed the portal and waltzed directly into the library out of habit.

The conversation with Aquaria from yesterday still swam in her head. Did the commander plan on cohabitation or annihilation?

If it was the latter, the commander asked her to represent a civilization that would ultimately spell the natives' doom. She was more than a delegate. She was a spy, a bringer of death. Shriveling inside, Eri wondered if she possessed such cool callousness. A thousand doubts clouded her mind. This mission struck a dissonant chord inside her. Even though it came directly from the commander, it wasn't right.

Thatched tree huts were hardly the handiwork of a mechanically advanced society. Commander Grier was overreacting to the threat, and Eri was her pawn. But did she have a choice?

You're going to have to decide…

Whether or not to warn them…

That's only a decision you can make for yourself…

She had no idea her sister was a closet rebel. All those pretend games they had played as kids suddenly had new meaning. One question rose above the rest. How deep did Litus's alliances lie? For once, Eri was glad she wasn't paired with someone like him, because she wanted a partner who shared her dreams, someone who was able to open up and tell her how he felt.

A burly man passed by, flicking his ID badge to open the arena portal. Eri stepped into a jungle. She reached out and her hand passed through a thicket of vines, feeling thin air. Holograms. Designed to resemble the environment they headed into. A shiver ran up her spine.

She moved to the center of the arena where a group of men and women congregated. Some were lieutenants in training, others special ops, and a few were the commander's highly trained bodyguards. All were built like they could wrestle a bull to the ground and eat its guts raw. She felt like a mouse cowering in their shadows.

A whisper hissed from the crowd of giants. "What's she doing here?"

"She's a linguist." The other voice dripped with sarcasm.

Eri turned to identify the speaker. A man with a buzz cut and bristles on his chin looked down at her like she was some annoying cleaning droid. "Going to talk to the aliens, huh?" He held up his gallium crystal void ray with large ionic chambers on either side, a weapon almost as long as she was tall. "Here's my medium of negotiation."

Everyone chuckled. Eri must have paled because one woman with thick eyebrows taunted her. One small braid stuck out the top of her shaved head. "Don't worry, we won't let them hurt you."

"Enough, Mars." Litus's voice resonated across the arena. He walked through a fern cluster to meet them. "We have a small team of ten and everyone's here. Let's get the show on the road."

The crowd quieted. Litus's leadership skills impressed her. She'd never seen him in action before. Wouldn't Aquaria feel lucky with her pairing now?

Litus waved his arm in an arc. Thatched tree huts littered the canopy. The scout droid flew down from a branch, collecting samples from the jungle floor. "These are pictures shot from our satellite droid on Haven 6. Pictures taken before this happened." He pointed to a section of the jungle. An arrow whizzed through the air and Eri ducked. The man behind her didn't flinch as the shaft flew through his body and out the other side.

Holograms.

Embarrassment flooded her and her cheeks burned. Someone laughed, but Litus's glare stifled any further derision. He raised an eyebrow at Eri. "Good instincts."

Another arrow followed, and a portion of the wallscreen fizzled out and went blank.

Litus turned to the crowd. "The video input feed was disabled. That's all the info we have."

The man with the buzz cut stepped forward. "Arrows. You've got to be kidding me."

"It does seem primitive, Tank. Still, you can never be too careful. That arrow knocked out our scout in one hit. That's why the commander is sending us first. Our mission is to collect as much data on our new environment, and on those who inhabit it, as possible. Eridani Smith is our interpreter, and everyone, and I mean everyone—" Litus glared at Tank. "Must listen to her."

Mars's voice purred like a lioness. "Why the target practice, chief?"

Eri watched Litus's reaction carefully. *Yes, why the humongous laser guns?*

Litus shifted, bringing the gun down to his waist. "Like I said, we can never be too careful. We're invading their planet, taking over their home. We don't know how our visitation will be received. There's a good possibility we'll have the same welcome party as this unfortunate satellite droid."

Taking over? Eri raised her eyebrows, sizing him up. Did he just give away an element of the plan? Or was he being overly dramatic to warn them of what the creatures might think?

Litus held up his weapon. "Everyone's laser is set for practice mode, which means you are shooting harmless light. But try to take this as seriously as possible. We wouldn't want friendly fire once we landed, so let's not shoot each other today."

No matter what the mission was, Eri questioned having her own laser. Would a leader of state attend a meeting with a laser gun? No. Having a weapon might make her a target.

Rustling disturbed the leaves behind her and Eri whirled around. "What is it?"

"A target." Litus stepped over to her and offered her a hand laser. "I've already input the code."

She took the laser in both hands and the weight dragged her wrists down.

Litus stood aside as a gray figure darted in and out of the foliage. "Target anything that moves."

Her weapon buzzed, vibrating her fingertips and warming the palms of her hands. Shots pinged around her, and she backed up against a holorock and cowered.

Litus joined her, crouching. "Eri, your weapon is set and ready to go."

The gray humanoids flitted by as the team followed them in a trail of fireworks. The smell of burned dust spiked her anxiety. "But I've never fired at anything before."

"You've got to try."

"I can't do it, Litus. I'm…frozen with fear." She hoped she sounded convincing.

Litus checked the surrounding area before turning back to her. "Believe in yourself, Eri. That's the only way you'll make anything happen in your life."

Eri shifted from foot to foot, wishing she could turn into a hololizard and slither underneath a holorock.

A gray humanoid sprung from the ferns but Litus continued, oblivious. "Or else you're just cosmic dust on the ring of a planet, waiting for gravity to pull you along the same old circular path."

Tank slid on his knees, firing, but the humanoid zigzagged against the changing stream. As it neared, its face came into view, making Eri shiver. The holographic image had no eyes or mouth, just a sheen of twilight for a face.

Is this what the aliens will look like? If so, could she bring herself to even utter a single word to them?

As the battle raged, Eri thought Litus would raise his own laser and stop the rampage, but he didn't notice the stray opponent lunge in his direction. There was no time to warn him.

Eri snapped her laser up and fired, the shot blasting her backward through the holorock. She slid on her back, feeling the gun pulse in her hands as it recharged. The smell of singed electrical wires choking her, she cringed and covered her face with her arms.

When she gathered the courage to open her eyes, the gray humanoid lay on his back. Litus walked over to her, respect and astonishment shining in his eyes.

Even Tank shouted a hoot of support. "Go, linguist."

Litus seemed to reassess her as he offered his hand and pulled her up. "You have more spunk than you let on."

CHAPTER FOUR
QUEST FOR KNOWLEDGE

Weaver trudged through the dense undergrowth, failure eating away at his insides like poison. Swamp water sloshed into his boots, making his toes curl with a damp chill that spread up his legs. He shivered, and the familiar feeling of inferiority hovered over him. Too long he'd lived in its shadow.

As he followed the battered army home, he replayed the battle. *How did I fail?* His bows had penetrated his former village's defenses, giving the men the lead time needed to scale the wall. Nothing could beat the Death Stalker's scope and aim.

Except Striver. Once again his brother had outshined him tenfold. By felling the first three ropes, he'd weakened the pirates' resolve. Death by leechers was a nasty, painful end, and Striver's aim guaranteed some would fall. If only his men had pushed through, letting the first wave of ropes go down while other attackers sprang up. The Lawless claimed they ate ferocity for lunch, yet they had the most spineless weasel worm hearts he'd ever seen.

He had to remind himself the pirates' shortsightedness was why he thought he could lead the Lawless, manipulating them to his own ends. Only then would he feel powerful. After he gained control of the Lawless tribe, he'd show his village how they should have chosen him, not Striver, to lead.

An unsettling snake of discomfort slid across his shoulders. First he had to report to Jolt.

People scurried from the tree huts, shouting to the survivors as they passed. Weaver didn't reply. They'd learn soon enough who'd died and how deeply they'd failed. These lands were ruled by a dictator, not a democracy like the do-nothing Guardians and the weak-minded council. He reported to one man alone.

The husk of a spaceship protruded from the ground just beyond the last cluster of fern huts. Cold, harsh metal cut through the soft leaves like a razorblade, reminding Weaver of the power of technology.

Two bodyguards nodded as Weaver passed. Snipe, the younger man on the right, shifted his predatory eyes under heavy lids, looking as mean as a cornered swamp boar. Crusty, the older man on the left, cracked a sad half smile, as if Weaver paced to his death.

Weaver stifled a shudder. *I can handle Jolt. He still needs me.* Stepping underneath the perpetually open hatch, he mustered his courage.

Torches lit the inside of the ship, casting flickering light on control screens long dead. The putrid scent of dank moss and rusty metal hung heavy in the air. Water dripped everywhere, forming muddy puddles on the chrome floor.

Jolt slumped in the cockpit, gazing through the cracked glass of the sight panel on a dead-end course to nowhere. He swiveled in the age-old captain's chair, the plastic cracking as he moved.

The flickering torchlight illuminated half his pockmarked face and tight-lipped frown. He ran his hands over a laser gun with photon chambers clogged with dirt. Hundreds of years ago, the gun had pulsed with energy. Now it was an empty trophy, a remnant of a bygone time.

"Humans were once a mighty superpower. We ruled Earth with our weapons of mass destruction, creating grand wars and great, mighty leaders. I've heard the stories passed down by my ancestors. The same people who once flew this very ship. Now, thanks to your technohoarding friends, all we have left are sticks and stones. They sit on top of lost technology, and they won't let us access it, won't let us progress beyond our primal means."

Jolt turned so the reddish light bathed his entire face. "Your weapons failed." A scar above his forehead twitched with his pulse, reminding Weaver of a weasel worm. His muddied brown hair twisted up in spikes.

Weaver bowed, gazing at the scuffed chrome floor. "For now."

"You promised me access to the *S.P. Nautilus*, and instead, we lost seven men."

Boy, the scouts ran quickly. Weaver had guessed word would reach Jolt before he could explain. He'd prepared for such a fight. He straightened, standing tall enough that he could reach the dangling wires above him. "Your army is a bunch of cowards who scramble at the first sign of death."

Jolt lurched and lunged, shoving his face into Weaver's. His lips quivered as his bitter breath fell on Weaver's cheek. "No one insults me and lives."

Weaver didn't flinch. He had to stand his ground, or Jolt would turn him into a pile of mush on the chrome floor. "It's not an insult. It's the truth."

Cold pricked Weaver's skin. He glanced down. Jolt had snuck an obsidian blade against his gut, slicing into his shirt.

"Give me one reason not to kill you right now."

Weaver's gaze strayed to the blank control screens. "Look at this ship. The circuits are corrupted beyond repair. Only I know the exact coordinates of the one working spaceship on Refuge, complete with data files on both the space pirates of Outpost Omega and the

Guardians' advanced technology from their home world. Only I can scratch the codes and mimic the claws of the Guardians to get you in."

"It does me no good on this side of the fence." Jolt narrowed his eyes. "All this failure has got me thinking. Who's to say you're not a spy?"

Weaver put both hands on his hips, jutting his thumbs through his belt loops. "Nothing worth having is without risk." He hated quoting his father, but the old man had been right about some things, even if he'd favored Striver over Weaver since birth.

Jolt eased, slipping his blade into a side sheath. "Of that, you're right. I'm giving you one more chance to prove yourself. Meanwhile, I have my eye on you. No ship, no place here in our lands. I can't let you crawl back to your brother's cheery little village. You know too much."

"I'd rather die than go back."

Jolt smirked. "So be it. But all in good time. I have another project for you."

"If it has to do with that scout droid you found last week, you can count me out. There's no way I can get it running again after your huntsmen skewered it. My expertise is with bows, not technology."

Jolt eyed him. Weaver cocked a brow. He had his ways of finding information.

But Weaver's knowledge of his secret didn't seem to intimidate Jolt. Something more profitable than a scout droid stirred in the depths of his dark eyes. He savored his words. "No, it's something much, much better."

❧ ❧

The scent of smoked boar filled the air. Wooden flutes trilled, accompanied by the heavy beat of leather drums. Striver stood apart from the festivities, watching Guardians thread strings of flowers through the trees in the twilight.

"You don't care to celebrate?" Phoenix appeared from the branches above him, proving to Striver that he could never truly be left alone. Although sometimes he resented the constant attention leadership thrust upon him, tonight the Guardians' presence soothed him. At least someone else noticed the discord slowly twining through their everyday lives.

Striver leaned against a wood railing. "What's to celebrate? The attack was too close this time. One of our men died."

Phoenix perched on the upper branch, giving Striver space. His voice was patient, kind. "Thrift gave his life to protect us. Tonight, we gather to honor him."

Striver clenched his fist. "I should destroy the ship, Phoenix. Then we'd all have peace."

"And erase our two people's histories?" Phoenix cooed softly like a parent warning a child against playing with fire. "How can we ever hope to live a better life on Refuge without learning from our mistakes of the past?"

"Sometimes I think it's better to start with a clean slate."

"Is it? Or will we fall prey to the same demons that led your ancestors to Old Earth's end?"

"Sometimes I think it's inevitable. The rise and fall of civilizations. Man's never-ending search for knowledge and power."

Phoenix shifted on the branch, his feathered wings rustling. "Such is the weight carried by the leader. Always thinking about the best interests for his people, always striving for the better course. You are true to your name."

Striver sighed, expectations burdening his shoulders.

"Sometimes you have to let your worries go. Only then will you see the right path." Phoenix dropped beside him and placed long fingers like twigs on his shoulder. His eyes shone the unchanging color of twilight. He squeezed lightly and fluttered off, joining the other Guardians in the sky. They flew in formation, uniform in appearance, attitude, and purpose.

Striver shook his head and tried to empty the riddles from his mind. The Guardians had no interest in leading themselves, but boy did they have a load of complicated advice. Still, he had to be thankful for their cohabitation. Without them, the entire colony may have fallen to Lawlessness, or used the knowledge on the *S.P. Nautilus* for their own ends. The Guardians were a constant voice of reason that echoed throughout centuries, providing their colony with a single vision in an otherwise wild land. Thank goodness Aries and Striker had hatched the eggs on the *S.P. Nautilus*, giving this remarkable species another chance at life. The videos on the Guardians' ship had shown their planet's sun was dying. It was possible the Guardians on Refuge were all that were left of their kind.

The music lulled and people congregated around the roasting boar as Carven began to cut a piece. "As per custom, the first serving of this feast is given to the hunter who felled the beast."

Applause and hoots erupted as Striver jogged to greet them. He'd rather someone else take the credit, but he also didn't want to seem ungrateful for their offering. Carven handed him a plate with steaming boar meat.

"A meal for a true hero, and our fearless leader!"

A chorus of approval rang out. Children chanted his name.

Striver took the wooden plate and bowed to them. A pang of remorse shot through him. He wondered if it were these moments where he shined that had caused Weaver to leave. If so, he'd rather have his brother back and be a nobody than lead a colony without him. Stifling his feelings, he pushed through the crowd, wanting to be left alone.

A young boy pulled on his sleeve. "Is it true the boar almost ran you over?"

Striver sighed, reminding himself that he had once been young. "You could say that."

"I heard you cut a rope with only two arrows." Another boy, this one with fuzz growing on his chin, gave Striver a hard look of respect.

"Luck, nothing more, my friend."

"Can you promise me the next dance?" The alto voice sang over the crowd. Striver whirled around, facing a young woman with hair, black as night and thick as the dense forest, trailing to her ankles.

"No, Riptide. Not tonight."

She traced her fingertip down his arm, stone rings glittering in the firelight. "Some other time, then?"

"Maybe so."

"Though a true hero deserves more than just a dance."

He looked away. "Tonight, I'll settle for boar."

It took him several minutes to work his way through the crowd to the rope ladders. He climbed, balancing the wood plate, hoping the meat hadn't gone cold in the chilled twilit air. Circling the tree hut, he pushed through thick vines, revealing a woven fern door. He opened the door to a small room, lit by the embers of a flickering torch.

"Mother, how are you feeling?"

A wispy-haired woman moved under the covers of a thatch bed. "I appreciate the visit, but you should be with your people." Her dark eyes sparkled as she took in the sight of him. "They need a strong leader like you in a time like this."

He handed her the plate. "Here, have some boar meat."

His mother pulled off a slender piece and chewed. She placed the plate aside. "It is good."

"Then why don't you try some more?"

Her thin fingers pulled the blanket up to her chin. "Maybe later. Tell me about the battle."

He sighed until his lungs emptied, summoned courage, and then took in another breath. "I saw him."

His mother shot upright, and her thin fingers grasped his arm so hard his skin turned white underneath her grip. The eagerness in the twitch of her mouth hurt him more than the sight of his brother had. He wanted to tell her Weaver was coming back, that he'd had enough of life in the Lawless lands. But that was a dream for another day. "He led the attack."

Either his mother didn't care or didn't hear him. "Is he all right?"

"As far as I could see. He didn't look very happy."

She shrugged. "He was never happy."

"Yes, but he looked downright miserable."

"Then maybe he'll come back to us."

"Let's keep hoping." He spread his hands, thinking of Phoenix's earlier speech. "We can't make him. If there's one thing our founders believed in, it was free will."

The shouting outside escalated, turning from celebratory hollers to screams of alarm. Striver stood, apprehension bubbling in his veins. *Not another attack.* He couldn't take seeing Weaver's miserable expression again.

"I have to go."

His mother squeezed his hand. "Don't try to save the world all by yourself."

Outside, the hollering died down. Everyone stood still as trees, all heads turned to a clearing in the center of the village. Striver slid down the rope ladder and ran to join them. As the clearing came into view, an object eclipsed half the second moon, casting a shadow over the gathering.

His heart stopped and his stomach sank to the ground. A ship. Not just any ship, but a mother boar of a ship, a hundred times larger than the *S.P. Nautilus*, hovered in the sky. An object shot from its belly, trailing flames as it cut through the atmosphere.

Oh, no. A bomb.

A thousand images flashed through his mind. His mother on her bed. Catching a trotter in the river with Weaver. His dad saying good-bye before his last mission. Was this the end? A current of anger and injustice flowed through him. So many things were still unresolved.

The projectile hurled through the air, leaving a streak of orange and gray behind it. As it neared, wings spread from the hull, steering from right to left. Its descent slowed.

That's not a bomb. It's a scout ship.

Striver ran his hands through his hair. *Holy Refuge.*

The scout ship dove straight into the Lawless lands.

CHAPTER FIVE
PLUNGE

Every molecule in Eri's body vibrated like she sat in a giant food congealizer turning into vegetable sludge. Anxiety rode through her in tidal waves as she grasped her seat restraints and held on until her fingers numbed.

How did I ever go from being an archival linguist to an interpreter and a spy on an exploratory team?

She wondered if she was more of a ticking time bomb than a friendly diplomat. The more she stewed over the training session, the more she suspected Litus had orders to eliminate these creatures on Haven at any sign of threat.

She studied him from across the circular drop chamber. *What did the commander tell you that she didn't tell me?*

He saluted her in response as if she'd just given him the next mission coordinates. Eri shook her head and sighed, closing her eyes.

Aquaria had said this was her destiny, but she felt more like a case of mistaken identity than any star-crossed heroine. *Lathos*, the Greeks would say. Major, *megalos lathos*.

The pilot's voice came on the speakers. "Prepare for landing."

Eri opened her eyes, the screeching sound of the landing gear scarier in the complete darkness. She'd rather focus on her boots.

Mars hollered a primal scream from deep within her throat. Her beady eyes teased Eri as she grinned beside her. Eri looked away, avoiding further eye contact. Why Litus situated her between the two hulking bodies of Mars and Tank, she had no idea.

Mars threw her head back, and her slender brown braid whipped in the breeze of the ventilators. "Bring it on!"

Tank snored on Eri's other side. Was the entire trip too boring for him to pay attention? Eri swallowed down bile, trying not to lose the remnants of her dinner all over his boots. She'd already gotten on Mars's bad side, and she didn't need any more enemies.

The other five members of the exploratory team checked weapons, slept, or typed messages on their wrist locators. Eri wondered what their messages said.

Send my love to…

Landing right now…

It was good knowing you…

She suppressed the urge to send a good-bye message to Aquaria. It would just heighten her sister's nerves. Later, when they'd landed and established base camp, she'd send her a reassuring note. *If we made it.*

Roaring wind turned into a screeching as the landing gear engaged, slowing their descent. The ship pitched sideways, and her stomach flipped. Real gravity pulled on her arms and legs, not the weak force simulated by the gravity rings. She thought her muscles would rip apart.

Real gravity meant a hard landing.

"Wishing you hadn't eaten that extra serving, heh?" Mars laughed.

Eri winced and looked away. "I feel fine." Just because she was small, with less than optimal genes, didn't mean she wasn't tough. *Now do something to prove it, macho woman.*

"Sure, you're just green as a cucumber every day."

"Green or not, at least no one mistakes me for a man."

Mars's face tightened and her arm muscles bunched in her restraints. Good thing the restraints held.

"Enough, you two. Can't a man get some shut-eye?" Tank shifted in his seat and pulled his newly camouflaged hat over his bristly face.

Eri closed her eyes, still smelling the reek of laser paint on her uniform. No one had thought they'd need camouflaged clothes for Haven 6. They had to scramble to dye their pristine white clothing with blotches of different shades of browns and greens. She felt like she wore one of those abstract paintings from Old Earth.

Better to be unfashionable than dead. She pushed away the thought of the gray humanoids and those arrows that had impaled the scout droid. High-pitched wheezing roared in her ears as the drop ship slowed. Her seat vibrated underneath her, chattering her teeth. Alarms sounded, and smoke choked her throat.

"Emergency fire in supply bay," a computerized voice warned on the intercom.

"Everyone stay in your seats. I'll tend to it." Litus undid his seat restraints and stood. He stumbled sideways as the ship pitched but regained balance and pulled the fire extinguisher from the wall. He pressed the portal panel and slipped into the corridor, following the trail of smoke.

"What's wrong?" Eri shouted over the din to Tank, whose hat fell and rolled across the floor.

"It's an old ship, been sitting in bay twenty-one for a long time," Tank explained. "Commander Grier didn't think we'd have to use it."

Eri quieted and held tight. The commander hadn't thought about a lot of things. Eri wondered if living in a tub of embryonic fluid drove a woman crazy. But she'd never voice her doubts out loud. Two of the commander's bodyguards sat across from them, and Eri didn't want the team to label her a rebel. She'd fought that prejudice her whole life.

Alarms beeped as the roaring of wind increased. Eri expected Litus to walk through the portal, but the particles had rematerialized. He'd left her alone with the grunts. If anything happened to him, she'd be the one in charge.

Like they'd ever listen to me. Eri stared at the portal as if her mind alone would bring him back. *Please don't die.*

The ship shuddered, and oxygen masks popped from the ceiling. Mars hollered as she slapped hers on. Eri's fingers shook as she fumbled with the plastic ties. Big hands pulled the elastics around her head and she whirled around. Tank had already secured his straps, and he tightened the sides of her mask.

The lights went out as they hit the tree line. The shaking turned into giant bumps, like they rode the back of an angry bull, as the ship skidded across the ground. Eri held her breath and squeezed her eyes shut. Someone screamed like they were all going to die.

Branches scraped against the hull until Eri thought the terrain would rip the ship to pieces and they'd have nothing to fly back on.

Her throat tightened. Going back wasn't the point. Soon, they'd all abandon the *Heritage* for a new life on this jungle world. She'd looked forward to their arrival for so long, and now she dreaded the moment they opened the hatch.

The ship screeched to a halt and her restraints pulled against her chest as she flung forward with the momentum. Curls from her head fell in her face.

The alarms trailed off and silence fell. Eri blew back her hair to see the damage. The smoke cleared to reveal a wary-eyed team. No one was hurt. The pilot's voice came on the intercom. "Landing sequence successful. Preparing for deboarding procedures."

A wave of relief flooded through Eri, and then she remembered Litus and the fire. Anxiety zapped her heart.

Tank pulled off his mask. "That was one hell of a ride."

"That was nothing." Mars slipped off her mask. "Ever sat on the flux injectors during central ignition?"

Ignoring the fact that it was against the rules to go anywhere near the flux injectors, Eri tugged off her mask, the elastic straps pulling her hair. The air reeked of burned circuits and smoke. "Where's Litus?"

"Haven't seen him since the fire." Tank shrugged, shedding his seat restraints.

"What if something happened to him?"

Mars jumped to her feet, her thick boots pounding into the floor. "Nonsense. Litus is indestructible."

As if to prove her point, the portal dematerialized and Litus stepped through, a smudge of soot across his forehead. "The fire's out. Prepare to de-board and set up base camp."

He stooped and picked up Tank's hat, dusting off the top.

Tank raised his hand. "That's mine, sir."

"Quite the ride, huh?" Litus threw the hat over to him and nodded to Eri. He scanned the team. "No one leaves the perimeter for any reason. If you see anything that can talk, you let me and Ms. Smith know."

Eri slipped out of her seat restraints, eager to stand on solid ground. She followed the team toward the back of the ship. This was it. She'd walk on a real planet, an alien world, for the first time in her life.

Mars cuffed Tank's shoulder and whispered under her breath. "Let's kick some alien ass."

Tank laughed and patted his gun. "Any day. Any time."

Their boasts fell silent as Litus pressed the panel for the back hatch. Eri held her breath, hiding in Mars's shadow but standing back enough to peer around her tree trunk of an arm.

The hatch opened slowly, humid air wafting in. A sliver of green peeked through, turning into a primordial sprawl of wild, tangled growth as the hatch lifted. Eri released her breath and took another, soaking in the dank reek of moss and stagnant water, reminding her of the compost heap in the biodome. The velvety air choked her, and she sucked in each breath like breathing through a tube filled with mold. How would she ever adapt to the higher oxygen levels? Litus gestured over his shoulder for them to follow and stepped down the ramp. The commander's bodyguards flanked him, pointing lasers into the savage wilderness.

A furry black animal shrieked and fluttered off, leaves falling in its wake. The guards pointed their lasers toward the commotion, and Litus held up his finger to stall them. Nothing else moved. Eri thought back to pictures of jungles from her history studies, but this chaotic, cornucopian paradise looked more aggressive than anything she'd imagined.

Litus whispered over his shoulder. "Press on. Tank, set up the perimeter fence."

"Yes, sir." Tank disappeared back into the ship.

The gravity pulled on Eri's feet and her boots stuck to the metal ramp. She strained to lift each leg, wondering how she'd ever get used to a force that made her feel twenty pounds heavier. A speck of black moved beside her cheek and she leaned back, watching a fuzzy ball the size of a pinhead with a slender tail land on her arm. The tail twitched, feeling the smooth texture of her uniform before it flew off into the forest.

Not like the flies in the biodome. Haven 6 was an entirely different world than the one they'd left. The original scout ships had discovered three hundred distinct species while researching the planet. None of them intelligent. But after seeing those thatched huts, Eri realized they could have overlooked any number of strange species. Species she had to establish contact with and pretend to befriend.

The team spread out, surrounding the ship. Tank strutted down the ramp with a handful of metal poles and thrust the first one into the ground. A blue light flickered on, signaling the energy field activation.

The artificial light cast the misted ferns around it in a spectral glow, making them seem sentient.

"Ten-meter radius," Litus called over his shoulder. He lifted a leaf with the tip of his laser and turned to Eri. "Ms. Smith, have a look at this."

Eri jumped off the ramp, her boots sinking into the soil. The ground crushed underneath her feet, like a cushy blanket. She stumbled, tripping over a root, and caught herself before her face crashed into a fern. The edges of the leaves looked so sharp, they could slice her skin. Her cheeks burned. How would she ever get used to uneven terrain after a lifetime of walking on chrome?

Not wanting to look incapable, Eri straightened up and tensed her legs. As she approached Litus, he handed her a hollow round pouch. "What do you make of this?"

Eri smoothed her fingers over the rough leather. Caked dirt stained her pale hand dark brown. She ran her fingers over the top. Using her nail, she dug out a hole the size of her thumb. The inside was slick. She overturned the pouch and a drop of water leaked out. "Looks like some sort of primitive canteen."

"That's what I thought." Litus raised his eyebrows. "Skilled hands made this."

His gaze flicked back to her. "The question is, who?"

CHAPTER SIX
MEMORY LIQUID

"We have to go after it." Striver pounded his fist on the meeting-room table, rattling a line of clay chalices long emptied. Two rows of elders on either side jumped in their seats. The torches, burned to stubs, cast a dim glow in a losing battle with the shadows creeping from the high crisscrossing rafters, each one thick as a girth of tree. Although the thatched roof blocked the view of the sky, the presence of the mother ship pressed down on Striver, and the sands of time ran thin.

"And put ourselves in danger to save aliens we don't even know?" Carven shook his head, settling back into his wicker chair. The dried cushion of swamp reeds creaked underneath him. "We're safe here behind the wall."

Striver picked up his fallen chalice with forced calm, running his fingers along the nicks in the rim. He expected as much from Carven. His loyalties lay with his large family. The hardest people to persuade were those with greatest risk.

Finding the ship might be the best way to protect all their families. How could he make them see?

Striver scanned the council. The table stretched the length of the meeting room, as long as the redwoods from which it was carved. The expressions of the farthest council members were hard to decipher in the dwindling firelight. "If everyone stayed where they were and lived with minimal risk, our ancestors would never have left Old Earth. They would never have battled to live on Outpost Omega or boarded that alien ship to a paradise planet only heard of in legends. If our ancestors hadn't taken risks, none of us would be here today."

A few members of the council nodded with reluctant accession. Several more held tight-lipped frowns. Beckon, an elder from Striver's grandfather's generation, furrowed his wiry gray brows from the head of the table. "What if they're hostile? Their technology is far more advanced than what we're capable of right now. The Lawless can fend for themselves."

Ignoring the shouts of protest, Striver pointed from across the table. "Exactly. Do you want that technology falling into the hands of the Lawless?"

Carven spread his palms. "If the Lawless can take it from them."

Striver pushed down his rising frustration. An unknown force within that ship called to him, and ignoring his instincts meant trouble. But a leader couldn't let his own emotions get the better of him. "We don't know they're even attacking. What if they can help us?"

"What if they want to take over? Shouldn't we be running for our lives? Finding a safe place in the mountains?"

Striver held out his hands to settle the anxious murmurs in the crowd. The last thing they needed right now was mass hysteria. Besides, running away would only delay the inevitable. If those beings in the sky wanted to conquer, Striver had to make a stand and fight, perhaps convince them to cohabitate. Sharing Refuge was his village's only chance, since their ancestors decided to forgo technology. "They could be delegates, missionaries. Do you want the Lawless to be the first humans they meet?"

"Let the Lawless deal with them. We have our own problems." Beckon waved his hand and sat back in his chair as if he'd said the final word.

Striver held Beckon's gaze, challenging him to stay in the discussion. "If they intend to conquer, wouldn't you rather know now so we can plan accordingly?"

"You just want to go back over the wall because of your brother!"

Striver whirled in the direction of the speaker. Riley, Riptide's older brother, glared at him from across the table. Ever since Striver had denied Riptide's affections years ago, the young man had been breathing down his bow.

Riley gripped the table with white knuckles, looking like he'd flip the whole thing. "You're not going to convince him to come back. He left because of you."

Anger and hurt rose up and churned in Striver's chest in a sour brew. For a moment he questioned his own motives. Was it because of Weaver?

No.

This situation did not concern his brother. A current of urgency in his gut drew him to that ship. Striver straightened, swallowed bile creeping up his throat, and spoke softly. "Weaver has nothing to do with this."

Arguments flew over the table, and the heat from the torches seared the back of Striver's neck until his skin dripped with sweat. This meeting had turned ugly, digging into his weakest places. His father's voice echoed in his thoughts. *Vulnerability makes you human. When you've lost that, you've lost your true self.*

Carven gave him an apologetic smile and stood. "We've said our arguments. If we draw this out, the meeting will last until morning, and there'll be no decision at all. We must vote."

Striver nodded, acknowledging the rules set in place by his ancestors. "How many say we don't get involved?"

Four out of seven hands rose and his stomach sank. They'd never know who or what was on that ship until it was too late. Anxiety tugged on his nerves. How could he lead if he didn't know what he was dealing with? Ever since they'd elected him, he'd feared losing the colony his ancestors had worked so hard to build. He didn't want to be the broken link that severed the chain, the generation that sent the world to hell just like on Old Earth.

He had lost Weaver, and then the Lawless attacked the wall. Now his greatest fear threatened to come true. A ship full of technology was heading into the enemy's hands.

Although he knew the outcome of the vote, in order to finalize, he had to ask the other side. "And how many say we go after the scout ship?"

Two hands rose besides his. Striver exerted all his will power not to pick up Carven's hand and make him change his mind. This was it. He'd said his argument and they'd outvoted him. All he could do was sit tight and wait. Every nerve in his body screamed for him to go after the scout ship, but he silenced all his instincts.

One of the torches flickered from the back of the room as a shadow walked past. Phoenix stepped forward and held up four long fingers, casting a branch-like shadow across the table. The shadow grew until a golden glow illuminated his whole feathered body.

The council turned toward Phoenix, silent. Guardians didn't usually involve themselves in the vote. But, when one did, people listened.

"Ignorance is more dangerous than curiosity." His large eyes met Striver's, and he seemed to wink in the glint of firelight. "I say we go."

Warm pride flowed through Striver's veins. He grinned at Phoenix before turning to the rest of the council. "That makes a tie."

Slowly, every hand rose until Carven was the only man with both palms on the table.

Striver shook his head. "I'm sorry, old friend."

Carven sighed and peeled his hand off the wood. His fingers shook in the firelight. "If you're going, then I'm going with you."

ॐ

Weaver followed Jolt into the jungle, wondering if the leader of the Lawless had brought him to the edge of their grounds to finish him off. They'd walked for hours, into the foothills of the northern mountains. Darkness had fallen, and Jolt had lit a torch, the flickering shadows bringing out the ghoulishness in his crooked features.

Surely if he wanted me gone he would have killed me in the ship. Unless he didn't want to foul up his floor.

Weaver pushed the thought away. He'd had numerous opportunities to run away on this meandering jungle trek, enough to wonder if he should blindly follow Jolt. Besides, spilled blood on the muddied, rusty chrome plates of that ancient wreck would make no difference. The ship would never fly again.

The terrain grew steep as they approached the foothills of the mountains, trees growing sideways to reach for a sliver of light. Hard rock jutted from the soil like broken shards of pottery, sharp enough to slice his pants leg open. Using a branch for support, he wished Jolt had waited until daybreak.

The jungle gave way to a valley of rocks. Jolt's torch flickered before a veil of blackness. A crumbling cave led into the bottom of a crag. Weaver stifled his doubts as he approached. "We're going in there?"

"Don't tell me you're afraid."

"I've got more courage than ten of your men combined."

"Good. Because it takes a real man to see what I've found." Jolt stepped into the cave, and the darkness engulfed his torch until it was only a small, quivering light up ahead. Afraid to lose him in the crux of night, Weaver scurried ahead.

Cool air stung his cheeks, making him shiver. The floor reeked of stagnant water and fungus. Weaver disliked any place away from the surface, away from the light. He slipped on the incline as he struggled to keep up. His night vision wasn't as acute as some, and the walls pressed in, suffocating him.

The cave narrowed, and Weaver held his arm out in front of him to slip by the rough edges. The ceiling had partially caved in, and he kicked away stray rocks to find firmer footing. Spidermites clutched his shirt and he brushed them off, their hairy legs tickling his skin. What had he gotten himself into?

"Jolt, you still there?"

Water dripped, breaking the silence. Jolt's gritty voice resonated from deep within the cave. "A little ways farther."

Pushing aside a rising current of fear, Weaver forced himself deeper into the cave. Jolt's torch had burned to a stub, and he wondered how much light they had left. Had Jolt gone crazy?

Weaver squinted in the darkness. Could he feel along the walls to find his way out? If he got trapped, Striver wasn't there to rescue him. Not this time.

Just as the ember of firelight died, a golden radiance illuminated the cave farther in.

Was it Jolt's torch? Weaver strained his sight to peer ahead. No. This light shone steadily without the flickering reds and oranges of flame. Curiosity outweighed his fear, and Weaver pushed ahead. The light grew stronger, making Jolt's torch unnecessary. Weaver expected warmth on his skin, like when he stood in the sunlight, but the tunnel grew colder and damp moss clung to his pants legs. What kind of light had no heat signature?

The narrow tunnel opened to a room lit by a golden glowing pool. Swirls moved on the surface, blossoming and disappearing like the substance moved with life. Jolt stood at the edge, his torch a weak flame compared to the radiance enveloping them.

Weaver stepped forward, leaning over the pool of light. "What is it?"

"Who knows? That's why I brought you here." Jolt pointed to the rim of the pool. The rock had been smoothed down. Strange scratchings and loops were carved into the stone in a language Weaver had never seen.

"You said you could read the symbols and work the controls of the *S.P. Nautilus*. Is this anything like those hieroglyphs?"

Weaver bent down, tracing one with his finger. Definitely not. The width of the scratchings was too skinny to match anything he'd traced on the *S.P. Nautilus*.

Weaver paused, thinking quickly. He knew better than to deny the resemblance. His familiarity with the *S.P. Nautilus* and the language of the Guardians was why Jolt kept him alive. Especially after Weaver's attack with the Death Stalkers had failed. He'd have to find a way to prove the bows were still useful.

"It's possible. I'll need some time to study the symbols."

"Of course. Just don't get too close." Jolt circled the pool, and the swirls followed him, churning at his feet. "A member of my crew fell in when we discovered it. He never resurfaced."

Weaver watched a golden swirl spin toward him and disappear. "It doesn't look very deep."

"Appearances can be deceiving, can't they?" Jolt narrowed his eyes, the scar of his forehead widening until it looked like his skin would break.

"I'll be careful."

"Good. We wouldn't want you disappearing on us."

Weaver met his glare, his muscles tightening like the strings of his bow. "I told you once already. I'm here to stay."

"Then get to work. Decipher the symbols and find out how we can use the goo to our advantage."

Jolt headed to the tunnel. Relief flooded Weaver's veins as he passed. Somehow, he had to find a way to beat this man and take control of the Lawless. Maybe the pool of golden light was the answer to his problems.

Jolt stopped at the entrance and craned his head to Weaver as if he could hear his thoughts on the wind. Weaver's pulse quickened. Was he that easy to figure out?

"One more thing. I should warn you about the side effects."

"Side effects?" Weaver shook his head. That's not what he expected Jolt to say. At all. He couldn't tell if it was better than another accusation of treachery or worse.

"I call it memory liquid. Seems to turn men sentimental over time. If you spend too long in proximity, the golden stuff will bring up all sorts of things you want to remember." Jolt tilted his head. "And some you don't."

Weaver set down his arrow bag. "What do you mean?"

"Ever want to relive a day of your life? Ever feel regret?" Mistiness clouded Jolt's eyes.

Sure, there were a lot of memories he wanted to forget, but ones he could relive again? Weaver pushed down the thought and lied. "Not that I know of."

Jolt shrugged and turned back to the tunnel. "Maybe you're too young for regrets. But maybe there's more to ya than you want people to know. You can't keep secrets from the memory liquid."

The sound of footsteps echoed down the tunnel, and Jolt flicked a warning in Weaver's direction. Weaver picked up his arrow bag and took out a long, slender shaft. The footsteps grew louder, soon becoming two sets of heavy boots. Torchlight flickered in the darkness.

Jolt slinked back along the entrance and prepared to take the intruders by surprise. Weaver cocked his arrow in his bow and pulled the string taut. The grooving in the handle reassured his blistered palm.

"Damn spidermites are crawling all over me," a tenor voice echoed.

"Shake 'em off. We're almost there," a deeper, gravelly voice answered.

Jolt's shoulders slumped, and Weaver loosened his hold on the bow. He recognized the voices.

Crusty and Snipe emerged into the golden light, looking like vagabonds stumbling upon the gates of heaven.

"What are you two doing here?" Jolt growled. "I told you not to interrupt—"

Snipe's hooded eyes widened so much, they almost looked normal. "You're gonna want to see this, boss."

"See what?"

"A ship." Crusty flicked a glance in Weaver's direction. "Headed right into our lands."

"A space ship?" Jolt's hand hovered over the sheath where he kept his obsidian blade.

"Yes, sir. A big monster, and it just sent a scout ship in our direction."

"Holy Refuge." Jolt clapped both men on the shoulders and grinned. "Get the team ready. We're gonna have an ambush."

CHAPTER SEVEN

SAVIOR

Leaves swayed in the wind above the thin beam of bluish light, the only thing separating Eri from the wilderness. She stared into the darkness over the perimeter fence. The jungle stretched around her forever, more sinister than the vast vacuum of deep space. The dim lights of their transport ship only penetrated so far.

Rustling raised the hairs on the back of her neck. A stray leaf wafted toward the beam. The electricity zapped it and it sizzled, a burning smell tainting the air. Eri hugged her arms around her chest. Would the beam work?

"Don't worry, strawberry curls; we've got it covered."

Startled, Eri whipped around. Mars smirked, and then returned to the fluorescent miniscreen in her lap. She ran her finger along the keypad and passed it to Tank. "Ha! Beat that, starship destroyer."

Anger simmered in Eri's throat. They weren't reviewing base camp conditions like Litus had instructed. They weren't even paying attention. Who knew when the aliens would find them?

Tank's fingers grazed the screen as he hurtled comets the size of raisins at virtual spaceships. The faint triumphant, techno music of *Galaxy Battlefield* played in the background.

Stupid thugs. Grier had handpicked *these* people to meet a new intelligent species and represent humankind? Eri walked around the back of the scout ship and found a container wide enough to sit down. At least they wouldn't bother her there.

Her legs kicked in rhythm against the plastic. *Thump, thump… thump, thump.* Litus had instructed the team to rest tonight so they could get an early start when the sun came up. She didn't think she'd sleep a wink. In fact, all she really wanted to do was get back on the ship and seal the hatch.

Branches snapped. Eri checked over her shoulder, expecting some gray humanoid to dart from the forest. Instead, Litus rounded the corner. He brought an extra packet of soybean wafers and a bottle of mineral water.

"Feeling okay?"

"As okay as I can in a strange jungle with unknown beasts surrounding us on all sides." Eri took the bottle and the wafer. "Thanks."

"No problem." Litus ignored her sarcasm and settled beside her. He unwrapped his soybean wafer and held it in his hand without taking a bite. She tore open her wafer and the wrapper crinkled in the wind. A stray piece of foil flew into the darkness, making Eri shiver. Would the jungle swallow the team just as easily?

"Have you talked to Aquaria?"

Litus's question caught her off guard. Was it illegal to report to family members? "I just sent her a message on my locator saying we landed safely."

"Has she written back?"

"Only to say good luck."

"Oh."

He checked his own locator and the screen remained blank.

For the Heritage's *Sake! He's not checking up on me; he's trying to get ahold of Aquaria.* Her sister had written to Eri before writing to her lifemate. Guilt trickling through her, Eri shrugged and pretended not to notice his disappointment. "She's probably stuck in the evening Guide ceremonies."

"Of course."

An uncomfortable shiver crawled up her back, and she felt like she'd spit out the bite of dry wafer that rested on her tongue. She'd rather wander alone with the jungle than talk with Litus about Aquaria. Her mind scanned all the different excuses she could come up with: *I have to get my coat in the ship. My feet are asleep and I need to walk it off. Mars wanted me to review the readings with her…* But Litus spoke first.

"Aquaria's been distant since our pairing ceremony."

The thin beam of light buzzed in the silence, making it seem like eons passed before Eri could think of an appropriate answer. "Give it time. You need to get to know each other."

Litus sighed, his broad shoulders slumping forward. "I wish she'd speak with me as openly as she speaks with you."

Eri fidgeted with her wrapper. Of course. Aquaria was a closet rebel, and she couldn't voice her thoughts to do-gooder Litus. Especially when he hadn't opened up to *her* yet. The guy was destined for lieutenant-hood. He probably studied the Guide every night before bed. What could Eri tell him? Loosen up and you'll be fine?

She shrugged. "We're sisters."

"Yes, but you have a special bond."

Heat blossomed on Eri's cheeks. "I guess I've never thought of it before. Or I didn't think anyone else could see it."

The corners of Litus's mouth curved with envy. "Her love for you is plain as black space."

"Aquaria's taken a social beating to associate with me, illegal pairing and all. I owe her so much."

"Listen." Litus turned toward her and his voice grew low. "Like everyone else on the ship, I know about how your parents…" He looked like he had trouble even saying it. "How they paired outside of the system. But their actions have nothing to do with you. You make your own reputation. Not them. Besides, I think it's kinda neat you were born of something that doesn't always happen in lifemate pairings."

"What?"

"What I'm trying to find with Aquaria: love."

Eri almost fell off the supply container. Litus talking blasphemy against the system? Had the universe turned upside down?

It must have, because he'd just told her he accepted her for who she was. She smiled tentatively at Litus. Maybe Aquaria had underestimated him. All of a sudden she wanted to help him win Aquaria's heart. "You know, you could be a little more—"

Movement blurred the leaves behind Litus's head. A slender black shaft pierced the air, careering across camp to lodge in one of the soywafer boxes.

Litus stood and whipped out his laser. "Take cover."

Another shaft whizzed through the air, knocking one of the perimeter poles to the ground. An ear-cracking *zap* made Eri cover her ears as the energy stream broke. A section of blue light fizzled out. Litus turned to Eri, his eyes alert. "We need to get back to the ship."

This isn't happening. Eri ducked behind the supply container and fumbled with her laser, yanking the gun out of the holster. What was the code? Her brain blanked. Arrows rained from the sky, three piercing the plastic where she'd just sat with sickening *thump*s. *That would have gone right through my leg.*

Litus returned fire, his laser light illuminating the darkness. Leaves and branches moved as if the trees themselves released the arrows. Maybe they did. Who knew what the aliens *really* looked like? They could have been spying on them this entire time while Mars and

Tank played *Galaxy Battlefield*.

And we're supposed to be the more advanced society.

The code: 66459. Eri finally remembered and keyed it in. Her laser buzzed underneath her fingertips. *Now or never.* She peeked around the side of the container, chancing another foray of arrows. Two more perimeter poles had gone down, making a gaping hole in their defenses, big enough for an alien the size of her wallscreen to run in.

"I don't see them!" Tank shouted from the other side of the ship. "What are we firing at?"

"Anything!" Litus shouted. "Just hold them back. Get to the ship."

Arrows hit the hull with *click*s and bounced off, raining on top of Eri and Litus. She covered her head with her arms as the shafts fell around her. One of the arrows bounced on the ground at Eri's feet. She picked up the slender wood and ran her fingers over the carved rock tip. It looked so human, like something right out of her texts about Columbus conquering the New World. But these natives were conquering her team.

Dark figures trailing leaves darted into the perimeter and rolled behind a stack of supplies. Eri nudged Litus's arm. "Over there."

Using the supply container as a shield, two sets of feet carried it back into the jungle. Feet. The bunches of leaves had feet.

Eri whispered, "What are they doing?"

Litus's voice hardened as his laser fire wove straight through their feet. "They're stealing our supplies."

Tank howled in pain from the other side of the ship. Litus gave Eri a hard stare. "We have to make it back. Are you with me?"

Her hands gripped her laser so tightly, she'd have to pry them off later. Eri nodded. "I sure as hell don't want to stay out here."

"On the count of three, we make a run for it. You stay on my right and use me as a shield."

"What about you?"

"You're much more important to the mission. Besides, Aquaria made me promise to protect you." Litus gave her a wink. "We can do this. One, two…three."

Litus pitched forward and tugged her with him. They ran against the hull as the arrows whizzed past, clicking when they hit the metal. As they rounded the corner, a member of the team lay on his back with two arrows protruding from his chest. Blood pooled around him. Eri's stomach clenched as she realized she hadn't even learned his name.

Litus crouched and felt for a pulse. He looked up at Eri and shook his head.

Dead. Eri's whole body shook with fear. She'd just seen the same man walking around camp twenty minutes ago. Anger sizzled inside her. These were the best the *Heritage* had to offer, and they'd already failed.

Was it really their fault? They were colonists not soldiers. For all their tough demeanor, her team had no real experience in combat. They'd lived their entire lives in a bubble in the sky.

Whoops and calls of triumph echoed from the forest around them. Litus grabbed her arm and dragged her forward. "We have to leave him." He shot his laser sideways into the jungle as they ran. Arrows whizzed from all angles, and Eri ducked as best she could, feeling like a big target was painted on her back.

The front of the ship was empty, containers spilled on their sides with debris blowing in the wind. Smashed energy cells tainted the air with an acidic smell. Eri stepped around the glittering pools of battery acid. Two hours into their exploration and they'd already contaminated the scene.

The ramp lay open and unguarded. Eri huddled with Litus behind a row of water jugs.

"Where is everyone?"

For once, Litus looked overwhelmed, and his wide eyes scared

Eri more than the arrows shooting from the trees. "I don't know."

"Do you think they made it?"

He shook his head. "They would have closed the ramp, or at least defended it."

Eri couldn't imagine those savage creatures firing arrows at their control screens or tearing through the wiring of the scout ship. There would be no way for them to get back to the *Heritage*. They'd have to wait in the jungle, in the dark, with no cover or reinforcements for who knew how long? "One of us has to get inside."

"Over there." Litus pointed to the edge of the jungle where a tangle of leaves dragged Mars's and Tank's limp bodies away.

"They're taking them!" Eri's voice croaked as fear suffocated her throat. "We've got to do something."

Litus's face turned solemn. "Head for the ship. When you get inside, close the hatch and buzz Commander Grier."

Eri paused. That all sounded like the kinds of things Litus should be doing himself. "What about you?"

"I'm going to buy you time."

The thought of an arrow piercing Litus's heart flashed in her mind. "No. It's too dangerous."

"Someone has to report and get help."

Scanning the empty camp, she and Litus were the only members of the team left.

"Tell Aquaria I love her." Litus's eyes burned with intensity. "Now go!"

He ran toward the jungle, firing in all directions. Eri scrambled, tripping over her boots. When she looked back, Litus had downed three clumps of leaves with legs and chased the remainder into the jungle. Eri zigzagged through the remnants of camp, trying not to look at the fallen bodies of her teammates. The air was ripe with the smell of putrid jungle rot and sweat.

Eri chanted the orders in her head. *Get to the ramp. Close the hatch. Notify the commander.*

One clump of leaves lay unmoving at the bottom of the ramp. Eri circled around it, curiosity getting the better of her. Legs, much like human limbs, poked out from the leaves. The skin was tan as a leather hide, and its feet wore rough leather boots.

Wait a second. Eri crouched down beside it, yanking off a fern. The leaves had been plucked and reassembled in a thick overgrowth, woven together with some sort of grassy reeds.

Her hands shook out of control as she dug into the leaves and pulled the covering free. A human face with a slight dusting of beard and brown eyes stared back at her, lifeless. He looked like the man who served vegetables in the cafeteria of the *Heritage*, missing a front tooth, with a very bad tan.

They're people.

She felt betrayed, tricked, hoodwinked. The odds of another civilization evolving exactly the same on an entirely different planet were…almost impossible. If not *entirely* impossible.

Litus's laser fire abruptly stopped, and Eri jolted into motion. Rainwater had made the ramp slick and she slipped, banging her elbow as she went down. Grime and green muck stuck to her hands as she scrambled. An arrow flew by her head into the loading bay. *Almost there.*

She reached the top, forcing herself not to look back. The panel glowed dim green in the night, beckoning her. Sweat dripping down the sides of her face, Eri hid behind the corner and read the screen. Outside, one of the leaf-covered men yelled like a hyena closing in on its prey.

Her mind raced as she tried to remember the hatch retraction code. *Seven seven eight two. Wait, no. Seven one-one-eight-two…*

She wiped her slimy hands on her pants and punched in the second code, her fingers shaking as they pressed the screen. The hatch moved above her head and she felt a wave of relief. *I'm going to make it. I'm going to get help.*

A beeping sound vibrated the bottom of her stomach and the gears stopped. The computer's monotone voice came on. "Warning. Object obstructing hatch retraction procedure. Please remove to continue."

Freaking nebula! Eri scanned the portal frame. A single arrow had lodged inside the space where the hatch closed. She chanced one look at the jungle. Leafy men poured from the trees, all running toward the ramp. Even if she stood out in the open and jumped, she'd never reach the shaft.

I'm doomed. We've all failed.

The ship was too small to hide. They'd find her. But maybe she'd hide long enough to contact Commander Grier. As Eri backed away from the ramp, another chorus of war cries joined the rest. Arrows flew across the battlefield, and the first wave of attackers fell head over heels, tumbling to trip the others in a massive crash.

What was going on? She stuck her head outside the ship. Another tribe of men with white feathers threaded in their hair emerged from the jungle. Their leader, tall, tan, and bare-chested, wearing simple leather pants, ran ahead of the pack like a gazelle, shooting arrows from a long black bow. His wavy brown hair shone deep chestnut in the ramp's emergency white lights.

He was gorgeous.

Pain pricked Eri's neck. Had a jungle bug bitten her? She raised her hand and felt a small dart protruding from her skin. Horror crashed through her. *I've been hit.* She plucked the dart from her neck and studied the thick black substance coating the tip. Poison. The substance mingled with her blood like oil on water.

The loading bay blurred, little red lights blinking at her like devil's eyes. She collapsed to the floor. Her mouth dried and she coughed back nausea, bringing her locator up to her face. The numbers swam on the screen. *Must…contact…Grier.*

Shrieks and other war calls rode the wind as pain exploded behind her forehead. Her world closed in until she could only see a pinprick of light. That pinprick blinked, winking at her before it went out.

CHAPTER EIGHT
SURVIVOR

Striver ran toward the mass of Lawless men and women pouring from the trees. Dim lights illuminated the artificial clearing where the ship had crushed a semicircle of foliage. The hull sat in a crater like a metal egg, repelling the arrows. The belly lay open, a ramp sticking out like a black tongue. The visitors must have already disembarked.

Striver stifled the doubt he'd arrived too late, shouting behind him, "Aim for the front. Drive them into the forest."

He checked the sky for Phoenix. Black shadows spotted the second moon in an arc. The birdman led an army of Guardians in battle-flight formation, their arms filled with reed nets to quell the Lawless. Until now, Striver's tribe had an advantage with the Guardians, but if the Lawless seized the ship's technology, the nets would be useless.

"We have to pick out the leaders." Carven ran beside him, unsheathing his cooking knives. He gave Striver a sidelong glance and headed for the front line. Striver covered him, felling the first few men before they could pump air into reeds filled with coma darts. A shiver ran up his spine. Coma darts meant one thing: they wanted to capture the aliens for interrogation, maybe even torture. Not a good start to intergalactic relations.

Striver didn't see anyone besides Lawless refugees. Where were the visitors? Their camp lay ransacked, containers spewing silver gadgets and tatters of golden foil. Had the Lawless beat their superior technology and taken them already?

Carven swung his blades at two Lawless men as they jabbed at him with flint daggers. Although he had size over them, they were fast, and Striver struggled for a good aim. Just as the one on the right lunged, the other backed up enough for Carven to fire at him without endangering himself. Striver pulled the bowstring back and aimed. Carven's arm swung, blocking him.

Almost…almost…

A pile of leaves rammed into his shoulder and the arrow ricocheted into the trees. Striver fell and the man crawled on top of him, pinning his legs. He lunged with his flint blade at Striver's neck. Striver dropped his bow and grabbed the man's wrist just before the blade cut through the skin. Adrenaline surged through him and he felt every pulse of his wildly beating heart. His strength lay as an archer, not in hand-to-hand combat.

They pushed against each other in a deadlock, the flint blade glistening blue-black in the moons' rays. Striver thought of Carven, wondering if the older man had managed to survive against two of these savage creatures.

"Technohoarder." The man spit into his face. Leaves hung from the pirate's hair, brushing against Striver's neck. But his disguise didn't fool Striver. He bled just as easily as any man.

Striver's muscles bunched under the pressure. The burn stung, and he didn't know how much longer he could hold him back. "It's for our own good."

Now was not the time for a lecture, yet he found himself wanting to educate the man. He spoke through gritted teeth. "You don't know how dangerous technology can be."

It was like talking to the trees.

The man glared, pressing the blade ever so close to Striver's neck. "Not for you to decide."

He'd shifted enough weight off of Striver's legs to allow him to move. Striver brought up his knee and kicked the man in the gut. The man's grip loosened and he fell back. Before he could recover, Striver had already picked up his bow and stood with an arrow tip aimed at the man's chest.

The man raised both his arms with a bitter half smile on his face. "You win."

A horn wailed from the trees. Striver scanned the campsite, keeping his quarry in sight. Lawless writhed underneath reed nets, and Guardians carried pouches of them into the sky, arms and legs sticking out. The few Lawless left retreated into the forest.

"What was your purpose in coming?" Striver pulled the arrow back farther. The familiar sound of bending reeds whispered in his ear.

The man turned and ran for the trees, leaves falling from his back. Striver lowered his bow. There was no sense in more pointless death.

Striver searched for Carven's familiar head of black-and-silver-streaked curls. If anything had happened to him, he'd never forgive himself. He stepped over bodies, fearing Carven's blank face lay among the unlucky ones.

This had all been Striver's idea. He'd wanted to secure the technology, meet the visitors before the Lawless made the wrong impression. Kicking away blood-spattered leaves, he wondered if going after the scout ship had been a bad idea after all.

So many dead. He'd have to report their deaths to the colony. Carven's family flashed through his mind with a pang.

"Ugly savages, aren't they?"

Striver whirled around. Carven stood behind him with blood and grit smeared on his forehead. Striver scoured every inch of the man but didn't see any wounds. "You're all right?"

"Yeah, but this time it came pretty close." He gestured toward a nick on his arm.

"Thank goodness for their poor aim."

Carven smiled, and then his face grew somber. "We'd better move. They'll be back in larger numbers."

Striver grabbed his arm and whispered, "Did you see Weaver?" He knew the others already blamed his desire to see his brother for their midnight excursion.

Carven shook his head. "He wasn't in the group. I'd spot him from a mile away."

Striver stifled a rising current of worry. The Lawless wouldn't kill Weaver; he was too valuable. Still, he couldn't quell the ripple of doubt that rode through him.

Two members of his tribe had captured a Lawless woman. She writhed as each man held onto one of her arms. Her hair was a tangle of dreadlocks, mud, and vines. Striver walked up to her and ducked as she spat at him. Her eyes were wild, painted with red and blue concentric circles spanning out across her forehead. She growled in one of the men's ears. "Go to hell."

Striver put a finger under her chin and raised her head to look into her gaze. "What were your orders? Tell us and we'll let you go."

She appraised him up and down, smiling. Her apparent attraction of him made him even angrier, and his jaw tightened.

"Steal everything." Her eyebrow arched as she caressed his chest with her eyes. "Kill some, take some as prisoners."

One of the men holding her tightened his grip. "That doesn't help us."

Striver put up his hand to stop him. "That's okay." He met her gaze again, seeing fiery, uncontrolled emotions. *Damn Lawless and their unbridled passions.* "One more question and I'll let you go."

She licked her lips. "Have at it."

"Was Weaver with you? Do you know who he is?"

The woman smirked. "Your lesser brother. Yes, I know of him."

Striver's fury intensified like a hard fist squeezing his chest. Only fools compared them in his presence. He spoke through gritted teeth. "Was he with you tonight?"

She laughed, a bone-shattering, high-pitched whinny that tore into Striver's heart. "No."

Relief flooded through him like fresh air.

"Where is he? Is he all right?"

She shrugged like Weaver's life didn't matter to her. "He went off with Jolt into the darkness." Her eyes teased him. "Never came back."

He waved her away in disgust. "Let her go."

The men pushed her from them like a disease. She rubbed her wrists where they had held her and gazed at Striver. He turned away.

Her voice brought him back to her mean-spirited gaze. "You should let him go, honey. He's not coming back."

Striver's heart ached like she'd stuck a knife in it and twisted. Suppressing the pain, he turned to her. "Go home."

He addressed the men guarding her. "Ignore her. Collect anything that looks valuable. Search for survivors."

As she waltzed into the forest, his tribe dashed around him, gathering the silver gadgets and other containers from the wreckage of the camp. Carven walked up beside him. "What about the ship itself?"

"We'll gut it. Take everything we can and set the controls on fire. We can't have the Lawless claiming the skies for themselves."

Carven nodded and joined the group. Just as Striver moved to help carry one of the containers, a young man ran up from the ship.

"Striver, sir?"

"What is it?"

"There's a survivor. She's unconscious."

Striver froze. *She?* "You mean one of the Lawless?" The last thing he needed was another conversation like the one he'd just had.

"No, sir." The young man gave him a knowing glance and pointed to the sky. Awe filled his voice. "One of them."

Striver stopped breathing. "Take me to her."

"Yes, sir."

This is it. The moment of truth. He'd finally meet the people from that mother ship and find out the ultimate reason why the foreigners had sacrificed so much to wander into Lawless lands.

Striver followed the young man up the ramp, feeling the strange solidity of the metal underneath his leather boots. The inside of the ship pressed in on him like a tomb. He wasn't used to an impenetrable ceiling blocking the star-studded sky and air that hung stale with no trace of a wind. Panels lit up in sickly green light, and flashing buttons made him dizzy.

The young man tugged his arm. "She's over here."

Members of his tribe parted, revealing a young woman with a head of pink curls. Striver stepped closer, reminding himself to breath. The survivor, wearing the worst camouflage uniform he'd ever seen, lay on her back. She never would have stepped ten meters into the jungle without being spotted. And that hair! He'd never seen such a bright color. It reminded him of pearl berries in midsummer.

"She has a steady pulse, sir. But she's been hit with a coma dart."

He knelt beside her and gently probed the wound. Her skin was pale as moonlight and dusted with freckles. She looked like she'd never seen the light of day. Striver turned her head, and a heart-shaped face with a cute upturned nose faced him.

"Never did I think the aliens would be this beautiful." Gil, a member of his team, gawked, and Striver gave him a stern look.

"She doesn't look like an alien to me." She looked human. Too human. Human enough for him to have an emotional reaction and a stirring of longing he'd never felt before. He gestured for some of the men to help him. "Come on, let's bring her back to camp before the Lawless return."

As he slid his arms underneath her, his heart raced and blood rushed to his neck. He wondered if the scout ship had drawn him in just to find her.

CHAPTER NINE

A REAL ALIEN

Eri's head throbbed worse than when she'd hit her forehead on the inside of her sleep pod. Her eyelids stuck, glued to her face. *Some night I must have had.*

She buried her head into the blankets. *Blankets?*

When did sleep pods have emergency blankets?

"She's moving. I think she's waking up," a male voice whispered across the room.

Eri jolted awake, prying her eyes open. The room blurred and she blinked away residual tears.

A frail older woman placed a knobby hand on Eri's head. Thatched roofing framed the old woman's wispy hair and firelight from torches illuminated her face. Her skin was tough as leather and wrinkles spread from the corners of her eyes. "She doesn't have a fever. I think the dart is wearing off."

Dart?

The battle scene came back to her in full force and her stomach heaved. She coughed, falling forward into the woman's arms. The old woman smelled like herbs and sweet blossoms. "There now, you've had a rough night. Those coma darts can put you under for hours."

She offered Eri a clay cup filled with water and Eri sipped, feeling the odd roughness of the uneven ridge on her lips. The water tasted cool and fresh with strange minerals, unlike the recycled water on the *Heritage*.

She glanced up and almost gagged as she swallowed. The gorgeous man from the battle stood in the back of the hut. His arms lay crossed over his bare chest, and his wavy chestnut hair fell around his strong-boned, angular face. His eyes sparkled with intensity, green and wild as the jungle. He seemed wary and hesitant, making her fidget with the blankets.

"Where am I?"

"She speaks English!" The older woman smiled and cupped her cheek like she'd performed some trick. "You're in the village, dear. The tribe brought you back from the battle."

"Where is the rest of my team?"

"You were the only one left." The young man stepped forward and uncrossed his arms. He spread his hands out in an apology. "The Lawless spirited away the rest. You're lucky to be alive."

She thought of Litus, Tank, and even Mars. Her heart clutched. "Taken them where?"

"To their hideout. For interrogation."

"Who are the Lawless?" The name sounded so foreboding, it sent a shiver across her shoulders.

The young man frowned as if their name dropped a bitter taste on his tongue. "Another tribe; people who refuse to live by our rules."

The room swam around her. The heat from the firelight pressed in, and the blankets itched. Vines thrust through the cracks in the floor.

She put both hands on the bed to steady herself. Her team was gone, and she was alone in what looked like one of the thatched tree huts Commander Grier had shown her from the control deck. Her gaze dropped to her locator. She had to contact the commander and tell her to send help. But not yet. She needed privacy in case Delta Slip came up.

The old woman's kind voice brought her back to reality. "What's your name, child?"

It was in her best interest to be friendly. "Eridani Smith, but my friends call me Eri."

"Nice to be together under the twin moons, Eri. I'm Nutura, Striver's mother. This is Striver."

Striver. What a strong, dedicated name. Perfect for such a gorgeous human being. Eri reminded herself not to stare.

Wait a second! They spoke with a strange bumpy accent and weird poetic expressions, but it was definitely English, and she understood it. "How is it you speak English?" The question came out as more of a demand or accusation. She'd studied too long and hard for her only mission to be this easy.

Striver stared her down with his green gaze. "Why do you?"

"It's my native tongue, from Earth."

The older woman turned to Striver. "Just what I thought. She's from one of those colony ships, the ones the *S.P. Nautilus* told us about."

Striver's face brightened with recognition before another deeply guarded emotion passed. He crouched down by her bedside, his face inches from hers. "So you've come to colonize our planet?"

Eri's heart broke. How was she going to tell them? *Yes, we're here to steal your home.*

She changed the subject instead. "Where did you learn English?"

The older woman patted the back of her hand. "We're from Earth as well, dear."

Eri shook her head, backing up against the bedframe. "That's impossible. We've been traveling for five hundred years to get here, to Haven 6."

Striver's face softened, as if he understood her confusion. "My ancestor found a worm hole, and he transported those remaining at Outpost Omega to this place, which we call Refuge."

She shook her head, trying to absorb all of the information. *There goes my job; no foreign languages here.* "So you're no more alien than I am."

Striver shrugged. "Let's hope not."

Eri tried to hide the disappointment sinking in her stomach. She'd trained her whole life to decipher foreign languages. Everyone considered her job to be a dead end. When the commander appointed her to the exploratory team, she felt needed, important. It turned out she wasn't necessary at all.

Aquaria's words flooded back to her: *Your job is much greater than you think. You're going to have to find out if these creatures are peaceful, and if they are, you're going to have to decide.*

Looking into the kind face of Nutura and the handsome face of Striver, she wondered if maybe she ought to stay around. Did these people deserve to be obliterated? Have their home taken away?

"Eri, are you all right?" Nutura put her hand back on her forehead. "You look peakish."

"I'm fine. This is a lot to absorb."

"I'm sure it is. We'd be happy to answer any of your questions if it would ease your discomfort."

"Not right now. I need some time alone to inform my commander of the status of the mission, if you don't mind."

Striver's jaw tightened, but Nutura nodded. "Of course. I need to go back to my bed and rest. Let Striver know if you need anything."

Eri glanced at Striver. She didn't think she could even speak to him alone, never mind ask for his assistance. But if it assured Nutura enough to leave her be, then she had to play along. "Okay. I will."

Nutura dragged up a cane from the floor and hobbled to the doorway, parting ferns with her free hand. Striver helped her balance as she left.

Eri realized she hadn't even thanked them for saving her life. "Wait."

Striver turned in the doorway, his face impassive.

"Thank you. For…for saving me, I m-mean." Eri stumbled on her words, feeling like a fool.

"You're welcome. I only wish I'd come sooner and saved your friends, as well." He gave Eri one last melancholy look before he disappeared behind the ferns.

Wasting no time, Eri brought up her locator and pressed the hail code. She squeezed her fingers so hard her fingernails stuck into her palms as the transmitter blinked, trying to find reception. The bar grew longer, then shorter, and then disappeared altogether.

No, no, no. She tried again, pressing each number with emphasis. Maybe she mis-keyed the code? Holding her arm up over her head, she brought the signal as close to the source as possible.

This time the bar appeared and stayed. Commander Grier's face fizzled above her locator, broken up by static fuzz.

"Ms. Smith. Thank goodness you've made contact. I haven't heard from the team in hours."

Eri struggled to collect all of her thoughts and form cohesive sentences before she lost the transmission. "The team is gone. Everyone but me. Humans from Outpost Omega found a wormhole and colonized Haven 6 before we got here. I'm with a friendly tribe right now, but the rest of the team has been captured by a hostile group."

The commander's lips tightened. "Humans? From Outpost Omega?" Disgust soured her features before she blinked her real emotions away. "This does complicate things. How many are there?"

Eri tried to think of all the people flooding into the campsite. "I don't know. Hundreds? A whole civilization? Please, you have to dispatch help right away. I'll send you my coordinates."

"Negative."

"What do you mean? Some of the team may still be alive."

"I cannot compromise more of our DNA pool. Not until I have further information. What weaponry did they use?"

Eri nervously tugged on a thread from the roughly woven blanket. Part of the weave unraveled and she blushed, glancing at the door. She hid the loose strand underneath a fold. "Arrows, I think, and darts that put you in a coma."

"They don't have the same technology we do?"

On second thought, Eri did find it odd that people who came in spaceships now lived in tree huts. "Apparently not, but I can't be too sure."

"Why didn't the lasers work against them?"

"They were camouflaged, and they ambushed us. They know the terrain and were able to use it to their advantage. Please, you have to send help."

Her image flickered and Eri's heart skipped. *Not now.*

Commander Grier's face solidified, her beady eyes cold. "Stay where you are. Learn as much as you can about these tribes. Report to me in six hours with accurate numbers and detailed descriptions of their weaponry."

"B-but…you're not sending a rescue party?"

"Ms. Smith," the commander snapped back. "You must befriend this welcoming tribe, get them on our side. We may need them before the time for Delta Slip comes. You are only to report to me. I'm blocking any further transmissions to others on the *Heritage*. I cannot allow widespread panic."

Blocking her locator? But what about Aquaria? How would she let her know about Litus? The image flickered out and Eri couldn't tell if the commander had ended the transmission or if she'd lost it. But one thing was for sure. No help was coming, and Litus, Tank, Mars, and the others might still be alive.

Using her locator, Eri searched for the members of the team. A weak signal came from Northwest, showing the life signs for Litus and Mars. Hopefully the others were just too far away to register. She refused to believe the rest of the team was dead.

Eri stood up. The floor pitched underneath her, but she regained her balance and took a deep breath. She'd have to ask that gorgeous man for help.

$\approx \ll$

"Do you think we can trust her?" Striver whispered as he led his mother into her thatched hut. The dim glow of the dying torch made the rings under her eyes darken with shadows. She shouldn't have left her bed, but he could only bring so much of the world to her. She wanted to meet the girl who'd descended from the stars. Her enthusiasm gave him hope that her own battle wasn't yet lost. Besides, he needed her advice.

"I looked right into her eyes. She has a good heart." His mother lowered herself into bed slowly and waved away his help. "You know I have a good gut instinct when it comes to people."

"Of course." He resisted the urge to roll his eyes at the mention of her psychic tendencies. No one had shown powers like that since the last generation on Outpost Omega. Either those old fortune-tellers were bogus, or those with the gift chose to stay behind.

Maybe they were right.

He shrugged off his doubts. Their colony hadn't lost anything yet.

His mother settled underneath the blankets. "She'll do the right thing."

"Yes, but for her people or for ours?"

"Gut feelings don't answer specifics, Striver. All you can do is spend time with her. Get to know her."

Impatience bubbled inside him and he clenched his fists. "I don't have time for that. There's a whole mother ship hanging up there in the sky, the Lawless seized who knows what from the colonists, and they're probably interrogating the rest of them as we speak. Our relations with this new faction are chancy at best, and I have to decide what's best for our people."

She gave him the same look she used when he cursed bad weather or couldn't wait until twilight to hunt—the look that told him he couldn't save the world all by himself. "Whether you have the seconds to spare or not, only time will tell."

Striver calmed his frustration by focusing on his mother. He took her hand, the bones thin as twigs, and squeezed her fingers gently. "Rest now. I'll come if I have any more news."

She smiled and closed her eyes. Her voice sounded sleepy, her mind already drifting. "The way she looked at you…"

The way who looked at me? The girl?

He opened his mouth to ask, but she'd already fallen asleep and he didn't want to wake her. She'd had a long day. Rarely did she leave the bed, never mind venture from her hut. The fatigue must have weighed on her, making her imagine things.

Shrugging off her comment, Striver parted the ferns and walked into the crisp morning air. He hadn't slept since they dragged Eri home, and the sleepless night had pulled on his muscles, making him feel like he had stones tied to his arms. Rest was not possible, though, because the young beauty lay in his bed.

He slumped against the outside of his own tree hut, trying to remember what he'd learned about the ships from his ancestors who'd founded their colony, Striker and Aries. Striker had been a space pirate from Outpost Omega, but Aries had escaped a colony ship called the *New Dawn*. Their strict rules of lifemate pairings and job assignments based on test scores had been too much for her. Aries had met Striker after she escaped, and with his help, they reclaimed his map to Refuge and transported the rest of the space pirates.

Those colony ships had strict objectives, and he doubted they'd change their plans to include descendants of the very space pirates who took over their space station and severed their communications with the other ships. Especially when the Lawless had already fired the first shot.

He rubbed his forehead, the situation worsening in his mind.

The ferns rustled behind him and Eri stuck out her head. "Excuse me, Striver, could I speak with you?"

His name sounded foreign on her tongue, like she'd found a different way to accent the syllables that he wasn't used to. At least she remembered it.

"Of course." He stood and gestured inside. "For privacy."

She ducked her head, and he followed her into his own room, feeling as though he were the intruder.

Eri paced, her small boots walking the same planks of wood he'd paced himself many times. She wrung her hands, worry creasing her pretty face. "I've spoken with my commander, and she's hesitant to send down any more teams."

He nodded, unsure what this new development meant for him and his people. Would these people just fly away, find another planet that was habitable?

"What are you going to do?"

"I need your help. Some of my team members are still alive. I've tracked their locators with my own, and they have steady life signs."

"Are you sure?"

"The locator wouldn't work if they didn't. It's embedded in our arms, a part of us. Our electrical energy drives it."

"I see." He cast a glance at the locator on her arm and stifled his usual distrust of technology. If she had such a fancy device, why did she need him? "What do you want me to do?"

"We've got to rescue them before something happens."

He shook his head, running his hand through his hair. "I don't know. We lost many good men and women just trying to get you."

"You don't understand. They took our weapons as well. Once they figure out how to use them, the combination of their camouflage techniques and our technology will be unstoppable. I mean, they already pummeled us with just bows and arrows. Imagine what a gallium crystal void ray would do in their hands."

She had a point. A gallium crystal void ray sounded pretty dangerous. It only meant one thing: these people came to conquer. "How many weapons did they take?"

Eri shrugged. "I'm not sure. Maybe twenty laser guns? Maybe more? How many did your tribe recover?"

"Counting yours?"

She nodded, eyes open wide in expectation.

"One."

"Damn." She stomped her foot, making a dent in the wood. His glance dropped to the floor and she looked up, the corner of her lips curling. "Sorry."

He raised an eyebrow. "That's okay. I was going to fix that soon anyway."

Eri looked around and Striver suddenly felt self-conscious about his clothes thrown in the corner and his shaving blade next to the stone washbasin. "This is your room?"

"Yes."

She touched the bead necklaces hanging from his mirror. "These are beautiful."

"Thank you. My mother threaded them. One for every year of my life." He walked up beside her, his heart beating faster with the close proximity. He reached out, selecting a blue bead carved in the likeness of a fish. "This year was the first time I caught a trotter with my father."

Eri touched the bead, running her fingers over the ridges. "We have nothing like this on the *Heritage*."

"I wouldn't think you would."

"So much is done by computers and machines, nothing by hand." She reached up and touched one of the beads woven into his long hair. Her hand brushed his cheek and sent a rush of warmth throughout his body. A flash of vulnerability shone in her features before she pulled away and her face hardened.

"So, we have to go after them, right?"

Striver had to pull himself together to realize what she referred to. Her team. He sighed, mostly talking to himself. "I'm thinking about it. It would mean gathering another force. And we'd have to ask the Guardians."

"Who are the Guardians?"

Striver smiled for the first time all night. Despite the warnings that screamed in his mind, a sudden urge to show her his world came over him. He offered her his hand. "Want to meet a real alien?"

CHAPTER TEN

NEWBIES

The last thing Weaver wanted to do was sit in a dark cave, tracing ancient scratchings with his finger. An alien ship in the sky? Sending a scout ship in their direction? And here he was lying next to swirly golden sludge.

Keep working. This liquid may be the key that gets you out of here. The ticket to taking over. He'd make the world what he wanted it to be. How it *should* be. With him in charge instead of Striver.

Weaver watched as a golden swirl eddied around the smooth outcropping, teasing him. He wanted to touch it, but Jolt's warnings held him back. He didn't need any of his old memories troubling him. Not when such an important job sat in his lap.

If only the writing matched the hieroglyphs on the *S.P. Nautilus*. But they didn't. Not even one symbol. This was an entirely different race, and he was no more of a forensic linguist than Jolt was a babysitter.

Rolling on his back, he closed his eyes. Golden swirls erupted behind his lids, and he wondered if he'd stared at the liquid for too long. Jolt's words haunted him.

If you spend too long in proximity, the golden stuff will bring up all sorts of things you want to remember. And some you don't.

A shiver slithered across his shoulders, and he struggled to shrug it off. There was nothing he did or didn't want to remember. The past was the past, and you couldn't change something that had already happened. So what was the point of traveling back in time?

Ignoring the strange sensation, he drifted to sleep.

∾∿

The river rippled, clear water bubbling and foaming around the upturned rocks and fallen branches. Weaver balanced by the shore, using his wooden fishing rod as a walking stick. A wave of cold water slapped at his boots, icy droplets stinging the bare skin on his arms. Wiping away the water on his shirt, he jumped to the next rock.

"Be careful, Weave. The rocks are slippery," Dad called from behind him.

"I'm as limber as a weasel worm, Dad." He chanced a look over his shoulder. His dad followed with Striver beside him, holding a pot of wriggling scrubber worms. Mom had almost kept him behind again, but today he'd prove he could fish with the men.

He used his rod to probe the next footstep, making sure the boulder wouldn't tip under his weight. If only his rod were as long as Striver's. When Dad gave it to him, the size was a smack in the face. How could he catch giant trotter in the middle of the river with a stunted pole? They'd given him a disadvantage from the start. The familiar swell of bitterness welled in his chest, and he swallowed it. They always tried to keep him down.

He jumped onto the boulder. No matter. He'd prove his worth anyway.

"Let's stop here. The rapids get worse below," Dad shouted.

"Don't get too far from us, Weave," Striver called after him.

"I won't." He took three more steps before he found a rock flat enough to sit on and set up his pole. The closer you got to the rapids, the more trotter you caught. He had a pocket full of scrubber worms, and he pulled out the longest one, its scaly skin catching the rays of sun. He stuck it on the hook and cast his lure into the water with a splash.

The rock grinded against his boney butt as he waited for the bait to lure the fish. The golden swirls in the water hypnotized him, making him slump forward sleepily. He sang the song his mother sang while cooking to keep alert.

Gentle, silent breeze
Lift me up
Where stars twinkle in the night.

Where no walls divide
Or laws abide
Where no one needs to hide.

Weaver's words trailed off and he fell forward. The rush of air on his face woke him up and he stuck out his hand, catching himself before his nose smashed into the rock. He checked on Dad and Striver, but they hadn't noticed. Fishing took longer than he thought.

Pulling himself up, he heard Striver shouting. "Got a bite!"

"Great job, son. Reel it in." Dad leaped up with pride beaming on his face.

Weaver propped himself on the heels of his hands, his neck and cheeks heating. Of course Striver caught the fish. He had a longer pole. Weaver's own bait flickered blue-green in the water, taunting him, untouched. His gaze shot back to his brother. Striver yanked, and a glorious trotter the size of his arm slapped the air, silver body flailing in the river mist.

Striver and Dad laughed together and envy boiled inside him.

He'd have to try harder to outdo Striver now. As they reined in the
trotter, he pulled up his pole and climbed down two more rocks to
where the current flowed much stronger, eddying around a log. He
stuck the end of the pole in the crevice between two rocks, the water
rushing around it. His bait swirled in the current, sparkling in the sun.

A fish was bound to see it now.

Weaver sat back just as a rushing wave dislodged his pole. He
threw himself on his belly and reached across the water grab it, and
the wood slipped from his fingers. The pole splashed into the water
and his heart jumped to his throat. He could hear Dad lecturing him
on responsibility as the rod bobbed and caught on a rock toward the
middle of the river.

The spray stung his face as he leaned over the rapids and
stretched his arm, wiggling his fingers. His reach ended centimeters
from the rod. He scraped his belly as he climbed forward on the rock.
One hand braced him while the other one reached. His fingers grazed
the slick pole.

Just a little farther.

The spray from the river trickled down the sides of his face and
underneath his shirt. The rock slipped below his sweating hands and
he began to slide.

"Weave, watch out!" Striver called after him just as he skidded
forward and plunged into the icy river.

Roaring water raged in his ears. His body tingled, turning numb.
He struggled to gulp for air, but the current spun him head over heels
and he couldn't tell the surface from the gravelly bottom. His lungs
threatened to burst as precious air bubbles escaped his lips.

Failure slapped him harder than the current against the rocks.
He'd die today as a nobody, just a clumsy kid who couldn't catch a
trotter in spawning season. A little voice nudged him to keep trying,
that there was more to life than excelling at trotter fishing, but under
the weight of his failure it seemed like too little encouragement too

late.

Hands reached around him and pulled him just as the last bubbles of air slipped from his mouth. He breached the surface and gulped in a deep breath, his entire body shaking.

"You…okay…Weave?" Striver struggled against the current, holding Weaver's head above the water. Weaver coughed and spat.

"My rod. I lost it."

"It doesn't matter as long as you're safe." Striver gripped him under his arms and swam them back to shore.

Embarrassed and defeated, Weaver felt like a pincushion with prickles sticking him everywhere. A deep, dark shame festered in his soul.

"I thought I'd lost you. But you're gonna be just fine." Striver dragged him to the shore and laid him on his back. Weaver hacked up water and hugged his arms close to his chest, shaking.

"Is he all right?" Dad ran beside them and draped his shirt over Weaver's shoulders. The warmth of the boar's hide blocked the biting wind but could not take away the sting in his heart.

"I think so."

"I knew he was too young to take with us. I should have listened to your mom. Thank goodness for your quick reaction and your excellent swimming skills, Striver. I couldn't have reached him in time with my bum leg." Dad's pride in his brother made Weaver feel like he'd eaten a whole bowl of pearl berries, the sweetness sickening him to the point of hurling. Every time Striver looked good, it made him look bad.

"I'm just relieved he's okay."

"You shouldn't have gone so far, Weave." Dad's voice was more plaintive than angry. "We can't watch over you if you run away."

"I don't need anyone to watch over me." Weaver's voice came out as a weak cry and he winced. "I can do things by myself." But the truth nudged him in his gut. He needed them more than they needed him.

Weaver buried his head in his arms and curled into a fetal position. He hated Striver for catching the trotter, for being better than him at everything, and for saving him. He would always live in his older brother's shadow.

"Sure you can, Weave. I'm just here to help if you need it." Striver placed a hand on his shoulder. Instead of comforting him, the gesture heightened Weaver's aggravation and he pulled away.

"Come on, help me carry him back to the village before he catches cold. Mom can brew him one of her herbal teas and wrap him in blankets." Dad's voice was tired and agitated, making Weaver feel worse. "She's going to whip us into swillow wisp stew."

Arms reached underneath him and he melted into their embrace, wishing he could climb under the water once again and freeze forever.

$\approx$ $\ll$

"Put them here." Jolt's rough-edged voice cut through Weaver's foggy mind. He sat up, eyes blurry from deep sleep. Remnants of his dream sent a shiver of disquiet through his gut. He felt like he'd traveled fifteen years into the past and back again in only moments. But somehow, the past wasn't exactly as he remembered it. His father's stern reproach from that day burned in his memory. Looking back through the dream, Weaver knew his father had just been worried about him and what his mother's reaction would be when he came home soaking wet. He'd probably gotten his old man in a bunch of trouble. Guilt and shame burned in Weaver's heart. He had gone too far down the river.

Crusty, Snipe, and a few other Lawless men carried two people wearing strange camouflaged uniforms into the cavern. Weaver stared, openmouthed, as they lowered the tied bodies to the cavern floor.

"Sleeping on the job?" Jolt turned toward him with a sly look in his dark eyes.

"No, I was resting." He wanted to tell Jolt how the golden swirls had affected him, too, but he didn't want to speak of such personal things in front of the other men, and he didn't think Jolt would be the best listener, anyway.

"Now you've got some friends to keep you company."

Weaver studied their pale faces. A man and a woman, although the woman looked more manly than any women he'd seen before. They were massive, with well-developed muscle tone, but their skin was soft and pasty like a baby's. "Who are they?"

"These are the visitors who fell from the sky." Jolt circled around them like a vulture around prey.

"But they look human."

Jolt bent down, hovering over the prisoners' faces. "My spies tell me these pale-faced newbies even speak English, which could only mean one thing." He pointed to the ceiling of the cave. "That mother ship hovering over us like some raspwasp's nest is a colony vessel. Those Lifers have traveled hundreds of years through deep space to reach what our ancestors did using their secret worm hole."

Weaver tried to wrap his mind around the thought of several generations living on a ship. "Impossible! After all those years, they're only just arriving now?"

Jolt felt the pulse of one of the men and nodded. "Yes, and generations on a ship have not been kind. Look at them. They'd die of sunburn and spidermite poison in one night out in the jungle. My spies tell me they even tripped on sticks and stones."

Weaver shifted uncomfortably. This whole setup didn't feel right. It was almost as if by stashing them here with their guards, Jolt was also keeping his eye on Weaver. He'd never glean the secret of the golden sludge and hoard it for himself with Snipe and Crusty breathing down his bow. "What do you want me to do with them? Why do they have to stay here?"

"Because I don't want anyone questioning them besides me.

They're suffering from the effects of coma darts, but when they wake up, they're gonna tell us how to use these." Jolt walked over to a plastic container brought in by one of his men. He pressed a front panel, and air wheezed as the lid rose. He reached in and brought out a laser gun two sizes bigger than the one he coveted day and night. This one shone like the eye of a predator and buzzed with activity.

"Holy Refuge." Weaver stared. "Have you tried it?"

"It's locked." Jolt's grin turned into a scowl.

"Can't you figure it out?"

Jolt gave him a mean glare. "It's harder than you think. There's some type of recognition code you have to type in to turn it on. Even the ones they were shooting don't work for us."

"Let me guess; you want me to figure it out as well?"

"You're the descendant of the famous Decoder from Outpost Omega, aren't you?"

Anger rose in Weaver's chest. Being compared to his ancestors was worse than being compared to Striver. He always came out lacking. But if he wanted to live, he had to play along. "I'll see what I can do."

"Good." Jolt smirked like someone with all his game pieces in place, ready to launch an attack. "Crusty and Snipe will stay here to guard. Send one of them if any of these mooncalves wakes up."

Weaver nodded, only half listening. If he could figure out the code and get those weapons, he wouldn't need the golden sludge. He'd already spent too long in its presence and the effects were playing with his mind. "Sure, Jolt."

"And one more thing—don't be getting any ideas of your own. Crusty and Snipe would slice you up like a roasted boar."

Snipe raised his hooded lips and Crusty nodded his head.

"Where are you going?" Weaver asked as Jolt turned his back on him.

He twisted around and grinned, teeth glowing in the golden light.

His scar seemed to writhe with life. "I'm thinking up a way to shoot that mother boar of a ship out of the sky."

CHAPTER ELEVEN

BLANK EYES

Eri slid her hand into Striver's and wondered if she'd made the worst decision of her life. He *was* considering rescuing her team, and meeting the elusive Guardians seemed like the only way. Besides, Commander Grier said she had to get to know the natives, so holding his hand was actually a direct order.

His skin felt like fire against hers and heat blazed in her cheeks. She looked down, trying to hide her reaction. "Where are we going?"

"To the *S.P. Nautilus*, the ship our ancestors piloted to Refuge. Phoenix is on guard duty today."

Guard duty? Why did the jungle seem more menacing with every hour? "Guarding it from what?"

Striver parted the ferns and held them up so she could step through without the palms touching her. "The Lawless."

She ducked, trying not to brush too close to him as she passed. "Oh, so they bother you, too?"

He looked away into the early morning rays of sun, his face falling into a grimace. "You have no idea."

Eri knew enough just from the edge to Striver's voice not to broach the particulars on that topic. Instead, she changed the subject. "How long have you lived here?"

He uncoiled a rope ladder and lowered it to the forest floor. "Several generations. The year is three hundred twenty-two."

She pushed away her fear and lowered herself onto the first rung. The rope ladder swung with her weight, and she tightened her grip, fingers turning white. *Cyberhell, I miss the elevators.*

Striver steadied the ladder and held his hands over both of hers. His skin felt warm and rough on hers, making her heat level spike. The rope ladder stilled, and he let go. "Try it now."

Eri chanced the first step down, making sure her boot fit snugly into the next rung. "You've abandoned Old Earth time?"

"We've abandoned almost everything from Old Earth. Look around you. No technology of any kind."

"Why?"

"For all the same reasons that destroyed Old Earth. We don't want history to repeat itself."

Wow. What must he think of her with her locator, her laser gun, and their scout ship? Did she represent blasphemy itself just by showing her face?

Eri climbed down another rung, breathless from the height. She tried not to look at the ground. "I'm sorry."

"Sorry about what?" Striver swung in an elegant arc and followed her down effortlessly.

Sorry that I've come to steal your home? No. She couldn't say it. "Sorry you have to go back into the Lawless lands."

"It's not your fault. You're just doing your mission, following orders."

Seven more rungs to go. "Yeah, but I'm sorry all the same."

She debated jumping the rest of the way down and decided against it, clinging to the rope ladder like she stood above the recycling compactor, sharp teeth grinding away. She could tell Striver waited for her, but he didn't seem impatient. If anything, he kept reaching down to make sure she was steady.

The ground squished underneath her boots, but at least it felt more solid than the tree hut or the ladder. *And to think—I've been in a metal bubble in the vacuum of deep space my whole life.* Which world was safer? At the moment, she wasn't sure.

"So, you're the star girl come to conquer us?"

Eri whirled around. A jungle beauty, a whole foot taller than Eri, stood beside her. Glistening black hair flowed to the beauty's feet and appraising cat eyes stared with a taunting grin.

Boy, word traveled fast. Had the whole village gossiped about her as she lay unconscious?

Striver's voice was almost a growl. "Leave her alone, Riptide. She's just woken up from a coma dart."

Riptide's gaze traveled from her curly-haired head to her plastic boots. "The visitors are certainly daintier than I thought they'd be. Never mind freckle-faced and pale."

Striver jumped the remaining feet down. He looked at Eri and sighed. "Eri, meet Riptide. She's the village gardener and an excellent chef."

Riptide glowed from his compliment, her tan skin reflecting the early rays of sunlight filtering through the trees. "Thanks, Striver. You have impeccable taste in chefs. I'm still waiting for you to stop by and try my latest creation." Her face grew serious. "So, I hear the Guardians have a lockdown on the whole fence. What's going on? Are the Lawless acting up again?"

"Not yet. But it seems they may have stolen valuable equipment from Eri's team, as well as some of the survivors. We're consulting Phoenix before deciding on a course of action."

Riptide stepped toward him and placed her hand on his arm, her fingers climbing over his muscles. Large glittering stones, some dark as space, others light as the moon, decorated her fingers. Eri couldn't imagine how impractical they were, along with her curtain of hair. No one on the *Heritage* would have had enough water rations to wash that rug.

"You know I get nervous any time you go out. I can't afford to lose both you and Riley."

"We're not going anywhere at the moment." Striver pulled away. "And it's Riley's choice whether to stay or fight."

"Yes, but he always chooses to fight. You know that. He's very much like you." Riptide's fingers moved as if she itched to touch him again, jewels clicking together. Eri felt like a third wheel, once again the spectator of others' relationships and love. Were these two lifemates?

"We do what we have to." Striver sounded gruff and Eri wondered if he was angry with Riptide, but she couldn't see why. Riptide was only concerned for his safety, and boy was she beautiful—even though she could use some lessons in manners.

Striver glanced at Eri, his eyes changing from hard emerald to soft velvet. "Come on, we should keep moving." He nodded to Riptide as he started walking. "I'll keep you and Riley updated."

Riptide called after him, her voice low and lusty. "Of course. I'll be anxiously awaiting our next meeting."

Eri followed Striver, shutting her mouth tightly against all the questions brimming in her mind. It wasn't her place to intervene, and yet the urge to get to know him better almost overpowered her good reason.

Instead, she settled on an innocent question. "Who's Riley?"

"Riptide's brother."

Oh, that's why she was worried about him. Maybe she felt the same way about Striver, like a sister watching over a brother or a cousin.

The question slipped out before she could stop herself. "Are you related to her as well?"

He gave her a curious look and returned to the path ahead. "No."

His answer piqued her curiosity even more. Pushing branches out of her face, Eri wondered why Striver kept Riptide at arm's length. Did he not want a lifemate of his own?

The forest thinned, revealing more golden sunlight. The trees tapered off to a meadow with long thin grasses white as the dual moons and dust-sized insects that spun on the wind. A torpedo-shaped ivory vessel sat in the middle like an egg. Green vines wove around the outer hull. It looked as though it hadn't flown in eons.

"The *S.P. Nautilus*." Striver waved his hand like a magician performing a trick. "I'm not supposed to show it to outsiders, meaning Lawless. But I don't think you're interested in stealing its technology." He gave her an appraising look. "You have your own."

"True, but I'd love to see inside." Eri walked toward it, awe spreading through her. "This is really an alien ship?"

"As certain as the twin moons. My ancestor found it on the desert planet of Sahara 354. He rebuilt it and used it to escape with Aries from the *New Dawn*. In exchange, he brought out the eggs preserved in its belly, and the Guardians hatched on this new world. Together, the races coexisted. The Guardians taught us how to live peacefully and logically. They are the main reason why we haven't fallen into the gang-run chaos of the Lawless lands."

Their past intrigued Eri. Every good linguist was also a historian. "Are the Guardians happy living with humans?"

Striver pursed his lips. "Happy isn't quite the right word. I'd say content. Guardians don't feel emotions as strongly as humans; I think that's part of the reason they lived on their planet in peace until its end. Whereas we destroyed Old Earth before its time."

She touched the ship's hull, the ivory smooth against her fingertips. Although the ship sat decommissioned, it still emanated life.

"The hull captures solar power, which is why it's outlasted all the other ships people used to colonize."

"There are other ships?"

"Oh yes, or what's left of them, anyway. Others from Outpost Omega followed my ancestors to Refuge. Unlike his mutinous crew, who wanted to keep it for themselves, he provided the coordinates to everyone. It's a legend here on Refuge. We tell it every year on the eve of the *S.P. Nautilus*'s arrival date."

Pieces of a puzzle fit together, giving Eri a glimpse into this mysterious world. Commander Grier had instructed her to find out as much as she could, and by talking to Striver, she learned things they couldn't discern with the scout droids. Aquaria's voice resonated in her thoughts. *You'll have to decide whether or not to warn them.* Eri pushed the thought away. There was so much she still didn't know.

Striver traced a hieroglyph in the hull, and a hatch opened on top. Eri stared, thinking this probably was way off from the technology Commander Grier had expected. But should Eri tell her?

Curling his lips, Striver offered his hand. "Inside tour?"

"You betcha." She grabbed his hand and he pulled her up to the hatch. Walking on the ship's hull was like walking on solid rock—it reminded Eri of the chrome floors back on the *Heritage*. Strange how she felt more at ease on an alien ship than on solid ground. *Because I've lived on a ship all my life.*

They stood on a platform with geometric shapes carved into the hull around it. Striver traced another set of symbols on the hull and the platform lowered like an elevator. Eri shrieked as it moved and grabbed ahold of Striver's arm.

He laughed. "It moves slowly. Don't worry."

She let go, feeling as foolish as a schoolgirl, and sobered. *Keep your mind on what's important. Remember, you need answers.* "How do the Lawless fit in with all this?"

The platform lowered and doors parted to reveal white walls and sapphire-blue light. Chirps, trills, and whistles echoed on the intercom and Eri remembered this was the Guardians' ship. Striver took her hand and led her to a control room where the entire meadow stretched out before them in a V-shaped sight panel. "Most of the space pirates from Outpost Omega chose to take their own ships and follow Aries and Striker to Refuge, but some of them didn't want to live in harmony with the Guardians. They didn't want to follow rules."

Eri ran her hands over the blinking screens, which showed a hieroglyphic language she'd never seen before. "And your ancestors didn't force them to?"

"No. Free will and choice are most important to us. Aries didn't have either aboard the *New Dawn*, so she made sure Refuge was founded on different standards."

"So no lifemate pairings?"

"Definitely not."

Interesting. Eri had wanted Haven 6 to evolve into such a world once they'd abandoned the strict conditions of the ship.

Striver's lips thinned. "You don't agree with our system. I can see it in your eyes."

"No, it's not that. Believe me, I have my own complaints about our system. But your world is so different. To tell you the truth, it's scary."

He approached her, placing his hand gently on her shoulder. He felt solid and certain, the one thing that made sense on this entire world. "Anything new is scary, but as my father used to say, you don't gain without taking risks."

Eri felt the urge to lean into his hand. She wanted to believe him, but after what happened with the scout team, she didn't know if she could. "Seems a big risk to me. I mean, people running around without laws? Doing whatever they feel like?"

Striver leaned in, his face a breath away. "Tell me the truth. Are you happy with your job aboard the *Heritage*? Your lifemate pairing?"

Eri backed up against the control board as the truth smacked her in the face. *I'm not happy with either.*

A shadow moved across the meadow on the sight panel behind Striver, drawing her attention away. He followed her gaze as the shadow traveled over his face. "It's Phoenix."

"I thought none of the ships could fly."

Striver gave her an impish smile, green eyes sparkling. "They can't. Too bad he's here. I wanted to show you the chamber that held the eggs."

"The eggs the Guardians hatched from?"

"Yes. There's a neat storage facility in the belly of this ship. Thank goodness Aries and Striker kept the eggs intact and carried them out to the meadow to hatch. I guess they felt obligated because they used their ship. Besides coming to Refuge, it was the best decision they could have made."

It sounded like a bedtime fairy tale. Haven 6 had such rich history, and Eri felt like she'd only seen the tip of the iceberg. She wanted to ask more questions, but Striver took her hand.

"Come on, we should get outside to meet him."

As they rode the platform to the fresh air, Eri titled her face up to the sky, shielding golden rays with her hand. A winged creature spiraled down in elegant circles. His feathers shone with pearly iridescence in the morning sun.

He landed swiftly, turning from a glide into a jog on spindly legs. Eri froze, blinking hard, as if she'd imagined it. He jumped to the top of the hull in one leap.

The birdman had long, branch-like fingers and slender arms. Gray eyes with no pupils stared back at her. A beak-like mouth trilled a shrill note on the wind. He reminded her of an angel from another world.

"I see your ward has awoken," Phoenix announced in a more manly voice than Eri expected, making her gawk even more.

The birdman talks?

"Yes, and she speaks English, Phoenix. She's from a colony ship, departed from Old Earth five hundred years ago."

Phoenix bowed and his feathered back ruffled in the breeze. "A pleasure to meet you."

Striver nudged Eri's arm and nodded encouragingly toward Phoenix. She quirked an eyebrow. *You mean you want me to talk to it?*

His face grew sterner, the wrinkles around his eyes saying: *You were the one who wanted our help.*

Phoenix waited, his blank gaze unnerving her. Did he feel the same emotions as humans? Could he sympathize? Eri took a deep breath and offered her hand. "Eridani Smith. Call me Eri."

His clawed fingers wrapped around hers, and she resisted the urge to pull away. Fear wasn't the most diplomatic emotion to convey. The claw was smooth and cold, reminding her of the ivory ship behind them. "Phoenix Highland at your service."

Did they always speak like an old English book? Eri shook his branch-like hand. "Nice to meet you, Phoenix."

"Are you going back to your ship?" He leaned forward and she could see her reflection in his eyes, a frightened and exhausted young woman who had stumbled upon a world she'd never dreamed could exist. Thinking about Litus, Tank, and Mars, she summoned courage and held her head up high to meet his emotionless gaze.

"No. I've come to ask for your help."

Just as she wondered how she'd explain everything, Striver stepped in. "She's located the surviving members of her team, and she wants to rescue them." He gave her a reassuring nod. "The Lawless captured several of their weapons, and I think it would benefit us both if we confiscated them before the Lawless have a chance to use them. Besides, they'll torture those colonists to death, and that doesn't look good for our intergalactic communications." He pointed to the mother ship, still hovering in the sky like a giant eye.

"Well thought-out, Striver." Phoenix extended one of his fingers to the other one, making a circle. His large, placid eyes blinked.

Striver shifted, his gaze darting to the rising sun in the sky. "We don't have time for another one of those town hall meetings. If we decide to save them, we must act now."

Phoenix disconnected his two fingers as if he'd come to his conclusion. "You know this may anger members of the council?"

Striver regarded Eri as if she were worth it. "I'll take my chances."

"And you know the Guardians can't help you carry out any act that may induce war or transfer anyone across the wall without the council's consent."

Striver didn't wait one beat to reply. "Understood."

"Very well. I'll send word to the other Guardians. You organize another infantry force."

Before Eri could thank Phoenix, he turned away and launched into the sky. A single feather drifted to the ground and Eri picked it up, feeling the soft hairs against the slender quill. Pure white fluff at the stem turned into a pinkish iridescence at the tip.

"That was easier than I thought." Striver slumped back against the hull and sighed. "The hard part lies ahead."

CHAPTER TWELVE
LOOKING BACK

Touching the keypad on the laser gun reminded Weaver of the antique mineral locator passed down for generations in his family. His dad, as his father's father before him, told him Aries Ryder used the device to find the missing piece of the *S.P. Nautilus* while on Sahara 354. As a boy, he'd hold it in front of him and pretend the locator still worked, trying to find precious minerals in the rock bed of the dried-up stream by their tree hut.

The way the laser gun's keypad clicked under his touch made him feel like he had power at his fingertips. If only he could find the code to activate it.

"I bet the kid's bluffing. He can't figure out anything at all." Snipe spit on the rock wall, and the drool trickled down, scaring away a spidermite.

Crusty waved his hand. "Give the kid a chance. What have we got to lose?"

"All our secrets taken back to those technohoarders, that's what." Snipe drew out his flint blade and sharpened it along the side of a rock with a *swhang*.

"What secrets? That pool of dreamy regret? Lasers we can't use? Colony Lifers who won't wake up?"

Weaver ignored them, punching in another series of numbers as he ran logarithms in his head. He'd always been good at math. But despite his progress, an ill seed of anxiety grew in Weaver's chest. Was it Snipe's teasing? No. People in his village had badgered him all his life. He was accustomed to snide remarks about not measuring up. Besides, no one was his friend on this side of the wall. Crusty and Snipe knew he was competition, and they'd take any chance they got to put him down.

This was a new feeling, an uncomfortable melancholy tainted by remorse. The feeling had started like an itch he couldn't scratch after the dream. Plunged back in time, Weaver felt all the same feelings he'd experienced as a boy. But new feelings along with the old put the memory in a different light.

Striver and his dad weren't holding him back that day. They never had. In fact, they'd convinced his mom to let him fish with them, and all he did was get them in trouble. Why did it take ten years to see his own selfishness?

Shaking his head, he tried the next set of numbers he'd systematically derived. *66459…*

The laser gun buzzed in his hands, and the screen flashed on.

Weaver stared, hope rising in his chest. *I did it. I cracked the code.*

His eyes flicked to where Snipe had been sitting against the rock wall. The floor was bare. Crusty stood, holding out his black flint blade.

"Nice job, Weasel." Snipe's voice echoed from behind him.

Weaver whirled around to the tip of an arrow aimed at his forehead.

"Give the gun to Crusty and we'll let you live."

He squashed down his fear. *Think. You've made it out of tough situations before this.* Weaver swallowed, keeping his tone even. "You have to let me live. I'm the only one who knows the code."

Snipe lowered his arrow to the right. "True. But you can live without your right arm."

Weaver's heart sped up, the muscles in his arms tensing. He needed his shoulder to use his bow. Without it, he was nothing.

"Wait!" Weaver placed the laser on the cave floor. His fingers lingered on the trigger before he slid it to Crusty.

"Good." Snipe grinned. "Crusty, take the gun to Jolt. Tell him Weaver cracked the code. I'll stay here and watch the prisoners."

The way he said *prisoners* made Weaver think he was one of them. *Great. I've managed to fall from disgraced brother to lackey to captive.*

"Sure thing." Crusty stumbled to his feet and dusted off his pants. He bent down to pick up the weapon, holding it away from his body like it was a bomb. Some pirates on Refuge still feared technology. *Ignorant idiots. Technology's the thing that's going to make me famous. All I have to do is steal back that laser.*

The back of the cave stirred with movement. Weaver checked on the prisoners. The man with light blond hair coughed and squirmed against his restraints. His voice was hoarse. "Where am I?"

"Interesting," Snipe muttered under his breath. He strutted over and crouched down to the prisoner's level to meet eye to eye. "You're in hell."

∽⁓

The wall rose in a slab of mold-coated concrete like the structure of a long-forgotten civilization, refusing to crumble. Eri tilted her head up, trying to decipher how tall the wall stood. The concrete ended in a tangle of branches and leaves.

Striver placed his hand upon the surface gently, almost in reverence. "Here it is—the one obstacle that stands between us and the Lawless lands."

"How do we cross it?" Eri scratched her arm, the new clothing Striver had given her irritating her skin. He said she wouldn't make it ten meters in the jungle without being spotted in her old gear, but she didn't know if she'd make it ten meters without stopping to scratch her back underneath the rough weave of the fabric. The embroidered green tunic made her look like some medieval minstrel from her old Celtic texts, and the tight leather leggings didn't exactly help. Thank goodness they let her keep her boots.

"We have to climb over it." Striver pulled back a cluster of ferns, revealing ladder rungs stuck into the cement. "There's only a few places on the wall equipped with these, and the rungs are only on our side. We'll have to use ropes to scale down."

Behind them, a small party of four of the village's strongest men and women scouted the area. Eri cast a glance over her shoulder, taking advantage of their moment alone. "Do you think three people are enough?"

"Phoenix thinks a smaller party can infiltrate the camp and steal your team and their weapons without causing a major battle and any further loss of life. Besides, they outnumber us three-to-one."

Eri swallowed down a current of panic. "Not many people want to live by the rules, eh?"

"We lose more over the wall every year. Faced with a choice, I guess not."

"Cyberhell. Your rules don't seem as bad as the ones aboard the *Heritage*."

Striver grinned. "You're telling me."

Eri caught Striver's green gaze and they froze, her gaze locked on his. *Maybe he isn't all that different after all?*

A bird rustled the canopy above, and the branches rained leaves. One fell in Eri's hair, and Striver brushed it off. A warm glow surged inside her.

"Striver, the coast is clear."

Eri and Striver whirled around. Riley stood with his arms crossed. Suddenly, three people seemed one person too many.

Although it took her a few seconds to recover, Striver didn't miss a beat. "You sure?"

"Phoenix did a sweep of the area. There's no Lawless on the other side."

Striver turned back to her. "Ready?"

She felt her laser on her hip and nodded.

"Good. I'll go first." He gave her a serious look. "When you're climbing, don't look down."

Riley stepped in, his blue eyes gleaming with distrust. "You sure we should bring her with us?"

Anger blazed on her cheeks and Eri waved him off. She didn't like him any better than his pushy sister. "I'll be fine. They're my team and rescuing them was my idea. Besides, I'm the one with the laser."

Riley looked up at the trees in disdain. "Why Striver gave that thing back to you, I haven't the slightest."

Eri hated being questioned. Not only did she have to prove herself, but he was right. They shouldn't have given the laser back to her. She could turn on them at any time—not that she would. They were helping her save her friends. To shoot them in the back would break every rule of decency. Striver trusted her—she could feel it. He believed in her, and that's all she needed.

She took a deep breath. She wasn't about to go into some big speech. "Because I can use it to defend us."

All Riley did was harrumph in response.

Ignoring Riley's tone, Eri turned to the wall. She'd climbed the plastic rock wall on the physical activity deck many times, and that wall had no ladder rungs for handholds. But it did have cables holding her up if she fell.

Eri breathed deeply, trying to calm the fury raging inside her. Why did she care so much about their opinions? Driven to show these tree-dwellers that she could survive on their turf, she bounced on her heels behind Striver, waiting for her turn.

What did they think the people on the *Heritage* did all day? Recline in their sleep pods?

Striver climbed, skipping every other rung, as if he'd scaled the wall a thousand times. Adrenaline pumped through her as Eri grabbed the first bar and leapt up. The metal was cold and slick underneath her palms, and she wished she had powder to keep from slipping. Riley followed behind her.

The higher she climbed, the sweatier her hands grew. She kept wiping them on her new tunic, wrapping her arm around the rung for balance. In between each set of ten, she took her time, catching her breath. *Remember what he said. Don't look down.* The last thing she wanted to do was fall on Riley's head. He already disliked her and she hadn't even said three words to him.

Eri climbed through the branches obscuring the top of the wall. Twigs with spiraling thorns pulled at her curls, and furry, pin-sized bugs kept flying in her eyes, ears and mouth. She needed both hands to keep her death grip and couldn't bat the insects away. *Twenty or so rungs left to go.* Striver had already reached the top and crouched down, offering her his hand. "Almost there, Eri."

It was the first time she'd heard him speak her name, and the way he looked at her, like he believed she could do it, made her think of Aquaria. Homesickness washed over her and she forced herself to toughen up. *I have to save Litus for Aquaria. I owe it to my sister and my team.* Eri increased her pace. The air thinned, and her heart beat hard, making her dizzy. She glanced down despite Striver's advice, and Riley's head popped out of the canopy of trees. He furrowed his eyebrows and she whipped her face back up. Clinging to her goals, she cleared her head and stepped up another rung.

Striver grabbed her arm with a firm grip and pulled her up. "Watch your step."

Jagged stalagmites of rock and glass jutted from the top of the wall. Eri held onto his arm until she could find a place to land both feet. "Jeez. Don't want anyone to come in, do you?"

"It's for our own protection. Lawless try to breach our lands all the time."

The jungle on the other side of the fence loomed darker than the side she left, even though the trees were the same tangled chaos of twisted vines and crisscrossing trunks that seemed to grow in every direction except up. Murky water surrounded the wall in a moat. A glittering tail writhed just below the surface before disappearing into the darker depths.

"Don't fall in. The leechers will eat you alive."

"Leechers?"

"Yeah." Striver took a minute to think about it. "Long, worm-like fish with teeth."

"What a nice planet you've got here."

Striver gave her a sly smile. "Wait until you see the swamp boars."

"Hopefully, we won't run into anything too aggressive on our way." Riley hoisted himself over the edge, once again ruining their brief moment alone.

"The coordinates on Eri's locator are far from the Lawless's homeland, deep within the mountains. We're going to have to trek through Soren's Bog to skirt their sentinels. We'll need to be alert."

"More than alert. We'll have to tread like ghosts." Riley wrinkled his broad nose.

Striver squeezed Eri's shoulder. "We can do it."

He turned to the jungle and brought up his bow, releasing an arrow trailing a rope behind it. The arrow soared through the air and pierced the nearest tree. A pink-and-orange-feathered bird cawed in protest then fluttered into the horizon. The rope swung precariously, hanging in suspension above the moat.

Eri almost choked. "We're using that?"

"Ever heard of zip-lining?"

"No."

"What did they teach you aboard that mother ship?" Riley asked as he tied a loop in a rope and secured it around his wrists.

"Manners." Eri wanted to add: *More than you or your sister have.* But she remembered Commander Grier's orders to make friends.

"I'll go first." Striver secured his own rope and stepped near the edge. He winked. "See you on the other side."

Before she could reply, he jumped, sliding along the rope. The rope dipped and Eri's stomach clenched as his boots skimmed the surface of the moat. Striver rose up again as he approached the tree. He braced himself with his legs outstretched. Eri's heart skipped as his feet hit the tree and he released his rope, jumping to the forest floor. She sighed and shook her head. *He made it look so easy.*

Riley gave her a weary look. "Having second thoughts?"

"No." She couldn't imagine staying in the village while they went without her. Her teammates would never trust her after what the Lawless did. They needed her.

"Courage is found in the least likely of places." Riley looked as though he humored her because he had to. He offered her a rope loop. "Your turn next. Just don't let go."

Her face must have blanched, because Riley shook his head. "You're the one that wanted to come with us."

Eri tightened her lips, lest an unfriendly comment spit out. She grabbed the loop and wrapped it around the rope bridge, making sure it was secure. *If only Aquaria could see me now.*

"Am I going to have to push you, or are you going to jump?"

Her heart pounded against her ribcage. "I'm going to jump. Just give me a sec."

She breathed in and out, watching Striver wave at her from across the moat. She trusted him. For some strange reason, she knew he'd do everything in his power to keep her from harm. Was it his way with everyone? He did seem like a hero in a messed-up world.

Her boot toes poked out from the ledge, thin air between both feet. She teetered forward, vertigo clutching her stomach. *Now or never.*

Eri jumped, the air whooshing around her as she slid down the length of the rope. The jungle blurred, nothing existing except the rope in her fingertips and the adrenaline racing through her veins. Fear and exhilaration hit her in a rush. The moat came up at her in a glassy black slate, stealing her breath away. She kicked her feet, ready to send those leechers back to the watery depths were they came from. She didn't weigh as much as Striver, so her feet cleared the moat with room to spare. Regaining her breath, she picked up her legs, preparing for the oncoming tree. The arc flattened, slowing her descent. Her feet touched the tree, and she bounced off. She hung above the forest floor, swinging like a pendulum.

"Way to go, Eri!" Striver called from below her, bringing her back to reality.

Eri looked up the rope. The monolithic wall cast a shadow over her head, the concrete covered in wispy moss and lichen. *I can't believe I did that. Two days ago I sat in my bubble office, typing old languages into my miniscreen.*

Striver stood below her with both hands raised. His fingers wiggled in the air. "Jump!"

She released her hold on the rope and fell. The ground came up fast, knocking the air out of her as she dropped and rolled onto her back.

Striver knelt beside her, his face hovering over hers. Worry wrinkled his angular features. "You all right?"

"Yeah. Now I know what it feels like to be a bird."

His face softened. "Or to be Phoenix." Striver stood and helped her up.

She dusted leaves off of her tunic. "Frightening." She gave him a mischievous tweak of her eyebrow. "But fun."

He smiled and looked away, as if deciding whether or not to tell her something. "He did fly you over the wall earlier last night when you were out."

Eri paused in mid swipe. "He did what?"

"Flew you over the wall. We would have needed a pulley system to lift you back up. Too bad you don't remember that, huh?"

Thinking about Phoenix's branch-like fingers, Eri decided she'd rather forget.

Riley followed, careering through the trees over the moat. He landed, giving her a nod. Either he'd run out of mocking comments about her lack of experience, or by zip-lining she'd earned a small amount of his respect.

"Come on." Striver picked up his backpack. "We don't want to waste the daylight."

Eri didn't argue. Every second her team lay in the Lawless's clutches felt like a weight on her heart. She followed him into the jungle feeling like a hero for the first time in her life.

CHAPTER THIRTEEN
CAMPFIRE TALES

"What do you want with us?" The light-haired prisoner squirmed until he could sit upright and stare Snipe down. His face was broad, his dark gaze calm and calculating despite his dire predicament.

Snipe raised his bow at the man. "Not for me to decide. One more question and I'll put an arrow in your leg."

Weaver remained silent, trying not to catch the man's attention. Pity and guilt mingled in his stomach. He felt bad for the prisoners, but at the same time, mistrust simmered in his mind. Since they spoke English, Jolt might be right about them being from a colony ship and coming to steal their world. If so, the pirates settled here first, and that should mean the planet was theirs, a universal rule in an otherwise lawless land.

Snipe walked over to his side of the cave and put down his bow. In a second, he held his blade instead, sharpening it on the groove in the rock. Weaver watched from the corner of his eye, wondering which weapon the bodyguard favored.

The hefty woman rolled over, anger flashing on her face when she noticed her bindings.

The blond man whispered to her, and Weaver listened carefully. "Don't ask questions. Don't move."

"Where are we?" She flicked her head around the room, and her single braid whipped back against her bald skull.

"Some sort of cave. They've sent someone to get their leader."

Her eyes narrowed, beady and intense. "Do you have a plan to get us out of this?"

"I left Eri with the ship and told her to notify the commander. She'll get us help."

She snarled. "The linguist. You've got to be kidding. She can't even zip her boots."

"She'll bring help. I know she will."

"Enough." Snipe leapt up and walked in between them, flashing his blade. "I don't want any whispered plans of escape. It's futile. You're a hundred meters into a mountain surrounded by dense jungle and thousands of pirates. There's no way out. No one's coming to get you except our leader, and I know for a fact he won't let you go."

Weaver stopped listening, turning back to the ancient symbols surrounding the golden pool. *A linguist?*

Jolt had the laser guns, and there was nothing he could do about it. No way could he get them back by himself. The golden liquid was his only bargaining chip.

Power emanated from the pool. The energy source tingled every bone in his body, vibrating to a pitch his ears couldn't quite hear, promising him greatness. He just needed to figure out how to harness it. Then, the weapons would be a consolation prize. Maybe he'd have to befriend these people, get their linguist to decipher the hieroglyphs. And take the credit himself. They were prisoners, so he could bargain with them, maybe even do a prisoner exchange. Where did they say she was? At the ship?

Weaver's gaze followed Snipe as he took his seat against the cavern wall. First, he had to get past Jolt's most menacing bodyguard.

Snipe glanced up and caught him staring. "Got a problem, Weasel?"

"No." Weaver kept his tone light, laughing inwardly. *I'm only plotting how to take over the world.*

↾↽

Doubts crept in as Striver trekked through the growing muck leading into Soren's Bog. Sure, they'd skirted every sentinel within ten kilometers, but the legend of Soren's disappearance still hollowed him out, ever since his friends had whispered the tale of tragedy over the embers of their campfire as little boys. The mist flowed in a thick carpet up to their thighs, and the trees drooped in mossy curtains into the sludge. Everything dripped, and the random *plink-plunk*s made it seem like someone followed you from behind. The whole place oozed creepiness.

Eri splashed behind him, her space boots protecting her better than their leather footwear. He envied her, even if she wore a byproduct of the technology he'd shunned. *If only she'd learn how to walk in them.* An overwhelming urge to protect her surged inside him, and he resisted again and again the impulse to offer his hand. Every time he touched her, a spark ignited in his chest, and he feared if he remained too close to her, his heart would catch on fire—one he couldn't control.

She stumbled forward and caught herself on a tree before her face could hit the water. She had a smudge on her left cheek, and his fingers itched to touch her fair skin and wipe it away.

"No bogs in space?" Riley passed her with a grin. His mocking irritated Striver, but he held his tongue. He had to stay on good terms with the man if they were to accomplish this mission together. Constantly defending the invader wasn't the most diplomatic tactic, as much as he wanted to be the shining hero who came to her aid.

Besides, as her personality unfolded, he noticed a good dose of spunk in her, along with a stubborn streak that made her all the more interesting. Eri had the guts to defend herself.

Pulling herself back up, she snorted. "No. Space is a whole lot of nothing. Besides, the gravity is stronger here, and I'm not used to walking on anything that isn't made out of some sort of chrome."

Riley laughed. "Some conquering party."

"I was on an exploratory mission," Eri spat back.

"That's why you came with so many laser guns?"

"The guns were for our protection." She laughed and muttered under her breath, "Some protection they were."

Striver caught her eye and flashed an apologetic smile. He kept his gaze moving before she mesmerized him again, looking to Riley instead. "Come on, we need to reach the mountains by nightfall or we'll be sleeping on a water bed."

Eri nodded, picking up a walking stick she'd found on a mossy incline. "Why's it called Soren's Bog anyway?"

Riley chuckled with a sinister undertone. "Do you think we should tell her?"

Striver turned around and Eri glared at him as if he'd haunted the bog himself. Sighing, he plowed ahead. "There's a legend in our village about a man named Soren. A century ago, he led a hunting party into this bog, tracking a herd of swamp boars. After several nights, his men were drenched and wanted to go home, but he'd had a dream of trapping the biggest swamp boar the village had ever seen."

Striver shrugged, trying to dismiss the man's irrational goal, even though he'd had similar dreams of his own when he was a teen. "I don't know if he was trying to prove something, or maybe to impress a woman in the village. Whatever the case, Soren wouldn't give up. His hunting party sloshed through the muck for days tracking the great boar. They ran out of supplies and got lost."

"What happened to them?" With the walking stick, Eri caught up to him, close enough to splash more water on his pants.

Striver didn't care. He watched her curls bob with each step. Somehow, in all this muck and gloom, her hair seemed even brighter. "Supposedly they came upon this pool of golden liquid, welling up from a spring deep within the bog. They walked right in, the liquid seeping around their boots and crawling up their legs. They started to have strange daydreams, memories of the past. Some of the older men had lost family members—wives and children—and they were able to relive happy times again and again. They became obsessed and didn't want to leave."

Eri grabbed his arm. "Wait a second. How do you know all this if they all stayed in the bog?"

Striver smiled. "One of the younger men, a guy named Blue from the Lawless lands, had no family, no memories he wanted to relive. He was able to crawl out of the liquid and found his way back home, almost starved to death."

"What happened to him?"

"He was fine. Grew up in our village, had a family of his own. In fact, isn't he related to you, Riley?"

Riley gave him a sarcastic smile. "Ha. Ha."

Striver turned to Eri. She'd smiled at his joke, and it made him feel so good to make her happy. "But the others were never found, nor was the golden liquid. The village council sent out search parties for months, but none of them was ever seen again."

Riley chimed in as he slung out his knife, cutting through a curtain of hanging moss. "They say Soren's ghost still roams this bog looking for the swamp boar he was destined to kill. If you're not careful, he'll mistake you for the boar, and one of his arrows will go right through your heart."

"Enough, Riley." Striver gave Eri a consolatory smile and shook his head. "That last part is just Riley's boar droppings."

Eri waved it off. "That's fine. You don't think I've heard my fair share of ghost stories aboard the *Heritage*?"

Riley scoffed. "I bet they're nothing compared to Soren's Bog."

Eri glared at him. "Much scarier, actually."

"Oh yeah? Tell me the scariest one."

Striver threw up his arms. Here they were, bickering like children, when both tribes had so much to learn about each other. If Eri's people did colonize Refuge, how would his tribe ever get along with theirs?

Eri glanced over at him and raised one slender eyebrow. He shrugged. "Go ahead. We have all day." Besides, he was interested in her life on the ship, and telling stories kept their minds off the sludge and kept them walking.

She hopped onto a mossy ledge and walked one foot in front of the other, her arms balancing with the walking stick.

"When someone dies on the ship, we eject their body into space in a small nanofiber coffin. They float for eternity into the unknown, drifting."

The ledge ended and she jumped back into the swamp muck, splashing Riley's boots. "A whole generation before mine, there was one family on the *Heritage* who lost their little girl, Lynex, to some rare disease. The computer tries to weed out such genetic deformities, matching the best pairs of people to create durable children who will live long, fruitful lives. But every so often, the calculations go wrong, and someone is born with a genetic weakness."

"Lifemate pairing. How utterly hideous." Riley threw a rock and it skimmed across the water.

Striver put up his hand. "Enough, Riley; let her tell the story."

Eri waited until the waves in the surface stilled, her gaze far off, like she saw it happening in her mind. "This family didn't want their little girl ejected into deep space. So, before the funeral, they switched the coffins and hid Lynex's body in their family unit. The authorities ejected an empty coffin into space."

"That's not very scary."

Eri raised her eyebrows tauntingly. "The scary part is coming."

Riley furrowed his brow and took another swing at the next curtain of moss. "I'll make sure to strap my boots on tighter."

She ignored him, kicking away a vine floating in the muck. "They hid her body in her sleep pod and kept the airtight container closed to preserve her. One night, when they checked on her, the pod was empty. When they opened the lid, they saw scratch marks on the inside."

Eri walked over to Riley and scratched his arm with her nails. To Striver's surprise, he recoiled.

Laughing, she walked back to Striver's side. "Anyway, they say her ghost haunts the decks at night, her malformed face scaring even the hardiest of men. They say she can manipulate technology, make your locator turn off like you're dead, shut off the lights, anything to tease people."

A shiver jolted up Striver's spine. Her story chilled and impressed him at the same time. "That's pretty scary, Eri."

"That's not all. One night when my sister and I played hide-and-seek in the abandoned corridors of the ship, I got lost. The lights flickered off, and I heard a scratching noise coming from behind me. At first I thought it could have been mice that had escaped the biodome. Then, as I listened harder, I heard a sniffle, like from some little kid's nose."

Striver was hooked. "Did you turn around?"

She smiled and shook her head. "No way. I used an alarm on my locater. I kept thinking she was going to turn it off, and then I'd be stuck, but the device kept wailing. Aquaria found me shaking in an air vent."

Riley had grown quiet, and he stood by a grove of trees ahead. Striver wondered if Eri's story had gotten to him. "Riley, you all right?"

"No."

He gave Eri a questioning look and ran up to join him. "What's the matter?"

Riley pointed to a broken branch and a place where the muck had been flattened in a large circle with two points at the top. "We're not alone."

CHAPTER FOURTEEN
MATCHING BREATHS

Weaver watched as Snipe's eyelids drooped and flickered. He'd sat in a nook in the wall where the golden glow couldn't reach, and Weaver wondered if Snipe rested better in darkness or if the substance affected him as well. One more minute and the man would fall asleep. Weaver inched over to where Snipe had kicked his bow.

Where was Jolt? Crusty had been gone for several hours. Had the old man gotten lost in the cave?

"Psssst."

Weaver whirled around. The blond prisoner flicked his head, inviting him over. Weaver paused, considering his offer. He wanted the linguist, but if Snipe caught him associating with the prisoners, he'd be a dead man.

He glanced at Snipe. The bodyguard's chin rested on his chest, rising and falling with his deep breaths. Snipe rarely slept, and not for long. Weaver had precious seconds at most.

He shuffled over and crouched by the blond man, hiding behind a wide stalagmite almost as tall as he was. White lugworms crawled on the slick rock at the base, and he kicked them away, wondering how the man could suffer being tied. Poor guy must have hundreds of spidermite bites. Weaver whispered so softly, the faintest breeze would cover it. "What do you want?"

"Free us, and we'll help you overpower him." His blue gaze sparkled with intensity. This was not a man who'd back down easily. *Jolt has his hands full with this guy.*

Weaver rubbed his chin. "What makes you think I'm not on his side?"

"I see the way you look at him, like you want something he has."

More like the position he's trying to inherit. Weaver bit his tongue, remaining silent.

"What's your name? Weasel?"

"Weaver," he growled. Snipe's demeaning nickname always bit him in the butt.

"Weaver, I'm Litus and this is Mars. Untie us and we'll help you in return."

Weaver knew exactly what Litus was doing: using names to make him more emotional, more attached.

"What's to say you won't just run away and leave me for dead?" One look at the man-woman told him he'd rather she remain tied up. Her eyes reminded him of the vicious mountain vultures that could pick out your eye in one swoop.

"My word." The blond man's face was set in stoic lines, making him look like some hero from the tales of Old Earth. He was a good guy; Weaver was sure of it, and the offer tempted him. Weaver's fingers itched to untie their bindings. It would be so easy. But what he really needed was that linguist, and he doubted once they were untied they'd usher her back to this cave for him. Besides, if he let the prisoners free, none of the pirates would ever trust him again. He had to work around Snipe, not take the man out. Weaver shook his head. "No deal."

Snipe shifted against the cave wall and Weaver shuffled back to his seat next to the pool of golden swirls. As Snipe turned his head to check on him, Weaver's finger traced a symbol of three intersecting lines.

Snipe raised an eyebrow, his gaze burning a hole in Weaver's forehead.

Don't. Look. Up. Weaver whispered the words, pretending he was deep in thought. He scribbled something unintelligible into the sand at his feet. The bodyguard sat back, balancing his blade on the tip of his finger and whistled a sour tune.

Too late. I should have moved when I had the chance.

But what would he have done? Even if he overpowered Snipe, he'd have to deal with Jolt and the other pirates. His only chance at power was deciphering the symbols of the golden pool, and he needed the linguist for that.

Weaver rubbed his temples, trying to ignore the swirls of golden liquid congregating around him, urging him to touch the surface and break the patterns with his fingertips. He didn't need any more of those sentimental dreams making him weak. He turned away, watching the prisoners instead. The glow danced along the cavern walls, revealing reddish swirls in the rock and then falling back to the shadows. Even with his back turned he couldn't get away from its call. *That* was power. If only he could harness it, turn its dizzying mysteries against his enemies.

Weaver had a fractured plan at best with no way to put together the pieces. If only the linguist would march right into his cave.

ఎ~ઠ

Eri stood on her tiptoes, gazing over Riley's shoulder at the broken branch. Her heart raced. Just when she was starting to feel comfortable, Riley had to pull the muck right from under her. "Is it one of the Lawless?"

Riley pulled a tuft of coarse black hair from a kink in the wood and felt it between his fingertips. "This hair belongs to no man."

Striver took the tuft and put it up to his nose. "It's boar hair, all right, but it's too high up for a swamp boar."

The broken branch was eye level with Striver, a good two heads taller than she was. "Maybe the boar jumped?" Her voice rose up in a high-pitched shriek as she imagined a monstrous hulk of that size.

Striver shook his head. "Boars don't jump. They're too heavy."

Riley reached behind him and pulled out his bow with an arrow. "How old are these tracks?"

Striver crouched near the muck and poked his finger through the surface. When he pulled it up, water filled the hole. "An hour at most."

"Good. If it's an hour away, we should just keep going." Eri's hand hovered over her laser as she rocked back and forth on her heels in the water.

"It's not that simple." Striver put a finger up to the wind. "It's going in the same direction we are."

Riley scanned the bog. "Should we circle around?"

"No. It would take too long, and we'd have to navigate deeper waters."

Eri nodded in agreement with Striver. She didn't want to delay the rescue any longer, and the thought of deeper waters made fear creep up her throat.

"What are we going to do, ride its tail?" Riley looked at both of them like they were crazy.

Eri put her hands on her hips. "What's the matter; you scared?"

"No." Riley scanned the jungle around them as if a massive boar would show up right then and prove them wrong. "I'm not stupid, either."

Striver shrugged. "The deeper waters may have leechers."

Riley's hand tightened on his bow. "Anything's better than leechers. You've got me on that one." His chest heaved. "Let's go, straight into its tracks. At least we'll have the advantage of surprise."

Striver nodded toward Eri's leg and brought out his own bow. "You may want to take out your laser. Just in case."

Oh, that's reassuring. She tugged the laser out of the holster and input the code to unlock it. The proton chamber buzzed and warmed underneath her fingers. Lasers used to scare her, but now the tingling warmth comforted her. "Lead on."

They walked until her feet felt like lead and her muscles ached. The swamp stretched on forever, an endless netherworld of mossy trees under hazy light. Her worry over the boar diminished with the monotony. To keep her mind occupied, she thought of all the questions she wanted to ask Striver, but Riley's presence kept her from saying anything.

"Why'd they choose you for this exploratory mission, anyway?" Riley asked. He turned his head in her direction and assessed. "I mean, you don't look like a warrior, or even a scientist."

"What do I look like, then?" Eri could have reported him for prejudice on the *Heritage. You're not on deck twenty-seven any more, though.*

"I don't know. Maybe a teacher?"

Striver slashed a path through a mossy overhang with his hand knife. "What *is* your job, Eri?" The genuine interest in his voice made her want to answer.

"I'm a linguist."

Riley wrinkled his broad nose. "What's that?"

Eri took a deep breath, knowing they'd probably think it was the most boring job in the whole universe. "I study all of Old Earth's languages. I can speak and translate Latin, Greek, French, you name it. The commander thought my team would need an interpreter. She had no idea you'd be from Old Earth, and would speak English, no less."

"English was the primary language on Outpost Omega." Striver brushed back a long branch. "But all those other languages—I can't imagine how much discipline it would take to learn them. That's really impressive."

"So you're not even necessary?" Riley's lips held a hint of a smile.

Eri looked at the muck caked on her boots. Riley had won this round. "Afraid not." Her voice came out gloomier than she'd expected.

"Hey, I bet you're more important than you think." Striver gave her a meaningful glance. "Look at you now, going to rescue your team. You're probably the most important colonist there is."

"Only if we succeed."

"*If* we succeed?" Striver shook his head. "If you knew me at all, you'd know I refuse to fail. We'll get your team out of there. I promise."

Before Eri could respond, the leaves rustled behind them and everyone froze. The stench of rot and mold wafted from the jungle. Eri covered her nose, holding back a gag.

"I thought you said it was in front of us," Riley hissed under his breath.

"It was." Striver brought up his bow and cocked an arrow. "It must have circled around to catch us off guard."

"Nonsense. A boar's brain is as big as a pearl berry." Riley brought up his own bow.

"Not this one's." Striver gestured for Eri to join them in a line. She brought out her laser and aimed it in the direction of the smell.

A snort exploded from the undergrowth, followed by splashing. The ground pounded under her feet, and waves spread in concentric circles around her legs. Eri's hands shook as she held up the laser.

Striver's arm muscles tightened. "Here it comes."

A snout, big as the front of Eri's drop ship, parted the trees and two tusks dripped water from either side. It stared at them with raging black eyes, and the hairs on its hide prickled up in a Mohawk.

Eri's whole arm shook as she tried to hold her laser steady. "Should we shoot?"

"Wait. I don't want to provoke it." Striver cocked his arrow.

"It already looks mad as all hell," Riley whispered beside them.

Stomping the water, the beast exhaled, and puffs of steam rose. It charged, looming over their heads, bigger than an Old Earth bear.

Striver shouted, "Shoot!" He released an arrow and the shaft sank into the beast's shoulder. Riley fired another one into its snout. Eri fired her laser, but the recoil sent the stream over the beast's head. The boar kept charging, undeterred.

"Spread out. Run for cover!" Striver grabbed Eri's arm and pulled her sideways. Riley ran in the opposite direction, disappearing behind a stand of ferns. The beast skidded past them, splashing water on Eri's back like a tidal wave. It snorted and squealed low and loudly as it circled back.

"In here." Striver pushed her toward a hole in one of the massive trees. Eri slipped in, cowering with her back against the inside of the trunk. Striver ducked in after her.

The boar's footsteps pounded in Eri's gut. Striver put a finger to his mouth and raised his bow toward the opening. The boar's snout collided into the trunk, sniffing. Drops of snot sprayed on Eri's chest. She fell backward, dropping her laser. The gun sank into the water at her feet. "Dammit! I hope it's waterproof!"

Striver shot an arrow into the nostril and the beast roared and pulled back.

"Do you think you got it?" Eri whispered, creeping forward and reaching into the water for her laser.

Striver shrugged, pulling another arrow out of the bag on his back. "You can never be too sure."

Eri inched forward, stretching her arm out as far as she could. Slimy grasses entangled her fingers and a scaly worm slithered against her arm. She instinctively yanked her hand out of the water. What had Striver said about leechers and their teeth? She couldn't remember, but now wasn't the time to think about it. Her laser was her only defense in this wild world. *Don't think; just reach in and feel around.*

The boar roared, the sound coming from only a few meters away. She didn't have much time.

She jammed her hand back under the water and reached down as far as she could, the water reaching her neck. Swamp reeds splashed in her face, and she spit them out, gulping down brown water. Her fingers brushed a hard, slick surface, and she grabbed onto the barrel of the gun. A hoof scratched at the bark of the tree right above her and Eri screamed. She turned the laser around and fired into the leathery foreleg as it came down. Pieces of bark rained on her face.

Striver yelled and fell toward her. "Eri, watch out."

Eri pulled the trigger again, and the light seared a black spot on the boar's leg right above the hoof. The creature wailed in agony, then disappeared back into the jungle.

Striver pulled her toward the inner trunk. He shook as he held her. "That was close. Too close."

She couldn't tell if her heart raced from the attack or because his arms enveloped her. "Where's it going?"

"Hopefully it's not coming back." They huddled, waiting for another sound. Eri welcomed his warmth against her bare skin. He smelled like fire smoke and pine, wilderness and fresh air. His chest was hard against her shoulder. She turned her head, her nose brushing the firm line of his chin. She met his gaze, and the intensity brewing in the green flecks drew her in. They breathed together in sync, her lips so close to his. If she was going to die, at least she'd die happy.

Riley screamed as the ground pounded again.

"Stay here; I'm going after him." Striver pulled away from her and her heart ripped in two.

He disappeared into the jungle and Eri bolted after him.

The boar had cornered Riley against a massive mangrove, the white tusks stuck into a trunk on either side. Pinned against the tree, Riley had no room to release another arrow. He kicked at its toothy mouth with his feet.

Striver fired at the boar's back, but the animal was too focused on his prey to notice.

Eri brought up her laser just as Striver jumped onto the boar's back and climbed, gripping handfuls of hair. He positioned himself on top of the boar and brought out a small knife. The beast pulled back, freeing its tusks from the tree and reared up, throwing Striver to the ground before he could plunge the knife into its back. Striver rolled over but didn't have enough time to get back up again before the boar charged him.

Eri's hand tightened on the laser. *This is it.*

Running alongside the boar and screaming her lungs raw, Eri aimed for its black eye and fired. The first shots missed by centimeters, but she kept shooting until the trail of light fired directly into its eye. The beast fell forward and slid against Striver, pushing them both toward the mangrove forest. Her heart shattered.

Oh no. I've killed Striver.

She ran through the water to where the beast stilled. Striver's hand poked from under its snout. She grabbed onto his hand and held it against her chest. *Please, please, please be alive.*

"Striver? Striver, wake up!"

There was no response, leaving an empty hole in her gut.

Riley came up on the other side. "Is he okay?"

Eri dropped Striver's hand and grabbed a tusk, the ivory smooth and slick under her fingertips. The beast didn't budge. "Help me. We have to lift the head."

She knelt in the muck and braced her hands under the beast's snout, feeling the course hair and leathery hide under her fingertips. The stench gagged her throat, and she held her breath to avoid choking.

Riley shouted, "On the count of three, push the snout toward me."

Eri nodded.

"One."

"Two," she chanted with him.

"Three."

They heaved, pushing the weight up enough to shift the snout to the side. Riley fell back on his butt, splashing into the water.

Striver lay on his back between two massive tree roots arcing up from the muck. His eyes were closed. Thankfully, the roots braced the brunt of the boar's fall. Eri fell on top of Striver, holding his face in her hands. "Wake up!"

No response. She slapped his cheek. "Wake up, dammit!"

His eyelids fluttered. "Ohhhhhhh, man. I feel like a ton of logs just fell on me."

Relief flooded her nerves. "Is anything broken?"

He moved his legs and his arms. "I don't think so. Eri, you saved my life."

"More like she dropped a huge-ass monster on you to squash you." Riley got up and wrung out his pants.

"Striver, I'm sorry. There was no other way."

"You did the right thing." Striver sat up slowly and hunched over. "It had to be stopped."

"One thing's for sure." Riley walked to the beast and patted its hide.

"What?" Eri helped Striver up and braced him against her until he regained his balance. He clung to her as if she were the last pillar on Refuge.

"We're going to feast tonight."

CHAPTER FIFTEEN
FAITH

Eri awoke to the flashing light of her locator. Grogginess from a grueling trek and a belly of boar's meat faded when she saw the sender. Commander Grier hailed her from the *Heritage*.

She wiggled out of her blanket and checked on the others. Striver and Riley lay asleep several meters down the mossy incline—one perk of being a woman was getting more privacy. She didn't want to accidentally wake them, but ignoring the commander would be toying with disobedience, as stated in section four of the Guide. Eri climbed farther up the ledge to ensure secrecy. She pressed the receiver button.

Commander Grier's face floated above her arm like a ghost. "Ms. Smith, you haven't reported to me."

"I'm sorry, Commander." Eri felt her face blush with embarrassment. "I don't have much to tell you. I'm getting to know them, as you said to do."

Grier's lips thinned and her features hardened. "I need numbers. How many people live on Haven 6? How many are of fighting age? Do they have an army? What is the extent of their weaponry?"

"I don't know. I'm on a mission to save the other members of my team." *Because you won't do it.* Eri put her hand through her hair and tugged until her curls straightened and fell through her fingers before bouncing back again. She wasn't even sure she wanted to tell the commander anything. Giving her any more information was betraying her new friends, people who were putting their lives on the line to save her and bring back her team. She'd procrastinated contacting the commander for those very reasons. Everything Eri did felt like a conflict of interest.

"I can't just ask direct questions without seeming suspicious. I'm supposed to be gaining their trust, aren't I?"

"My patience wears thin, Ms. Smith. The *Heritage* can't hover in orbit forever. Our biodomes are overtaxed due to unfertile soil, and the colonists grow anxious to start their new life. I must take action, whether you supply me with information or not."

Guilt plagued Eri like a disease. Aquaria and her parents counted on what she did on Haven 6. Her people waited up there, and here she was, exchanging ghost stories and romancing their leader. "I'll try to do better, Commander. I promise."

"Project Delta Slip is top priority. Don't expect me to tell you again."

The image flickered out. Eri sat under the moonlight, gazing at the massive mother ship through open patches in the jungle canopy. What was she going to do?

She breathed in deeply, calming her prickly nerves. *Rescue Litus and Mars first, and then think about how to handle the commander.* If only she could speak with Aquaria. She'd know what to do.

"Eri, what are you doing up?"

She whipped her head around. Striver stood behind her, framed in moonlight. How long had he been standing there? The shadows on his face concealed any emotion.

"My commander hailed me. I had to check in with my status."

"In the middle of the night?"

"There is no day or night for her. She's a brain in a box."

He sat down beside her and shook his head as if rejumbling her words would allow them to make more sense. "What?"

"She's from the generation that left Old Earth. She's got to be at least five hundred and seventy years old. When her body started to fail, they connected her brain to the mainframe."

"Wow, and you chose the little girl ghost story as the scariest one?"

Eri laughed, the tension easing. "I guess growing up with something like that, you take it for granted."

"Let me tell you, that's not a common thing here on Refuge."

"Neither is living your life on a colony ship, but my ancestors did it for generations, and here I am today."

She shivered outside her sleeping blanket and he put his arm around her. "Yes, here you are." The silence thickened. Did he think her arrival was a gift or a curse? Judging from all the problems she gave him, probably the latter.

Striver squeezed her shoulders and released her. He stood up, offering his hand. "Come on, let's get you back to sleep. Tomorrow's another long hike into the mountains."

Eri took his hand, glad he didn't ask what the commander had said. She didn't know if she could lie to him. As he led her back to her blanket, she wondered if she should just come clean and tell him the truth.

"Striver?"

He bent down and tucked the blanket around her, making sure the edges were sealed so snakes and insects didn't crawl in. His face hovered over hers. "Yes."

If she told him, would he still help her rescue her friends? Would he cast her out? She felt like she'd swallowed a rock and it stuck in her throat. She wasn't ready to say good-bye. "Thank you for everything."

"Thank *me*? You saved my life, remember? Every swamp boar from here to the mountains fears you now."

Eri smiled. "Thank you for helping me rescue my team."

Striver's face crinkled. "I'm going for the weapons also, remember? We can't have such technology in the Lawless's hands."

"You say technology as if it's a dirty word, but it's what saved your life today."

"Technology can be dangerous. It brought about the fall of Old Earth."

"Yes, but it can be helpful when used the right way."

"That's the key." Striver put up a finger. "Who's to say what the *right way* is? Some people can't be trusted. When faced with power, they lose sight of their own humanity."

Eri thought about his words. The idea of Lawless men with uncontrollable power scared her, but she still wasn't able to shun her own world and their ways. "I still believe people can harness power and do the right thing."

"Then you're an optimist." Striker gazed at her. "I wish I had such faith. Good night, Eri."

"Good night." Eri smiled, hiding her trembling lips under the blanket. She watched as Striver walked down the incline and settled under his own blanket. It took all of her self-discipline not to follow him.

❧

Striver tossed under his blanket until his face stared up at the mother ship in the sky. He traced the outline of the hull with his finger. He liked Eri, and he wanted to believe she and her people came to coexist. Something about her conversations with her commander stuck a thorn in his side, though. What did they mean by 'Project Delta Slip'? And why all the secrecy?

At first he'd wondered why the commander herself hadn't come to establish contact, but after talking to Eri and hearing about how she was confined to the ship, at least that made sense.

What was the commander doing up there? Planning an attack? If so, how did that affect his relationship with Eri? Would they be enemies? Could he convince her to stay on his side?

No, that would be selfish. If it came to war, Eri would have to choose for herself where she belonged. Hopefully, it wouldn't come to that.

But could his people live with technology? They'd shunned it for so many years, living in a healthy relationship with the land. Could he stand by and watch the colonists strip the planet's resources like humans had on Old Earth? What would Aries and Striker have done?

All of the unknowns stirred in Striver's mind until the first rays of dawn touched the sky.

Riley rolled onto his back beside him, yawning. "Today's the day."

Striver nodded, eager to focus on something other than his turbulent thoughts. "We'll reach the mountains by nightfall. Perfect timing to cover our escape."

"Should I wake Ms. Boar Hunter?"

"No, let her sleep while we pack."

Riley turned and shoved his blanket into his backpack. "You favor her, don't you?" His voice was soft and low, almost a growl.

"What?" Striver froze, feeling like he'd been caught with his finger in the pearl-berry jam.

"The young woman."

Maybe he did, but he hadn't treated her any differently than anyone else who would have dropped out of the sky. "I'm just trying to make her feel at home. The last thing we need is an angry colony ship hanging over our heads."

"Sure. You always do the best thing for our people."

Why did he sound sarcastic? "I try to, yes."

"Just like the raid on the drop ship?"

Anger simmered inside Striver and he pushed it down. "You were there. We decided as a council it was the best thing to do."

"Riptide tells me you're a great leader. She believes in you more than anyone else. You could at least show her the same attention you show to this space girl."

Striver glanced back at Eri to make sure she was still asleep. Why was Riley bringing his sister into this? Why now? Somehow he had to turn the conversation away from Riptide.

Striver stood, challenging him. "Is this why you came? To look over my back and judge my decisions as a leader?"

Riley backed down, returning to packing the leftover boar meat. "No, no, no. I'm just suggesting, be careful. Don't say I didn't warn you."

"I won't." Striver turned back to packing, shoving his knife and their cooking tools into his bag with a *clang*.

"What are you guys arguing about?" Eri stood, hugging her blanket around her shoulders, a large pinkish curl falling in front of her face and making her look so adorable Striver had to turn his eyes away.

"Nothing. We're preparing for the hike ahead. We should reach your coordinates by nightfall. That is, if they are still in the same place."

Eri pressed a few buttons on her locator. "Yup. They are."

"Good." He threw her a package of salted boar meat. She weighed it in her hands and gave him a questioning look.

"A snack for the journey."

"How much do you think I eat?"

Striver shrugged. In his village, a woman who ate well was a blessing. "Consider it a trophy, then."

"Enough flirting!" Riley threw his hands up in the air. "I'm sick of the both of you." He strapped his backpack on and started down the incline to the path of muck.

Striver blinked in dazed confusion. Flirting? Was he flirting?

Eri watched Riley leave with daggers in her eyes. "What's gotten into him?"

Striver tied up his backpack and brushed away the ashes from their fire. "I don't know. He thinks he knows what's best for the colony, what's best for me." He didn't know how that last part slipped out, but it did, and he couldn't take it back.

"What do you mean, what's best for you?"

A memory of Riptide running from his tree hut in tears flashed through his thoughts. "Never mind."

He helped Eri fold her blanket. "Looks like we're all packed up. You ready for another day of sludge?"

"If it's going to get me to my team, yes, I am."

They slid down the incline together and splashed into the swamp. Sunlight filtered through the trees, creating golden splotches on the water's surface. It reminded Striver of Soren's tale. He didn't think any part of the story was true, but after meeting that boar, he had reason to rethink everything.

"What does he mean by *flirting*, anyway? I don't seem to recall the word in my old texts. Not all vernacular words make it into my files."

Striver pushed aside a mossy branch. *Thank goodness this one didn't.* "It's kind of like fooling around, shooting the breeze, in a way, so to speak."

"I think we've been fairly serious and on task." Eri sloshed beside him, adjusting her backpack.

"We're making good time." Striver wondered if she had any idea how much she distracted him.

CHAPTER SIXTEEN
ABDUCTEE

The swamp water dribbled off into thick mud and long grasses that tickled Eri's thighs as they hiked north. Jagged rocks took the place of mossy knolls, and the jungle thinned into patches of spindly trees. The blue sky overhead gave Eri a naked vulnerability. Could the commander spot her from the control deck?

The ship hovered over her like a parent over a child, and she avoided glancing up. The commander still awaited answers, but giving her what she wanted might bring an attack on Striver's village. Either way, Eri wanted to know what they faced, whether she'd tell the commander or not.

"Striver, how many people live on Haven 6?"

"Haven 6? Oh, you mean Refuge?"

"Yeah, whatever your people call it."

Striver jumped from one rock to another and held out his hand for her to follow. "I'm not sure. We do a rough census of our village frequently, but who knows how many Lawless have multiplied throughout the years."

"Do they have an army?"

His face darkened. "More like a horde of mercenaries."

She jumped onto his rock beside him. "Jeez. Have you ever tried to control them?"

He scanned the landscape in front of them, searching for the best route. "No. It was my ancestors' dream for everyone to have the luxury of choice." He jumped down to a patch of sandy ground and waved for her to follow.

Eri steadied herself by gripping a gangly tree trunk as she slid down to join him. "Aren't you afraid they'll overwhelm your village at some point and take over?"

Striver nodded, helping her up as she fell against him. "It's a growing concern. We have the wall and the Guardians, but if the Lawless's numbers continue to rise, someday it won't be enough."

Eri noticed his hands linger on hers, and she struggled to keep her mind level. "Who built the wall? The Guardians?"

"They helped, in part." Striver let go and a small current of disappointment swam through her.

"What do you mean?"

"My ancestors, Aries and Striker, built the wall with the Guardians' help. They wanted everyone to be able to choose for themselves, but they also didn't want their choices ruling others."

Eri put a hand on his arm. "They were brave and wise. But what will you do if the Lawless breach the wall?"

A black tuft of fur took off beside them, its wings fluttering like a butterfly's. Eri watched it disappear over the horizon, farther into the Lawless lands. *Poor animals have no idea what awaits them with so many factions vying for their resources.*

Striver shook his head. "I'm not sure. The council is hard to budge in any direction. They follow our forefathers' wishes to the letter."

"But what if your ancestors couldn't predict the Lawless's rise? I'm sure they'd change the bylaws to save the colony they started."

He climbed up a ledge to another series of rocks. "True. But how? By cultivating technology? Then we'd be just like our predecessors on Old Earth, using weapons against each other until we destroyed our new world. I'm not willing to lead them down that same path."

It was like trying to reason with her linguistics program. Frustration boiled inside her. They had technology in the palms of their hands and they refused to use it. How could she teach him that people can change, learn from the mistakes of their past? That technology did more good than harm?

Striver stopped on the ledge and gazed down at her. "Tell me about your commander."

"Commander Grier?"

"The woman whose brain sits in the box."

Eri nodded, climbing up to join him. "I don't know much about her, really. I've only met her face-to-face one time, if you could call it that. I spoke to a computer screen, an image of what she used to look like on Old Earth."

"What did she do on Old Earth?"

"She held a bunch of political offices before the planet's collapse. When she left, she was governor of a place called New York City. Gangmen attempted to assassinate her, and she managed to survive, but her family died in the firefight. Commander Grier believed in furthering humanity, that we shouldn't have to die out along with our world. She used all of her life's savings to build the *Heritage* and follow her dream."

"Do you have faith in her as a leader?"

"On the *Heritage*, she's revered like a god. Commander Grier's the only one of us who remembers the Old Earth days, giving us a singular vision for our future."

"But you didn't answer my question. What do *you* think?"

Anxiety rushed up Eri's legs. They were already far behind Riley, and standing around wasn't getting them anywhere. "To say anything against the commander—"

Striver put a gentle hand on her cheek, holding her face to his. "You can trust me."

His touch, the closeness of his face to hers, and his smell of fire smoke and pine disarmed her. She closed her eyes and pressed her cheek into his hand, feeling the warmth spread through her face and down her neck.

Who cared about the commander? Why couldn't they just stand there like that forever?

Eri pulled herself back from her intense longings and opened her eyes. Her team needed her; she had to stay sane.

Looking into Striver's gaze, she faced her own fears. "Sometimes I think the commander has forgotten what it's like to be human, to walk around and relate to others. I wonder if she's lost touch with reality."

Relief coursed through her. She hadn't told anyone about her misgivings, and it felt good to shake her concerns from her own shoulders, to share the burden with someone else, an unbiased party. *Well, not totally unbiased.*

"Whatever happens, Eri, we'll work it out together, all right?"

She wanted to believe him so badly, she denied all the secrets brewing inside her and the fact she spied for people plotting to steal his home. "All right."

His hand traveled to the back of her neck, his fingers interlacing with her curls. She leaned toward him, losing herself in his touch. His mouth was only a breath away. Her heart fluttered. Just a little closer…

Something stomped on the rock behind them and they jumped apart. Riley crouched down, like he'd just jumped three meters to where they stood. He chewed on a piece of long grass, and his blue eyes twinkled like magic. "Hey guys, I found the cave."

❧

Dusk came sooner than Eri expected, the mountain casting a dark shadow over them. Riley led her and Striver to a ledge where they could peer down at the mountainside without being seen.

"Where is it? All I see is rock." Striver squinted as he lay beside Eri.

Riley pointed. "Look by that shrub. See the crack in the facade?"

Striver inched near the edge to get a better look. Eri resisted the urge to pull him back. She wasn't his mother, and he'd been able to take care of himself all these years before she met him. So why was she feeling so overprotective?

"Boy, if it wasn't for the coordinates on Eri's locater, I would have never guessed anyone could even fit in there, never mind use it for a hideout."

Eri placed her hand on her laser. "No guards?"

Riley spit out a piece of chewed grass. "Nope."

"Why do you think they chose this spot?" Striver scratched his head. "It doesn't make any tactical sense."

Riley shrugged. "Who knows? I'm guessing this entrance is the only way out and in. It could be a trap."

Eri checked her locater. Her teammates' life signs blinked just beyond the rock. So close, yet so untouchable. The urge to save them welled up inside her. "They're here, all right. We've got to do something. We can't just shake our heads and turn back."

Striver rubbed his chin with his fingers. "They may fight us with the lasers."

"That's *if* they got them working, *if* they figured out the code. Besides, I have a laser, too, remember?"

"It's a gamble." Riley crept up to the edge of the ledge with Striver.

"How could they possibly know we've come for them?" Each second of inaction pressed on Eri's chest, squeezing out her last breath. Now was not the time to argue.

"We all know you guys have techno-gadgets that can do almost anything. What if they bet on you having something like that locating thingamajig on your wrist?" Riley picked up her arm and her locator flashed fluorescent green in the dim light.

Eri touched the screen and the light flashed off. "There's no way they'd know what it did, or that mine connected to theirs, or that you guys saved me."

"We're going in." Striver pulled his bow off his shoulder. "Like Eri said, we've come too far to turn back."

"Under the earth, the Guardians can't help us," Riley warned.

"Good," Striver shot back, sliding down the ledge. "Let's prove we can accomplish something on our own." As much as he cared for the Guardians, sometimes he felt their presence suffocating. It was like having your parents around you all the time.

Eri followed Striver, hoping Riley would come along. They could use his help, but if he didn't believe in going, she wasn't going to force him. Her feet touched the ground and she heard Riley sliding down the ledge behind her.

She turned her head as he landed beside her and gave him a questioning glance.

"I can't leave you and Striver to go alone, now can I?"

Eri smiled and cuffed his arm. Maybe she didn't hate him after all. "Thank you."

"You can thank me once we get in and get out." Riley shook his head. "*If* we make it."

"We're going to make it." Striver adjusted his arrow bag tighter to his back. "Stop being all gloom and doom. You sound like you're telling the tale of Old Earth." He pointed to a circular route, his eyes flicking to Eri. "We're going around this way. Keep low to the ground and follow my lead. Skirt the foothills. Stay out of the open."

"Yes, sir." Eri saluted him like a lieutenant. Striver smiled and slid down the nearest rock. Riley waved his hand for her to go next, so she checked on her laser and followed Striver into the shadows.

Her heart beat so fast, she thought it would fly out of her mouth if she gasped for too long. So many things could happen, and she didn't want anyone to get hurt because of her. She feared what the Lawless had done to her teammates, and she feared what they'd do to her if they caught her. Surprisingly, she feared losing Striver the most. Was it because he'd risked everything for her? Or was it more than just his sacrifices?

They closed the distance, and Striver put a finger to his lips and waved them back. Eri huddled with Riley behind a jutting rock as Striver crept to the mouth of the cave. She bit her nail backward as he snuck in with an arrow raised.

"Always the hero." Riley sighed and settled back on his butt, crossing his arms. Eri remained silent, too nervous to reply.

Two second later, Striver emerged and signaled for them to join him. Eri and Riley ran across the naked expanse and slipped in.

Darkness swallowed them as the air cooled, leaving goose bumps on her skin. The crack cast a sliver of light behind them.

"We need light to go on." Riley shuffled in the dark. "I should have thought ahead."

"No problem." Eri raised her laser gun and pressed a button on the side. White light erupted, illuminating walls dripping with water and moss. A multilegged bug skittered across her boot and she kicked it off, jumping back.

"What in cyberspace is that?"

"A spidermite." Striver kicked it away and placed his hand on her shoulder. "Their bite is poisonous, but it would take thirty of them to make you sick."

Eri cringed. "I don't even want one to bite me."

Riley took up the lead. "They swarm, so we have to move fast."

The cave narrowed until Eri had to squeeze against slick walls crawling with spidermites. She brushed one off her shoulders, stifling a shriek. This was worse than the air ducts she used to crawl through as a kid. These critters were ten times as large as the little brown spiders on the *Heritage*.

Don't think about the bugs. Think about your team.

"You doing okay?" Striver whispered into her ear.

Eri nodded, aiming the light ahead so Riley could continue in the lead. The walls pressed around her, and all she could think of was a cave-in, of the rock trapping her underneath its weight and her never again seeing the light of day. What if the tunnel narrowed so much they couldn't squeeze through?

Stop being stupid. If they lugged Litus and Mars through, you can fit easily.

The group rounded a bend and Riley turned. His face shone white as a ghost in the light of her laser. "There's something ahead."

Eri's throat tightened. *Judgment time.*

Golden light leaked from a source beyond the tunnel. The radiance grew so strong, Riley didn't need the light from her laser anymore. Eri turned it off, not wanting to announce their presence. She made sure the laser still buzzed with energy.

Riley gestured over his shoulder for them to join him behind a stalagmite in a pool of stagnant water. Eri and Striver waded behind it, huddling next to Riley. Peering around the rock, Eri saw the tunnel open to a larger cavern.

"Why are we stopping?" Striver whispered to Riley.

Riley held up his finger and they listened. Voices.

Eri couldn't make out the words, but she could definitely hear a man's voice. It wasn't Litus. She squelched her disappointment. Litus was still in there. Locators never lied.

She glanced at Striver. "What should we do?"

He'd already pulled out his bow and a long, slender arrow, the end decorated with what she recognized as a Guardian's iridescent feathers. "We catch them by surprise."

Riley brought out his bow and nodded in agreement. Eri's grip on her laser tightened, the weight straining her wrist. She didn't think she'd ever get used to holding it, always feeling like a child wielding her parent's weapon. *Remember—you killed the alien in the simulation, plus the giant boar. You can do it, even when you don't want to.*

They tiptoed toward the light.

Striver and Riley released the first volley of arrows. They ducked as shouts rang out and the men inside returned fire. Striver gave Eri the signal, and he and Riley distracted the attackers as she snuck forward to get a better look.

Hope bubbled through her limbs. "They're alive! They're tied up in the back." She wanted to run to them, but two men shot at Striver and Riley from different points. In the center of the cavern, a golden pool of light glimmered like a basin for the gods.

"Get to your friends," Striver shouted, throwing her a black blade. "We'll hold them back."

The weapon skidded to her feet and she picked it up. Eri nodded and slid it into her boot. In the distance, Mars and Litus shouted, sending more adrenaline through her limbs. She bolted to the next stalagmite, every moment she was out in the open tingling on her skin. She ducked behind the rock gasping for air. Two more and she'd reach her team.

She jumped out of hiding just as an arrow whizzed across the cavern toward her. She rolled and came back up behind the next rock. Panic made her squirm, feeling around her body for the end of an arrow, but she hadn't been hit. Another arrow flew over her head and hit the rock wall behind her. They knew she was there.

Striver yelled—in pain or frustration, Eri couldn't tell. Her heart tore as she cast a glance over her shoulder. She couldn't see if he'd been hit. Was he drawing the attention away from her? Should she go back?

No. She was too close now. One more rock to go.

Waiting for another volley of arrows to end, she fired in the general direction of the men and scurried between the two stalagmites, keeping close to the ground. She reached Litus first, pulling out Striver's blade to cut his ties. His camouflaged uniform sagged on his body like he'd lost weight.

"Eri?" he whispered through dry, cracked lips. "Is it really you?"

"What are you doing wearing their clothes?" Mars looked at her with a mix of incredulity and distrust.

"I've made friends." Eri pushed the thought of a wounded Striver from her mind. They were there to save her team, and that's what she had to do right now.

Litus rubbed feeling back into his wrists. As he fumbled with the bonds on his legs, she cut the ropes around Mars's hands.

"Where's Cursor and the rest of the team?" Her locator had registered them as gone, but she refused to believe it.

Litus shook his head. His shoulders slumped with failure.

"Damn bastards." Mars stood and stretched her legs. She'd already kicked off the ropes. "We're all that's left."

Eri swallowed a lump in her throat. *All that's left.* Even though she'd found Litus and Mars, she still felt empty-handed. Tank had helped her with her oxygen mask. Even now she could see him playing Galaxy Battlefield with Mars. *Don't think about the others. Save the people still alive.*

"Come on." Eri rubbed her nose with her sleeve. "We have to get back to the tunnel."

"Not until I've given him a dose of his own medicine." Mars hurled herself into the arrow fire, running directly at one of the men. He saw her coming and reached behind him, into his arrow bag for another arrow.

"She'll never make it." Eri brought up her laser, but Mars stood in the line of fire.

"You don't know Mars," Litus said from behind her. "Give her a second. She's been waiting for this chance since she woke up."

Just as the man pulled the bowstring back, Mars lunged, hurling through the air. She rammed his chest before he could release the arrow. Eri's heart sped as they fell in a tangle to the ground, wrestling.

"Push ahead!" she heard Riley shout from across the cavern. Striver and Riley ran and hid behind a stalagmite in the middle of the cavern. Striver was still alive and well enough to keep fighting. That much kept her going. As they closed in on the younger man, Eri watched Mars fight the older pirate on the ground. He managed to get the upper hand, pushing his weight on top of her.

Eri held up her laser.

"Can you get a good shot?" Litus's voice was hoarse and weak.

"I'll try."

While Mars looked like she'd stored her energy up on the floor of the cave, Litus looked as though they'd leaked his energy from him. Eri wanted to help him, but she had to make sure Mars didn't get killed. She focused on the man's back just as Mars punched him in the jaw and they rolled over together, limbs entwined.

"Nope."

The man pulled himself from Mars's grasp and stood, reaching in his shirt. He pulled out a black blade and swung it as Mars regained her footing.

Mars jumped back as the blade swung a millimeter away from her gut, slicing her camouflaged uniform. She turned and side-kicked the man in his belly. He stepped back, teetering over the golden pool. Mars recovered from the kick fast enough to land another punch in his chest. Flailing his arms, he fell backward into the liquid.

Litus cheered, pumping his fist into the air. Eri shouted across the cavern, "Way to go, Mars!"

Instead of splashing, the golden substance enveloped the man like gel. He screamed as molten ooze covered his face. The surface lay placid a moment later.

Eri and Litus joined Mars on the edge, staring into the golden liquid.

"What happened to him?" Eri offered them her water pouch. She checked across the cave for Striver and Riley. They stood with their bows raised, cornering the other man. To her relief, they looked unharmed.

Mars took a swipe of water. "Sent him back to where he came from."

"Where's that?"

Mars's eyes looked like they could shoot lasers of their own. She handed Litus the water pouch. "Hell."

"Hey, Eri, look at this." Litus took the pouch and pointed to strange symbols carved along the side of the pool. "Can you figure out what it says?"

Eri crouched down, tracing her fingers over them. "It's nothing I've ever seen before."

"You're the linguist." Mars joined her by the symbols. "I bet with enough time you could."

For a moment, she forgot about the battle, intrigued. Besides the *S.P. Nautilus*, this was the find of her life. Any linguist would be excited to get a chance at something this foreign. "With enough time, I'd figure out the whole language."

"Tie him up." Riley's voice echoed from across the cave. Eri tore herself away from the symbols. *Striver.* She had to check on him and make sure he was okay. She left Mars and Litus and ran across the cavern.

Riley tied the man's hands behind his back. "Stupid, betraying weasel worm."

Striver watched with such strange pity and emotion in his features, it made Eri's stomach quiver.

"You guys okay?"

"We're fine." Pain tainted Striver's voice.

"What's the matter?" Eri placed a gentle hand on his arm. "Are you hurt?"

"Only by his traitor brother," Riley said, yanking on the ties. The man he'd bound fell to the cave floor with a *thud*. Brown hair covered his face and he blew it back with defiance. His nose was broader than Striver's, his features softer, but he had the same green eyes. *His brother?*

She turned to Striver and he pulled away, not able to meet her gaze. "Are your friends okay?"

"We're fine. What's left of us," Mars answered from across the cave. Although she'd just won in battle, her shoulders slumped. "Where's the fastest way out? I have a date with the leader of these savages. We're going to a nice little spot I call *revenge*."

"Enough, Mars. You and I need to rest. To eat." Litus held up his hand. He looked at Riley and Striver. "Can you help us?"

"Where are the laser guns?" Striver scanned the cave.

"They took them back to the main camp." The man tied on the floor struggled against his restraints. "You'll never get them back with your ragtag army."

Riley moved to kick him and Striver grabbed his arm. "Not now."

"I want to show the little traitor just how much it hurts to leave your people."

The man on the floor coughed and spat as if Riley's words sent a blade to his gut. "You have to get out of here. Jolt's coming back with more men. They'll be here any minute, and you will all be boar's meat."

"He's right." Litus stepped forward. "I heard them talking. He is coming."

"Why don't we wait here and take him out now?" Mars punched her fist into her palm.

"Because he'll bring more men with him. He'll block the entrance once he knows you're here and send for backup." The man on the floor stared at Mars, looking almost amused by their predicament.

"We'll be trapped like a weasel worm in a hole until they dig us out." Riley tightened the strap on his arrow bag. "And these two need to rest. They can't keep fighting without food or medical attention. Let's get out of here."

"I agree." Litus looked at Mars as if she'd stay behind by herself just to get at revenge. "That's an order."

"Then it's settled." Riley walked toward the tunnel. Litus followed along with Mars, muttering curses.

Striver didn't move. Eri tugged on his arm, but he stared at his brother. "Weaver, come with us," he pleaded.

"Are you crazy?" Riley shouted from across the cavern. "You can't trust him."

Striver ignored Riley, focusing on Weaver. "Jolt will kill you once he sees you let us get away."

Weaver shook his head. "You'd better leave now." There was a hint of concern in his eyes and Eri wondered how much he cared for his brother. He could have kept his mouth shut and let them be found.

"I can't leave you here like this. Come on, Weave." Striver bent down to touch him and Weaver whipped his head away. Red blotches of anger covered his face. His lips trembled with rage.

"Get away from me. You've done enough as it is," he shouted, spittle flying from his lips.

Eri stepped back. She couldn't imagine the pain Striver was going through. What if Aquaria joined the enemy?

"Come on, Striver, we have to go," Riley shouted. "Eri, I need your laser light to guide the way."

Eri checked her locator. They'd been in the cave for forty minutes and it would take them another twenty to get out. "Striver…"

Desperation shone in his gaze. "I can't leave him."

Time pulled on Eri until she felt ripped in two directions. Litus and Mars needed her. They probably hadn't had food or water for days, and another fight might be too much. But she owed her life—and theirs—to Striver. She couldn't bear seeing him in pain.

She dropped her laser to the floor and slid it over to Riley. "You lead them out. The light's the button on the right side. I unlocked it, so be careful."

Riley picked up her laser and nodded. Litus shouted after her, "Eri, what are you going to do?"

"We'll be right behind you." Eri turned to Striver. There was no way Riley would help him, and Mars and Litus were too weak. If she wanted Striver to move, she needed to take initiative. Eri put a hand on his shoulder and whispered, "I'll get his feet. You get his shoulders. We'll drag him out."

Striver's eyes reflected hope and fear. "You know he'll slow our escape."

Eri squeezed his shoulder. "You helped me rescue my team. I'm going to help you recue your brother."

Striver nodded and breathed out in relief. He ripped off pieces of his shirt and gagged Weaver before he could react. Eri avoided the blind hatred in Weaver's gaze as she tied his feet with another strip of fabric.

"You sure you can lift him?" Striver asked.

Eri wasn't sure of anything except that she wanted to help Striver more than anything in the world. "We'll see."

They hefted Weaver up, Striver bearing most of the weight, and carried him to the mouth of the tunnel. Eri yanked at Weaver's feet to catch up to the others, but Striver turned back. "What is it?"

"The golden liquid from Soren's tale." Striver's face paled. "The legend is true."

Eri resisted the urge to yell. Yes, it was pretty neat, and she'd love to stay and decipher the symbols, but Jolt would be here any minute, and they needed to get Mars and Litus to safety. She spoke in a careful, calm voice, with an underside of authority. "Striver, we can't stay."

"I know, I know." He tore his gaze away, blinking as if the light were too bright.

Weaver struggled at first, but he gave up as they entered the darkness. Eri wondered if he realized he could do nothing to stop them, or if he had crafted another plan of escape for later on.

It didn't matter. Carrying him was the only way to get Striver out of that cave.

The others were so far ahead they couldn't see their light. Eri stifled a current of worry and pressed the keypad on her locator. Her arm lit up with the dim neon glow. "That's all I have."

"It's plenty." Striver sounded so thankful, it warmed her heart. He'd helped her for so long, it gratified her to help him in return.

Striver entered the tunnel first, stumbling ahead using her dim light source.

Carrying a full-grown man through the tunnel was more difficult than she thought. Sweat dripped down her forehead as she followed Striver, gripping Weaver's feet. Every step was a hurdle, trying to balance Weaver's weight, step around jagged rocks, and stomp away the spidermites. She kept glancing at her locator, still set on Litus's life signs, to see how much longer they had to go.

When the signal stopped moving and blinked in the same place, she knew they waited for her outside the cave. Huffing, she whispered to Striver, "We're almost there."

Relief trickled through her when she spotted the slim crack of silvery moonlight. They emerged from the cave into the night, and the humid air of Haven 6 had never smelled so fresh.

CHAPTER SEVENTEEN
ESCAPE

"Over here." Riley's whisper carried through the darkness like a beacon of light. Striver whipped around in the direction of his voice, his tired muscles tightening as he hauled Weaver down the slope and into the night. He didn't want Eri carrying the brunt of the weight. He already felt guilty accepting her help, but he couldn't have left his only brother in that cave to die.

Eri followed him, hefting Weaver's feet. Her actions back in the cave and her perseverance carrying Weaver to safety knocked his boots off. This was not the work of someone trying to steal his home.

In the dark of night, Striver realized he trusted Eri even more.

"They're over there, behind that thicket," Eri whispered. "I can see Litus's locator blinking."

"He should turn it off."

"He kept it on for us."

They reached the thicket, pushing through the ferns to relative safety. Riley pounced on them. "You brought that scum with you?"

"What did you think we were doing back there? Fishing?" Striver glanced at all the faces waiting for them to emerge from the cave and guilt spread through him like poison. "They'd kill him if we left him behind."

Riley jabbed a finger in Striver's chest. "That's a choice he made when he left us. What are we going to do, throw him in some village jail? Watch him every minute until he jumps the fence again?"

"Enough!" Mars pushed herself between him and Riley. "Which way to safety?"

Riley sighed as if they'd already been caught. "This way. We'll sneak back through the swamp and skirt their sentinels."

Eri peered through the ferns. "They'll chase us until we reach the fence."

"Then we'll move fast and hide in the thickest trees." Riley gestured toward Eri. "Let me take the weight." He sounded weary, resigned to the inevitable.

Eri glanced at Striver with a questioning look.

"It's fine, thank you, Eri." Striver nodded over to what was left of her team. "You've done more than enough. See to your friends. Take them to the jungle, and we'll catch up."

She nodded, hefting Weaver's feet into Riley's arms. "Careful. He kicks."

Disgust soured Riley's face. "I wouldn't be surprised."

"Lower him." Striver gestured toward a patch of moss a half meter away.

Riley waddled over with Striver and crouched down just enough to throw Weaver's feet on the ground. He landed with a *thump*. "What? Now you're going to leave him?"

"Look for two branches." Striver pulled a blanket out of his backpack. "We're making a stretcher."

"Great idea, doctor." Riley's voice dripped with sarcasm, but he found one long branch and cracked it in half. "Wouldn't it be easier if we forgot he even existed?"

"Leaving him is not an option." Striver tied the ends of the blanket to the branches. "You can either help me or wait while I finish."

Riley harrumphed as he bent to help. When the blanket was secure, they hefted Weaver on and hoisted up the stretcher. The weight was more evenly distributed, and Striver could walk much easier. "See, now let's catch up to the others."

~∞~

Eri chatted with the other members of her team as they led the way across the plains to the jungle.

Striver hoped to learn more about her by studying her interactions with her team. She seemed happy to see them. Mars kept her distance, but Litus hugged her close to him, sending a current of jealousy through Striver's chest. Who was this man she'd risked so much to save? As Striver and Riley caught up, snippets of their conversation rode the air.

"I knew you'd save us. I just didn't think you'd come yourself. Look at you! You've turned into quite the warrior." Litus sounded so proud, it made Striver wonder what Eri had been like on the ship.

"I had to. Commander Grier refused to send help." Eri couldn't hide the bitterness in her voice. Striver knew she didn't like the commander, but he thought he was the only one that she confided in.

"Why?" Litus's voice fell to a whisper and Striver had to shuffle forward faster to hear him over the mating calls of swillow wisps penetrating the night.

Eri glanced back at Striver and Riley, almost as if she was checking to see if they listened in on their conversation. Striver gazed down at Weaver, pretending to tighten his brother's gag.

"She's afraid more of our people will get hurt or killed."

"I'll hail her and report in when we get to safety." Litus tripped and Eri caught him. The imprisonment must have weakened him. Damn the Lawless for driving a wedge in their relations with the newcomers.

Eri opened her mouth to say more and snapped it closed. She nodded. "We'll speak of this later."

Their conversation cast a storm cloud over the whole rescue. Striver had gone from developing feelings for her, trusting her, and now to this. There was so much about Eri and her life aboard the *Heritage* he didn't know. As a leader he couldn't allow his feelings for Eri to affect his decision making. Already, it had made him swoon like a fool.

They reached the jungle by dawn, the entire party lagging. Muscles aching, Striver stopped and called out, "We need to rest."

Eri, Litus, and Mars turned around, waiting for them to catch up.

"What if the Lawless are right on our tails?" Riley whispered as they pushed through waist-high ferns, approaching the rest of the party.

"I'll go back and scout the area. Watch over the others and make sure they eat and get some rest."

"What about you?"

Striver shrugged. "Guess we'll have to take turns."

They caught up with the rest of the party before Riley could disagree. They placed Weaver down on a mossy slope. "Watch over him, and don't untie him, no matter what he says." Striver gave his brother a steely eye.

"Where are you going?" Eri stepped forward, her forehead wrinkled in concern.

"Someone's got to make sure they're not on our heels."

Litus nodded in agreement and Mars plopped down by Weaver, giving him a wary look.

Eri stepped toward Striver. "I'll go with you."

"No, you need to rest with the others. Besides, two people will make more commotion than one." He turned, facing the long path they'd taken into the jungle. The thought of more walking made his legs scream in protest, but someone had to make sure the Lawless weren't pursing them.

"Striver." Eri grabbed his arm and tugged so hard he turned back around. "It's dangerous. Are you sure?"

Her cheeks were flushed from exertion and her lips pouted, slightly open. For a lingering second he wanted to bend down and kiss her good-bye. His logical mind kicked in just in time and he settled for placing his hand on hers with a small squeeze. Her fingers were so cold he wanted to blow warm air on them and hold them close to his chest to warm them. "I'll be fine."

"Don't worry about Striver; he's silent as the dead and swift as the wind," Riley muttered.

Striver wondered if all this communication with Eri was giving his feelings away. He pulled back and straightened his arrow bag against his back. "If they come, don't wait for me."

❧❦

Eri's chest ached as Striver disappeared into the jungle. He hadn't had any food or rest since the previous morning, and he sacrificed his own safety for the rest of them. No wonder his village had elected him as ruler. She'd only known him a few days, and in her eyes he was a hero.

A little too heroic, handsome, and charming.

"Boar's meat, anyone?" Riley announced, opening his backpack.

"I'm starving." Mars pulled off her boot and rubbed the sole of her foot.

"Me, too." Litus breathed heavily and Eri wondered if he'd caught a sickness while imprisoned. Hopefully Striver's tribe had been able to save her team's medical equipment, so she could check him when they returned to the village.

Riley pulled a piece from his stash and threw them the rest. "Help yourselves. I'm going to keep watch." Chewing on the meat, he climbed the nearest tree.

After watching Striver leave, Eri wasn't hungry, but she knew she needed to eat to keep up her stamina. Finding a seat on a rotting log, she dug in her backpack and pulled out the massive package Striver had packed for her. Out of the corner of her eye, she saw Weaver watching her. Maybe he was hungry? "What about Weaver?"

"I guess, but one of us will have to feed him, 'cause I'm not going to undo his bindings." Balancing on a wide branch, Riley popped another piece of boar's meat in his mouth.

"I will." Eri volunteered on Striver's behalf. This was his brother, and Striver loved him enough to carry him through hundreds of meters of swamp even after he deserted the village.

"Go ahead." Riley flicked his fingers like tossing trash on the wind. "I only hope he doesn't spit at you when you take off his gag. He's known to backstab."

"Or give away our location," Mars growled.

"If he utters anything above a whisper, I'll shoot an arrow in his neck from where I sit." Riley unpacked his bow and hung it on a nearby branch.

"Why do we have to take him with us, anyway?" Mars chewed on a piece of meat. "You said he's a traitor."

"Because Striver doesn't give up on anything or anyone." Riley chewed and swallowed hard, as if he had trouble swallowing the whole idea of Weaver even being with them.

Mars shrugged. "Should have killed him when you had the chance."

Riley shook his head like someone beaten in a game. "I couldn't. It would have killed Striver as well."

Litus swallowed and waved his hand at Mars. "It's like our people on the *Heritage*. We value each life and the precious DNA held within it. Our mission is to further our species. When someone does something wrong, they aren't killed, but conditioned and taught until they understand their place in our society."

"Sounds like tyranny to me." Riley sat back, spreading his legs out on the branch in front of him.

"Yes, but we don't have renegades out there to tie us up and kill us," Mars shot back with a mean half smile.

Eri stuffed another piece in her mouth, the cold, salted version not as tasty as freshly roasted. She kneeled in front of Weaver. He stared at her with intensity in his eyes, looking like he'd curse her, bite her, or worse. He didn't have the same distinction in his features as his brother, but he could be considered handsome if he wasn't so mean.

She reached behind his head and undid the knot, pulling the gag out of his mouth.

He took in a breath and she suppressed the urge to cringe, expecting him to swear or spit at her. "Are you hungry?"

Weaver chuckled. "Striver gets all the lovely ladies, doesn't he?"

Eri blinked. "I have no idea what you mean."

"Don't listen to him; he's just trying to get under your skin," Riley called out behind her.

"Don't give him anything." Mars spat into the mucky water. "He doesn't deserve it."

Eri's cheeks heated with the same shameful embarrassment she'd experienced when Mars teased her in the training session. She felt ridiculous allowing some young savage to rip away her composure. How could he know how she felt about Striver? Did Striver have other girlfriends back in the village? Riptide's catlike eyes and luscious hair came to mind.

The best thing to do is to not let it show.

She pulled out a piece of meat and held it in front of his mouth, feeling like she'd rather chuck it in the swamp water. "Well, do you want some or not?"

He shook his head, giving her a wicked smile. "I'd rather die."

"I can make that happen." Mars stood up, flexing her arms.

"That's enough." Riley dropped from the branch with a splash, walked over, and took the piece of cloth from Eri's fingers. "I'll stop this rotten hole back up."

Eri sloshed back to her spot on the mushy log. No one had ever spoken to her that way on the *Heritage*. She didn't know how to take it. Part of her pitied him, but she couldn't help but feel annoyed and violated, too. What circumstances had made him so mean-spirited? Or had he been born with a chip on his shoulder?

Something must be good about him, or Striver wouldn't work so hard to have him back.

Weariness weighed her down, and she lay on the log, using a tuft of moss as a pillow. Patches of stars shone through the jungle canopy. The *Heritage* hovered above them like a bloated eye watching her every move. Eri covered her eyes with her arm, blocking the ship. There was one place Commander Grier could never go: inside her mind, inside her heart.

ॐॐ

Water splashed on her face, waking her up. Dawn light shone through the canopy like a promise of better days to come.

"Striver's back." Riley jumped over her as she lay on the log.

Eri yanked herself up, feeling her heart gush. *Striver's back. He's okay.* She wanted to see him so badly it hurt.

Striver sloshed into camp, his breath heaving like he'd sprinted the whole way back.

"Get up." He spoke through gasps of breath. "They're in the jungle looking for us."

Mars leapt up and helped Litus stand. "Which way?"

Striver waved his hand in a semicircle. "They're combing the entire swamp with several groups."

Riley studied Mars and Litus. "Looks like you guys are more important than you think—"

"That, or Weaver is," Eri interrupted. "We have stolen a member of their tribe."

"Leave him. You can't keep up carrying him through the swamp." Mars sounded more like a commander ordering her troops than a rescued prisoner.

"He'll die in the jungle tied up like this." Striver's face creased with worry. Eri didn't know how he'd handle this, but Mars was right. Weaver slowed their escape, and today it could mean life or death.

"Cut his ties and let him run back," Litus suggested.

"No." Riley's voice was hard. "He'll give up our location." Riley put his face right next to Striver's. "How far back are they?"

Striver ran his hand through his hair, pulling until his scalp turned white. "Eight hundred meters at most. We don't have much time."

Panic rose up from Eri's stomach into her throat. She didn't want them to force Striver to leave his brother behind, but she also didn't want those Lawless people to get ahold of them. "What are we going to do?"

"I'm thinking." Striver put up both hands to stall them.

"We don't have time for thinking." Riley hefted his backpack. "I'm leaving. Anyone who wants to stay with Striver and his traitor brother, stay by all means."

A melancholy caw echoed over them, reminding Eri of the Yellowstone Park videos with the bald eagles back on the *Heritage*. She glanced up through the canopy. A gigantic bird swooped in a circle before spiraling down to their position.

No, not a bird. A Guardian.

Eri stared as leaves rained around them. The Guardian broke through the treetops and landed on a branch just above their heads. His long wings folded behind his back as his clawed feet wrapped around the branch.

Mars ducked. "What in cyberspace?"

Litus stood by Eri, whispering under his breath, "Holy mother of black holes."

"I'll handle this." Striver waved them back. The last of the leaves trickled down, floating in the swamp waters as Striver walked underneath the branch. "Phoenix, what are you doing here?"

"Allow me to take Weaver back to the village. My services will enable your escape."

"I thought you said you can't help us."

His blank eyes reflected the jungle around them. "I can't aid you in any act that would induce a war. However, Weaver's another story. I am allowed to pluck Lawless from their posts if they interfere with our objectives."

"Thank goodness." Striver bowed so low his chin touched the water. "Please take him back to the village. I'm eternally grateful."

Phoenix glided to Weaver and lifted him like a baby in his winged arms. He scanned the group, his gaze resting on Eri just a little longer than the rest, making the hair on her arms stand up. "Good luck to all of you."

Before anyone could speak, his legs bent and he leapt into the trees, spreading his wings. They pulsed once, the sound like the folding of a giant quilt, before he plunged through the canopy and the leaves rained again.

Mars turned to Striver. "Do you mind telling me what in the hell that thing is?"

"There's no time now." Striver pinned Weaver's makeshift stretcher under a log in the water. He waded through their camp, handing Eri her backpack from the end of the log. "We must run."

CHAPTER EIGHTEEN
ODD ONE OUT

The jungle blurred around Eri as she hurtled through the swamp, tossing away an endless slew of leaves and vines as they whipped in her face. Her waterlogged boots and pants slowed her down, making each step awkward. All she'd ever dream about from now on was murky water and muck.

Riley and Striver scouted ahead, leading them through the densest patches of jungle to mask their escape. Litus dragged in the back, slowing so much the last time Eri looked over her shoulder that he wasn't there at all.

"Litus!" Eri shouted, not caring if the Lawless heard her. The jungle hung silent and still behind her. Even the waves from her own sloshing footprints had dispersed.

"Litus!"

"I'm here." His voice sounded so weak, it squeezed her heart.

Panting to catch her breath, she pushed through the thick ferns until she saw him, stooped over like he'd just thrown up.

"Don't stop for me. I'll make it just fine." Litus wiped his face and waved her back. Sweat dripped from his forehead, and his cheeks paled whiter than the hull of the *Heritage*.

"You're sick. I can see it." Eri put her arm around his waist. "Let me help."

He slumped down against her, allowing her to take some of his weight, and her knees almost buckled under the pressure. Eri winced and gritted her teeth, standing straight.

Jeez, he's heavier than he looks.

"Come on, Litus, the others are just ahead."

Eri stumbled through deeper waters, thick vines wrapping around her boots. *They couldn't have gone this way.* A long, slithering worm that looked like some monster's tongue slid underneath the surface and she kicked it away.

Litus coughed beside her. "Don't take time for me. I'm fine."

She didn't have the heart to tell Litus she'd lost her way. "Just give me a moment to get my bearings."

Litus put up his finger, the tip shaking in the wind. "Wait. I hear voices."

Voices from our party or voices from the Lawless?

Eri forced herself to calm down enough to strain her ears and listen. A woman's deep voice cut through the mingling of men's whispers. "Enough talk. We have to decide."

"It's Mars." Eri never thought she'd be so happy to hear her voice.

They pushed through the ferns into a clearing surrounded by a circle of giant trees so tall and thick nothing could grow in their shadows. Mars, Riley, and Striver stood in the center of the mangroves, arguing softly.

Eri helped Litus to a rock and joined the semicircle. "Why are we stopped?"

"They're gaining on us." Striver shook his head. He whispered near her ear, "With Litus in that condition, there's no way we'll lose them."

"So we're just going to give up?" Eri threw her arms in the air. "We have to keep going."

Riley's hand tightened on the strap of his arrow bag slung across his chest. "It's not that simple. They have teams crisscrossing. We'll run right into one of them if we're not careful."

"Then we split up." Mars put her hands on her hips. "At least some of us will get away."

Fear bubbled up Eri's legs until they shook. They had to stay together. She'd risked everything to save her team, and she wasn't about to surrender anyone to the Lawless again.

Think. She peered around the mangrove. Could they climb the trees? Litus leaned against the rock, barely holding himself up. Even if the others could make it far enough into the branches to hide, there was no way any of them could haul Litus up there.

Hoots rang out as the Lawless closed in, reminding Eri of a pack of lions from the nature videos she watched of Old Earth. They were the predators and she was the prey.

"Scatter!" Mars whispered. "I'll run toward them and create a diversion—"

"No." Eri's voice rang out, loud and low like a command. She tugged her laser from the holster and input the code. The gun buzzed with energy, reassuring her.

Striver turned toward her, desperation stretched in his features. "I'll go. The rest of you run toward the village."

Over my dead body. "Enough talk of leaving someone or splitting up. We're all in this together, and we're all going to stay behind."

Everyone turned to Eri, staring at her like she'd gone insane. Ignoring them, Eri aimed at the largest tree and fired, blowing a hole in one of the twisted roots that poked up through the muck. Bark scattered, flinging against her chest and plopping into the swamp water at her feet. Smoke cleared to reveal a hollow underside. Even if the lawless were close enough to hear the gunshots, they'd think Eri and the others were trying to hold them off, not create a hiding place.

"Get some moss and drape it over the hole," Eri ordered the group. "We'll hide."

"That tree isn't big enough for four people." Riley stood his ground while the others ran to pull moss from the branches.

"I know." Eri turned to another tree and fired again. When the smoke cleared, she gave Riley a smug smile. "Two in one, three in the other."

"Well done, Eri!" Striver cheered from behind her, his hands full of moss.

Riley glanced at the hole with a wary eye. "Striver and I should split up in case your idea doesn't work." He scanned the forest surrounding them as if the Lawless would pour out any time.

"It'll work." Striver pulled a veil of moss across the hole. "But Riley's right. If they find one of us, the others should make a run for it, and only the two of us know our way back to the village."

Riley pointed to Eri. "I'm not sharing a tree with her."

Striver rolled his eyes. "I'll go with Eri. Riley, you go with Mars and Litus."

"Fine." Riley gave him a strange look. "Don't get too cozy." He jogged over and helped Mars carry Litus to the other tree.

Striver turned to Eri. "Looks like you're going with me."

They sloshed underneath the root system, ducking through the hole Eri had made with her laser. Cold water soaked her clothes as she dragged her pack behind her. Trying not to think of all the slimy swamp creatures she couldn't see, Eri took a deep breath and sealed her lips shut. She submerged herself nose-deep in swamp water to clear the branch. Striver followed her. He reached up and pulled the moss down across the hole. Eri thought it would cover them completely, but the strands bunched up, leaving slender cracks where sunlight trickled through. Striver waved her back from the veil of moss.

"Don't worry; they won't see us," he whispered and gave her a thumbs-up. "Good idea."

We'll see about that. She wiped swamp muck off her mouth as splashing came from the other end of the clearing. Eri peered through the crack, hoping the others had concealed themselves in time.

"Damn technohoarders. Why do they have to lead us through this swamp mess?" One of the men kicked the water and droplets splashed across the clearing on the tree where the others hid.

"Just to aggravate you, Stray, because the whole world revolves around you." Another man turned in their direction and Eri backed away from the moss until the bark of the tree roots pressed into her back.

"Shut up and keep looking." A taller man sauntered into the clearing and stood in the middle. His broad forehead was cut in half by a white scar and a crooked nose that looked like it had been broken a number of times. His mud-caked hair stuck up at all angles.

"That's him." Striver whispered so softly Eri wondered if he'd actually spoken.

"Who?"

"Their leader, Jolt."

She inched forward enough to get a clear look. Something glimmered silver in his sun-tanned hands. "He's got one of our laser guns."

Behind the man, a piece of muddy camouflaged fabric glistened on the rock face. Eri put her hand to her mouth and squeezed.

"What's the matter?" Striver whispered.

Her heart sped up. "Litus left his coat on the rock."

"Cyberhell." Striver clenched his fist. "And he's supposed to be your leader."

"It's not his fault." Eri's nails dug into the skin of her palm as she clenched her fists. "He's sick."

"Right." Striver sounded more than annoyed and Eri wondered what his personal vendetta was against Litus.

"Maybe they won't see it."

"Let's hope."

The water rippled beside her, and she felt a slimy fish brush her arm. Eri slapped her hand over her mouth to stop from screaming. Hadn't Striver mentioned something about fish with teeth?

Jolt scanned the circle of trees and leaned against the rock, centimeters away from Litus's coat. He sipped from his water bag, the excess dribbling down his cheeks. Although the scar intimidated Eri, the deadness in his eyes, dark as the centers of two black holes, disturbed her the most. He looked like someone who could shoot a laser right through a man's head and feel no remorse. She did not want such a villain deciding her fate.

And they wonder why we have rules…

A young man sloshed through camp, his breath heaving. "The trail goes dead here, boss."

"Nonsense. They can't just disappear. You're not looking hard enough." He raised the laser, but Eri noticed he hadn't input the code. The gun was dead weight in his hands.

The young man backed up all the same, falling onto his butt in the swamp muck. "I'll try harder, sir."

Jolt jiggled the end in the air. "You'd better."

One of the other men came up beside Jolt as the younger man scurried back into the jungle. "Why do we need them that badly anyway, boss? We have all their guns."

"It's that traitor kid." Jolt's voice dropped so low, Eri had to lean her ear against the moss to hear him.

"What about him, sir?"

"He figured out the code to unlock these fancy guns. If he dies, the code dies with him."

Eri's heart jumped in her throat. Weaver was more important than she thought. Good thing they hadn't left him behind.

"What makes you think they didn't kill him on the spot?"

"These law abiding technohaters, they have soft hearts. Too soft for their own good."

Striver's face fell, his gaze traveling to the water at his feet. Eri put a hand on his arm. She crouched next to him and whispered in his ear. "You're doing the right thing."

"What the…" Jolt trailed off.

"What is it, boss?"

Eri's attention shot back to the scene outside the tree. Her chest tightened and she held her breath.

Jolt threw the camouflaged fabric into the muck. "It's one of those invader's coats."

"They were here." The other man scanned the circle of trees. Striver wrapped his fingers around her palm and squeezed.

"Get up!" Jolt ordered the men. "Spread out in all directions. We must be close."

They waded through the water, and the ripples from their footsteps traveled right to Eri's thighs. She bent down, huddled against Striver, and froze. The only thing moving was her racing heart.

As the Lawless left the mangrove, Eri released her breath. "Why's Jolt so mean?" No man on the *Heritage* compared to his ruthlessness.

"There're a lot of rumors." Striver shrugged. "People say he was born with such an ugly face, his mother left him in the Lawless lands to fend for himself. Others say he killed both his parents."

A shiver crept across Eri's shoulders and she checked her back to make sure there weren't any spidermites nesting in the tree. "What about his scar?"

"I've heard several stories. The most believable, in my opinion, is that he got it in a fight for leader of the tribe."

"So the Lawless do have a social structure?"

"Not really." Striver stuck a stick in the water and twirled it around, making little waves that touched her legs. "Unless you call gangs villages."

"So how's he in charge?"

"He has the most followers, people who are too afraid to go against him and others who want to steal his power for themselves."

Eri shook her head. "Sounds like a nasty way to live."

"You're telling me."

"And I thought my life on the ship was bad."

Striver gave her a questioning look, but he didn't follow up with any questions, so Eri let the topic drop. "What do we do now?"

"We wait," Striver whispered, settling down on an upturned root.

"How long?" Eri already felt suffocated by the underside of the roots and the high water. She couldn't imagine spending a night cramped inside the tree.

"As long as it takes."

"Ugh." Eri's legs ached. She couldn't stay bent over like this forever. Joining Striver on the root, she gave up, letting the murky water seep around her to her waist. She checked her locator for Litus's life signal. So far, his heart still beat.

Striver took her wrist in his and ran his fingers along the screen. "Did this hurt?"

Eri laughed. "Not at all. Doctors attach the locators to us at birth. The plastic is actually synthetic bone, which grows along with the bone in our wrists. I'm sorry if it bothers you. I can't take it off."

His fingers brushed along the keypad, continuing up her arm. "No, no. I'm curious, that's all. It's a part of you, and I don't want to change who you are."

Suddenly, the humid air in the hollow tree grew hot, almost suffocating. Eri changed the subject. "I was checking Litus's vital signs. What do you think's wrong with him?" She stretched her legs until her toes hit the other side of the roots. Her knees were still bent, but it felt good to relax her muscles.

"Some sort of infection." Striver pulled his arm away and shook his head. "I'm not sure. Could be the side effects of the coma dart.

Some people have an allergic reaction to the poison.”

Eri suppressed a rising current of panic. Litus was a strong young man. He could withstand a lot. “Did you manage to recover our medical equipment from the scout ship?”

“We took several containers, but I’m not sure what’s in any of them. Like I said, we don’t use technology.”

“When we get back to the village, I’ll go through what you have and see if I can find our tissue regenerator.”

“So many gadgets.” Striver handed her his water pouch. “What does that one do?”

Eri was surprised he showed interest, considering how he felt about technology. “Repairs damaged cells in our bodies. Why?”

“Just thinking.” Striver’s voice trailed off. “You care for Litus, don’t you?”

“Of course I do.” Eri brought the pouch to her lips and sipped, coolness trickling down her raw throat.

“Is he your lifemate?”

Her throat constricted and she choked on the water, spitting it out into the swamp muck. “No. Litus is my sister’s lifemate. Everything I do, I do for her.”

Striver sat silently for several heartbeats and she wished she could see his features better in the shadows. “I see.” His voice was hushed, yet intense.

“I don’t know why I’m trying so hard. She doesn’t even seem to like him. I guess I’m hoping she’ll grow to. I want her to be happy.” Eri knew she shouldn’t have said it, but she trusted Striver, and this wasn’t the first time she’d confided in him. She needed to get her frustration off her chest, anyway.

“What about you, Eri. Do you like your lifemate?” Striver voice was soft and careful.

Eri swallowed hard. “I don’t have one. I’m the only female in my generation without a lifemate.”

"For Refuge's sake, why?"

She'd told him so much already, what was a little more? Eri doubted he'd look at her any differently, even though everyone on the *Heritage* did except Aquaria. "I'm the product of an illegal pairing. My parents got together before their lifemates were chosen."

"That's horrible." Striver patted her hand. "I mean, not that they got together, but that it prevented you from having a lifemate."

"I don't blame them. I love them both very much."

"What happened to their love?"

"They were placed with different lifemates. Aquaria, my half sister, shares my mom. Although my parents aren't together anymore, I'm proud to be a product of love, not one of science. I guess it's the rebel inside of me, passed down through my parents. It's pretty cool, except for the way everyone looks at me like I'm some kind of freak."

"You're not a freak. You're probably the most normal person on the *Heritage*."

Eri laughed. "Normal to you, not them."

Striver ran his thumb over the back of her hand. Her skin tingled underneath his touch.

"Do you want a lifemate?"

"Are you kidding? It's one of my dreams. Besides finding a better job. Linguist was not my first choice." Although her job had earned her a seat on the exploratory team. It had brought her to him.

He squeezed her hand. "I'm so sorry. I'm all for rules and a structured society, but the more I hear about your life aboard the ship, the more I want to take you away from it."

Eri leaned in, half excited, half afraid. What if she wanted to go with him? "Take me where?"

His hand traveled from her hand to her chin. He cupped her cheek in his palm. He opened his mouth to reply, and she pressed into his touch.

The water splashed outside their tree and someone brushed aside the veil of moss. Riley poked his head in. "Coast is clear."

How long had they been under the roots? Tearing herself away from Striver, Eri got up and walked to the hole. "You sure?"

"I sneaked out and scouted around. No one's here but us and a whole lot of muck."

Eri looked over her shoulder to Striver and he nodded encouragingly. But she didn't want to leave. Not yet. They had been in the midst of something important, momentous, at least in Eri's world—even if she didn't know exactly what it was. Striver never did get to answer her question, and she had so much more left ask.

"Well, are you coming out, or are you going to make a home in there along with the weasel worms?" Riley sighed and shook his head.

"We're coming," Striver growled as he stood up from the root. When he pulled back the rest of the moss in front of her, his face looked resigned to obey Riley, but his gaze smoldered with interest, making Eri's cheeks burn. "After you."

CHAPTER NINETEEN

HOMECOMING

Relief charged through Striver as the bristly spikes of the wall towered over the trees below the ridge. Not only was he coming home, but if Phoenix made it back safely, Weaver would be there as well. Even though they'd be holding his brother against his will, Striver felt like his family was complete once again. *As complete as it could be without Father.*

"We're almost there." He hefted his backpack, ignoring the pain in his muscles. The Lawless stilled trailed their scent, and they couldn't afford to let up their pace.

"Good, because I don't think he can take another step." Riley hoisted Litus's arm across his shoulders. Mars braced his other side, sweat dripping from her forehead.

"I can make it." Litus spoke through gritted teeth.

"We're almost there, and once we get to the village, I'll find the cell regenerator." Eri walked beside them, touching Litus's hand.

Litus turned his head in her direction and spoke under his breath. "I need to contact the commander."

"After you recover," Eri pressed.

Noticing Eri's reluctance, Striver decided to push the issue with Litus. "We don't have time. We'll be safe once we cross the wall." Striver turned and pushed ahead, wondering why Litus was so eager to talk with the commander and why Eri delayed it. Striver had won this round, but it still seemed as though a war hung imminent in the air. Maybe it was just the giant mother boar of a ship hovering over their heads, but unease sat like a sharp rock in his gut despite their homecoming.

Leaves rained around them as Guardians fell from the sky, meeting their party in a semicircle of iridescent feathers. The Guardians must have spotted them a kilometer away. Striver had expected some sort of greeting, but still, relief flowed through him with the familiar sight of Phoenix's wingspan blocking the blinding rays of sun.

Mars muttered under her breath, "Oh no, here we go again."

Phoenix landed last at the circle's arc. Although the Guardians had no chosen leader, Striver guessed Phoenix influenced most of the decisions. He was over three hundred years old and one of the original hatchlings from the eggs brought to Refuge by Aries and Striker.

"Greetings, Striver and friends." Phoenix bowed and his fellow Guardians followed, feathers ruffling as they folded their wings behind them.

"Hello, Phoenix." Striver turned back to the others, they didn't have time for formal greetings. "You met Phoenix briefly in the swamp. The others are Raven, Dove, Eagle, and Glider. They're here to help."

To his relief, Eri bowed and the others followed. At least her team was treating them civilly.

Striver wasted no time. He had to know. "Is Weaver safe?"

Phoenix straightened and nodded, his eyes serene as the surface of a lake. "He's in captivity. Guards watch over him. He'll speak to no one, but he's physically unharmed."

Striver rubbed his chin, deep in thought. He'd have his hands full when he returned. "Thank you for taking care of him."

"My pleasure. Your ancestors brought us here and gave us life. Protecting their offspring is the least we can do. You know that."

"Yes, but I appreciate your efforts all the same." Striver smiled before turning back to the others. "We're eager to get back. Lawless still hunt us, even this close to the border. Litus isn't feeling well, and the rest of us are weary and hungry."

"That is why we've come." Phoenix had a glint in his eye. "We're received permission from the council to fly you over the wall."

"So they couldn't fly us over when we left to get my team, but they can fly us over now?" Eri put her hands on her hips, eyeing them skeptically.

Striver opened his mouth to respond, but Phoenix put his long fingers on Striver's arm. "Let me explain." He turned to Eri. "We are a peaceful species, and we discourage any act of violence or anything that might encourage war. We also have no wish to rule. The council decides the fate of our village, and the Guardians are under their discretion. Without their permission, we can't help you if you cross into Lawless lands. But I've obtained their permission to carry you back over the wall."

"No way," Mars erupted behind him. "No way I'm letting one of those…birdmen touch me."

"Fine." Striver reached into his backpack and pulled out a coil of rope. He threw it at her feet. "Have fun."

He scanned the nervous faces of the others. "Anyone else?"

Eri shook her head. Her eyes were steady, but under the tough exterior, her hands trembled. Striver brushed her arm, whispering under his breath. "Don't worry. I've done this a thousand times."

"I trust you." Eri met his gaze and the intensity between them deepened. Longings resonated inside him, and he turned away before the urges grew out of control.

Branches cracked and shouts pierced the woods behind them. Striver whirled around. "We must go now!"

"Wait!" Mars's voice wavered. She kicked back his rope. "I'll go."

"Excellent. You will not be disappointed." Phoenix spread his wings and the other Guardians followed. Each of them took their place behind a human in preflight formation. Striver glanced at Eri and smiled. *You can do this.*

The Guardians' wrapped their branch-like arms around each human's waist. Phoenix lifted Striver, and in a heartbeat the pair broke through the canopy and soared. Below them, arrows from the Lawless arched up and fell short, plummeting back to the canopy of trees.

Wind whipped Striver's hair back and cooled his warm cheeks. Freedom and excitement pulsed through his veins. He glanced over as Eri, flown by Dove, broke free of the trees. His chest burst with pride as he shared this experience with her and her team. Sure, they'd flown in space their whole lives, but nothing compared to riding the air currents above the lush vegetation on Refuge.

Eri spread her arms in the air as if she had wings. He could picture her as an angel, descended from the sky to save him and his people. *If only that were true.*

She turned her head and blinked as she caught him staring. Dove hoisted Eri higher in the air. Striver wondered if the Guardian showed off just a little to make a good impression. Humans were prone to flaunting, but Guardians, he could only guess.

Tree huts protruded from the lush greenery like mushrooms. Even though he'd only left days ago, it felt like ages had passed since he'd been home. *What will Mother think of what Weaver has become? Can we convince him to stay?*

His stomach pitched as Phoenix dove for the middle of the village. They landed effortlessly, and his feet touched the ground as if he weighed no more than one of their feathers. The rest of the Guardians landed beside him. Mars's face was green as the grass, but exhilaration lit Eli's features, bringing out her beauty. Striver's heart quickened. *Maybe she'll like it here on Refuge after all?*

The villagers in his tribe descended from their tree huts to meet them, carrying water pouches and fruits. Riptide ran to Riley and he embraced her, twirling her around.

At least she's not running to me.

"Done it again, have you?" Carven came up behind him and punched him in the arm. His face had color, and he looked well rested and fed. Striver laughed, the sight of his friend calming him.

"We rescued the remaining prisoners, but no sign of the weapons," Striver whispered under his breath, accepting a handful of nuts from a little girl.

"Still reason to celebrate. You've returned unharmed and made friends with the owners of that hulk in the sky. Besides, the villagers need something to lift their spirits. Ever since that ship decided to park over our turf they've been anxious."

Striver murmured under his breath, "They have good reason to be."

Carven put his arm around him and smiled. "We'll have a feast with dancing tonight."

Riptide's head whirled around when Carven mentioned *dancing*. Striver avoided eye contact, guiding Carven to the woods behind them for privacy.

"Fine. But not in my honor, not again." *Not with Weaver here.*

"Okay, we'll honor our new friends."

"And Weaver?"

Carven shrugged. "You can try to talk to him yourself, but I don't think he'll join in the festivities."

A bomb sank in Striver's stomach. How was he ever going to convince his brother to stay on their side?

Carven clapped him on the back and turned him around to the rest of the village. "Here's one of our new friends now."

Eri smiled as she joined them, but her face turned serious a moment later. "Excuse me, but my teammate is very sick and needs a place to rest."

"Of course." Carven gestured over his head, and members of the tribe eased Litus onto a stretcher they'd carried from one of the storage huts. Striver thought she'd go with him, but Eri tugged on Carven's arm. "I need to go through what you salvaged of our supplies. I'm hoping to find a device to help him."

"Certainly." Carven released Striver and offered Eri his arm. "Come with me."

"Thank you." She jogged to the villagers carrying Litus away. "Take care of him."

An elder from the council nodded. "He's in good hands."

"Thank you." Eri moved to leave, but she halted in midstep. She turned to Striver, and the way her eyes sparkled made him feel like he was the only man on Refuge. "See you later." It sounded more like a promise than a statement.

"I hope you find what you're looking for."

Eri wiped a smudge of mud off her cheek. Her shoulders slumped with weariness, and Striver curbed the urge to comfort and embrace her. "I hope so, too."

Striver watched Eri leave, wondering when he'd get another chance to be alone with her. There was so much he wanted to ask her, so much he still didn't know. But his duties as leader came first. He had to tend to the villagers' worries and his brother's broken spirit first.

❧◆❧

Eri dug through the containers, throwing out broken pieces of equipment. She'd trained in the medical bay for two days before the mission, learning how to work all of the life-saving devices. At the time she didn't think she'd ever use the knowledge.

Cyberhell, I wish I'd paid attention.

A small oblong device poked from the pile and she pulled it out, flipping up the lid. The screen blinked on, fluorescent green light illuminating the inside of the tree hut where they'd stashed the supplies. Words flashed by.

READY TO SCAN SUBJECT.

"Did you find it?" Carven shouted from outside. Eri wondered if he'd stayed for her own safety or to spy. At least he'd given her privacy to go through their supplies without breathing over her shoulder.

Her hands shook as she held it. It calmed her to hold a remnant of technology in such a wild, savage place. The plastic was so white, so prefect compared to her mud-caked skin. "I think so."

She poked her head through the ferns covering the door. Riley leaned on the tree, arms crossed. He gave the device a hesitant look, reminding Eri of their distrust for technology.

"It's meant to heal, not kill."

"I'm sure it is." Carven narrowed his eyes and turned before she could interpret the change in his features. "Come, I'll take you to your friend."

He led her across a bridge to another tree hut toward the back of the village. "We've segregated him from the rest of the population, just in case he's contagious. I hope you understand."

"Of course."

Eri pushed aside the ferns and entered the tree hut, her sight adjusting from the bright daylight to the dimly lit room. Light trickled out of a small triangular hole in the thatched ceiling, shining on Litus's long legs. He slumped on top of a bed, propped up by the wall at his back. His eyes were closed, and Eri's heart sped. *I hope I'm not too late.*

His chest rose and fell, and she took in a deep breath, clicking on the screen. Carven joined her, watching with skepticism in his gaze.

READY TO SCAN SUBJECT.

Eri stood above Litus and pressed her finger to the screen. A loud beep rang out.

INCOMPATIBLE SUBJECT.

What? What if it had broken during landing? Eri flipped the regenerator over. Caked mud covered the screen. *For the Guide's sake!* She wiped the bottom on the blanket beside Litus and tried again.

The device cast a fluorescent blue light across his body.

SCANNING MODE ACTIVATED.

She held the light over his lungs, his stomach, and his lower body, waiting for readings.

"What's it doing?" Carven whispered behind her.

Eri didn't know exactly, but she'd listened to enough of the regenerator lectures to give him some sort of answer. "Searching for damaged cells or infection."

The device beeped.

INCREASE IN LYMPHOCYTES DUE TO A VIRAL OR FUNGAL INFECTION. DIAGNOSIS: PNEUMONIA.

She read it out loud to Carven.

"Sounds bad," Carven muttered.

"Not at all." Eri clicked a few buttons on the screen and the light changed from blue to green. The device buzzed in her hands. She held the scanner steady as the light moved from Litus's throat to his waist. "It will take a few moments."

"To do what?"

"Kill the infection. Make him well."

Carven jumped up and joined her at the side of Litus's bed.

"Amazing. Does that thing work for arrow wounds as well?"

"It depends on how bad it is." Eri watched as the oxygen levels in Litus's blood rose and the color came back to his face. "It can heal and regenerate cells, but it can't bring people back from the dead."

"How does it work?"

Eri shrugged. *Where to start?* She had no idea how educated these people were. They seemed to know enough about technology, so she leveled with Carven. "I'm not a doctor, but I think it has to do with the radiation waves. They enter his body and the device monitors the radiation given off as a result. Once the diagnosis is complete, the waves change the structure of the damaged cells."

Carven's face dropped as he stepped back. "Will it affect us?"

"No. The regenerator emits nonionizing radiation, which is considered harmless at low powers and doesn't produce a significant temperature rise."

Carven nodded as though he were considering her words, then he shook his head. "It still seems dangerous."

"Not when you use it properly."

The device clicked off and Litus stirred, taking in a deep breath. His eyes flickered and opened. Eri hovered over him, holding her breath.

"Eri?"

Her knees weakened with relief. "How do you feel?"

Litus rubbed his eyes and squinted into the dim sunlight where she stood. "Much better. Where am I? What happened?"

"You're in one of the tree huts, segregated from the rest of the village in case you were contagious. Striver's tribe recovered some of our supplies from the crash site. I went through the containers and found the regenerator."

He tried to sit up, but her hand rested firmly on his chest. "You need to rest. You had pneumonia. I killed the infection with the regenerator, but the process will leave you feeling weak."

"I know the side effects. I was at the class myself, remember?"

She pulled her hand away. As the second in command, she should concede to him. "I'm just reminding you."

He pushed himself up and blinked, offering an apologetic smile. "Eri, thank you for all that you've done." His features hardened as he looked to Carven. "I need to talk with the commander."

Anxiety ricocheted through Eri. By saving Litus, did she condemn Striver's village? She stared into his eyes, beseeching him. "I need to talk with you first. In private."

Carven eyed them both and nodded his head, suspicion stirring in his gaze. "I'll leave you two. Please join us tonight for the celebration."

"We will." Eri waited until Carven's footsteps faded before speaking. "Careful what you tell the commander." Her voice dropped to a whisper. "She's planning to annihilate these people. All she needs are numbers and a plan of attack."

Litus's lips tightened. "I'm only trying to do my job. What the commander does with the information is not for me to decide."

"How can you give her information against them after all they've done for us?"

Litus rubbed his temples as if the argument reared a headache he wasn't ready for. "Because I'm a team expedition leader, Eri. I believe in the Guide and the commander. She has our best interests at heart."

"She might have our best interests, but what about the others here on Refuge?"

"Did you see what they did to our team? To Mars and me? I have to tell the commander of the dangers here, along with the people who *are* friendly. My job is to look out for those on the *Heritage*—and especially for Aquaria."

Frustration boiled inside her. "Don't you see? Your single-mindedness is keeping you and Aquaria apart. She doesn't speak to you because she's afraid she'll say something against the Guide and you'll turn her in."

Litus's eyes widened. "I'd never do that. I love her."

The word *love* struck a resonant chord in Eri's heart. Maybe there was hope for Litus after all. Love—something that didn't happen all that often on the decks of the *Heritage*. And Litus felt that way about her sister. "Learn to think for yourself. A leader with a spine would impress Aquaria more than a blind follower who doggedly sticks to the Guide."

"Are you sure?"

"Believe me. I've known her all my life."

"Why didn't you say something back at camp?"

"I tried to, but we were attacked. Now it's even more important, not just to impress Aquaria but to do the right thing. Our actions influence a great deal of people: humans like us who have lived here for hundreds of years, along with a new species—the first alien contact humankind has ever known. Isn't that worth fighting for?"

Litus's shoulders slumped forward. Eri felt like she'd beaten him with a tree branch all afternoon, but she pushed the guilt away. He needed to step up if Striver and the others were to have any chance. "I have to report back," he said. "We can't ignore the commander forever."

"All I'm saying is consider what you tell her, what our mission here *should* be."

"If she sees these Lawless people posing any threat to our colonization efforts, nothing I can say will change her mind. I'll put in a good word for Striver and his village, but I can't promise you anything."

Eri nodded, weariness from all the frustration and anxiety bogging her down. She felt like she'd thrown herself at a wall and hadn't even made a crack.

"I'm glad you were chosen for this team, Eri." Litus's voice grew soft and gentle. He stood with his whole body creaking like an old man after a long nap and put a hand on her shoulder. He looked like he'd aged ten years in three days. Eri only hoped he'd gained wisdom as well.

"At least try to save us all from a war we don't need."

Litus squeezed her shoulder. "I'll do my best."

CHAPTER TWENTY
HOPE

Guards paced around the circumference of one of the back storage huts, bows cocked and ready to fire. Mixed feelings of hope and fear comingled in Striver's heart as he walked across the hanging bridge connecting the center of town from the residential offshoots to the storage huts in the back. The sun sunk low in the forest and the celebration loomed. Villagers had already lit the candle boxes dangling from low branches, making their own tiny galaxy with golden twinkling stars.

Despite the decorations, Striver felt anything but festive.

Beckon hunched over his walking stick, watching the guards like an eagle surveying his brood. The old man turned and gauged Striver's approach with a keen eye and a crescent frown.

Of course the council would supervise Weaver's return.

Striver knew it was only fair, but part of him dreaded butting heads with the close-minded elders doggedly adhering to custom and outdated laws. Talking to them was like talking to the rocks by the riverside.

Striver bowed before the village elder, then stood and met his gaze. "I want to see him."

Beckon didn't move, rooted to his spot like an ancient tree with his long gray beard stirring in the breeze. "Save your voice. He won't listen to you."

Striver's jaw tightened as he took in a deep breath. "I have to try."

"Tend to the others in the village. Their spirits are low. They need a leader to show them these visitors bring no harm."

"We don't know that yet," Striver corrected him with a tilt of his head. "In my opinion, we celebrate too soon."

Beckon nodded his head slightly. "You may be right. Still, if a war is upon us, we will need strength, courage, and unity. Our spirits should be unbreakable."

"Five minutes," Striver commanded him with strength in his voice.

Beckon nodded. Resignation weighed his voice down. "If anything, one conversation will quell your hopes."

Refusing to believe him, Striver walked past the guards and entered the hut, heart pounding. Weaver sat on a tweed chair, bent over like a rag doll. A plate of half-eaten trotter rested beside his bound feet. They'd tied his hands to the chair with just enough give to reach the food and water.

At least he's eating.

Weaver looked up, hair falling around his face. He frowned in disappointment as if Striver were the last person on Refuge he wanted to see.

Striver swallowed the hurt down. "It's good to have you home with us."

Weaver cleared his throat. "So you're going to keep me here, like a pet?"

"I'm hoping, in time, you'll want to stay."

Silence. Weaver's gaze stared to a place Striver could never go, even if he wanted to. Striver stepped forward, the floorboards creaking under his feet. *This shelter will not hold him forever, no matter how many guards stand at attention.*

"You have nowhere else to go. Jolt won't take you back. You failed him, and he'll kill you for it. He's got a reputation."

Weaver flicked his eyes up under heavy, brooding lids. "You have no idea what my arrangement with Jolt is."

"Weaver, whatever it is, it can't be good. That man is evil. He's out for power and to sate his own greed."

"I'm not planning on submitting to Jolt forever."

"What are you planning to do, then?"

Again, silence. Silence so sharp it cut Striver in pieces. Did his brother have a plan at all, or would his reckless behavior only lead him to a dead end?

Striver spread his hands. "You could have a great life here with us."

Weaver laughed bitterly. "Always living in your shadow? Watching Mom slowly waste away? Suffering as Riptide throws herself at your feet?"

Striver resisted cringing at Riptide's name. "I don't have feelings for her, and I never have."

Weaver's eyes glittered with bitterness. "That doesn't stop her from having feelings for you."

If only he could wish her feelings away. Striver spread his hands in helplessness. "I'm sorry, Weaver."

"What do you have to be sorry about? You're perfect. Heck, you even look like the legendary Striker, savior of our people and the Guardians. A spitting image. Who wouldn't want to follow you?"

Striver crumbled inside. He couldn't win. Weaver had nothing, and he had it all.

Holy Refuge, I don't even want half of it.

Striver wished he could hand the world to Weaver on a plate, but one had to earn the admiration Striver had. Respect only came with time, and Weaver had failed everyone he loved.

"This is why I won't let Mom see you. You'd break her heart all over again." Striver shook his head in disappointment.

"Her heart was broken a long time ago, when Dad left."

Weaver always knew how to spread the blame, and there was no sense arguing with him. In his head, he did no wrong; everyone else in the world wronged him. Striver turned toward the door. "I'm always here if you need me. Let me know if you change your mind."

Weaver spoke to his back, his words sharp as thorns. "You can't make the world perfect, like you. Refuge will always be divided. It's human nature."

Striver paused. Now three factions battled for their planet: the Lawless, his village, and the ship in the sky. Was there a way to bring all three together? If so, he'd find it.

"Not if I can help it." The crackling of torchlight followed Striver out.

⊱⊰

Striver's failure with his brother ripped a hole in his heart, and the pain of reporting Weaver's recklessness to their mother heightened the hurt tenfold. He stood outside her hut, searching for words that weren't there. He hadn't seen her since his return, but Carven had given her the news of his homecoming, along with Weaver, as Striver made arrangements for Mars and Litus and answered the villagers' questions.

Now he had to face her with bad news.

The candlelight shimmered from inside, calming and welcoming him. Whenever he spent time with his mother he felt centered, focused. She taught him what was really important in this world. He needed her to ground him again.

He parted the ferns and stepped in. His mother lay in her bed, arms and legs thin as twigs. His heart broke all over again.

"Striver, it's good to see you." A smile touched her thin lips.

"How are you feeling?"

She shrugged, propping herself up on her knobby elbows. "The same."

Her condition was worsening. He could see the listlessness in her body, the pain in her tensed muscles. Eri's regenerator flashed in his mind. Carven had told him how she'd saved Litus, eradicating the sickness tearing through his body. Could she do the same for his mother?

"What of Weaver?" Her question brought his thoughts back.

He came over by her bed, took her hand in his, and kissed the back of her palm. "He's home, Mom. He's safe." *For now.*

"Is he going to the celebration?"

"No." Striver ran a hand over his hair. "They've locked him up."

"Has he harmed anyone in the village?"

"No, but the council sees him as a threat. They think he'll run away again. He shared our secrets with the Lawless in return for shelter."

Her hand tensed underneath his fingers. This information was not good for her, especially in her weakened condition. He wished he had good news to cheer her up, but the recklessness of her son eclipsed her world.

She met his gaze. "Look after him, will you?"

"I'll do my best. I tried to talk to him, but he won't listen to reason. He's jealous of me and everything I've become. I can't blame him."

She patted the back of his hand. "Anyone would be. You've turned into a handsome young man and a brilliant leader. You've made me proud."

Heat spread through his chest. He loved his mother so much, he was willing to take a chance, even if his actions defied everything he'd ever learned. "If you could heal as a result of technology, would you give it a try?"

His mother blinked and shook her head. "I have no idea. I've never thought of such a thing. Why?"

"Eri has a device able to regenerate cells. She used it on her teammate, and he healed right before Carven's eyes." Anxiety bubbled up in Striver's veins. "Will you try it?"

She swallowed, looking like she was drowning in her bed sheets. "What will the villagers think of you?"

He suspected she'd argue as much. "A new age is upon us—if anyone argues that, all they have to do is turn their heads to the sky. Perhaps this will bring our peoples closer together. We can't continue to live in the old ways. The Lawless are strengthening, and that ship in the sky isn't going to go away."

"Yes, but is it the best way? Accepting the visitors' technology?"

Striver shook his head, stomping out the defeat creeping in. "I don't know. But I do know it's the best way for you, for us."

"A leader must always think of his people before himself. You know that."

"I've thought it over, and we must make the first steps to welcome these people and unite our tribes. Besides, you are one of my people." Striver squeezed her hand. "And I won't let you waste away any longer. With Father gone, you're all Weaver and I have left."

He knew Weaver was the soft spot that would get her to change her mind.

"All right." His mother clung to his hand, putting on a brave smile. "Let's give this device a try."

CHAPTER TWENTY-ONE
A GREAT CATCH

Eri dug out a package of soywafers from the bottom of a cracked supply container. She held it in her fingers, feeling the hard, bumpy surface underneath the packaging. Her mouth used to water with the feeling of the crinkling wrapper, but after eating fresh, roasted boar meat, the snack seemed artificial and stale.

"For people who shun technology, they seemed to have saved a lot of our supplies." Mars knelt on the floorboards beside her, rummaging through another container. The crude cotton tunic and green leggings muted her aggressive nature; she looked more like a forest giant than a highly trained bodyguard. Glancing down at her own blue tunic, Eri knew she shouldn't judge. *I look like an elf.*

"They weren't going to use it." Eri dropped the uneaten wafers beside her and pushed back more damaged wires, looking for anything they could use as a weapon. "They didn't want it falling into the Lawless's hands."

Mars nodded, picking up Eri's discarded soywafer. "Techno hoarders. That's what I heard one of the Lawless call them."

"Yup. They sit on top of a ship that can still fly, holding back secrets that would send Refuge into the industrial era."

"They're afraid. Fear holds them back." Mars split open the wrapper, popped the whole thing in her mouth, and chewed. Eri wondered if she was hungry because she lost her breakfast after the flight. Who knew the toughest member of the team was afraid of flying? Mars didn't let her fear hold her back, though, and Eri respected her for confronting it.

"That's how I got them to save you and Litus. I told them the Lawless have the rest of the laser guns."

Mars regarded her with a raised eyebrow. "Good thinking, Eri." She wolfed down another soywafer and stared up at the thatched roof. "You know, at first you came off as a scared, self-doubting gene-mutt, hiding in her work cell, unable to confront the issue of her birth. I thought you were a poor choice for the team, a weak link."

Eri looked down at a frayed wire, pulling on the ends. It hurt to have Mars reference the teasing she'd endured her whole life. On the *Heritage* she'd felt like a second-class citizen. Here on Refuge, she'd made something of herself. She'd found the courage to save her team, to make friends with the natives, and even to develop feelings for one of them, feelings that could possibly lead to this mysterious thing called love. She wouldn't have done any of this in her work cell, playing with words.

Mars brought all that baggage up again. Baggage she'd rather leave behind. "I was a weak link. I started believing what people said instead of believing in myself."

"I wasn't finished." Mars crumpled up the wrapper and threw it into the container. "I'm glad the commander chose you. We were put to the test, and you were the strongest of all of us." She stared at Eri, her chin twitching like she still had trouble believing it. "You saved my life."

"Don't worry about it." Eri waved it off. Inside, healing warmth flowed through her. Never in a million years did she think she'd win Mars's respect.

The ferns rustled behind them and Eri turned. Striver stood in the doorway, making her heart speed. She hadn't gotten a chance to talk with him alone since the swamp, but her feelings had brewed.

"Am I interrupting?" He'd changed from his swamp clothes to a chestnut-colored shirt, partially buttoned, revealing his smooth muscles underneath. He'd washed his dark hair and pulled it back in a ponytail so it glistened in the torchlight. One free white feather dangled from a string of beads, kissing his tan neck.

"Not at all." Eri stood, wanting to gush about how glad she was to see him. Thank goodness Mars's presence stopped her from spouting anything embarrassing. "Your people saved so much. Thank you."

"We did the best we could." Striver came over, his mouth downturned in a complicated frown. "There's a favor I need to ask you."

Eri gripped the wire hard in her hands, the end sticking into her palm. He'd done so much for her she couldn't imagine saying no. However, Mars knelt behind her and she had to be careful. Mars had a locator as well and access to the commander. "Yes?"

"My mother has been sick for some time. I wondered if you could try using the same device on her that you used to heal Litus."

Use technology? Had Eri heard him correctly?

He stared, waiting for an answer.

She nodded so hard, curls fell in front of her face. "Of course I can." This was her chance to show Striver technology could be used for good. She couldn't believe he'd allow it after all he represented. *He loves his mother more than their silly ideals.* He must trust Eri. Did that mean she could trust him?

Striver breathed in deeply in relief. "Thank you."

Seeing his vulnerability brought a surge of compassion and something deeper, a yearning to make him happy, to fulfill his desires.

Her whole body gravitated forward, leaning to him.

Forget Mars. She slipped her hand in his. His calloused fingers grazed her palm, tingling her skin as they wrapped around her fingers. He brought his forehead to hers, his breath on her lips. "Tell me you can save her."

She trembled all over, wanting to make everything right in his world. "I'll try."

ॐॐ

Switching off her locater to keep Commander Grier from interrupting, Eri followed Striver to the same cluster of huts where she'd woken up after the battle. That whole morning had seemed like a blur, but Eri remembered Nutura's kind nature and how she reached for Striver's help as Eri left.

Clutching the regenerator in her hands, Eri hoped more than anything she could heal her. "How long has your mother experienced symptoms?"

Striver turned back to her, concern etched in the perfect angles of his face. "A year. Maybe longer. She tries to hide her pain because she knows how much it makes me worry."

They reached the rope bridge and Eri clung to the railing, trying not to look down. "How does your father feel about us using the regenerator?"

Striver stopped, the bridge creaking under his feet as it swung with their weight. A furry black bird took off in the distance, crooning. Striver waited for the bird's calls to fade before answering. "He died a long time ago, when Weaver and I were young boys."

Pain seared through Eri's chest. *I shouldn't have asked.* "I'm sorry."

Striver shook his head. "It's not your fault. My father took risks for the village: staying out late to check on the wall, exploring new territory for hunting, charting the regions in the mountains in the north. He'd leave for days and come back with an awful rash or a broken leg. The Guardians couldn't keep up with him."

"He sounds brave." *In fact, he sounds a lot like Striver.*

"He was." Striver glanced up at the sky and smiled. "Too brave."

"What happened to him?"

Striver paused, running his fingers along the rope, his touch delicate and tentative. "Don't get me wrong—he wasn't a failure. He accomplished many wonderful things for this village." His face grew grim. "But one day he didn't come back. The Guardians looked everywhere for him, from the meadows to the mountains. They never found a trace."

His story ate a hole in Eri's heart. She was honored he'd share such difficult memories with her, but she didn't know how to react. No one disappeared on the *Heritage*. It was a simple matter of buzzing their locator. With all its beauty, Haven 6—or Refuge—was a perilous world. She scanned the leaves fluttering in the breeze. The jungle seemed as though it could swallow her whole. "Maybe he's still out there?"

Striver shook his head. "No. He loved us too much to not come back." He stepped closer to her, his voice falling to a whisper. "I have my own suspicions. But I've never told anyone this before. Not anyone."

Eri held her breath as Striver's eyes narrowed and he spoke. "Sometimes I wonder if he encountered the same golden liquid Soren did, the same liquid that man fell into in the cave."

The strange symbols flashed in Eri's mind, tantalizing her in a puzzle she was dying to solve. That's why Striver had wanted to stay. If only she'd had more time to decipher them. "He doesn't sound like someone who would abandon the present for the past, especially with two young kids at home."

"No." Striver swallowed as if a bitter taste swirled in his mouth. "He doesn't." He blinked and turned around. "Come. I don't want my mother to suffer any longer than she already has."

"Of course." Feeling all shivery from the mystery of the liquid and guilty about bringing up the past, Eri followed him across the bridge and into the hut.

The room smelled of sweet blossoms, fresh ferns, and cooked meat. Bell-shaped flowers decorated the floor. *Are they all from Striver?* A table stood in the center with a mug of water and pieces of smoked boar. Striver's mom lay in her bed, barely making an impression in the fern mattress.

Can I really save this woman? Or am I giving them both false hope? Eri shook off her doubts. She needed to focus to use the device effectively.

Nutura gazed up at Eri with amusement on her face. "So, Eridani Smith, how do you like our world?"

"It's beautiful." Eri stood over her, taking her hand. "Scary, but beautiful."

"Yes, like a great many things in this universe." Nutura patted her hand. "Thank you for helping me."

"It's the least I can do after what Striver did for my people and me."

Her eyes twinkled. "My son is a great catch, isn't he?"

Eri lost her count on the pulse. *Great catch? What does she mean by that?*

Striver ran a hand over his hair, looking frazzled. "Now's not the time for chitchat, Mother. Eri's brought the regenerator."

"The device that's supposed to heal me?" She didn't look very hopeful.

Eri squeezed her hand. "That's right."

Nutura chuckled. "Guess it can't make me feel any worse."

"Mother." Striver gave her a stern look.

Nutura smiled and turned her head to Eri. "Do your best." She winked and tossed off her sheets, showing a bony body underneath a thin underdress.

Eri's heart skipped when she saw how skinny the woman was. She nodded, trying to keep a stoic face, and flipped up the lid. "Close your eyes and relax. You'll feel warmth, but nothing more. Most people fall asleep."

READY TO SCAN SUBJECT.

Yeah, as ready as I'll ever be.

Eri glanced at Striver and he nodded his approval. The hope mingled with worry in the lines of his face gave her all the courage she needed to start the scan. The device illuminated the small room in sapphire light.

Minutes passed with silence except for the crackling of the torches on the walls. Nutura slept soundly as the scan finished. Eri read the results, her chest aching.

Striver came up beside her but he didn't look at the screen. Instead he looked directly into her gaze. "What is it?"

Her tongue numbed until she could hardly speak. "Tumors. Cancerous. Spreading through her body."

He winced as if she stuck him with a knife. "Can you fix it?"

"I'm not sure. We never let such a thing get to this stage on the *Heritage*."

He balled up his fists and Eri put a hand on his arm. "I'm going to try."

Holding the regenerator in both hands, she set the scan to optimal power. The device buzzed under her fingertips as the green light traveled from Nutura's head to her toes. She repeated the process over and over until the regenerator grew hot as fire in her hands and the muscles in her arms shook from holding it steady. The energy cell read low, but Eri pressed the scanner button down with all her force. The heat traveled up her arms until drips of sweat rolled down her cheeks. The reek of burning plastic filled the room.

INSUFFICIENT CELL REGENERATION.

Eri pressed harder. *Insufficient, my cyber butt.*

The light weakened to a sickly pastel green, flickering out as the energy cell depleted. Eri shook the regenerator in her hands until the light came back on. The device beeped, the sound loud and foreign in such a dark and primal hut.

SCAN COMPLETE. CELLS RESTORED.

The heat faded as the regenerator buzzed off.

Eri dropped the device and it hit the floor with a *thud*. Dizzy from concentration, she fell backward and Striver caught her in his arms.

"Are you okay?"

"I'm fine." Eri breathed deeply as Nutura shifted under the blankets.

His voice was hushed, his words hesitant. "Did it work?"

Eri forced the hope down before it got out of control. "I think so, but I'm not sure."

"How can you be sure?"

Striver held onto her like they were the last two people in the world. She melted into his embrace, drawing on his strength. "We wake her."

He released her and they approached the side of the bed. Eri was hesitant to touch Nutura, so Striver bent down and whispered over her ear. "Mother, wake up."

Her eyelids fluttered and she rolled away, her back facing them, bones protruding from the nightdress.

Eri tried to ease his worries. "Sleep is a byproduct of the healing process. She'll feel weak and lethargic for the next few days."

Striver shook her shoulder gently, pulling her toward them. She groaned and rubbed her eyes. "Is it morning already?"

"No, Mother. Eri used her regenerator to heal you, remember?"

Nutura blinked as if she saw them for the first time. "I remember. It seemed so long ago."

"We just finished." Eri swallowed, not sure if she wanted to hear her answer to the question resting on her tongue. "How do you feel?"

Nutura scrunched up her eyebrows and wiggled her toes. She prodded her stomach with her finger, traveling from her navel to her chest. She shook her head, and Eri's hopes fell through the floor.

"No?" Eri's voice cracked.

Nutura smiled, and her eyes twinkled. "No pain." Her voice was incredulous.

Eri's emotions did a one-eighty. Her heart almost burst. "You sure?"

"Certain of it. In fact, my joints move much easier now." She bent her legs and sat up. "I haven't felt this good in ages."

Striver collapsed to the floor, tears watering his eyes.

Eri dropped beside him, taking his hand. Had she done something wrong? "What's the matter?"

He glanced up and shook his head like he couldn't believe it. "All this time we've shunned technology. Think of all the people we could have saved."

Guilt crushed down on her. Eri wanted to prove technology's worth, but she didn't want to give him regrets. She put a comforting hand on his arm. "You were following the rules set up by your ancestors. It's not your fault." Thoughts of the Lawless flittered through her mind. "Besides, you could be right about people. They may not learn to control it."

He traced his fingers along the back of her palm. "After what you've shown me here, we have to try."

"Blending our cultures may be the only way to coexist on Refuge." Eri hoped Litus's talk with the commander had gone well. Maybe Commander Grier would spare Striver's village. They provided a new pool of DNA and knowledge of the planet. If anything, she could contact the commander again and try to persuade her herself.

Striver's hand traveled up her arm to the back of her neck. "Eri, you've shown me so much. You've rocked my world."

Eri blushed, feeling self-conscious and tingly all over. *Rocked his world? What does that even mean?* "All I did was press a button. A child could have operated that machine. That's the miracle of technology."

Wiping his eyes, he smiled for what Eri suspected was the first time since they got back to his village. "No. I saw you hold onto that thing even though it looked about to explode in your hands. You didn't give up, Eri. You're the miracle."

Drums erupted below them, followed by shouts and laughter. Nutura's fern bed rustled as she sat up. Striver pulled his hand away as if he realized they weren't alone. Eri turned to Nutura with embarrassment flaming in her cheeks.

Nutura didn't seem to notice their attentions. She scanned the room. "Find my good tunic. The celebration has begun, and I'm going outside to see it."

Striver stood, offering his hand to Eri to help her up. "Finally, we have something to celebrate."

CHAPTER TWENTY-TWO
JUST ONE DANCE

Striver and Eri emerged from the hut propping his mother between them. She grasped each of their arms with bony hands. The villagers had gathered below, and all heads turned up as they reached the railing. The crowd began to chant Striver's name. Although it pleased his mother, he hoped Weaver couldn't hear them over the drums.

"Let go of me, please," she whispered. "I can stand on my own."

"It's too soon, Mother." He didn't want her to fall in front of everyone in this triumphant moment. Eri had warned the healing process would take time.

She squeezed his arm. "Trust me."

As the chant grew louder, she pulled away from him and Eri and held her arms up to the sky where the ship hovered over all of their heads. Nutura shouted, "I am healed!"

The crowd roared in applause. Voices rang out. "It's a good omen!"

The drums increased in pace, and a bone flute entwined in and out of the rhythm, the shrill tones dancing in the air. Trotters sizzled above the fire, the smell watering Striver's mouth. Carven stood, turning the silver-white fish with a wooden spatula. He signaled a wave of encouragement to Striver as people called out for a speech.

Striver glanced over at Eri and she nodded. She stood within arm's reach, but she felt a world away. *If only I could speak with her alone.* The glory of this moment was all because of her, and he wanted to show her his thanks; he wanted to tell her how much she meant to him, to hold her tight against him and show his feelings in a way he'd never done before.

Striver shoved his feelings away. It would all have to wait. His village stood before him, awaiting the speech of the century, words that would change the history of Refuge.

He'd thought on his decision for a long time, and the way he felt about Eri along with his mother's healing had sealed the deal.

Striver held up his hands and the shouting quieted. The music lulled to a low ostinato. He took a deep breath. "My fellow villagers, I present our newest friends, Eridani Smith and her team, Mars and Litus, descended from the ship in the sky."

Litus and Mars stood from the group below him, waving to the crowd. Eri climbed down the rope ladder to join them. His heart tore to see her leave, but she had to take her place for the festivities. She wasn't a member of his tribe. *Yet.*

"We must welcome them."

The music faded. People shifted uneasily, their expressions hard to read. Nervous anxiety jolted through Striver. Would they listen?

He raised his voice. "A new age is upon us, and we must embrace change. These visitors brought technology with them. I know we've shunned any advances for hundreds of years, believing technology to be the ultimate downfall of humankind on Old Earth. But technology can heal as well as destroy."

He held up his arm, pointing to his mother. "My mother is proof. These visitors have lived peacefully, in harmony with technology, for hundreds of years. Their lives depended on it. I believe, with the visitors' help, we can learn to accept their technology, integrate it into our society, and in turn, accept them."

The crowd shifted restlessly, weighing his words. Striver kept a straight face. *Hopefully they'll understand.* The alternative, to live in the jungle apart from this new colony, would only divide them more. He trusted Eri, and through that trust he'd build a whole new world.

No one argued with him, so he continued. "Lawless continue to multiply. We lose people to their ranks every year." He pushed Weaver away from his thoughts. *Not now.* Members of the council stood with their arms crossed, frowns weighing down their faces. Striver knew he couldn't convince them alone. He had to drive the issue home where they'd understand the full implications.

"I'm not asking you to decide tonight. I'm asking you to think about it. Speak with the council members at this celebration. Tell them how you feel. We can live in the dark while these colonizers descend and live in the light, or we can integrate both our societies, providing a united front against the Lawless."

Silence rang out after the echo of his final words died away, clutching his throat until he could no longer breath. Striver hoped he was right. He needed to provide a secure front for his people, but doubts lingered in the back of his mind.

A single clap broke the spell. Striver scanned the crowd. Carven had dropped the spatula, and he brought his hands together faster and faster until a little girl beside him joined in. Soon, the entire village roared with applause. The music began again in a lively jig with a boy shaking a tambourine.

His mother put a hand on his shoulder. "Well done, Striver."

He turned toward her and muttered under his breath, "We'll see if it works."

"They'll follow you anywhere." As his mother settled into a seat on the balcony, Striver searched for Eri. She talked with Litus behind a line of people waiting with empty plates for trotter. Others danced in the center square. He'd never liked dancing, but tonight his legs itched to move, and he had just the person in mind to ask.

He kissed his mother's cheek. "I'll bring you some trotter."

She nodded, bobbing her head to the beat. Color had come back to her face, and her gaze shone bright and clear without pain. He hadn't seen her so lively since she'd first gotten sick.

Striver descended the rope ladder two rungs at a time and leaped the remaining half a meter to the ground. With his mother healed, and the relations between the visitors strengthened, part of the weight on his shoulders had lifted, even with Weaver incarcerated. *At least he's home.* He'd deal with his brother later, when Weaver had cooled off. Maybe reality would finally set in and he'd realize Jolt wouldn't take him back.

Now to ask Eri to dance.

A hand grabbed his arm, snaking through it with surprising strength to pull him in the opposite direction. "I've been waiting for you."

Striver turned, meeting Riptide's golden gaze. She pulled him under the balcony in the shadows, pressing her body against his. She was almost as tall as he was, and he found it hard to wiggle away without blatantly shoving her away. "You promised me a dance, remember?"

He glanced back, making sure Eri hadn't seen Riptide steal him away. Eri still talked with Litus, her back to him. Seeing him standing in the shadows with her was one thing, but to dance out in the square in front of everyone? He couldn't do it. Not when such strong feelings for Eri thrived inside him, wanting to break free.

"Riptide, I need to tell you something."

Her eyes glowed in the darkness as if her dream had finally come true. "Yes?"

Striver ran a hand over his hair. *Holy Refuge, can I bring myself to tell her?*

One look back at Eri cemented his decision. "We've been friends for a long time."

She put her hand on his chest, her fingers twirling in the ties of his shirt. "Since childhood."

They were practically destined to be together, almost like the lifemates on Eri's ship. The thought made his stomach cringe. He cleared his throat. "You've grown into such a well-respected member of this village and a striking young woman."

She hung on his every word, eyelashes fluttering. "Yes?"

He exhaled and shook his head. "I can't keep you waiting for something that's not going to happen."

Her eyebrows creased. Behind them, the music took a melancholy turn. "What do you mean?"

Striver forced himself to meet her gaze. "At first, I kept my distance because I knew Weaver had feelings for you."

Riptide scoffed and tapped her slender fingers on his chest. "Yes, but we both know I don't like Weaver." Her eyes grew wild and intense as her hands traveled up his arms. "I want you."

He stiffened under her touch, resisting the urge to recoil. He'd always thought of her as a social climber, wanting him for who he embodied and not for who he really was. But how do you tell a person her shallowness turns you off?

"Now I have a real reason." He took her hands and brought them down between them. "Riptide, I have feelings for someone else. Feelings I can't ignore."

Her flawless face cracked into a spiteful frown. Her hands turned to ice under his touch. He wished he could warm them and make everything okay, but she'd have to find someone else.

"I don't understand." A tear ran down her cheek.

"It's not your fault. You did everything right. It's just…this was unexpected."

"Unexpected is right." Her tone turned sour and she yanked her hands away, her stone ring scratching his skin.

"I'm sorry." Striver felt helpless, guilty, but also free. Why had he waited so long to tell her? He had enough courage to hunt a boar, fly over the wall, battle the Lawless, but not enough to tell her the truth. *Because hurting Riptide would have angered Weaver even more.*

"Yeah, I am, too. Sorry I wasted so much time." Riptide whirled away and disappeared into the crowd.

కొ~స్

"I talked with the commander while you were healing Striver's mother." Litus pulled Eri aside as the crowd cheered around them. Eri's heart thumped against her ribs, yearning to find Striver, but she couldn't blow off this conversation. She followed him to the back of the celebration, far enough from eavesdroppers but close enough to avoid suspicion, even Carven's.

"What did she say?"

Litus had an anxious twitch in the vein in his neck. He shifted like a snake was slithering over his shoulders. "She appointed me first lieutenant."

"No way. That's the direct position underneath her on the ship, right?"

A little boy burst from the crowd and shot between them, stumbling and laughing. Litus smiled at the boy and waited for him to scamper off before he acknowledged her question with a nod.

Eri shook her head, speechless until she realized saying nothing would disrespect him. "Congratulations, Litus. You just won the most coveted job on the *Heritage*."

"Just because I'm in the right place at the right time. The commander wants more power down here on Haven 6, and it's the only way to see her orders are carried out. I'm supposed to supervise everything that happens on the planet and report back to her."

"That's because I wasn't doing my job. I haven't been reporting anything, Litus. I can't give her information that she could use against these people. But you have real power as a first lieutenant. You can make a difference, bring our peoples together."

Litus shook his head. "I'm not as powerful as you may think. She still has the ultimate say." Behind them, the music slowed to a minor waltz, the tune haunting her like a reference to the future.

"Did she mention any attack?"

"No, but the questions she asked lead me to believe she's planning one soon."

"Cyberhell." Eri threw her hands up and turned away, watching the villagers celebrate their imminent doom like naive children. "How can we stop it?"

His blue eyes were cold as ice. "I don't think we can."

She pointed her finger into his chest, pushing him back despite his towering stature. "That's not good enough."

He held up both hands in an apology. "Eri, I did my best. I've steered her away from our current coordinates for now. If they're going to attack, it will start in the Lawless's lands."

Eri crossed her arms and flicked her eyebrows up. "Yes, but for how long?"

"Depends on the success of the attack on the Lawless, I'd assume."

"Can the Lawless fight them off?"

"With their current weapons along with the lasers they seized? No. I don't think so. Although the Lawless have sheer numbers, the *Heritage* has far more advanced weaponry. And with my advice, they'll be better prepared this time."

Eri stared at him open mouthed. "How could you?"

Wiping sweat from his forehead, Litus glanced at the ship in the sky. "Eri, those are our people up there. You don't want more of them to die, do you?"

Eri glanced down, unable to bring her gaze to where the

commander's brain floated in the control room. "No. I don't want anyone to die. That's what I'm trying to prevent."

He jerked his thumb back to the shadows in the forest beside them. "It's better them than us. You saw for yourself how savage those Lawless can be."

"But after the commander conquers the Lawless, what then? Will she continue her conquest to this village?"

"I don't know. All I can do is inform her of their value, of how they can help us with their knowledge of Haven 6. Only she can decide."

Litus's loyalty to the commander made ire boil in Eri's stomach. She tried to calm her anger before she spit out something she'd regret. She had to give him credit for swaying the commander to attack the other side—at least he was trying to think for himself. Was it enough to grab Aquaria's attention? Probably not. Her sister would never agree with this plan. If only Litus had consulted Aquaria about it…

"Have you heard from Aquaria? The commander blocked all my communication through my locater, except to her."

"I'm waiting to hear—" Litus's gaze moved above her head to the crowd behind them as his words trailed off. Eri turned, ready to glare at whoever spied on their conversation.

Striver broke through the last row of twirling dancers. The urgency in his steps piqued her interest. His lips broke into an eager smile as his eyes met hers. Firelight danced across his chest, making his skin shine like gold. Her heart jumped to her throat and she gulped it down.

Brushing back a few strands of dark hair tied to a white feather, he offered her his hand. "May I have the next dance?"

It took Eri a moment to realize what Striver was asking. All the talk of war filled her head with clutter and weighed down her heart. She almost felt guilty indulging during such a dire time. "I don't know."

He brushed back a curl, placing it gently behind her ear. "Please?"

Eri needed this more than anything. She glanced at Litus and he waved her away as if they had been discussing the weather and nothing more. "Go." Litus grinned. "Have fun."

What is the harm in one dance? She'd danced numerous times at lifemate pairing ceremonies. How different could this be? Eri slid her hand into his. "As long as you don't make me dizzy."

After saying it, she knew it was already too late. Her head swam with his proximity as he pulled her against his hard chest and they broke into the dancing ring. Low drums beat in her stomach, eliciting a primal need for release. The bone flute trilled and sailed on a high note and she burst into uncontrollable laughter as Striver twirled her around.

He brought her back to him and his arms wrapped around her until she could feel every muscle in his chest. They didn't dance like this on the *Heritage*.

Holy mother of a black hole, we've been missing out.

Eri's hands moved up his shoulder blades to his neck. His ponytail tickled the back of her palms. She threaded her fingers through his silky hair and pulled his head down close to hers. Between the laughter, the shouts, and the music, it was impossible to tell him how she felt. Instead, she pressed her lips against his. He tasted wild and sweet, like everything in the jungle she wanted but couldn't have. She closed her eyes as he reacted to her kiss, his hands cupping her chin to prolong their embrace.

Blood pounded in her ears as heat rushed from her lips to her toes. Her whole life on the ship seemed only a dream, and for the first time, she awoke, her body energized. In all the lifemate ceremonies, she'd never seen a couple kiss with such passion.

This is real. Is it love? It flowed through her veins until all she cared about was melting into him. Becoming one.

Only after her hands had explored his chest and his hands roamed through her hair did she realize they'd stopped dancing. The crowd blurred around them. They were the only two pillars of constancy in a changing world. Gazing into his eyes was like peering into a forest only meant for her steps. His strength, his intensity persuaded her that together they could conquer both worlds.

"My sister isn't good enough for you, but this space girl is?" Riley broke through the crowd reeking of sickly sweet sweat. His shirt was pulled half out of his pants and his hair stood up on one side.

Eri grabbed Striver's arm. "What's wrong with Riley?"

Striver shielded her with his arm. "Don't get too close. He's had too much pearl-berry ale."

"Sure, blame it on the ale and we'll see just how trustworthy these visitors really are." Riley stared at her, spittle flying from his lips with his words. "Go ahead. Tell him why you're really here."

Eri's insides clamped up until she felt like she'd hurl worse than Mars. She stepped back into the crowd and shook her head. "I'm trying to help."

"Leave her alone," Striver shouted, pushing his face right up into Riley's. "Your argument is with me."

"My sister has been waiting for you for almost a decade, and you go after the first visitor you meet. What kind of a leader chooses an enemy over one of his own people?"

"Someone who believes in a new future."

"What about Aries and Striker? What would they say if they were here now?"

"They're not here. All you've got is me, and I choose her."

Riley bolted forward into Striver's stomach, knocking them both into the dirt. He rammed a fist at Striver's head. Eri's heart stopped. Hitting him was a direct blow to herself.

Striver deflected the blow with his arm and kicked Riley over. Riley pushed himself back at Striver and they rolled over and over until the dancers stopped, parting around them in a circle. The flute trilled off and the drums pattered out.

Eri clutched her stomach, fingers digging into her ribs. "Someone pull them apart before they hurt themselves."

A man moved to separate them and Riley flung him back into the crowd. A young girl threw a reed bucket of water on them, and they fought through the splash, oblivious.

"Stop it!" Eri shouted until her lungs grew raw. She reached out for Striver's arm and Riley whacked her backward, not knowing whom he'd just sent flying. Eri landed hard on her butt, the air knocked out of her and her chest throbbing.

They're going to kill each other.

Just as she considered going back in, movement rustled the hairs on the top of her head. Phoenix and two other Guardians descended like angels from the sky. They slipped through the crowd and ripped the young men apart. Riley continued to writhe in the Guardians' arms as Striver caught his breath, a red scratch running across his cheek.

"We will settle this like civilized people," Phoenix announced to the crowd. He and the other Guardians lifted both young men to the tree huts.

"Where are they going?" Eri turned to the nearest villager, an older man with a white beard as long as his arm.

"The council room, where all disputes are resolved," he answered in a resigned voice, his face unmoving.

Eri watched the Guardians disappear around the tree huts. "Can I follow them?"

The older man gave her a tired frown of condemnation. "I think you've done enough for tonight."

CHAPTER TWENTY-THREE
EAVESDROPPING

As soon as the drums began, Weaver had slid his hands through the loosened bindings.

Soon.

He'd wanted to throw his plan in Striver's face when his brother visited, but he couldn't give away his strategy. *If only I could see the look on his face when he realizes who's gone.*

Weaver had listened for the familiar shouts of laughter. *Idiots.* They celebrated while their doom hung over their heads. He'd be the one to save them, not Striver. He'd do what the others were too afraid of. He'd take on the visitors singlehandedly. All he needed was the power behind the golden liquid. Even then it called to him, igniting memories he'd rather have dead.

Imagine how it could manipulate the minds of others. The symbols were the key.

Guards who were outside his door cast flickering shadows through the ferns. The music had grown louder, and Weaver broke the leg of the chair in the rhythm of the drums. He gathered dry fern leaves from the floor and rubbed the end of the stick into the wood with both hands. His father had taught him well.

A spark caught, the golden-red flame reminding Weaver of the golden swirls. *No, not now.* He blinked, trying to refocus, but the swirls danced in his vision. *Damn it. I'm not even next to the pool.* Would his exposure to the pool affect him forever?

"Come, son. Hold the stick in the palms of your hands and rub them together." They sat underneath an open sky, the river gurgling beside them and the stars shining down. Striver hung the trotter from the day's catch as Weaver sat with their father.

His skin turned raw and red as the wood cut splinters into his hands. The sense of failure lurked, always imminent. "It's too hard. Nothing's happening."

His father placed a reassuring hand on his shoulder. "Have faith, Weaver."

Weaver glanced up and his father smiled in encouragement. Even though Striver usually started the fire, this time his father had chosen Weaver for the task, not his brother. Pride surged up and he rubbed harder.

A thin ribbon of smoke wafted up. Weaver shook his head, flinging the memory from his mind. He'd always thought his father had given Striver all of the honorable tasks. He'd forgotten this particular memory until now. *My father meant well; he wanted me to succeed, just like Striver.*

Stay focused. You'll never achieve leadership with such a mushy heart.

Weaver kicked the plate over, trotter flinging across the room. The pungent odor of the fish masked the reek of smoke. The guards wouldn't detect anything until he was long gone. Using the beat of the drums to hide his steps, Weaver kicked the weakened floorboard until it broke. The hole was jagged and narrow, but his wiry body slipped through with only a few scrapes. Using the bindings, he swung to the nearest tree. Branches provided handholds as he climbed down and slid into the darkness.

Unlike Striver, Weaver blended in. He could morph into part of the wall, melt into the shadows behind the fire, or sneak underneath the covers until no one knew he listened to the conversation. While Striver shined, Weaver hid. He got so used to blending in, now that was all he knew how to do.

Skirting the celebration, Weaver climbed a thickly branched tree. He curled up against the trunk, the bark cutting into his back, and waited. The music and the shouts of laughter had ceased. Weaver watched the paths below, a current of uneasiness slipping through him. It was too early for the celebration to end. Something must have triggered a prompt conclusion, and he wondered if they fought over the visitors. Maybe someone with half a brain stood in the crowd.

Was he too late? He couldn't stay another day in the village, so he had to claim his target now. He'd overheard the guards, and he knew the hut where they'd stored the visitors' equipment. That's where she'd stay for the night. He hovered above the main path, searching the dirt for footprints caused by ridges from her plastic boots. Surely she wouldn't seek an alternate route through the undergrowth.

Weaver shifted, dangling his foot toward a lower branch when voices penetrated the night.

"I want to help him. It's my fault he got into a fight."

Weaver froze, then slowly pulled his leg up, recognizing the voice right away, the same voice that had said: *With enough time, I'd figure out the whole language.*

"That was his choice, Eri. You heard what the Guardians said. They'll resolve the issue. Wait until morning, then seek him out."

Damn mother of a boar herder. The other voice was Mars, the woman who'd pushed Snipe into the golden liquid like he was a toy. Weaver flexed his sore arm muscles, feeling weak. With no weapons, he'd never stand a chance against her.

Eri stopped below his feet and Weaver practiced his art of blending in, allowing the leaves to silently shift between him and the path below, turning him into shadows.

She pulled on a leaf until it tore from the tree and ran her fingers over the surface.

Damn visitors have no respect for our world.

"You go ahead. I need some time to clear my mind."

"You're not going to storm the council room, are you?"

Eri shook her head, pocketing the leaf. "No. I just need to think."

Mars leaned on the tree and Weaver held his breath. "Gotcha. You're in a tough spot, between this young man and your mission. I can see it tearing you apart."

"What would you do?"

"Me?" Mars laughed, the sound like the inhalation of a mother boar. "I've never been in love. My lifemate is adequate, but he's not someone I'd fall head over heels for. Suppose it's good, keeps me logical, on track."

"Don't you ever feel like you're missing out?"

A swillow wisp took off above him and Eri glanced up at the branch where he hid. Weaver closed his eyes, afraid the sheen of his dark retinas would reflect the moon's light.

"Hell, no. Look what love is doing to you."

Weaver flicked his eyes open. Were they talking about Striver? If his brother had picked a fight over this space girl, then he cared about her. Weaver's plan took on a new meaning. This would turn personal when he'd only meant it to be a minor slap in the face. Could he really steal his brother's newfound love interest?

Why not? Striver stole yours. Whether he meant to or not.

Weaver threaded his fingers together in thought. It wasn't just to annoy Striver. He needed her to decipher the symbols.

Did he dare betray his brother so deeply?

Mars shifted off the tree below. "Take all the time you need. I'll be back in the tree hut going through the rest of our supplies."

"You can have the soywafers. I don't want them."

Mars waved over her shoulder. "Suit yourself."

Weaver leaned over, watching Mars disappear into the darkness. His chance dangled in his face like a grubber on a lure. Reaching into his shirt, he ripped open a secret pocket and pulled out the last of his coma darts. The venom was mostly dried and stale, but it would subdue her long enough to drag her to the other side.

Blocking his mind, he switched to combat mode. He dropped from his branch and slid down the tree faster than a Guardian descended from the sky. The bark scratched at his back and legs, but he ignored the pain, reaching Eri just as she turned toward the rustling leaves. Her pretty face blanked in shock as he brought his arm down on the back of her neck, knocking her to the ground. As she struggled to rise, he stuck the coma dart into her neck.

Adrenaline rushing through him, Weaver whirled around, searching the forest. Darkness and silence. No one had seen the struggle. He dragged Eri into the shadows, heading directly for the wall.

༄ ༄

Striver stared into Riley's harsh face, pleading. *Just say you apologize. You don't even have to mean it. Anything to get us out of here.* Every cell in his body yearned for Eri. Their kiss had been a moment of pure ecstasy, and he wanted to know if she'd felt it as well.

Phoenix paced across the floor of the high-lofted Guardian meeting room, his clawed, tri-toed feet scratching lines in the wood floor. The Guardians had painted geometric symbols all over the walls in the hieroglyphs of their native tongue. Striver had already read all of them, each one a riddle of a proverb offering wisdom with no true kernel of advice. At least for him today.

Guardians were patient enough to watch a sprout unfurl from the soil. They could be here until the swillow wisps sang.

Riley shook his head, bending a white feather he'd found on the floor and whipping it back up again. "I'm not going to give in to this madness. These visitors are here to take over, and Striver welcomes them with open arms."

Phoenix's head turned to Riley and he stared with his blank, silver-eyed gaze, reminding Striver of the glow of their moons. "You don't think I'm aware of the impending attack?"

Striver stiffened. *Impending attack?* Surely Eri would have warned him of such danger.

Phoenix spread his long arm, wing unfurling like a cape behind him. He pointed to the skylight where the *Heritage* hung. "These are turbulent times. Any number of paths could be taken. As the weaker of the two factions, we must choose the path of least resistance. We must work our way into the visitors' minds and hearts if we are ever to survive extinction."

Striver swallowed. Maybe Eri didn't know? Or maybe Phoenix was wrong? His gut told him no. Guardians were seldom, if ever, wrong. Which meant he had to talk with Eri as soon as possible.

"Striver works to befriend the visitors and show them our world. Only through his alliances can we achieve salvation. Riley, you must not get between him and the young woman."

Riley clamped up and clenched his fists. He was a fighter until the end. Unfortunately, his inclinations didn't help either of them get out of the council chamber any sooner.

"I don't need an apology." Striver appealed to Phoenix with a friendly smile. "I promise I won't let our differences come between us again."

"You won't, but what about Riley?" Phoenix's head twitched and a feather wafted on the breeze, lilting in the morning light. "We need to unify in this common cause."

Striver leaned forward. "Which is?"

Phoenix spread his branch-like fingers. "Survival of our colony."

Riley spoke through gritted teeth. "Why can't we fight? Send these visitors back to space. Let them find their own planet."

Phoenix stepped to Riley, bent down, and whispered by his ear. "Simply because we won't win. Perhaps if we joined forces with the Lawless we'd have half a chance, but with access to our secrets, they'd overtake us after the final battle, and we'd lose in the end."

Riley glanced up with a skeptical frown, "How do you know all this?"

Phoenix remained silent, as if such a question didn't warrant an answer. Striver stepped in for him. "They're Guardians, Riley. You have to trust them."

"They may have the power to fly, but they're not gods. They can't decide our fate."

The first ray of morning sun warmed Striver's skin, and he resisted the urge to throw back his head in disdain. How long would they argue?

Phoenix pointed an elongated finger at Riley's chest. "Your actions decide your fate."

The floorboards outside the hut creaked with footsteps. Hope rose in Striver's chest. Maybe Carven had come to bail him out—he could think of a millions reasons Carven could fabricate to whisk him away from these circular arguments. Or maybe it was Eri herself? His heart jump-started.

Mars rushed in, the broad woman pushing through the ferns, and Striver's stomach sank. Not only was it not Eri, but from the crushing look on her usually stoic face, something had gone terribly wrong.

Phoenix straightened up. "Dear visitor, what brings you here?"

"It's Eri." Mars caught her breath between words. "She didn't come back last night, and I can't find her anywhere."

A thunderbolt jolted through Striver, almost stopping his heart. He leapt up from his seat, knocking over the tweed stool. "When was the last time you saw her?"

"After the celebration. We were walking back to our tree hut and she said she needed time to think. I thought she'd snuck into this council chamber to go after you, so I came to look here first."

"She's not here. Nor has she stopped by." The feathers on Phoenix's wings prickled out behind him as if he itched to fly. "I'll check the surrounding area."

A sick feeling stung Striver's gut. *Weaver? Has he escaped?* It made perfect sense his brother would attack the one person who had come to mean everything to him. Striver knew just where to look. "I'll check for Weaver."

CHAPTER TWENTY-FOUR
EVENT HORIZON

Eri awoke bleary-eyed to the jungle pressing in on all sides in a vicious tangle. Had she passed out before she reached the hut? She didn't remember drinking any pearl-berry ale. *Unless someone slipped it in my water canteen.*

"Morning, curly locks."

Her sight adjusted to the bright light as she recognized the edged voice. Weaver sat cross-legged beside her, twisting reeds around a long black branch. No, it wasn't a branch any longer; he formed a bow. Sharp-tipped arrows were strewn around him.

Eri yanked her arms and kicked, but he'd tied her hands and feet. Nausea rose swiftly and she coughed, dry heaving until her stomach settled. Her neck throbbed as the attack came back to her. After saying good-bye to Mars, she heard something above her head and thought it was another one of those cute little furry black birds that Striver called swillow wisps. As she looked over her shoulder, an arm collided with her neck. She ducked, feeling like she moved in slow motion. A heavy weight landed on top of her, knocking her to the ground. Pinned down, she felt the familiar prick of the coma dart on her neck.

Anger rose inside her. "What are you doing? Where are we?"

He grinned, tightening the ties on the bow. "We're on the other side."

"The other side of what?"

He pulled the bow back and released an arrow into the jungle. The shaft tore through a giant leaf and landed in the hollow of a trunk. "The wall, boar brain. What other side is there?"

Eri tore her gaze away from the arrow to glare at him. "The other side of sanity. You're going to get us both killed."

Weaver hung the bow over his shoulder, looking like he'd done it a thousand times. He probably had. Whereas Eri's laser gun felt like a foreign substance in her hands. She checked her holster, but it was empty.

"Calm down, sweetie. I got it covered. Jolt can't hurt a hair on my head, and once he finds out you're the only one who can decipher those symbols around the golden liquid, he won't touch you, either."

"You're crazy. People have lost themselves in that stuff for centuries. Didn't you hear Soren's tale?" *And your father's, for that matter.* But she didn't want to make him angry by bringing up touchy subjects.

"Yeah, and with you, I'll finally unlock the code. I'll learn how to control it."

"Then what? You'll push in everyone from the *Heritage*?"

He gave her a sour glare. "I'm not about to give away my whole plan to you."

Which clearly meant he had no further plan at all. Eri wiggled around, trying to find a weakness in her bindings. The ropes cut into her skin, rubbing it raw. She couldn't feel anything in her right thumb, and her left foot had pins and needles prickling all over.

Cyber freaking hell.

And she had been so close to telling Striver the truth. After the intimacy they'd shared in that dance, she knew she could trust him. If only they'd had more time alone. Even now she could taste the saltiness of his lips on hers. She licked her bottom lip, feeling cracked skin. Dehydration, along with the other effects of the coma dart, would continue all day if her last episode were any indication. Even if she tried to run, she'd pass out and fall flat on her face.

"Striver won't let you get away with this. He'll come after us."

"Let him. We're going straight into the Lawless territory. He'd be a lunatic to follow us."

Weaver whipped out a knife and adrenaline coursed through Eri's body. She bit her tongue to keep a tough look on her face.

Weaver bent over her and cut the bindings on her legs. "Now you can walk. I was getting tired of carrying you all the way. You're not as light as you look."

Eri moved her feet, feeling blood rush to her toes. The thought of him touching her sent a feeling like spiders crawling all over her back. She couldn't imagine being nice to him ever again, even if he was Striver's brother.

"You're not as bright as you look."

"I'll consider that a compliment." Weaver kicked over the remains of his campfire. "Time to meet your new family." He hoisted her up and her head spun. It took all of her concentration not to vomit again as she steadied herself and stood without his help. She didn't want to give him the satisfaction of seeing her helpless.

He scanned the woods behind them. "We'll be near the patrols soon. Let me do the talking and don't say anything."

He pulled her ahead, and she fought to keep her balance with her hands tied behind her back. Using the tip of her finger, she clicked on her locater, muting the sound. Now it would transmit the coordinates of her location to Litus and Mars back in the village. Thank goodness the device had been embedded in her arm since birth. Weaver would have to cut through her skin and muscle to pry it out, and she doubted he'd go that far. *Unless he sees me using it.*

Eri paused. Did she really want them coming after her? If Weaver was right, Jolt wouldn't lay a hand on her, and she could get information they or the *Heritage* might need. All she wanted to do was ask Striver to save her, to see him again, hold him again. Eri stopped her heart from gushing; she needed to be brave. Signaling him would only put him and his village in more danger. Now *she* needed to be the hero.

Eri typed slowly, feeling the buttons and counting the right number to reach each letter behind her back. *I ok. I spy.*

Weaver yanked on the rope tied to her waist. He gave her a suspicious glare and she pretended she was adjusting her boot with her knee.

"No wasting time."

Biting her tongue to avoid spewing out a mean response, Eri raised her nose up in the air and followed him. She hadn't wasted a second.

❧❦

Striver fell to his knees in front of a hole in the wall that was twice his height. Not only had Weaver taken the one person who meant everything to him, he'd also destroyed the only obstacle holding the Lawless back.

Event horizon. The point of no return.

This time his brother had gone too far. For the first time in his life, Striver didn't think he knew him anymore. He'd failed him—they all had. Sadness rose up in dual amounts with the anger edging its way in.

"How did he do it?" Mars walked ahead and ran her hands along the crumbling edge.

"He used Eri's laser." Litus spoke up behind them. "If you set it to the right frequency, it can blast through anything."

Litus's arm beeped and he held up his locator. "Hold on. Eri's trying to send me something."

Striver rose and stood beside him, looking over his shoulder. Anything connecting him to Eri was invaluable. Numbers flashed by along with some sort of code.

It was his turn to look to Litus for help. "What does it mean?"

"It's her coordinates!" Litus's face lit up then darkened. "They're on the move."

"Where are they?" Striver stared at the screen. "Where are they going?"

Litus brought up a mini map of the area and pointed. "Here. Bearing due west."

Damn Refuge and all its leaves. "They're heading directly into the Lawless city, not to the cave. He's too smart. He knows we'll follow him there."

"What's he planning to do? Kill them both?" Mars stomped over like she could pull Weaver right out of Litus's locator and eat him on the spot.

"Revenge?" Striver ran a hand over his hair. "I'm not sure."

"No, it's got to be more than that." Litus stared at the screen, narrowing his eyes. "Eri has something that he needs."

"Her laser?" Mars thought aloud. "No, they already have a bunch of those, and he could have just taken it from her and left her here."

"It's my fault." Striver gripped his bow against his chest, pain rippling through him. "I shouldn't have trusted him."

"Hey, now." Litus put a hand on his arm. "We do the same on the *Heritage.* We tend to our own no matter what undesirable symptoms they exhibit. Every life is precious. Every one of us holds the history and the future of mankind in our DNA."

"Enough with the lecture, Lieutenant." Mars peered through the hole. "We need a plan."

"We can't just storm in there." Striver tried to calm his frustration.

Every second, Eri slipped farther away from them. "They outnumber us. Even if we brought our entire village, and they were all experienced warriors—which they aren't—we couldn't win. We can't sneak in; Weaver knows all our faces."

Litus's locator beeped again. "Wait. There's more."

This time the locater displayed a simple message. Striver read what she'd sent and a kernel of pride formed inside him. Eri was fighting back.

"I say we wait it out. Let time take its course." Although Litus stood tall and still, a storm brewed in his eyes.

"What do you mean?" Striver put his face right up to Litus, standing on tiptoes. Phoenix's observations from the council room rushed back to him. "What are you not telling me?"

Litus sighed and rubbed the sides of his head as if weighing whether or not to speak. "The *Heritage* will attack the Lawless lands. With their fire power and technology, coupled with my own tactical advice, there's no way a less-advanced civilization, no matter how savage and brave, can withstand such an onslaught."

Mars shook her head. "And Eri's going to be right in the middle of it? I don't think so. What if they torture her for information?"

"If they wanted information, they would have targeted me. I was alone and unguarded all night."

"What could that weasel possibly want with her?" Mars's braid had fallen in her face and she blew it back.

"It's got to have something to do with what she does." Litus ran his finger over the screen. "No offense to Eri, but why would anyone want a linguist?"

"The symbols," Mars growled. "The stupid etchings around the golden liquid. I heard Weaver talking to one of them. He's supposed to crack the code."

"Can she do it?" Striver's heart sped. If she failed, they'd kill her.

"If anyone can, she can." Litus's faith in Eri showed right in the hard edges of his chin. "The question is: Do you want them to know?"

"Who cares about the liquid?" Mars shrugged. "I just want Eri to be safe."

"Cracking the code of a language takes time. If they want her to decipher the symbols, she'll go back to the cave. None of the fighting will happen there." Litus put a hand on his heart. "You know this is hard for me as well; she's my sister-in-law. All I want to do is rush to her aid. But realistically, those Lawless lands are going to be a warzone, and Eri's smart enough to use any attack to her advantage. Besides, once the forces are on Refuge, they answer to me. I can give a team her coordinates and send them right to her."

Striver's insides twisted as he stood in inaction. He was the leader of his people, and he had to weigh that against his own personal agenda. When he took the position, he never thought those two responsibilities would collide, and that's all they'd ever done. "How soon is this attack going to happen?"

Litus raised his eyebrows. "Soon."

"So we do nothing, even after she saved us?" Mars kicked a stone, and it bounced off the wall.

"She wouldn't want us rushing to our deaths." Litus crossed his arms.

"I can't do it. I can't sit by while Weaver takes her into the most dangerous place on Refuge." Striver felt like jumping right out of his skin, becoming a Guardian and flying himself over those woods to find her. If only he had the freedom of choice.

Litus turned to Striver. "I've thought a long time about this, and I think you should gather your own people together with any weapons you might have. No matter what happens, whoever wins this war will come after us next."

CHAPTER TWENTY-FIVE
SWIMMING WITH LEECHERS

Weaver tugged on the rope tied around Eri's waist, leading her across the Lawless lands to their sprawling metropolis west of the wall. Guilt weighed him down more than her floundering steps.

I'm not going to kill her. Just use her to identify the symbols.

So why did he feel like the worst criminal to ever steal on Refuge? He glanced back as she stumbled over a tree root and caught herself on the next trunk, leaves falling in her hair. She looked like a fairy-tale character stuck in the wrong story. Like Pearl Berry Jamboree thrown into Isaac the Swamp Monster's fester pot.

Isaac the Swamp Monster. He hadn't thought of him in years. It was his favorite fairy tale growing up. Isaac was a castaway. No one liked him, and the other animals called him names. Weaver pleaded with his mother to recite the story every night, making the *squish squish* noises as Isaac stomped through his swamp.

What are you doing reminiscing? Weaver shook his head. It was that cursed golden liquid, making him remember things he'd rather keep buried and making his heart soft as swamp sludge. Bottom line was he needed Eri, and her people invaded Refuge, so he shouldn't feel a shred of guilt for making her decipher those symbols.

But Striver cares for her. Taking his brother's girlfriend made him feel like the slime on the underside of Jolt's boots. Striver was still making him look bad after all these years. Weaver's resentment swelled, predictable as the tide.

Striver should have let me be that day in the river. He would have died. Think of all the suffering he wouldn't have had to endure.

"Are we almost there?" Eri whined behind him like he was dragging her to the harvest fair. "My feet hurt."

"We're close." Weaver turned just as Eri tumbled forward. He caught her in his arms, his face inches from hers. Dark circles ringed her eyes, her forehead was creased in worry, and her face was eerily pale.

I did this to her.

Remorse panged in his gut. He squeezed her shoulders and helped her up. "You okay?"

She pushed him away, disgust curling her beautiful lips into a frown. "Get away from me." The thought of taking her back to the village and giving her back to Striver crossed his mind, just as an arrow cut through the leaves and dug into the earth in front of them.

Weaver's heart sped. *Too late for redemption.* He straightened, stiff as a statue, and spoke without turning to her. "Don't move a muscle."

Holding up both hands, Weaver waited. People concealed by headdresses of leaves emerged from the forest and surrounded them in a semicircle. Crusty led them, and Weaver focused on his attention. The old man seemed to have a soft spot for Weaver, and maybe he could use that to his advantage.

"Come back for more, eh?" Crusty chuckled as the others pointed sharp spears at Weaver's gut. Crusty clapped his shoulder. "Thought you were dead, weasel."

"That's Weaver."

He chewed on some tobacco root and spit into the forest. "What happened to Snipe?"

Weaver shook his head. "Didn't make it. He fell in the golden liquid."

"Poor bastard." A glint of excitement traveled across Crusty's eyes. Since Snipe hadn't made it, Jolt would promote him. "Gimme that shiny laser of yours, and we'll call it even."

Weaver handed over the laser. "I've come to speak directly to Jolt."

Eri seethed.

Crusty shook his head, oily gray hair falling around his face. "Jolt's been looking for ya like a mother boar over a younglin'. You'd better have something good for him."

"This is real good. But it's real secret as well."

Crusty put up his hand and the people with spears backed away, giving them privacy.

Weaver leaned forward, suppressing the urge to gag as he smelled the man's sour breath. "Not only can I give him the codes to the guns, but I have a linguist."

Crusty rubbed the gray stubble on his chin. "A what?"

Weaver waved his hand in the air. He'd always thought Crusty was a bit slow. Although, no one in the Lawless lands lived to that ripe old age without some amount of cunning. "Never mind. A girl from the ship who can decipher those symbols he wanted me to learn."

The old man blinked in surprise. "You sure 'bout that? 'Cause Jolt'll rip that sweet little thing to shreds if he feels like it."

An undercurrent of anxiety lined with guilt shot through him. Weaver took a deep breath. "I'm sure."

"May fate work its will." Crusty signaled the others and they walked toward camp in a rag tag parade, Weaver leading Eri like a new pet. Lawless leered at them as they passed, some making snide remarks about a curly red head. Although Weaver had been through this before, he couldn't help uneasiness from creeping under his skin. Protecting himself was one thing, but babysitting a young woman, his brother's potential love interest, was another. This time he was in over his head in waters filled with hungry leechers.

～◦◦～

Eri tried to ignore the lewd comments that could only refer to things she'd never heard of in her sheltered life aboard the *Heritage*. Men dressed in rough leather breeches with sticks through their nose, ghoulishly painted faces, and muddy dreadlocks lined the streets, looking like a ragtag bunch of savages. As she passed ramshackle huts and muddy pathways filled with garbage and animal excrement, she wondered, for a moment, if it actually might be best for her people to take these guys out.

No, I'm not going there. Everyone deserved a life, and what they did with it was their choice. Too long had she lived on a ship where everything had been decided for her, predestined. Now that she had a taste of free will, she didn't want to let it go. Even if her awakening meant stumbling through a village of chaos and poverty.

Eri covered her nose with the side of her arm, blocking the dank smell of mold mingled with sweat. Compared to Striver's village, this place looked like hell. People argued in the streets, calling out profanities, and children cried from the darkness of muddy, moss-covered huts. They walked to the back of the settlement where the husk of an old space ship protruded from the earth like a broken toy.

Holy Refuge, it must have come from the original space pirates.

She hadn't believed it when Striver had told her there were other ships on Refuge, and the one they protected was the only one that could still fly.

Half buried in the ground, with moss draped over its wing, the ship looked like a forgotten dream, a remnant of a lost civilization.

Maybe it was. As a man slapped a small boar on a rope, and a little boy stole a broken pot from a windowsill, she wondered if these Lawless people were civilized at all.

A guard stood on each side of the entrance to the ruined spacecraft. The one on the right whispered to Crusty. The guard jogged up the ramp.

Eri had a crazy hope that Jolt wouldn't want to see them.

A minute later, the guard sprinted down the ramp, faster than he'd gone up. He nodded to Crusty and turned to Eri and Weaver.

"Jolt will see you now."

A shiver tickled her spine. She remembered Jolt's unforgiving, dead eyes from the swamp where she'd hidden with Striver in the tree.

If only I could go back to that moment and warn him about Delta Slip, tell him that I'm with him and not the people storming Refuge from above.

Weaver pulled the rope tied around her waist and she jerked forward, feeling unprepared for what lay inside.

Humid air reeking of smoke and mold bathed Eri as she stepped in. Her tired reflection stared back at her on wallscreens long dead. The technology was centuries old and outdated, with thick, clumsy wires leading into the ceiling and running along the floor.

"I thought you were dead," Jolt growled from the captain's chair.

Eri whirled around, feeling as though an icy hand clutched her heart. Jolt slumped in his chair, his face covered in shadows.

Weaver stepped between her and Jolt. "You lucked out. I survived."

"Only to take my secrets back to the village."

"They asked me nothing. It's not their style to torture and interrogate."

Jolt shifted in his seat, the plastic creaking. "Naive softies, don't know what's good for 'em. So they learned nothing of my plans?"

"Zilch."

"And the code for the guns."

Weaver pointed to his head. "Right here."

Jolt held up Tank's gallium crystal void ray, still shining without a scratch. "Give it to me now and you'll regain my trust."

Eri suppressed the urge to latch onto Weaver's arm and tell him not to. Fear stalking the edge of her consciousness warned her not to draw attention to herself.

"Six, six, four, five, nine."

Eri's insides shriveled in defeat. Jolt pressed the buttons on the keypad and the laser buzzed to life. He pointed the gun straight at Weaver's head and chuckled. "What's to stop me from testing it out right now?"

Weaver pulled Eri beside him and she slanted back as far from his head as possible, not wanting his blood to spew all over her hair. "This girl here."

Jolt leaned forward into the light. He grinned and the scar on his forehead glistened with a sheen of sweat. He lowered his laser. "What have you brought me?"

"A linguist. Using my knowledge of the Guardians and her skills from the ship, we can decipher the symbols of the golden liquid."

Jolt scratched his chin. "Interesting. Very interesting."

Weaver placed his arm around her. "Now if you'll excuse us, I'd like to get right to those symbols in the cave." Although Eri wanted to shrug his arm off like it was a cobra, she remained still. In this particular circumstance it was better to be *with* Weaver than against him. Weaver moved them both toward the ramp for the entranceway.

"Hold on." Jolt's voice sliced the air like an obsidian blade.

Weaver turned them around. "What is it now?" Although he sounded annoyed, Eri could feel his fingers shake against her arm. Why would he expose himself to this man? This village? It made Striver and his hometown seem like a dream.

"Crusty will accompany you. You've helped me out, I'll grant you that. And returned with a promising piece of the game. But I still don't trust ya."

"Fair enough." Weaver bowed his head. His hair tickled the side of Eri's cheek and she tilted her head away again.

"And a message for pearl-berry curls." Jolt's gaze stung her composure and her skin crawled with prickles. She wanted to flee from that hunk of junk space ship into the jungle and climb a tree to get away. "If you fail to decipher that code, I'll have Crusty knit a nice sweater with your hair."

She must have winced because he laughed at her response and waved his hand. "Out with ya. We don't have all day."

They walked down the ramp and Eri pinched Weaver.

Weaver shrugged his arm off her shoulders. "Ow, what was that for?"

She grabbed him and pulled his ear close to her lips, whispering, "I can't believe what you've gotten us into."

"Just decode the symbols and you'll be fine."

"Fine?" She wrinkled her nose at him. "After I decode the symbols we'll both be *dead*."

His voice fell to a whisper. "Didn't you hear me the first time when I said I had a plan?"

"If you don't tell me what it is, I can't help either of us."

Weaver opened his mouth to respond, but Crusty met them at the bottom of the ramp and growled. "Looks like I'm your babysitter."

"More like warden," Eri spat out, frustration bubbling up inside her.

Crusty smiled, undeterred. "Whatever you want to call it. Come with me."

They stomped through dense jungle to the cave. Eri's feet already hurt from the day's trek, and now they swelled in her boots. She started daydreaming about her sleep pod on the *Heritage* and had to remind herself that she'd probably never sleep in it again.

If she wanted to be with Striver.

It was a big *if* hanging on so much: her ability to escape, what Commander Grier had planned, if they both survived this planetary war. She needed to take her life one step at a time. Decode the symbols, get herself out of the Lawless lands, and then think about her feelings for Striver. The seemingly insurmountable odds made her stomach churn with doubt.

Just take it a day at a time. Step one: don't get yourself killed.

The last thing she wanted to do was crawl through the cave infested with spidermites.

Again.

Eri braced herself, summoning courage from the deepest corners in her heart. With Crusty's spear stuck in the hollow of her back, there was no way out of it. If she wanted to see Striver again, she had to decipher those symbols, or at least look like she was working on it. Besides, the symbols had tickled the back of her mind ever since she laid eyes on them, and the linguist part of her wanted to know what they were.

She entered the cave, following Weaver's torch as it cast flickering shadows on the rock. Although she had more light to find her way, she decided she preferred the dark. Every flicker showed cracks full of spidermites' legs and walls crawling with colorful beetles and white worms squiggling up trickles of water.

The golden light leaked from afar, and she scrambled toward the glow. Crusty followed close behind, cursing the spidermites.

The cavern looked like it had the night they'd invaded, with laser blasts blackening the rock. Eri felt as though she'd taken ten steps back instead of forward. Just a few days ago, they were all free, and here she was now, a crumb in the Lawless's jaws.

Use your predicament to your advantage. Remember, you wanted to spy.

Swirls in the liquid followed her as she walked along the symbols.

Eri couldn't decide where to start.

"Does any of it mean anything to you?" Weaver whispered.

Eri cast a glance at Crusty. The old man found a hollow in the rock and slumped down, whistling to himself. Together, she and Weaver could take him, but first she needed Weaver on her side.

"Not yet. Give me some time."

She knelt down and traced her fingers over a Y symbol with spikes coming out of the right side.

Using the sand around her feet, she began scribbling notes. "You told Jolt you knew the Guardians' language. Show me what you know."

Weaver shrugged. "It's not anything like these symbols. I only told him to keep myself alive."

"Show me anyway." Eri stared into his dark eyes, pleading. "I'll need all the help I can get."

Weaver sighed and plopped down beside her. "Okay. But we've got to make this quick. I'm not sure how much time Jolt will give us…"

CHAPTER TWENTY-SIX
THE DARKNESS WITHIN

Lavender blossoms drooped to his knees underneath a whispering breeze. The low harvest sun cast the meadow in a sheet of amber gold. Weaver held a bouquet, stems pricking his palm. His fingers bled as he removed every thorn. He sucked on his cuts, wondering how he'd summon the courage to speak with Riptide.

Shouts from the village elders carried on the wind as they set up the stalls along the main square of the village. He didn't have much time. He sprinted down the slope toward the village, careful not to damage any of the blossoms. They had to look perfect. Perfect like her sharp features, the curve of her cheeks, and the shine in her dark hair.

He ran through the village to Riptide's family hut. He stuffed the bouquet between his teeth and climbed the ladder, his heart speeding. I can't believe I'm doing this.

He'd waited all summer to show her his feelings, bottling them up like pearl-berry juice. The festive atmosphere of harvest time excited him and gave him the confidence he needed. Besides that, he hadn't felt the darkness flare inside him for a long time.

Now or never. *He pulled himself up.*

Riptide's mother shuffled over to greet him, wiping her hands on her apron. "Weaver, what brings you here right before the celebration?"

He pulled the stems from his mouth. "I have something for Riptide."

A complicated emotion passed on her face before she regained her composure. "She's not here."

"Where is she? Is she all right?"

Riptide's mother gave him a tightlipped frown. The older woman had never liked him very much, but Weaver didn't let her ill will stop him. Not this time.

"She's at your family hut."

Weaver's heart stopped. Had Riptide come to ask him? She'd been hanging around him and Striver since the last few long summer days—going fishing, picking berries, and sharing her mom's favorite recipes. She had a killer arm and could spear trotter from the riverbank.

"Thank you, ma'am." *Remembering his manners, he bowed his head before stuffing the stems back into his mouth.*

As Weaver jogged through the village, he passed Beckon firing up the coals for the boar roast. Golden swirls moved in the embers in between the coals. The old man shouted over the growing flames, "Remember what we talked about concerning you joining the council. We'd really like to have you."

Weaver waved. "I'm considering your offer."

He passed under Carven's wife, Lista, who stood on a ladder, threading lace through branches. "Hello to the new arrow maker!" *she called down, her long brown hair blowing with the leaves.*

Weaver slowed and jogged in place. "Nice to see you, Lista."

"So are you excited about being Carven's new apprentice?"

"I sure am. And I'll work real hard. You watch. I'll be making bows before you know it."

"I'd like to see that." *She held onto her stomach.* "I'm expecting *another child, and Carven really needs the free time to help me out at home."*

Weaver glanced at the bump in her tunic. He hadn't even noticed. "Congratulations, Lista."

"Thank you. Give my regards to Striver and your mom."

"I will."

As he approached his family's tree hut, a sense of belonging and acceptance overcame him, something he hadn't felt in a long time. He was moving up in the world despite living in Striver's shadow. Striver could only do so much, leaving other opportunities for Weaver to pick up. And now he'd spend the day with Riptide. Life had turned sweet.

Riptide and Striver stood on the circular balcony surrounding the tree hut. Weaver opened his mouth to shout up to get their attention and froze. Such intensity lay in her eyes, it stopped his heart.

She placed her delicate hand on Striver's wrist. "I want you to go."

What did she mean? Go with her to the harvest fair?

Weaver's chest cramped up and a weight squeezed out all the air in his lungs. Had she spent all of that time with him to get to Striver?

Striver shook his head. "I have too much to attend to. The boars need to be skinned, and my mother is ill. I must stay behind to tend to her. Why don't you go with Weaver?"

Weaver clutched the rope ladder, feeling the twine of the braid cut into his skin.

Riptide pulled away from Striver, frowning in disgust. "Weaver is still a boy. He's got so much to learn."

Weaver felt like nothing, small as an insect or a grain of dirt. Was he really that miserable to be around?

Striver stepped toward her. "He's a good person and you should consider him in your thoughts as well."

Riptide leaned over the balcony and Weaver ducked underneath the ladder to avoid being seen. "You're making excuses."

Striver didn't move to comfort her. "I am not. I'm being responsible."

"You have a responsibility to yourself as well, Striver. You have to allow a little fun now and then."

"You speak the truth. But today is not the day."

"When?" She practically swooned, making Weaver sick.

He climbed a few rungs to hear Striver's response. "I-I can't tell you. I really don't know."

Diplomatic enough to keep her at arm's length, but vague enough to keep her waiting, Striver left her on the balcony without so much as a good-bye. Riptide clung to the railing and shed silent tears.

Weaver was tempted to comfort her, but she didn't want him; she wanted Striver. Dropping the bouquet, he stumbled away from the hut. The flowers spread and sunk in the mud.

A familiar pain stabbed his chest. The darkness within him welled up and spread through his veins until he raged with pain and hate.

He felt hurt, used, betrayed. Why did Striver have to take everything he wanted?

Weaver stumbled over to the tanks of fermenting pearl-berry ale pulled from the distillery for the fair. He poured himself a jug and gulped the sour liquid in three gulps, red trickling down his neck to stain the white tunic he'd washed and pressed so carefully. He poured another, and another after that, wanting to drown in it, like he almost had in the river. The liquid spread through him, dulling the pain but not obliterating it. The darkness would always be inside him, and he'd never be free.

Stumbling into the main square, Weaver kicked over chairs and market stands. Fruit rolled on the ground and he kicked a pearvacado at a swillow wisp regarding him with a little black eye. The bird took off squealing.

Beckon tried to help him up. "Weaver, what's happened, is everybody all right?"

Weaver pushed the old man away. The darkness enveloped him, tendrils spreading over his heart, rooting inside his soul.

"Go to Hell!"

Beckon had always been so calm and collected. He had no idea what true pain was. He'd never understand. The old man stared at him like he'd turned into a monster. Weaver shied away, feeling the beast inside him rear up to wreak its revenge. If he stayed, he'd hurt someone, maybe worse.

Weaver bolted into the jungle, tearing through the undergrowth. People called after him.

"Weaver!"

"Weaver!"

He ignored their pleas.

ॐ◌ॐ

He woke up with Eri's angelic face hovering over him. She shook his arm. "Weaver, are you okay?"

He shriveled away from her touch. "I'm fine." Crusty snored across the cavern, so at least the old man hadn't seen his vulnerability.

Eri raised her eyebrows. "You were tossing and turning, mumbling Striver's name in your sleep."

"Bad dream." But it wasn't. It had been a memory, real as the day it had happened. So real, he noticed things he hadn't paid attention to the first time. When it had happened, he'd hated Striver, wishing his brother had never been born. After experiencing the memory again, he realized Striver had tried to protect him from the truth. Not only did Striver suggest Riptide go with Weaver instead, he turned the village beauty's affections away. All for him.

Weaver's heart hurt like he hadn't exercised it in years and only now did it begin to feel again. He'd made an ass of himself that day, and Beckon had outlawed him from the council, citing his unpredictable nature. He'd thought the punishment harsh, but now he understood. He deserved every bit of the shame.

"Eri, I have a question for you."

She poured over her notes in the sand, not even looking up as she answered him. "What is it?"

"Have you had any memories lately?"

"Like what?"

"You know, recollections of the past."

She pulled herself away from the symbols and glanced at the stalactites dripping water from the cavern's ceiling. "Come to think of it, I have. Visions of my sister and me when we were little keep flashing in my mind."

"Are they the same as you remembered them to be?"

"No." She pulled her curls out of her face. "They're clearer."

Weaver ran a hand through his hair, thinking. The golden liquid wasn't warping his memories; it was displaying them through a clearer lens, a perspective outside of himself. "Do the memories make you feel guilty?"

Eri shook her head. "Not at all. They make me want to keep reliving them, over and over again. I have to remind myself of the symbols, or we'll never get out of here." She gave him an incriminating glare and muttered under her breath, "Unless you want to overtake Crusty now. He's sleeping on the job."

"And go back to the village? No way. The key to everything lies in those symbols. Besides, Crusty can see everything. He'd wake up right before you tried anything. Believe me, I've watched him."

She stared back at him with intensity brewing in her eyes. "We could take him, you and I."

"That's not part of my plan. I abducted you, remember? We're not on the same playing field. You're still my prisoner."

"Seems like we're both prisoners." Eri's jaw jutted out and she flared her eyes before returning to the symbols, whispering dead languages under her breath.

"Have you made any headway?"

She hesitated, as if she were deciding what to share with him.

"Yes."

Holy Refuge, why didn't she say anything sooner? "Well, what is it? What do they say?"

"The language is a lot like the hieroglyphics used by the ancient Egyptians."

"Who?"

"A race of people who used to inhabit Old Earth."

Ancient Egyptians? Why hadn't he ever heard of them? Doubt teased him. Maybe this young woman had no idea what she was doing. Maybe she was making it up in an effort to win her freedom. "That doesn't make any sense. Why would they be here, parsecs away?"

Eri blew dust off of a pyramid with an eye in the middle. "Actually, it makes perfect sense. Their ancient mythology talks of visitors from the heavens, and these aliens could have been whom they referred to. Whoever carved these symbols worshipped this golden substance."

She pointed to a symbol of a ramp with a ball in the middle. "Look here: this is an Ahket. It represents the horizon from which the sun emerged and disappeared. It's also a representation of the passing of time." She pointed to a cross with an oval on top of it. "And look at this one. It's an ankh, the symbol for eternal life."

The more she talked, the more Weaver believed her. "Yes, but what do they have to do with the golden liquid? What do they mean?"

"If I'm deciphering the inscription correctly, the golden liquid is an extremely volatile energy source, existing outside of time. Perhaps that's why it triggers memories in all of us."

He thought of Snipe falling into the liquid, and of the suspicions Striver had of their father's disappearance. Even though Striver had never spoken to Weaver about it, Weaver knew Striver thought their father's disappearance had something to do with the golden liquid. His heart quickened, eager to learn the truth. "So when people fall into it, where do they go?"

"Another dimension?" She shrugged. "I don't know. I'm not a

philosopher. All I can tell you is what the symbols allude to. They say this substance contains all of time, and simultaneously, it's the exact opposite, existing without the boundaries of time. Outside the ribbon of time itself."

Weaver's head swam with nonsense. "Hold on, where are the beings who carved the symbols now? Why would they just leave it behind?"

Eri pointed to a stick with two branches on either side, pointed up. "This is *Ka*. It means soul or spirit. The ancient Egyptians believed their *Ka* would live on, even after they died."

She followed the symbols around the perimeter of the pool "Now look here." Two-legged beings with strange animal heads stepped onto a platform and disappeared. Above the hieroglyph was that ancient symbol for soul. "I think they stepped into the liquid, hoping they'd live forever in the undoing of time."

Weaver pointed to the liquid. "You're telling me they're in there?"

"Gives you the creeps, doesn't it?"

"No." Weaver shook his head, trying to absorb everything she told him. "This is all very interesting, Eri, but none of it helps us. What can the golden liquid do?"

Eri sat back on her heels and tapped her finger on the last symbol. "I don't know. In my opinion, this substance is too dangerous to mess with. It cuts through the fabric of time and space."

Weaver's stomach churned with this new information, his mind ticking away, mulling over how to use this powerful, dangerous substance for his own purposes. "Can it be contained and controlled?"

"Obviously it's movable." Eri stuck the stick into it and when she pulled it out, the end dripped golden tears on the cavern floor. "But how it reacts with other energy sources, I have no idea."

Weaver's eyes widened, unable to contain his excitement. "Whatever it does, it's powerful stuff."

CHAPTER TWENTY-SEVEN
INEVITABLES

Striver tightened the swamp reeds along the Death Stalker bow he and Weaver had designed. His skin burned, rubbed raw by mending every used bow in the village, but the pain was nothing compared to the hurt twisting inside of him from the betrayal of his brother and the loss of Eri. He shoved the agony back to the deeper part of his soul, blockading his emotions for a later time. A battle loomed, and he had to protect his people first. The two hundred Death Stalkers he'd spread on the floor of the council room seemed like a minuscule lot.

A ruffle of feathers came with the wind. Phoenix appeared as a winged shadow in the doorway. "May I come in?"

"Certainly."

The birdman had been present the day he was born, and every day after that, so it was fitting he'd be there on the day when it would all end. "You can help me distribute the bows."

Phoenix walked by the weapons as if they meant nothing and put his long, clawed fingers over Striver's shoulder. "You are brave to stay and fight."

Striver shrugged. "Brave or stupid. I've evacuated most of the village to the caves. Those who stay and join us do so by free will alone."

Phoenix nodded. "That is why I am here. The Guardians will fight by your side."

Striver stopped weaving the reeds and glanced up at the birdman. "What?"

"The Guardians have always followed you, deterring the Lawless as much as we can."

"But this is different." Striver shook his head. "You can't get involved in anything violent toward another living thing."

Phoenix spread his wing. "Who said we'd be violent? We're just bringing our nets."

Striver sighed with frustration. Phoenix sacrificed too much. "This may be our end, and yours as well. You have more to lose. Humans will take over this planet, whether we win or not, but the Guardians are scarce. Who knows if any other colony ships made it to other planets from your dying home world?"

"We'd like to have a say in which humans we choose to share our planet with." Phoenix tilted his head and his eyes sparkled.

Striver sighed, shaking his head. "We're not going to win, no matter who comes for us."

Phoenix whistled a melody followed by a gentle cooing sound. "You cannot predict the future. Many strands of the tapestry have still yet to be linked for an accurate picture to develop."

Striver collected the first row of bows. "I wish I had your faith."

Phoenix ruffled his feathers. "I wish I had your passion."

Striver paused, glancing back at the Guardian with a questioning look. They never even so much as showed a hint of wanting something that humans had. They could fly, for Refuge's sake! And live for hundreds of years.

"Why? My emotions tear me apart."

"They make you who you are. They give you strength, conviction of purpose."

"You have those already."

"Yes, but mostly through logic. Passion is a powerful driving force. Don't hold your emotions back. Use them to achieve success."

Phoenix's speech stirred determination in Striver's heart. He put a hand on the birdman's wing, feeling the soft features that covered a soul with a hard, iron will. Phoenix was both gentle and strong, a true asset to their colony. "If it will keep you safe, old friend, I'll try my best."

❧❦

They descended the rope ladder to meet the others who'd chosen to stay. The main square was full of villagers. Striver's chest swelled and tightened as he scanned the crowd. So many had come to fight, and he was responsible for every one of their lives. Had he made the right decision?

Riley stood with his bag full of poison-tipped arrows and an apologetic look on his face. Striver approached him carefully, still feeling the sting of the welt on his cheek. "You sure about this?"

"Sure as anything. I want to defend my home."

"What about Riptide? How is she doing?"

"You can ask me that yourself, because I'm right here." Riptide walked into the moonlight from the shadows with camouflage painted across her face, holding a spear. "Although I question your romantic choices, I've never questioned you as a leader."

"Thank you, Riptide." She kept her distance, respecting his space. Maybe someday she'd come to respect whom he'd chosen. If they ever saw Eri again.

I will find her. I have to.

Carven pushed through the crowd and Striver shook his head, raising a hand to hold him back. "Not you, old friend. You have a family to watch over."

Carven smiled a sad smile, adjusting his belt of carving knives he used to prepare the roasted swamp boars. He took Striver's hand in his own. "That's why I'm here."

"We can't win this."

Carven patted him on the back. "Don't count your swillow wisps before they hatch. Besides, we have Mars." He gestured over his shoulder. The burly woman had carved a spiked hammer out of wood and flint blades. Holding the weapon with black streaks painted across her face, she gave Striver a ferocious grin. "She looks like she could eat Lawless for dinner and spit them back out again."

Litus broke through the crowd, checking his wrist locator. "The commander asked me to hold tight for now, but I'm to meet up with her forces if need be."

Striver had grown to trust Litus, and now he relied on him to provide vital information. He reminded himself the man walked a thin line between helping them and staying true to his own people. Striver would not want to stand in Litus's boots. He had his own thin line to walk between saving Eri and protecting his tribe. "When do you expect they'll attack?"

Litus glanced up at the ship in the sky and shrugged. "Anytime."

"How will we know when they move?"

Riptide gasped behind them. Striver followed her gaze to the sky. The ship moved, growing larger with each second. A deep rumbling stirred his gut, making him feel tied to the ship and its fate. The hull broke through the atmosphere, red and orange flames licking at the nose as it barreled down on Lawless lands.

❧❧

Eri watched the swirls of golden liquid eddy around the rim of the pool. Time. Oodles of it, stretching backward and forward into the future. If only she could borrow some, freeze the moment to make a plan. She had to get to Weaver before their time ran out.

Weaver sat by her scribbles in the sand, resting his head in both hands with his elbows propped on his knees. She still had no idea what his plan was, but it didn't look like it was going well.

She could tell the golden liquid made him feel guilty about his past. Which meant there was still hope for him.

Just get right to it. Open the wound and see if he reacts. Get him where it hurts most to wake him up, make him feel again. Eri took in a deep breath. "You know Striver would do anything for you."

Weaver cast her a suspicious glance.

"He saved your life in this very cave. He dragged you all the way back home, and look what you did in return."

Weaver's shoulders rose and fell as he sighed. He didn't look up again. "I don't want to talk about him."

"Fine. We won't talk about him." She kicked her boot against a rock, feigning interest in the etchings. She had other tactics up her sleeve. "You think you're special, that no one else knows your pain." She traced a symbol and blew the dust off the tip of her finger. "I know what it's like to be on the outside, to be the odd one out."

He spat in the sand. "You don't know nothing."

"Don't I?" Anger hardened inside her and she clenched her fists together. "I'm an illegal DNA crossing, a product of a mismatched pairing. Don't tell me I don't know what it feels like to be thought of as inferior my whole damn life."

Weaver sat up, staring at her as if seeing someone else in disguise. Her adrenaline surged. She'd grabbed his attention.

"What do you mean, illegal DNA crossing?"

"Everyone is paired with certain lifemates on the *Heritage*, and each pairing is based on the conditions that will create the strongest genes without inbreeding. When you have such a small DNA pool, you have to be careful." She checked to make sure he was still listening. He watched her like a child finding videos of Old Earth for the first time.

"Well, my parents weren't careful. They fell in love, defied the system, and created me without any genetic engineering at all. Do you know what that does to a person? Thinking everyone else had an advantage, that they were somehow smarter, taller, stronger?"

Weaver exhaled like he had been holding his breath. "Wow, that sucks boar droppings."

"You bet it does." Eri actually felt better getting her feelings off of her chest. Although she'd told Striver, he wouldn't understand like Weaver would. The difference between her and Weaver was how they took it. She overcame her prejudices on Haven 6, whereas he still fought with his. As much as she despised him, she pitied him as well. Now she understood why Striver had fought so vehemently to keep Weaver with them. It must have been hard for Weaver to follow in his brother's footsteps, always falling short. She wanted to help him, bring him back from despair to a place where he could find peace.

Eri pointed her finger at him, then at herself. "We're alike, you and I. I'm trying to find a way to live in Striver's village, and you're trying to find your place here among the Lawless. We're both shedding our previous skins, attempting to live without preconceived notions getting in the way." She walked up to him and whispered under her breath, "Maybe we can help each other?"

Weaver shrugged, a spark of interest in his emerald eyes. "I don't know."

At least it wasn't an absolute "no." Eri placed her hand on his arm, pressing the issue into the wound in his heart. "You owe it to Striver to keep me safe. You know that."

"I owe no one nothing." He pulled his arm away, a flicker of remorse crossing his face.

She was so close. A few more minutes and he'd come around.

Voices echoed from the tunnel connecting to the cavern. Eri snapped her head up. Crusty stood with his bow cocked and ready to fire. "Don't try anything rash, little lady."

How long had the old man been awake? Eri bit down on her lower lip.

Too late. Time's run out.

Weaver rose to his feet beside her. He whispered under his breath, "Don't tell Jolt anything. You open your mouth and we're both dead."

Eri clenched her fists until her nails dug into her skin. Maybe it wasn't Jolt. Just another watchman to replace Crusty.

The first thing she saw was the golden light reflecting off Jolt's white scar, making her insides squirm. The leader entered the cave carrying Tank's gallium crystal void ray. His eyes were wild, his muscles tensed. Sweat glistened in the pockmarks of his face. Behind him, other Lawless men and women carrying her team's lasers filed in. The air crackled with hushed voices, anxiety, and fear.

Crusty lowered his bow. "What's wrong, boss?"

"I'll tell you what's wrong. That mother boar of a ship is coming straight for us, and all we have are a few lasers." His piercing eyes traveled to Eri. "I need to know how the golden liquid works, and I need it now."

Eri stared, frozen with inaction. She had to trust Weaver. *Don't say a thing.*

"Did you figure it out or do I have to blow your hand off?"

"She's got it all decoded, boss." Crusty gave her a wink.

Eri cast a wicked stare toward him. He hadn't been sleeping. He'd listened in the whole time.

Jolt walked across the cave and Eri backed up until she stood beside the golden pool. One step back and she'd be reliving her thirteenth birthday party for all eternity.

His free hand grabbed the front of her shirt and he picked her up until her feet skimmed the floor. "If you send someone into this liquid, can they come back?"

Eri squirmed, the pressure on her chest increasing until she couldn't breathe. "I don't think so."

"Not good enough. Can they come back or not?"

The Egyptians didn't believe in their bodies continuing on forever, only their souls. If you entered the liquid, you lost your physical home and entered another dimension entirely. It was the only way it could work.

She shook her head. "No."

If she were wrong, he wouldn't know it until she was long gone or dead.

His grip tightened, pulling her tunic tighter around her chest. "Does it work with your weapons' capacity?"

"What?"

He shook her until her teeth rattled. "Will it ruin these weapons or make them stronger?"

The liquid could be moved, because she'd seen it drip on the cavern floor. The symbols alluded to an energy source, so it was possible it would react with the gallium crystals in the weapons, intensifying their magnification. Depending on the absorption properties, it could even change the nature of the crystals and make the gun more powerful than she or Jolt could ever imagine.

Eri paused. If she were wrong, Jolt would be a puddle of sludge. But if she were right, he'd have more firepower than anything on the *Heritage*. In one shot, he could make ten men disappear. As much as she didn't like her people invading, she didn't want the Lawless to win.

"It would ruin your weapons, and you'd be lost to the liquid."

Jolt eased her down. "Just what I thought I'd hear."

He turned to the golden pool. Crusty called out from behind them, "Boss, what are you doing?"

"Making sure we win." He dipped the energy sphere of the void ray into the golden liquid and held it there until the chamber filled with golden light. He pulled the weapon from the pool and gave Eri a mean smile, like he'd bested her in a game. "I'm not dead."

She swallowed, backing up. The void ray pulsed with life, buzzing in his hands. "And this weapon still seems to work." He pointed it toward her with a devilish sneer on his face. "You lied."

Weaver stepped beside her. "Jolt, you don't want to do that. She's the only one who can decipher the symbols."

"Who needs the symbols? I never liked directions anyway." Jolt hefted the gun up higher, targeting her forehead. "Besides, I need to try this thing out."

Fear clutched Eri's throat with icy fingers until she fought for air. She hadn't felt so incapacitated since she was a girl scurrying through dark corridors with the ghost of Lynex. *Wait a second! The ghost of Lynex...the alarm saved me before.*

Eri pressed a button on her locater and a high, keening noise brought everyone to their knees. Blocking one ear, she grabbed Weaver's arm. Holding both hands over his ears, he followed her past Jolt. Jolt had dropped his laser gun to cover his ears, and Eri contemplated going after the discarded weapon. But that was the opposite direction of escape, and she'd still have to fight Jolt for it. No, it was better to take advantage of the surprise. Dragging Weaver behind her, she bolted for the tunnel.

Crusty lay across the path to the tunnel, writhing. Eri bent down and tore her laser from his belt.

Laser fire erupted behind them. Jolt had misfired, and the beam of light exploded like shrapnel, cutting through six of his men. In seconds, they were gone. Not even dead. Just gone. Eri pulled herself away and ran. The mouth of the tunnel loomed steps away with stalactites pointing down in jagged teeth.

A high buzzing noise grew as the photon chambers charged. Jolt fired another shot behind her and the stalactites fell from the ceiling. She dove for the darkness of the tunnel as rocks crashed behind her and the wind rushed over her head.

Eri scrambled forward. Her ears rang as she tore through the tunnel, not caring if she swallowed a spidermite on the way out. Sound returned in time, dull and foggy, like she wore thick headphones. She touched her earlobes to make sure they didn't bleed. Her head felt like someone had stuck a pin in each ear and turned it over and over again.

She checked behind her and Weaver followed her through the narrow cavern. He shouted, but all she could hear was ringing in her ears.

"What?"

"What was that noise?"

"Just an alarm," Eri shouted over her shoulder as she jumped over rocks blocking their path and landed in a puddle. Using her locator, she illuminated the narrow space between the rocks ahead.

"Why do I feel like my ears are going to fall off?" This time she heard him more clearly, which was a good sign. It had taken two days to regain her complete hearing after the hide and seek incident.

"The echo in the cave intensified the sound waves." She hadn't thought the alarm would work, but death stared her in the face and she had no other ideas.

"Why did you save me?"

She slipped against the rock and pulled herself back up again, her heart pounding. "Because Jolt's going to kill you, Weaver. I can see it in his eyes."

"What if I deserve to die?"

"No one deserves to die." *Except for Jolt, maybe.* She grabbed Weaver's arm and pulled him forward. "Come on."

The laser fire pinged through the rock behind them. Flashes of light illuminated the cave and sent them into darkness once again. Eri had stored up energy, drinking from a water canteen and stretching her muscles while studying the symbols. She wished she'd thought of the alarm sooner, but then she would have never found out about Jolt's plan with the lasers. *I have to warn Litus and Striver.*

With the weapon upgrade, the Lawless would give the team from the *Heritage* a run for their money. After witnessing their savage civilization, she didn't want the Lawless in charge of Refuge, even if it meant enabling the commander's attack.

As Eri ran from the laser fire, the commander's past flashed through her mind. Eri's short time with the Lawless illuminated the assassination attempt in a new light. The gangs on Old Earth had killed Commander Grier's family. The survivors stole a colony ship and settled at Outpost Omega, and their descendants traveled here. No wonder the commander wanted them all dead.

But they aren't the same people who killed her family. Not all of the people on Refuge are Lawless. Striver is a good person. His village can coexist in harmony with the people from the Heritage. *If only they could be given a chance.*

The commander had to be stopped, and only Eri was sane enough to do it.

She and Weaver broke through into clean air and the vast expanse of star-studded sky. Eri looked over her shoulder. The cavern behind them lay dark and silent.

They ran over the jagged rocks. Eri expected laser fire to erupt at any moment, but she reached the nearest strand of trees unharmed.

"Where are they?" Weaver huffed by her side, peering through the leaves.

Relief spread across Eri's shoulders. Jolt didn't need her and Weaver any longer. Although he'd probably revel in killing them, he had bigger problems on his hands. "They don't have time to pursue us. They need to dip their weapons and meet the others for battle."

"Are your people really invading?"

Eri gave him a cold stare. What else could she say? "Yes."

"Are they going to take over the planet?"

"Most likely. But I have a plan." Eri smiled. "One that had better work more effectively than yours did."

"What are you going to do?"

She put up her arm and started typing into her locator. "I'm going to warn them."

"Will they still attack?"

Eri sighed. "I don't know. I feel like I'm trying to stop a tidal wave from crashing down on all of us."

Litus's face popped up, hovering over her arm. "Eri! Are you okay?"

She slowed down and spoke between gasps of air. "I've escaped. Weaver is with me. I have some bad news."

Nodding gravely, Litus's face hardened. "Bring it on."

"Jolt has upgraded our weapons using the golden liquid in the cave. Anyone who's near the lasers when they go off will disappear to another dimension, never to return."

Litus ran a hand over his mouth. Eri knew she sounded crazy, but there wasn't any other way to explain it.

"You mean, they just disappear?"

"Yes. It has a wide range, too. He misfired and I saw it take out six of Jolt's men."

Litus rubbed his temple with his free hand. "This will make the Lawless harder to beat."

"You're telling me."

"I'll notify the commander." He moved to turn their communication link off.

Eri held her locator screen up to her nose. "Litus!"

"What?"

"I just saw one of our guns work with the liquid. I don't think the people on the *Heritage* will win this."

Litus didn't seem to believe her. "I'll take care of it, Eri. I'm sending your coordinates to a rescue team. When they hit down, they're coming right after you. We're going to get you out of there."

"Tell the team not to come out. Tell them all to stay inside the

Heritage."

"I can't stop our commander's orders." Litus's shoulders rose and fell. "I can only help our people myself."

"What do you mean by that? Are you going to fight as well?" Eri slammed her palm to her forehead. Her plan had backfired. "Litus, no!"

The transmission clicked off.

She tried reestablishing the link, but he was already busy hailing the commander. "Dammit!"

Weaver stood patiently by her side. "What are you going to do now?"

"Plan B. I'm going back to the ship to stop the commander myself."

Weaver rubbed sweat from his forehead, giving her an incredulous look. "How are you going to do that?"

Eri reached down to his belt and took her laser back. "Serious negotiations."

CHAPTER TWENTY-EIGHT
CONVERGENCE

Striver's heart broke as Litus switched off the locator.

She's still alive. She's safe. She escaped. And she's with Weaver.

The last part caused a current of unease to sting his gut, but she seemed to be in Weaver's company by choice, so maybe they'd worked something out. Maybe Weaver had changed his mind and saved her? Who knew the depths of his brother's heart?

The second part of the conversation gripped Striver's stomach and twisted. He'd spent his life keeping technology from the lawless, and now they faced the one evil he'd worked so hard to avoid. "Why did you shut her off?"

"I have to notify the commander immediately." Ducking underneath a branch, Litus left just as Commander Grier's alto voice rang out from his arm. For the first time, Striver wished he had his own locator to talk to Eri. *To think, I used to hate technology.*

"Did you hear?" Carven tugged on his sleeve. "The Lawless may have the advantage."

"Yes, but do we really want them to win?" Striver watched the trees for Litus's return. He raised his voice so everyone in the main square could hear. "Think about it. The Lawless would surely kill us if they won, but if we help these visitors, they would owe us their lives. I can't imagine such a well-developed culture going against a life debt."

"You want us to fight their war?" Riley crossed his arms. "Because of Eri?"

"It has nothing to do with Eri." He put his fist up to his chest. "It's our war as well. We've allowed the Lawless to amass over hundreds of years, threatening our own village. Now, we have a chance to make a difference. If we go with Litus and fight by his side, we have a chance to prove ourselves. If we let them die at the hands of the Lawless, the savages will not be as forgiving. Especially if they steal the visitors' technology. They'll blow us to bits."

"Who's to say the visitors won't turn on us once the Lawless are taken care of?" Riptide tilted her head, her blue gaze catching the moon's light.

"Because Litus and Eri won't let that happen."

"I won't either." Mars stood at the back, swinging her new weapon. "You've got my vote."

"As much as I *love* Eri"—Riptide rolled her eyes—"what if she can't convince her people to accept us?"

Striver shrugged. "It's a chance we'll have to take."

"I still don't trust them," Riley murmured as he shook his head. His gaze flicked to Mars sharpening her weapon. "Eri's sweet, but she has her own job to protect. If it came down to it, do you think she'd give up everything she has to save us?"

The certainty rose up inside Striver, giving him courage. "I know she will."

Riley's voice fell to a whisper. "And what about Litus? He has more power than she does."

"Litus is a good man and he'll do the right thing. If not out of love, then out of moral responsibility." Striver turned to the crowd. Most of them were already listening. "Hear me out."

He leapt on top of a stump so everyone could see him. "I'm going with Litus to the battle, and if anyone wants to come with me, you are welcome. If you want to go to the caves with the others, then so be it. I won't stop you. Those weapons sound powerful, and you may not make it back."

As Striver spoke his final words, Litus stepped from the forest. "I've spoken with the commander. The attack is on as planned. She underestimates their abilities, I'm sure of it. That's why I'm leaving to help my people."

"I know." Striver adjusted his bow on his shoulder. "I'm going with you. We've fought the Lawless for centuries. They are as much our burden as they are yours."

"You can count me in." Carven nodded his head, his hand resting on the hilt of one of his knives. "I've wanted to give those pirates some of my own medicine for years."

"Me, too." Riptide held up her spear. "Riley and I are both in."

"I'm with you, too." Mars stood and the spikes on her weapon shined in the moonlight.

A low thunder drew Striver's attention. Whispers and questions filled the air and he raised his hand to calm them down. "Listen."

The sound grew louder until it roared in his ears. A screeching noise keened above the din, and the earth rumbled underneath their feet. Striver clung to a tree trunk, helping Carven stay upright while others fell to the ground. His teeth rattled and the leaves on the trees shook like nervous observers. The booming earthquake stopped suddenly, and the cries of startled swillow wisps filled the night.

Above them, the sky was clear except for a V-shaped congregation of arcs sailing in the direction of the crash. "Look, the Guardians!" Striver pointed to the sky, hoping the site would bring courage to his people.

෴

Weaver gripped a spongewood tree as the ground shook like the planet tore apart underneath them. *They are planning to take over.* Anxiety shot through Weaver's legs. "Was that what I thought it was?"

Eri hadn't been as quick to respond. She'd fallen to her knees in swamp muck. "I'm not sure what you thought, but that, most definitely, was my colony ship."

"Why the hell would the entire ship land, and right in the middle of the enemy territory?"

Eri stood up and wiped off the brunt of the mud. "We're not a warship; we're a colony vessel. The ship is not equipped with weapons. Besides, she doesn't want to nuke the planet and destroy our new home. She'd rather take the Lawless out gorilla style and keep the environment intact as much as possible. If Commander Grier wants a fight, she's got to come to them."

All this talk of war made Weaver anxious. They needed to cut through the battle and reach to the ship before a victor emerged. The best time to take control was during a period of flux. "Come on." He offered his hand.

"I can walk on my own." Eri cast him a warning and he dropped his hand to his side like a dead trotter on a string. He had to admit, the more he got to know her, the more he liked her. He could see why she'd caught Striver's attention. As much as Riptide was gorgeous, Eri was clever, vibrant, and spunky. She fit Striver's personality like pearl berries with pie.

And I stole her away.

Guilt dripped down his throat until he could hardly swallow. Somehow he had to make it right. He'd lost his control of the golden liquid and he'd betrayed the one person on Refuge who still believed in him. His only chance lay in seizing the ship from the commander. He'd control everything: the technology, the team attacking, Striver's village, and the Lawless. He'd be the most powerful man on Refuge. Then he could make the world what he wanted it to be.

"Why are you coming with me?" Eri's eyebrow rose in suspicion as she wiped off her knees.

He shrugged. "I don't want the Lawless to win, either."

She narrowed her eyes. "Who do you want to win, then?"

Weaver glanced down at the ferns brushing against his legs. *Me.*

"I thought so." Eri trudged ahead.

Could she hear his inner thoughts? "You thought what?"

"You can't pick a side."

"That's not true. I could pick if I had to."

"Really? Or can you only think about yourself?" She stopped and turned toward him. "Wake up, Weaver, and smell the swamp sludge. There's something happening that's bigger than all of us, and we have to fight for what we believe."

She spun around, turning her back to him, and sloshed ahead. Weaver followed her, speechless. He didn't know what he believed. He hadn't taken the time to really think about it. He'd been too involved in his own woes. *Eri was right. I am selfish.* Now he had a new emotion to add to the already miserable bunch: shame.

She kicked a clump of moss and mud from the toe of her boot. "You're no less than Striver, just as I'm no less than any of those genetically planned people on the *Heritage*. The only thing holding you back is self-doubt."

"Self-doubt is the story of my life, but I didn't give it to myself, those around me —"

"Stop blaming them." Eri's voice came out harsh and she turned and gave him an apologetic look. "When you start taking responsibility for yourself, you'll control your own destiny. It happened to me. I used to let all those people on that ship tell me who I was, what I did for a job, and how I couldn't have a lifemate."

She snorted in disgust. "Once I stopped listening to them, I found myself, and I found Striver."

The mention of Striver made a hole ache in his gut. Here he was with his brother's love. Striver didn't deserve this.

Eri walked toward him and put a reassuring hand on his shoulder. "I believe in you, Weaver. I think you can figure things out and do the right thing."

Lasers pinged through the trees. They ducked, listening to the direction of the fire. Eri whispered, "We're close."

She moved, but Weaver caught her arm. "Don't go in too fast. They'll think you're one of the Lawless."

Eri held up her arm, showing her locator. "I have this."

"What if they don't see it until they've shot you dead?"

"I know my own people. I'll be careful."

They inched closer to the laser fire. Weaver realized if he wanted to take responsibility for something, he should start with Eri. He was the one who'd taken her out here, putting her in danger. "Wait. I know a better way."

She creased her eyebrows in suspicion. "We don't have much time."

"You won't have any time if you get yourself killed. Now come on."

They backtracked into the forest. He led her up an incline to a ridge where the battle sprawled below them in all directions.

The *Heritage* cut into the ground, leaving a path of destruction in its wake. All of the trees a mile around had collapsed or burned to ash. The earth steamed, smoke rising in strings to the twilight sky. Bush fires illuminated the clearing in a molten red light. Bodies lay everywhere, bent and curled up, some on their backs staring blankly at the sky. Lawless fired at the belly of the ship where members of the attack team pushed toward the jungle. To Weaver, it looked like pandemonium at the end of the world.

Eri pointed to her people spreading in a semicircle from a ramp connected to the ship. "Look! Their uniforms blend with the foliage much better than mine had, and they're wearing helmets and vests that repel the arrows. Litus advised them well." Pride filled her voice.

"Maybe they won't have such a hard time fighting the Lawless?"

A deeper buzzing sound came from the forest and a stream of golden light shot out, spreading in all directions as it spiraled through the air. The first row of men spun into particles of swirly light and disappeared.

"Holy Refuge."

"Jolt." Eri uttered his name as if the man were an inevitable evil. She wiped sweat from her forehead, her jaw tense.

Just as Jolt's forces pushed ahead, Guardians dove through the sky, dropping nets to slow them. Weaver clenched his fists as anxiety crept up his spine. It wouldn't be enough. Unlike the Lawless's usual bows and spears, the lasers could fire through the netting, so even if they lay tangled, they could still cause damage.

"We have to help them." Eri tugged on his sleeve. "Or Jolt will make them all disappear."

War cries rang out from the east. Another force emerged from the forest. At first Weaver thought it was more Lawless, then his heart clenched in recognition. Striver led others from his village into the thick of the battle. Carven and Riley followed him, and behind them, Riptide ran with a spear.

Not her. Anyone but her.

Weaver leapt up, adrenaline spiraling through his limbs. "Let's go."

Eri nodded and scrambled to her feet. She whipped out her laser and input the code. Her eyes shone with fierce determination as the gun buzzed to life. "I'm ready."

CHAPTER TWENTY-NINE
RESPONSIBILITY

Striver bellowed a war cry as he led his team into the pandemonium of lasers, arrows, and death. Fires crackled around them, casting faces in a hellish glow. The air stank of smoke, scorched leaves, and blood. The soles of his feet burned as he crossed the charred ground to ambush the Lawless from the side. His heart coiled like a tight fist. This was the end-all to centuries of war. *Do or die.*

Ash stinging his tongue and throat, he turned to Carven and Riley running beside him. "Take out the Lawless men with the lasers. One by one."

Adrenaline surged through his body. He'd waited his entire life for this moment, his chance to face the Lawless and ensure the safety of his village. They'd had skirmishes in the past, but this battle encompassed the brunt of both their forces. Without the attackers on the *Heritage* to even out the odds, their dwindling army could only hide behind their crumbling wall.

"Over there!" Riptide pointed to a man shooting golden light from a high-tech gun. The front line of colonists disappeared like dust in the wind. Striver slowed, stretching his arms to hold his army back.

"Holy Refuge!" Carven wiped his forehead. "The men. They're gone."

Eri had warned them. Still, seeing men reduced to thin air stole his breath away. Striver turned to Carven. "Can we beat this?"

"We have to." Carven tightened his fingers around his bow.

Striver scanned the battlefield. "Not from a direct assault. We'll have to break into teams and distract them."

Carven nodded. "Riley and I will sneak up from the back and clear you a path. We'll meet in the center."

Striver put a hand on Carven's shoulder. "Be careful."

"It's not me you need to worry about." Carven winked and took off into the forest.

Riley nodded at Striver. At least they were civil enough to fight together. "Look after my sister."

"I will." Striver checked the rest of his team. Litus and Mars ran down by the ramp, rejoining their team. Hopefully they could merge their forces in the middle. Fighters from his village waited on his command. They'd follow him to the end of Refuge, if they weren't already there.

"I'm going to take him down." Riptide tightened her grip on her spear.

"Wait for the group," Striver shouted, but Riptide had already run out of earshot. *Dammit!*

He circled past a clump of Lawless releasing arrows at the ship's hull. The Lawless on the edge of the fight turned in their direction and shouted warning cries to their friends.

That's it. We've been spotted.

Was it enough of a head start to get close to the men with lasers? *It has to be.*

Arrows whizzed by Striver's head, and he ducked as he ran. He had to reach Riptide in time to cover her assault. Carven and Riley had disappeared in the chaos.

A man with a green-painted face and leaves threaded through his hair jumped in Riptide's path. He brandished his flint blade and grinned, exposing yellow teeth. As he ran at her, Riptide brought her arm back and threw her spear. The weapon sailed in an arc and landed in the man's chest. He crumpled to the ground face-first. More Lawless surrounded her, blocking her path from the targeted gun.

Striver raised his bow and sent twin sailing arrows in two different directions. Two attackers fell before reaching Riptide, giving her time to reclaim her spear. A third man threw a blade at her throat. She ducked and lunged with her spear as Striver reached for another arrow.

Riptide was too close to the Lawless man, giving Striver no choice but to put his bow down. He sprinted forward, hoping to reach her before more Lawless crowded around them. Heart pumping on overdrive, he watched the man grip her spear and try to yank it from her hands. Riptide screamed, pulling the spear toward her chest. Still gripping the spear, the man pushed her back.

"Riptide!" Striver threw himself forward through ash and embers. "I'm coming!"

The attacker tossed Riptide into a stand of ferns that had somehow survived the crash. He jumped in after her. All Striver could see was the palms shaking as they moved.

Striver leapt over a dead colonist's body and slid down an incline. *Weaver would never forgive me.* Somehow, even though his brother had betrayed him and stolen his own love, he still couldn't bear to fail him.

When he reached them, the man lay on top of Riptide, lifeless. Shock stung Striver's gut. Had they killed each other?

He pulled the body off her. Riptide opened her eyes and grinned. She held her cooking knife, the end bloodied.

"I don't think he'll go with your famous boar roast stew." Striver offered his hand and she gripped it. He pulled her up.

She smiled, and her white teeth shone wild in the firelight. "I guess I'll have to keep looking, then."

Carven and Riley had cleared a path to one of the Lawless men equipped with a laser gun. Striver retrieved his bow and nodded at Riptide and they ran toward the gun before the Lawless man turned the barrel on them.

A woman clothed in leaves turned, eyes widening. "Techno hoarders! Take them out!"

The man with the laser gun quirked his head and whirled in their direction, vines flying around him as his disguise came apart.

"We're not going to make it!" Riptide shrieked as she ran.

"Oh, yes we are." Striver still had the arrow he'd drawn before. He slid to a halt and brought up his bow. As the barrel of the laser zeroed in, he focused on the hand attached to the trigger.

One shot, that's all I need.

Taking a deep breath, Striver released the arrow, and it soared across the battlefield, severing the man's finger when it reached its target. He screamed, dropping the laser. Golden light shot into the sky, dissipating as the laser hit the ground.

Riptide had reached throwing distance of her spear. Not wasting a second, she pulled her arm back, muscles bunching, and let the weapon sail. The shaft pierced through the Lawless man's neck, and he went down, holding his own blood in his hands.

Carven and Riley reached the gun and disabled it, pulling the energy cell from the back and emptying the golden liquid until it seeped into the earth. Striver breathed a sigh of relief, but his reprise was short lived.

One down, nineteen more to go.

❦

Eri followed Weaver, scrutinizing every step he took with a skeptical eye. Deep down in the secret recesses of his heart, he had some amount of good, yet she still doubted his shifty intentions. Why would he help her after throwing her to the Lawless like he didn't care whether she lived or died?

Unless she had something he wanted.

The ship. Of course. He wants access to the ship.

The sickening truth soured her stomach. If it came down to it, she'd be forced to fight him. No way could he gain control of the *Heritage*. She bit her lip, hoping that time would never come. For now, he was the only ally she had by her side.

They emerged on the southern side of the battle, just underneath the *Heritage*'s right wing. Eri and Weaver snuck underneath the metallic frame, hiding in its shadow. Eri ran her fingers over the metal. She'd lived her whole life inside that frame. Although the ship took up a large patch of what had been dense jungle, it looked insignificant compared to the wild world of Haven 6.

Laser fire pinged around them and they ducked instinctively, although no one fired at them. *Yet.* The one thing the colonists had in their favor was the Lawless's inexperience with lasers. Their aim was as good as their manners.

"Over there." Eri pointed to the ramp. "I need to enter the ship through that hatch." She had to slip through the guards and confront the commander—alone.

"All right, all right. I'm thinking." Weaver rubbed his chin, eyes skittering across the battlefield.

Eri tried to follow his gaze, but the chaos was thick and ever changing. *What's he looking for?*

Jolt and his team of laser-wielding Lawless had pushed ahead, meters from the ramp. Eri counted eleven lasers besides Jolt's. Pride swelled in her chest. Striver and his group must have taken some of them down.

Colonists fired lasers from inside the ship. If Jolt reached the ramp, they wouldn't be safe for long.

"We have to distract Jolt." Eri shook her head. "If he sees me run for the ship, he'll fire."

"Look! There's Striver." Weaver pointed to the far side of the battle, where Striver and a team from his village picked off the laser-wielding men from the back.

Relief coursed through her. Striver was still alive and fighting, but he had no chance against the commander's blind rage. She had to reach her, stop her from giving the Delta Slip order. "We can't wait for them. We won't make it in time. Once Jolt gets to the ship, he'll be unstoppable." Eri suddenly felt protective. *Aquaria is in there.*

"What do you want me to do? I have no weapons besides my bow."

Eri shrugged. She wasn't about to hand over her only laser. "If we don't do something now, the battle is lost."

"Doesn't your ship have more firepower?"

"Like I said before, it's a colony ship, not a galactic battle cruiser. We didn't come to fight a war."

Weaver spread his hands out over the battlefield. "Could have fooled me."

Eri pulled on her hair. They were wasting time bickering like children. She moved out of the shadows. "I'm going by myself. You don't have to help me." She checked her laser, making sure the weapon buzzed with a charge.

"Yes, I do," Weaver stated coolly, adjusting the bow on his back and pulling out a handful of arrows.

"What?" Eri choked like she'd swallowed a bug. That was the last thing she expected form his mouth. "Why?"

"I can't stand seeing Riptide and Striver out there, sacrificing their lives. This is all my fault. I figured out the code to those weapons, I unleashed the golden pool's power. I owe it to you, to Striver, and to every damned person in that village I betrayed."

He pulled out the longest arrow from the bunch and smoothed the feathers in the back. Eri could only stare. She'd never seen his eyes like this, deep and full of emotion, remorse.

He gave her a soulful glance. "Tell Striver I'm sorry."

A blast hit the hull above them and sparks rained down. Eri covered her head to keep her hair from lighting on fire. When she looked up again, she stood alone.

Weaver ran into the thick of battle, heading straight for Jolt.

She covered her mouth with her hand, fingers digging into her cheek. *It's a death mission.*

Lawless swarmed him like flies on a piece of meat. He deflected the first couple with arrows, but as he ran closer, he had to bludgeon them with his bow. The bowstrings snapped as he whipped the weapon into a man's neck. Another ran at him from the other side holding an obsidian blade. Weaver raised his bow against the man's arm and the wood cracked in two.

Eri snapped out of her trance. Weaver was doing this for her. This was her diversion.

Get moving!

She sprinted around the main conflict and ran toward the ramp. Colonists raised their lasers as she approached. "Eridani Smith: Lifer 39723. Don't shoot." She held up her arm with the locator, shining the fluorescent green light. Personal body energies and heart rhythms controlled each locator. If her locator shined, then she was the real deal.

The colonists held their fire. A man Eri had seen before at Aquaria's pairing ceremony stepped forward. "We have orders to take you back to the ship."

"I know. I can go by myself." Eri pushed through the front line before he could argue. The last thing she needed was an escort to keep her from visiting the commander.

She climbed the ramp, but a gut-twisting feeling turned her

around before she reached the hatch.

Weaver brought up his ruined bow and hit Jolt's arm as the man fired at another bunch of colonists. The golden light sprawled into the night sky, but Jolt didn't lose hold of the gun. He recovered quickly, turning in Weaver's direction.

"Weaver, no!" Eri screamed her lungs raw, but no one could hear her over the din of shouts and lasers.

Jolt's face twisted into rage as he mouthed Weaver's name, spittle flying. He brought his laser up, spraying golden light in an arc. The trail took out everyone around him, including Crusty and others in his Lawless army. Weaver ducked and rolled, and the light skimmed the hairs on his head before swirling away. Bare land surrounded him as everyone within a meter of Jolt disappeared. Weaver scrambled up and launched himself in Jolt's direction.

Eri froze, paralyzed. *I wish I'd given him my gun.*

With Weaver's bow broken, running at Jolt was his only chance, but he'd rolled farther away to avoid the golden light. Jolt glanced in Weaver's direction as his arm moved to fire the gun again.

No one could run that fast. Her whole body shook with the truth.

He's not going to make it.

CHAPTER THIRTY

VENGEANCE

Jolt squeezed the trigger. Striver had to shoot now. He brought the arrow back so far some of the reeds broke, aimed the tip up, and released it within half a second. The shaft glided through the air. The speed was fast, and the arc was high, but not high enough. The arrow landed half a meter from Jolt's feet.

"Noooooo!" Striver bellowed as the light encompassed Weaver. His brother's face glowed like some golden god before he blurred into swirling particles and disappeared.

Striver's world shattered.

He collapsed to the ground with the battle still raging on all sides. His heart folded in on itself, so tightly he couldn't breathe. He'd failed his brother for the last time.

Shock incapacitated him as ash rained from the sky, blurring his eyes. In a world of heat and flame, Striver thought of the river's icy touch when he'd found his brother's hand. He'd pulled him up through the current. He'd saved him. This time he was too late.

Weaver's words rushed back at him like knives in his throat: *You can't make the world perfect.*

Yes, but I can make it a better place. Anger coursed through Striver as he dug his fingers into the steaming ash. *Jolt.* This was Jolt's fault.

Striver pulled himself together and stood up, yanking out another arrow. Jolt had alienated himself from the rest of the battle by blasting his cohorts into the unknown. He was unprotected. Growling in anger, Striver barreled toward him with one purpose in mind.

Jolt turned in his direction. Recognition lit his features as he raised his gun. The end of the barrel shone red, reflecting the flames around them.

Striver had reached firing range. He slowed and released an arrow just as Jolt pulled the trigger. A current of air rushed around him as Striver dove for the ground. The golden light tickled the hairs on his arms, missing him by millimeters. For a brief second, a gentle finger of placid peace brushed his hair, quenching the pain in his heart. Striver yearned to reach out and pull that feeling back, to live in it forever.

Jolt's voice brought him back to reality. "I'll send you where I sent your brother." The pirate aimed the gun at him and grinned.

Hand shaking, Striver reached for another shot. The gun needed seconds to recharge, and Striver only needed half a second to pull the bow back and release his own powerful weapon. Aiming for Jolt's heart, he sent the shaft ripping through the air.

Living in the Lawless lands his whole life had given Jolt the reaction time needed to step sideways before the tip hit. The arrow slipped by, slicing through the leafy covering of his shirt. A thin streak of blood blossomed on his bare chest.

He chuckled as if they tossed a ball back and forth. "Let's play another round."

Golden light exploded from the barrel, and Striver covered his head, closed his eyes, and rolled backward into a dip in the earth. The golden current passed over him again, calling to him like a song from his childhood. Despite all his good sense, he opened his eyes. The golden swirls moved over him, dancing in the wind before coalescing into an image. A face. But not just any face; it was his father's long nose and high forehead.

Striver's eyelids fluttered shut, blocking it out.

Soren's tale was right. The golden liquid brings back your past.

But right now he wanted to live in the present to give Jolt what he deserved. Striver lay closer than Weaver had, and he'd counted how long the gun took to charge. He had three seconds to make it.

Striver stood and Jolt's gun buzzed. *One.*

He sprinted toward Jolt, kicking up ash. *Two.*

Jolt's face hardened into a frown, and he tried the trigger, but the chamber hadn't reenergized and nothing happened. Striver rammed into him, knocking them both to the ground. *Three.*

Striver landed on top of Jolt's hard chest, knocking the air out of his lungs. He grabbed Jolt's neck with one hand, while the other bashed the pirate's wrist into a rock, trying to loosen the gun from his grip. Jolt's face reddened as he reached for Striver's neck. He gripped Striver's shirt, and the pirate yanked him down. Striver had braced his legs against the ground, and it kept his balance. He smashed Jolt's wrist into the rock again and the gun fell from his fingers. Striver kicked it into the flames, making sure that's where it stayed.

When Striver looked back, Jolt's fist smashed into his face, knocking him over. Striver blinked, sucking in ash as pain exploded in his jaw. Jolt squirmed out from under him and stood, looking for the gun. Forcing himself up through the pounding pain in his head, Striver scrambled toward Jolt. His fingers slipped down Jolt's leg and grabbed hold of his pants cuff.

Striver jerked him back. "We're not done."

Jolt whirled around and snarled, the scar on his forehead pulsing with life. His pockmarked face gleamed in the firelight. "You're stronger than your brother. I wish you'd come over to my side instead of him."

Comparing him to Weaver sent Striver over the edge. He yanked so hard, Jolt's knee gave out, and the pirate tumbled on top of him. They rolled in the steaming ash, Jolt punching and kicking. Striver caught Jolt's leg as it came up to his stomach. He spoke through gritted teeth. "My brother was a good man."

Jolt laughed and ripped his leg from Striver's grasp. "Your brother failed."

Anger flowed like molten lava in Striver's chest. This man had led attacks against his village since Striver was a young boy. He'd ruled the Lawless like a greedy dictator, and now he'd taken Weaver away. In Striver's book, that was one bad move too many.

Striver and Jolt pitched down a hill toward one of the larger fires. Jolt wrestled his way on top, and his hands closed on Striver's throat. Striver pulled at Jolt's wrists and the pirate tightened his grip. The fire danced in Jolt's dark gaze as the corners of his lips curved up.

"Now you'll die, too."

Striver struggled to suck in air as he spoke in a raspy voice. "This one's for Weaver." He turned his body sideways, pulling Jolt into the fire beside them. The hot flames seared Striver's face as they licked up Jolt's back. Jolt screamed and released Striver's neck. Striver turned away from the fire as the pirate squirmed and rolled, trying to put the blaze out. The dead leaves he'd threaded in his clothes for camouflage fed the flames as the fire spread throughout his body.

Jolt's dying screams did not satiate Striver's pain; they only added to the horror of the battle surrounding him. Emptiness sucked a hole in his chest. Refuge seemed like a smaller, more barren place without his brother. He could kill as many Lawless as he wanted, but none of them would bring Weaver back.

☙❧

Eri pulled herself together and trudged up the ramp. Weaver had given his life for her to make it, and the least she could do was try.

Tears streaked her face as she bolted through the familiar corridors and buzzed an elevator. She gasped back a sob, trying to calm herself enough to speak with the commander as a person and not a blubbering mess.

How am I ever going to tell Striver?

Weaver's death was her fault. She was the one who'd lectured him about responsibility, playing the guilt card. She was the one who needed the diversion.

The elevator beeped and the doors parted to an empty corridor.

Where is everyone?

Fighting outside in the battle or locked in their rooms hoping for the best? At least, that's what she needed, because someone had to help her gain access to the commander.

Eri shot down the corridor and buzzed the door panel, bouncing on her tiptoes as she waited for a response. Aquaria's face flashed on the screen, her eyes widening. "Eri? Is it really you?"

The sight of her sister brought her comfort she'd not had in a long time. She soaked it up, collapsing against the screen. "I need your help."

Aquaria rushed off screen to press the panel. "Of course. Come in."

The door dematerialized, and Eri collapsed into her sister's arms. Aquaria smelled like soap and perfume, all the luxuries Eri had left behind. Those smells used to be so natural to Eri, but compared to the scent of real blossoms they seemed fake, one dimensional, and derivative.

Aquaria held her close, squeezing all the air out of her lungs. "I thought I'd never see you again."

"The commander blocked my communications, so I had no way—"

Aquaria smoothed over Eri's hair. "I know, I know. Litus told me."

"You know everything going on?"

"Litus has kept me informed since you rescued him."

Eri breathed a sigh of relief. This wouldn't take as long as she thought.

Aquaria looked her up and down. "What are you wearing? You look as though you've been trampling in the jungle all this time."

Brushing dirt off her crudely knit clothes, Eri shrugged. "I have."

"Look at all the scratches on your arms, and your boots are torn up beyond repair. What's this? A leaf in your hair! Come, sit on the couch. I'll get you some water and antiseptic spray."

"I don't have time." Eri slumped onto the couch. It wouldn't be long before someone emerged the victor outside the ship. But she had to take her time convincing Aquaria to help her break into the commander's control deck. She still didn't know how deeply her sister's rebellious streak ran, and she couldn't have Aquaria turning her in.

Her legs ached and her cheeks burned from the flames outside. She hoped Striver was all right.

The plastic felt oddly sterile against her skin after sleeping on fern beds and the ground of Haven 6. She felt like wherever she touched, she smeared dirt. The room looked as though Aquaria hadn't changed anything since the last time Eri visited. The same holopainting of daises undulated on the wall, and the plastic couch had a shiny green gleam. It was a dream in a chaotic world.

"Nonsense." Aquaria rushed back in with a bottle of mineral water and a soywafer. Eri chugged the water and threw the wafer on a side table. As Eri gulped, Aquaria sprayed her arm and rubbed it down. "Litus has changed so much since you first landed. And I owe it to you, Eri. You're the one who saved him from the Lawless. You opened his eyes."

"You know about our conversations?"

She nodded, folding her hands in her lap. "Litus told me

everything. How you bravely went back into the Lawless lands to save him and how you taught him to question what's truly right for us as a colony."

Eri wiped water from her chin. The last time she'd had anything to drink was in the cave, several hours ago. "He loves you."

Aquaria nodded. "When he left, I was glad he was gone. I ignored his messages when you'd landed. But as the days went by, I missed him. After you rescued him and he finally wrote again, I was so relieved. We've been talking through our locators every night."

Eri grabbed her hand, time pressing in. "You have to help me if you want him to be safe."

"Why? What's going on?"

"The people who rescued us are fighting alongside Litus and his team, helping them beat the Lawless. But the commander plans to turn on them once the Lawless are defeated. She doesn't want our two societies mixing. Litus will be stuck in the middle. He won't stand for the mass annihilation, and there's a chance he'll be labeled for treason and killed with them." Eri felt the weight of the world on her chest. So much of it was her fault. She'd convinced Litus to take her side.

"Oh Eri, how can I help?"

Eri's thoughts flitted a kilometer a minute, and she had to calm them down to form coherent sentences. "First of all, I'll need a toothbrush and a small makeup mirror."

Aquaria rolled her eyes. "That's easy. What's the hard part?"

Eri breathed deeply. If Aquaria didn't agree with her, she may have to fight her own sister. "I'm going to talk to the commander. If she doesn't bend…" Eri touched her laser. "I'll take over command of the ship myself." She paused, gauging her sister's reaction.

Aquaria looked as though she'd swallowed a large, bitter pill. Then she breathed deeply, nodding her head and glancing at the daisies before her gaze returned to Eri. "I'm going with you."

CHAPTER THIRTY-ONE

ETERNITY

Blinding light.

Weightlessness.

Profound, all-encompassing peace.

Weaver's eyelids fluttered open. The river coursed beside him, water cresting around the rocks, spitting puddles of white foam. The rapids used to grip him with fear, but today he calmly teetering over the banks. The spray had lost its icy touch, and the rocks were solid and level under his feet. The sunlight cast everything in a haze, and the world seemed muted, as if it were finally at peace.

A fishing rod lay on the rock beside him, the dark lumber contrasting with the gray stone. Weaver bent down and ran his fingers over the smoothed wood. A silver grubber dangled at the end on a hook, thousands of legs wiggling in the air. Recognition hit him like a splash in the face. *This is my rod; the one I'd lost that day when I tumbled into the freezing water.*

Holding the lost rod in his hands gave him a sense of completion, like he'd found the one item that had been missing his whole life. *Silly, it's just a branch with a grubber at the end.*

A trotter leaped from the rapids, gleaming silver-pink in the sunlight before plunging to the pool below. Today was a good day for fishing. The slight angle of the sun and the chill on his arms assured him trotter season was in full swing. The waters were probably littered with throngs of fat specimens as they swam toward the breeding grounds in the lower plateau south of his village.

But he never went fishing alone. Where was Striver? A current of unease shot through his gut. He'd been involved in something before this. Something important. Striver had been there.

A high-pitched whistle echoed from upstream, distracting him. The call of a swillow wisp, sweeter than any sound he'd ever heard. Thinking about roasted wing made his stomach gurgle. Maybe he'd set a trap instead of fishing. Clutching the rod, Weaver jumped from rock to rock upstream.

The swillow wisp gazed at him with a skeptical black eye and launched into the canopy.

Where there's one, there's more. Weaver scanned the banks for swamp reeds to tie into a trap. The rocks he stood on were bare, but a thicket of reeds sprouted farther upstream. Weaver leapt distances he'd never broached in the past. His legs stretched longer, and he landed with ease. Wiping his dry forehead, he glanced at his shirt. No sweat. A trek upriver like that would have surely, in the least, quickened his heart. But today the muscle beat steady and calm. He bent down to pull the tough casings from the reeds and they slipped off effortlessly in his fingers.

It felt good to be doing something he was familiar with, unlike whatever or wherever he'd just come from. He thought he'd smelled fire and ash only a moment ago, but the sweet lily pad blossoms overpowered any scent from his memories. Had there been a fire?

Low humming rode the wind. Weaver mouthed the words to the tune.

Gentle, silent breeze
Lift me up
Where stars twinkle in the night.

Where no walls divide
Or laws abide
Where no one needs to hide.

Gentle, silent breeze
Lift me up
Where my heart reigns free

Only then will I see
How to live in harmony
And be who I'm meant to be.

The song eased the worries prowling in the back of his mind. The humming grew fainter and Weaver shot up, dropping the reeds on the rocks below.

He followed the tune farther upstream to the foothills of the mountains. The trees grew dense, and the river widened until he knew he couldn't swim to the opposite bank. What did it matter? The wall was on the other side. *No one wants to go behind the wall, do they?*

A silhouette stood farther up the riverbank, a tall man casting a lure with a fishing rod of his own. Weaver ran, and the warm wind pushed him along. The man turned and blinked as if he wasn't expecting to see another soul on that bank with him. Weaver froze, paralyzed by disbelief and hope.

"Father?"

The man stepped toward Weaver, placed his rod in a crevice between the rocks, and rubbed his thumb over the stubble on his son's cheek. Searching Weaver's features as if he didn't recognize him, his father whispered, "You've grown so much."

All these years, and his father stood not a minute older than the day he disappeared, with no apparent injuries to hold him back. Weaver felt betrayed. "Where have you been?"

"Wandering." He spread his hands over the river expanse.

Wandering? What kind of an answer is that? Weaver's jaw tightened in anger. "While you've been fishing, Striver and I had to grow up on our own. Mom got sick, and you weren't there."

His father narrowed his eyes, like Weaver spoke in riddles. "I've only just set out a while back."

"A while back? You mean ten years back." Weaver felt a mixture of wanting to put his arms around the man and hug him and wanting to shake some sense into him.

"Funny you speak of years, Weave." Dad spread his hands out before him. "I'm not a day older than when I left."

Weaver's shoulders tingled as he realized what should have been apparent from the start. "You're right."

His father put a hand on his shoulder. "Sit down, catch your breath. It looks as though you've been running from something." Golden swirls danced in his father's gaze.

The scene of the battle rushed back to him. Jolt had hit him with his gun. The golden light had gushed around him, entering his head and his soul until he couldn't block it out, until the golden mist became part of him and he vanished into its stream. He was in the place of nontime, the other dimension Eri had talked about. But this wasn't a memory.

Weaver had never met his father like this on the upper banks of the river. They always came together, fished together, and left for home. Besides, his father would only notice his aged appearance if… if he was the real deal.

"You're really here, aren't you?"

"It's good to see you, son."

Striver had been right. He'd argued with his brother over their father's disappearance all their lives. Weaver thought their dad had grown restless and joined the Lawless, while Striver remained adamant he'd never leave them if he could help it.

Was he stuck here forever? There was so much left unfinished, so much he'd wanted to do.

"Take me back!" he shouted to the placid, uncaring sky. "I wasn't finished yet."

The rush of the rapids was the only muted voice answering his pleas. Weaver kicked a rock, and it skipped across the clear waters. He ran his fingers through his hair, tears rolling down his cheeks. His life had been so short and so full of hate. All those moments he'd lost when he could have enjoyed himself and those around him. What an utter waste.

I wish I had a chance to talk to Striver one last time, to tell him I'm sorry.

Would Eri do it for him? He trusted her. If she succeeded, she'd tell the whole village about how he sacrificed himself to get her to the ship. Weaver closed his eyes, hoping she made it, hoping he'd helped someone for once in his life.

His eyelids fluttered open, and his father still stood before him with both eyebrows raised in expectation. Weaver had always wanted to live free of Striver's shadow. He'd fought for his father's unending attention. Now he had it. For the first time in his life, Weaver released the pain and hate stored up in his heart. There was no place for it here, and he didn't want to waste any more of his time on self-destructive thoughts. He had one more chance to make the most of it.

Weaver put his arm around his father. "Let's see how many trotters we can catch."

CHAPTER THIRTY-TWO
DELTA SLIP

Eri's heart sped as she directed Aquaria through the restricted corridors leading to the commander's control deck. She'd only been once before, when the commander had asked her to join the exploratory team. Back then, she'd been a timid, inexperienced follower, lacking confidence. Now, she stormed the corridors as a battle veteran, ready to take over the ship.

They reached the end of the hall undetected. They paused, catching their breaths. Eri extended a mirror glued to a toothbrush to peek around the corner.

"Ten guards, all with gallium crystal void rays."

Aquaria turned the ring on her finger over and over. "You'd think the commander would order them out to the battlefield to help the others."

"Guess she's not taking any chances with her own safety." Eri shook her head. They could have used those void rays on Jolt. Maybe then, Weaver would still be alive.

Aquaria's third finger was turning red. "It's going to be hard to convince them all to leave."

Eri put her hand over her sister's before she twisted her finger off. "Are you sure you want to do this?"

Aquaria nodded. "I'm just thinking out loud. That's all."

"If this fails, we'll both be branded as rebels."

"I'd rather be in a category with you and Litus, and save those poor people, than live on this ship in an exclusive society."

"Okay." Eri pocketed the toothbrush and stepped into the doorframe of a storage unit, pressing her back against the wall to hide. "Do your stuff."

"One more thing." Aquaria squeezed her hand. Resolution shone fiercely in her oceanic eyes. "Do what's necessary to keep all those people, including Litus, safe. Okay?"

Eri nodded, reassuring herself this act of treason, something she'd never thought of doing in all her life on the *Heritage*, was warranted. She fought for Striver and his village, and their right to exist. Failure was not an option.

Aquaria took a deep breath and let out a spine-tingling scream. She winked at Eri before scrambling around the corner. Eri scrunched up against the doorframe, waiting for her cue.

"Please, you have to come help. All of you." Aquaria's voice shook.

"What's the problem, miss?" a deep baritone voice rumbled.

"I'm Mrs. Muller." Aquaria knew how to use her connections to their advantage. Litus's wife would have more credibility than any unknown colonist.

"Oh, Mrs. Muller. I didn't recognize—"

"It doesn't matter. Some of the natives snuck on the ship. They're heading to the reactor core." Aquaria sounded so authentic, Eri almost believed her for a second. All those times they played pretend as kids must have improved her plausibility.

The sound of thumping feet and buzzing guns echoed down the

corridor. "How many did you see?"

Eri bit her nails while Aquaria paused.

"Ten, maybe twenty."

Good thinking, Aquaria. That will mean the whole brigade has to go.

"Hurry!"

"We're on it, Mrs. Muller. Show us where you saw them."

"Come with me."

That was Eri's cue. She waited until the foot traffic faded before extending the toothbrush mirror again. Two men had stayed behind to guard the control room entrance.

Cyberhell!

Now it was up to her. Eri switched her laser gun to stun. After witnessing Weaver's horrible demise on her account, she didn't want any more deaths on her head. These guards were just following orders.

Taking a deep breath, she thought about her next move. She only had seconds to shoot, and both shots had to be accurate, or they'd return fire. Checking their positions one more time in the mirror, she took a few deep breaths. *You can do this.*

Aquaria could only keep the guards busy for so long. Eri tightened her grip on her laser. *Now or never.*

She leaned around the corner and zapped the guard on the left before he knew what hit him. He fell back against the wall and slumped. What she didn't count on was the time it took her laser gun to recharge. She pulled the trigger as the high-pitched buzz grew louder, but nothing happened. The guard on the right raised his void ray.

She ducked back around the corner as a laser blackened the opposite wall. *His gun is definitely not on stun.*

It took all of her courage to throw herself back out there, aim at his midsection, and shoot again. This time the trigger worked. But this guard moved quickly. He ducked and rolled toward her, and her shot hit the wall behind him. She ducked back around the corner.

Damn!

Eri held her breath and listened. She'd grown used to the chirps of jungle birds and the rustling of leaves, so the silent stillness made her uneasy. The guard breathed heavily. Plastic creaked, and clothes rustled. He was closer this time, and both of their guns had recharged. It was going to be a shoot-out, just like in those westerns from Old Earth she'd studied for linguistics jargon. Only she didn't think she had the faster trigger finger.

Yes, but my laser gun is smaller. The trigger is faster. Maybe that's enough.

It had to be, or that void ray would turn her into burned toast, the commander would order the attack on Striver's village, and they would all die. *No pressure.*

Each second felt like torture, her heart beating wildly, her throat constricting until she fought for breath, her sweaty hands gripping the laser. At least it would be over soon.

Eri turned, shot in the direction of the heavy breathing, and dove. She didn't stop to see what happened, scrambling across the open space for the other corner. She hit the chrome floor and rolled. Squeezing her eyes shut, she waited for searing pain, but none came.

I'm alive. Elbows throbbing, Eri scrambled up and crouched against the wall. Her hand shook as she pulled out the toothbrush and spied on the adjacent corridor.

The other guard was face down on the floor.

Could he be playing dead?

There was only one way to find out. She crept around the corner and aimed her laser at his back. He didn't move. Another stun might kill him if he was already out, so she had to be careful. She inched toward him holding the laser. He curled his fingers around the trigger of the void ray.

Eri nudged his shoulder with the toe of her boot. No response.

She slowly bent down, still holding her laser, and yanked on the end of the void ray. His grip remained firm. Heart beating out of control, she reached over his body and pried his fingers loose one at a time. His hands were still warm, and his fingers felt fat and soft under her skin. Striver's hands were hard and calloused. *Guess that's what living in the jungle will do.*

The weapon was heavy as all hell. Her wrist strained to keep it up, but a rush of relief came over her as she held both guns.

After one more nudge with her boot, Eri stepped over him and gently kicked the other guard near the door. Both were unconscious. Stuns usually lasted twelve to twenty-four hours. She had time.

Eri pressed the door panel and the screen beeped.

IDENTIFICATION REQUIRED.

Panic shot down Eri's legs. She looked around, but neither guard had an ID tag. Precious seconds ticked away as she scrambled for an answer. *On second thought, I shouldn't have knocked them both out.* She tried to remember when she'd visited the commander. The guard had stood at this very door and…placed his finger on the screen!

A finger. She needed a finger. Eri leaned both guns against the wall and hauled the closest guard to the door. Dragging a six foot man at five foot two wasn't easy, but she wasn't about to cut his finger off. She raised his arm and plopped his finger on the screen. The panel beeped.

INCORRECT IDENTIFICATION.

Cyber freaking hell. She didn't have time for this. Eri lay the first guard down and dragged the other one. He was heavier, and sweat ran down her cheeks as she tried his finger, hoping luck was on her side. The panel beeped again.

ACCESS GRANTED.

Thank the *Heritage* the other guard who'd stayed behind had access. As the particles disintegrated, she grabbed both weapons.

The control deck lay eerily silent and still in stark contrast with the main sight panel, where the battle unfolded below them. Eri rushed over and scanned the ground. No sign of Striver or Jolt. Litus and his team were working their way toward the middle, along with the others from Striver's village. Only two Lawless with lasers remained.

The sight of their victory brought a degree of triumph, but the joy faded just as quickly as it had come. This would give the commander unlimited power. Eri had to tear her gaze away from the battle to avoid distraction. "Commander Grier, I need to talk to you."

The pink tank of embryonic liquid sat on a pedestal at the room's center, wires sticking into a fleshy brain. She stared at it, wondering how aware the brain really was. Could it sense her presence when she entered the room?

The door solidified behind her. Panels rose from the walls and a low buzzing hummed through the room. Eri tensed. *Did I just walk into a trap?*

The lasers shook in her hands. She tightened her grip as a magnetic force from the panels pulled her guns from her fingers. She held onto the weapons as her hair clips yanked from her hair. The force increased, ripping both guns from her hands. They clunked as they hit the panels. Eri ran over and tried to pry them off, but the force was too strong. Holding the guns, the panels lowered back into crevices in the floor. Eri scrambled on her knees, fingers digging into the metal, but the crevices closed, and the chrome looked smooth as a newly polished floor.

"No, no, no."

The screen lowered in the center of the deck, and Eri whirled around. The commander's sharp features flashed on, her eyes narrowing. "Eridani Smith. You have failed to report back to me. I have relieved you of duty. You are no longer necessary to this colony's exploratory efforts."

Is that all she's got? Did she not notice how I just took out her main guards? Suddenly the commander didn't seem so all-powerful, and Eri's courage boosted. She put her hands on her hips and stared her down. "I couldn't care less about my duties. Let's talk about Delta Slip."

"Consider yourself off the project. It is no longer your concern."

Eri voice hardened. "It's my main concern, Grier. Those people down there are helping us win the battle. They have so much they can teach us, besides contributing to our dwindling DNA pool. You know it's in our best interests to keep them alive."

"Your opinions are unwarranted, Ms. Smith. Return to your family cell and wait for further orders."

"I'm not going anywhere until you call off Delta Slip."

The commander's eyebrows scrunched up. "If you continue to disobey orders, I'll have to charge you as a sympathizer."

Gears turned behind Eri, and she glanced over her shoulder. A robotic arm emerged from the wall along with a needle on the tip. She ducked and rolled across the floor as it swung at her. "I told you, I'm not going anywhere."

A second robotic arm dislodged from the opposite wall. Eri jumped sideways as a rotating blade sliced a lock of her hair. The arm with the needle jabbed behind her, and she fell forward before it could pierce her arm.

"It's the assassination attempt, isn't it? Lawless gangs killed your family, and now you want revenge."

The commander blinked like Eri'd hit her in the nose. Her virtual face blanched. It was the first time Eri had seen her vulnerability and a glimpse of her humanity.

"People must have order to their society. Without rules, evil can manifest in physical forms."

The robotic arms swung around the room and Eri scrambled to

her feet, watching them as she spoke. "Evil is here whether we have rules or not. Besides, this village has a social structure of their own. They're not like the Lawless."

"They are descendants of the gangs who stole Outpost Omega, space pirates. I can't have their rebellious blood mingling with ours."

"These people didn't kill your family. Their ancestors, many, many years ago, did. You can't hold them accountable." *Man, talk about a grudge.*

Litus's voice came on the intercom, stealing the commander's attention. "Mission accomplished, Commander Grier. The battle is won." Eri's head snapped up. She side-kicked the arm with the blade as it dove for her leg. The needle hung over her head, and she jumped and grabbed onto the arc before the tip could prick her. Dangling from the robotic arm, Eri hoped Litus had done the right thing.

The commander's lips stretched into a pleased smile. "Excellent. I'll send a team to hunt down the stragglers. Commence with Delta Slip."

৵৵

The villagers cheered around Striver, throwing up their bows, drumming on the ground, and leaping to the sky. Carven and Riley lifted him on their shoulders and the others chanted his name. The last of the Lawless scattered into the jungle, and they'd disabled every laser gun loaded with that golden substance. He'd killed Jolt. The Lawless had no leader and their numbers dwindled. They'd done it.

Disbelief and shock hit him in duel slaps. *We've triumphed, but at what cost?* Weaver was gone. Right now he was in survivor mode, but when the truth sank in, grief would swallow him whole. He still thought he'd see Weaver emerge from the forest like nothing had happened. It would take time to realize he'd never see his brother again.

A sense of disquiet quivered in his gut, and he scanned the

battlefield expecting one more man to run at them with a laser, or for Jolt to get back up as a blackened corpse and hunt them down. Everything looked in order; the colonists lined up in rows, the people from his village tended to the wounded, and the Guardians circled in the sky above. Maybe it was all of the death around him sending anxiety through his veins. Death that included Weaver's.

No, this is something different, something not yet resolved.

Had his mother's psychic tendencies gotten to him, making him believe he had another sense as well?

He tapped Carven's shoulders, and his friends lowered him down.

"What's the matter?" Riley shook his head. "We won."

"Did we?"

"Give the man some room." Carven pulled Riley back. "Go tend to your sister." He motioned to Riptide bandaging a cut on her upper arm.

"All right. But I think she proved today she can fend for herself." Riley left with a prideful grin on his face saying, *Look what you're missing out on.*

Striver didn't care. His heart was too full of pain to cultivate any more anger or annoyance.

Once Riley left, Carven squeezed Striver's shoulder. He looked worn, blood and dirt smeared across his forehead, and a few more wrinkles now creased around his eyes. "I'm sorry about your brother."

Striver's throat tightened. He could hardly speak. "It's not your fault. He made his own choices."

"I'm sorry all the same."

Striver looked past Carven to where Litus stood in front of the ranks of colonists. The unease in his gut grew so strong, he swallowed down bile. "Something's wrong."

"What's the matter?" Carven tensed beside him.

He trusted Litus. So what was the problem? "I'm not sure." Striver pushed by Carven. "Stay here and don't say anything. Let's not cause panic." Men all over the place with weapons and death in their eyes were dangerous enough without assumptions.

As he approached Litus he overheard that familiar term *Delta Slip*. Eri had never had a chance to tell him the truth. He should have asked her outright, but he realized he loved her too much to push her away.

Litus didn't look up at Striver. He spoke into his locator, eyeing the men around him. "I cannot continue with Delta Slip."

The commander's harsh voice spit back at him. "Why?"

"These men aided us in the battle. We owe them a life debt, and I'm not about to go against morality."

"Lieutenant, my rules *are* your morality. If you do not order them, I will myself."

"Commander, these villagers are armed. We can't have any more loss of life."

"It's a small price to pay for a stable society. Carry out the orders."

"No." Litus clicked a switch and the screen on his locator went blank. He put his arm down. "Everyone here, listen to me."

Before he could go on, all of their locators flashed on, beeping simultaneously. The colonists scanned the message, and then, one by one, they raised their guns at Litus. Anxiety gripped Striver's chest. Mars would never let this happen, but he'd seen medics bring her back to the ship with a leg wound. There wasn't enough time to go and get her. Besides, this was bigger than both of them.

Litus backed up. "What are you doing?"

One of the men's hands shook as he held his laser. "Sorry, sir. J-just following orders," he stammered.

Litus shook his head in disbelief. "What does it say?"

One of the men spit on the ground. "That you're a betrayer. You side with them."

"Don't you see? There is no *them*. We're all in this together now."

The man kept his gun raised. This time his voice was stronger.

"It's the commander's orders."

"What are you going to do, shoot me?"

Their silence was answer enough.

He glanced back at Striver with desperation in his eyes.

Damn the Lawless and all their doings. Even though they'd helped the colonists fight, they looked no different than the enemy. Striver drew out his bow, an arrow cocked and ready to fire within seconds. "The first person who shoots is a dead man," Striver growled. Behind him, Carven ordered the village to raise their bows.

It was a standoff to the death. Even the Guardians couldn't save them this time.

Striver had frozen the colonists for a moment in indecision, but it wouldn't take them long to realize they outnumbered the people in his village by three to one. Even if he picked off the first shooter, the rest of the team would kill him in seconds. Swallowing, Striver resigned to his fate.

I wish I could see Eri one last time.

CHAPTER THIRTY-THREE
MESSAGE FROM THE GRAVE

Eri dangled from the robotic arm, swinging away from the rotating blade. Her sweaty fingers slipped on the metal, and she struggled to keep her grip. If she fell, the needle could stick her while she was trying to fend off the blade. Litus, Striver, and everyone from the village who'd survived the battle were about to die if she didn't gain control. Frustration squeezed tears from her eyes and she gritted her teeth, trying not to cry out in anguish. She had to pull herself together. This couldn't be the end.

As the blade came back toward her, she kicked at the arm instead of swinging away. The toe of her boot caught the serrated edge, and the metal sliced through her sole. She scrunched up her toes and yanked her foot away as the blade cut millimeters from her skin. She kicked again, this time hitting the arm, and the blade broke off, sailing through the air. It hit the screen, and the commander's face splintered into shards, glass raining on the floor.

The needle arm bent toward her, the tip glistening a centimeter from her face. Eri needed both hands to hold onto the arm, and her feet couldn't reach the needle to kick it away. Gears squealed as the arm bent in farther. A drip from the needlepoint fell to the floor.

If she let go, the arm would chase her around the room. She had to get it now while the needle was right in front of her. Wishing she'd done more pull-ups on the workout deck, Eri released one of her hands and grabbed at the needle. Her arm shook as the muscles strained, trying to support her weight.

She wrapped her fingers around the needle and broke it off, throwing it across the room.

There was only one thing left to do. Only one way to stop the bloodbath riding on the commander's orders. Eri slipped from the arm and landed on her feet.

The pink brain tank stood unprotected at the ship's helm, the commander's umbilical cord to the controls. Eri launched herself toward it. She leapt to the pedestal and kicked with the heel of her boot. The outer level of the glass cracked.

Pain streaked down the back of her head and she fell to the floor. One of the broken robotic arms had hit her. Eri touched her face. A streak of warm blood ran down her cheek. The arm came at her again, and she pulled herself back as it crashed into the floor between her legs where her stomach had been.

She forced herself up and kicked at the tank again. The crack widened, and the brain shuddered with the force, but the glass didn't break. Eri ducked the robotic arm and came around the other side. Both arms followed her, and she slipped onto her knees and skidded underneath their broken fingers as they met in the middle. One of the arms snagged her tunic and lifted her off the floor.

Eri kicked her legs and reached behind her neck, trying to dislodge from the arm. It swung her back and forth until her tunic tore and she flew across the room. Eri smashed against the main viewing panel and slid down in a heap. Stars blossomed in her eyes and the room darkened.

No.

She blinked back the pain and shook her pounding head. Out of the corner of her eye she saw the metal arms coming for her. *Get up.*

Eri stumbled to standing, fighting dizziness, and circled to the other end of the room. She gave herself a running start, gaining momentum, and hurled herself in the air. She kicked the glass with both feet.

The tank shattered and cold embryonic fluid flowed over her. The lights went out as the ship's power fluctuated. Eri fell and her head smacked the chrome floor, knocking the air from her lungs. The commander's brain bounced beside her and oozed liquid onto the floor, deflating into mushy flesh with a long sigh, as if centuries of pressure, hate, and revenge finally abated. The room stank of pungent chemicals, and Eri covered her nose, hoping she wasn't too late.

ॐॐ

Striver tightened his grip on the arrow, scanning the crowd of men. *Who will shoot first?*

The colonists looked wary and anxious, not knowing what to believe. They'd followed the commander their whole lives, and Striver knew they couldn't disobey her now. But would they fire against their own lieutenant?

Whatever the case, he'd take out as many as he could before the lasers blasted him away. Anything to give his villagers a chance to escape. But deep down, he knew the laser's range and the length of battlefield stretching out before the cover of the forest. No one would stand a chance.

Glancing at the sky, he saw Phoenix circling with the other Guardians, perhaps deciding when to intervene. Arrows poked from his torso, and he flew in crooked arcs.

Don't try it, old friend. Stay in the sky where it's safe.

The colonists' locators blinked off, depowering. They glanced at their arms, and Striver wondered if he should take his chances and start shooting. But he didn't want to be the one to start the war. His father's words came back to him: *Wait for opportunity to show itself.*

His arm muscles screamed in agony, yet he held the arrow cocked, waiting to fire.

The locators beeped back on again. Eri's voice rang out. Striver couldn't believe it.

"Drop your weapons. There will be no more fighting." Her voice was deeper and more confident than the last time he'd spoken with her.

The men gave each other questioning looks. "Who is that?"

"That's not the commander."

"Commander Grier is dead, leaving Litus Muller in charge. You are to follow him for further orders."

The transmission clicked off and everyone stared. Litus raised his gun. "You heard her. Drop your weapons. This ends now."

"The commander can't be dead," someone shouted from the back of the crowd.

Striver whispered to Litus, "Is there any way to prove it?"

Litus nodded. "Check your locaters. See if she registers."

Striver's arm began to shake, and he willed it to hold. Who knew what really happened to the commander? Maybe Eri was bluffing?

"It's blank," someone called out.

"She's not registering," another voice answered.

"What do we do?" A man in the front row lowered his weapon.

Litus's shoulders eased. "You follow me, that's what you do. As the first lieutenant, I'm in charge now, and I'm telling you all to drop your weapons or I'll have to open fire."

A young woman in the front dropped her laser. "I don't want to die here today. I have kids and a husband, and all I want to do is start my new life." The men beside her did the same. Striver gave Carven a nod, and the villagers behind them lowered their bows. When the entire team of colonists had obeyed, Litus placed his weapon in the ash at his feet. Striver dropped his bow and the shaft bounced once before falling to the ground. Standing before Litus, he bowed until his hair brushed the ash.

"You kept your word, and for that I am forever in your debt."

"It is us who are in your debt." Litus bowed. "Without your help we would have never won this war."

"A truce, then, between our two peoples?"

Litus shook his head. "More than a truce; a friendship, a cohabitation that will strengthen both sides."

They shook hands, and the colonists and villagers around them cheered. A profound sense of resolution trickled through Striver like warm summer rain. He'd secured Refuge for his people. Aries and Striker would be proud. He hoped, somewhere in the nether land of that golden liquid dimension, Weaver and his father were proud as well, and that they found peace in their hearts.

A woman wearing a colonist's uniform, much like the one Aries wore in the pictures he'd seen on the *S.P. Nautilus*, ran up to Litus and wrapped her arms around his neck. *That must be Eri's half sister. Holy Refuge, she doesn't look like Eri at all.*

Litus slid his arms around her waist and whispered, "I love you."

They started to kiss, and Striver turned away, giving them their privacy. His people celebrated around him, yet an emptiness he didn't think would ever be filled sat in the pit of his stomach. People shouted in triumph, while others knelt beside their fellow comrades in mourning. So many of them gave their lives for the survivors to live free. He only hoped this peace lasted throughout the eons on Refuge.

A figure emerged on the ramp of the ship. The small person waved and ran toward the battlefield. *Eri?*

Ignoring his aching muscles, he sprinted to meet her. The ship's light illuminated a head of curly pink hair. Striver increased his pace, kicking up ash and jumping over a wall of fire. They collided into each other's arms, and for the first time in his life, he felt complete.

He ran his hands up her back to her neck and through her hair, as if convincing himself she was real. She placed both her hands on his cheeks and pulled his face to hers, kissing him fiercely.

The fires burning around him didn't compare to the flames raging in his heart. Eri ran her hands down his neck to his bare chest, sneaking underneath his open shirt. Her touch ignited heat until he felt like his whole body was on fire.

He needed her so badly he could barely stop for air. She quelled the pain inside him and unleashed a primal urge to be close. He felt the curves of her waist and drew her against him, losing himself in waves of desire.

Eri pulled away from him, breaking the kiss. "There's something I have to tell you."

He placed small kisses on her cheek and her neck, wanting to travel back to her lips. "Don't worry. I know about Delta Slip."

"It's not about Delta Slip." The storm brewing in her eyes held him back. "It's about Weaver."

He stopped as if she'd stuck a knife in his gut. The pain returned in full force, knocking him back a step. "He's gone, Eri."

"I know." Eri ran a hand through her hair, worry creasing her forehead as if what she'd tell him would change everything. "He died because of me."

Her words sucked the air out of his lungs. "What do you mean?"

Tears rolled down her cheeks. "I didn't mean to. I was lecturing him about taking responsibility, being a better person. When we got to the battle, I needed a diversion to get onto the ship and stop the commander. He attacked Jolt so I could make it on board, so I could save you."

That's why Weaver took on Jolt all by himself. A wall of emotion hit Striver, overcoming him with melancholy. He was right about his brother. Weaver had been a good man, and he'd died a hero—he'd just needed the right circumstance to prove it. Striver grasped Eri's arms to stay upright. "I knew he'd do the right thing."

Eri stared into his gaze, giving him strength. "There's more."

Striver looked at her. What could she possibly tell him that would ease the pain? Did he want to hear it? No matter—he had to, or he'd always wonder. "Go on."

"He gave me a message before he took off into battle." She took a deep breath. "He said to tell you he's sorry."

The breath caught in Striver's throat. For so long he'd wanted his brother's love, and there it was in two words. *He's sorry*. The world swayed around him, the emotion so strong he couldn't hold it back.

"Striver, I wish I hadn't judged him. I'm so sorry."

"No. Don't be sorry." Striver glanced up at the sky as if his brother resided in the stars. "This is long-awaited news."

CHAPTER THIRTY-FOUR
CLOSURE

"Fire!" Striver pointed to the cliff above the cave and Litus's army of colonists raised their lasers, releasing a cascade of loose rocks. The earth rumbled under his feet as the debris slid and settled. Dust wafted up, pluming above their heads until Striver couldn't see anything but his own hands in front of his eyes.

"Halt!" The laser fire stopped, and Striver waited for the dust to disperse. He needed the time for his own emotions to settle, time to say good-bye.

The clouds thinned around him, the world coming back into focus. A pile of rocks filled the entrance to the cave. Striver stepped over the rubble and placed a purple blossom, Weaver's favorite, on a center boulder.

He'd tried so hard to keep Weaver beside him all these years, and his brother had fought against it. He should have let Weaver pave his own path instead of suffocating him. It had been a month since the battle, and now Striver had to let him go.

Rest in peace, Weaver, and good luck, wherever you are.

Phoenix stepped from the dust cloud behind him. His torso was bandaged in two places, where arrows had hit him in the sky. He would have died that day but thanks to a regenerator from the *Heritage*, he was recovering quickly. Soon, he'd be able to fly again. Striver looked forward to taking another trip into the sky. "You don't regret sealing off the cave? What if it's the only way to contact Weaver?"

"Not at all." Striver shook his head. "As much as I want to see him again, I know not to mess with time. What's done is done, and we have to look at building our future, not to the mistakes of our past."

Phoenix nodded, folding his long arms to his chest. "If it wasn't for your lack of feathers, I would have thought you to be one of us."

Striver laughed. Yes, he'd gained wisdom in the last few months, but he was far from lecturing anyone on the subject. "You will assign a Guardian to watch over it, won't you?"

"Of course. This will stop people from entering the cave, but the substance still oozes through the ground every so often. The golden liquid is part of this planet, as much as the water and the air."

"We'll deal with it when it happens." Striver put a hand on Phoenix's shoulder, for the first time reassuring the Guardian. "For now, we are safe."

"Spoken like a true leader. You have grown into your own, Striver, son of Tallis, descendant of Aries and Striker."

Striver took a deep breath. A question he'd never had the courage to ask lingered on his tongue. "You knew them. Would they approve of what's happened? The direction this colony is headed…"

Phoenix glanced up to the sky where a swillow wisp perched on a mountain ridge. "They would be proud." He ruffled the feathers on his back and took a seat on a rock, bending his long, branchlike legs. "Sometimes I miss them. They were like parents to me. After I broke free of my shell, I leaped into the rays of the sun, spreading my wings for the first time. When I looked down, Aries stood in the meadow, watching me fly with a joyous smile on her face, her arms reaching toward the sky."

Striver hung on every word. Rarely did the Guardians speak of their first days on Refuge, and never such personal memories or feelings of their own.

Phoenix drew a circle in the sand, then a tree with branches spiraling out: the Guardian symbol for *legacy*. "But whenever I grow saddened, all I need to do is look at you."

To have a Guardian open up and share such a touching sentiment was unheard of. Speechless, Striver took a seat next to Phoenix. He bent over and, using the tip of his finger, traced his own symbol in the sand. His strokes were much fatter and clumsier than Phoenix's perfect lines, but the image was clear: two branches intertwining, the Guardian symbol for *friend*.

Phoenix trilled a soft tune. Perhaps he was impressed by Striver's knowledge of their language, or maybe he found the gesture just as meaningful. Phoenix scratched his feathered head. "Do you think the people in your village and the colonists will get along?"

Striver sighed and shook his head. "Let's hope so. The ceremony tomorrow will be a step in the right direction."

"Something tells me intergalactic relations are not the reason why you're going through with it."

Striver laughed and the heavy weight of the day's task dissipated. He winked at Phoenix. "Guardians always know the underlying truths."

❧❦

Aquaria adjusted the blossoms in Eri's hair. "You look ravishing."

Eri blushed. "I just want to look presentable, so don't overdo it, okay?"

She stuck another stem above Eri's ear. "Just one more of these cute pearl berry flowers. They are absolutely adorable. And they match your hair."

"Adorable isn't what I'm going for either."

Aquaria shushed her. "Not you! The flowers. Shouldn't a linguist know what ravishing means?"

Eri shook her head. "Ex-linguist, remember?"

"Of course, Eri, coleader of the native clan." Aquaria circled around her. "You're going to be much busier trying to work with Litus to blend our customs and make sure no one gets jungle fever."

Eri smiled. Both of her dreams had come true. She had the lifemate she'd always wanted and an essential job where she could make a difference to go along with it. "I like it that way."

Aquaria tightened the back straps of Eri's dress until her breasts shoved up like a table in front of her. She wore the ceremonial lifemate pairing gown from the *Heritage* embroidered with beads made by the women in Striver's village. "Ouch. What are you doing?"

"Making you less adorable."

Bone flutes trilled and a low drumbeat began. Anxious excitement bubbled in Eri's veins. "That's our cue, Aquaria! I don't want to be late."

"Showing up a few minutes late is fashionable. Besides, it increases the expectation."

"Ugh! I should have picked Uncle Ral to walk me down the aisle."

Aquaria took her arm and they headed up a mossy incline. "Nonsense. You picked me because you knew I'd be the best."

"Or because I had two sets of parents and couldn't choose between them."

Aquaria slapped her hand and they crested the hill. Rows of people turned to watch Eri descend. On the right sat the villagers who'd lived on Haven 6 for hundreds of years, wearing their crudely knit clothes, blending in with the long grasses of the meadow. Carven sat with his large family, two toddlers squirming on his wife's lap. Behind them, Riptide sat with Riley, matching heads of midnight hair.

On the left, the colonists wore their white flight uniforms from the *Heritage*, matching the ivory hull of the *S.P. Nautilus* behind them. Eri spotted her birth father sitting with his assigned lifemate and her birth mother, three rows ahead, sitting with hers. For a moment she wondered if her mom and dad still loved each other today, but she put it aside to honor their rightful matches. No longer would such pairing pains arise, no longer would any child feel second-class.

Eri's gaze gravitated to the center row, where Striver waited. He wore a loose white shirt and leather pants with new black boots, shined to catch the rays of the sun. He'd threaded white feathers through his long, wavy hair.

She remembered the day she first saw him, running at the Lawless to save her. Eri's heart skittered. He was standing there for her. To be with her. Her own lifemate, a better fit for her than anyone on the *Heritage* could ever be.

The flutes rose in pitch as she approached and the drums quickened, in synch with her heart. Only months ago, she'd been a nobody, punching keys in deep space, and now she was a hero, a warrior, and a future wife.

Aquaria kissed Eri's cheek as they reached the platform. "Good luck."

Eri glanced at Striver and the intensity in his emerald eyes made her feel like he saw no one else. She turned back to Aquaria and smiled. "Thanks, but I don't need it."

The music trailed off and Phoenix stepped to a stone podium decorated in climbing vines. "This is the exact spot where Striver's ancestors, Aries and Striker, took their first steps on this world, the spot where I flew for the first time. Now it will be the first union of your peoples, where they will take their first steps united on Refuge." He glanced at the colonists. "Or as you call it, Haven 6."

Eri wove her fingers through Striver's. His hand felt warm and reassuring in hers. He whispered in her ear, his lips tickling her lobe,

"I love you."

His fingers pushed a small, hard-edged object into her hand. Making sure Phoenix wasn't paying attention, Eri glanced down and opened her palm. A bead carved with two figures holding hands stared up at her. The man had a bow across his chest and the woman had short, curly hair. She had no idea how Striver could put so much detail into something so small.

She glanced back at him and mouthed, "I love you, too."

Phoenix gave them a questioning tilt of his head.

Striver laughed and bowed. "Go on."

Ruffling his feathers, Phoenix gave them an admonishing quirk of his beak before continuing. "This is the first *chosen* lifemate pairing ceremony; the first of many yet to come. As our cultures blend, you have agreed to uphold the prime directive of our founding ancestors, and freedom of choice will reign."

Applause erupted behind them, and Striver squeezed Eri's hands. Her dream and his were one.

EPILOGUE

As the universe expanded, humankind spread across the stars, sprinkling the galaxy like dandelion seeds in the wind. Some civilizations reverted to simpler means, living in the solitude of their chosen star system, while others developed new ways to speed travel through deep space, thereby reconnecting with the colony ships strewn across paradise planets.

The people of Haven 6 lived in symbiotic codependence with nature and the Guardians, developing a democratic society with deep philosophical values and pure ideals. The mysterious golden liquid continued to draw dreamers into its grasp, but fewer and fewer ventured each year to make the choice of an eternal, though hollow, life. Tundra 37 became a bustling metropolis as the planet warmed, and scientists worked for generations to build another colony ship to complete the voyage they had abandoned so many years ago. After five hundred years, a *New Hope* embarked for Paradise 18. Paradise 21 turned out to be less than paradise, with poison pod plants, and wars with aggressive alien species for planetary rights.

All civilizations shared the same past, a common thread binding them together. In the darkest of times, when battles had still raged over resources, it had been this single heritage that brought the different factions together, instilling peace before the wars raged out of control like on Old Earth.

Made cautious and wise, humans learned from their mistakes of the past and flourished.

ACKNOWLEDGMENTS

I'd like to thank my agent, Dawn Dowdle, for believing in my manuscript and finding such a wonderful publishing company. Also, thank you to Liz Pelletier and Heather Howland at Entangled Publishing. Thank you to Kerry Vail and Stacy Abrams, my eagle-eyed editors, who worked so hard to polish this manuscript and find more depth in every plot strand. My beta readers come next: the best sister in the world, Brianne Dionne, and my mom, Joanne, for giving me support and intriguing insights. My awesome critique partners deserve numerous thank-yous: Cherie Reich, Theresa Milstein, Lisa Rusczyk, Kathleen S. Allen, Lindsey Duncan, and Cher Green. My flute teacher and life mentor, Peggy Vagts, comes next, for encouraging me to pursue writing and flute as dual dreams. And lastly, my husband, Chris, for allowing me the time I needed to work on edits, do research, and most of all, write.